Brother Nature

ROBERT LLEWELLYN

Brother Nature

FLAME
Hodder & Stoughton

Copyright © 2001 by Robert Llewellyn

First published in 2001 by Hodder & Stoughton
A division of Hodder Headline

The right of Robert Llewellyn to be identified as the Author of
the Work has been asserted by him in accordance with the
Copyright, Designs and Patents Act 1988.

A Flame Book

2 4 6 8 10 9 7 5 3 1

A CIP catalogue record for this title
is available from the British Library

ISBN 0 340 75113 4

Typeset by Hewer Text Ltd, Edinburgh
Printed and bound in Great Britain by
Mackays of Chatham plc, Chatham, Kent

Hodder & Stoughton
A division of Hodder Headline
338 Euston Road
London NW1 3BH

For Holly and Louis

Acknowledgements

I have to thank Professor Kevin Warwick at the Cybernetics Department of Reading University. He was very generous with his knowledge during the research period of this book. Professor Warwick is the first human being to insert an active computer chip into his body, directly connected to his central nervous system. Proof that this story is not science fiction.

1

Slowly at first, and then a little faster, Ingrid Neilson touched her right thumb and forefinger together for the first time in five years. She was crying a little as the digits moved. Not big sobs – Ingrid had proved herself to be very brave – but there were tears streaming down her cheeks as she watched her hand. It was, without doubt, a very big moment in her life.

She glanced up at her father, who sat opposite her in the stark laboratory. He stared in amazement as his daughter's new hand actually moved. At a glance it looked utterly real. On closer inspection the nails were just slightly wrong, the wrong shape more than colour, but who was complaining?

'Can you feel anything?' asked Nina as she turned to look at a flat-panel monitor resting on a stainless-steel trolley behind her.

Ingrid didn't answer, so engrossed was she in the movement of her arm. Nina stretched forward and gently touched her on the shoulder.

'Ingrid, can you feel anything?'

Ingrid turned to Nina, looked her right in the eye as only a twelve-year-old can. She nodded.

'It's a bit tingly.'

'Okay. Where do you feel the tingly sensation?' asked Nina, now staring at the monitor as the readings came flooding through.

'I don't know,' said the child, and she started sobbing.

Her father leaned forward to comfort her. 'It's okay, darling.'

'I don't know where I feel it,' Ingrid went on between pitiful sobs. 'It's really confusing. Sort of in my arm, sort of in my head, but really I know it's in my fingers. Is it my fingers?'

'That's good,' said Nina as kindly as she could. She was on the verge of tears, but she struggled to maintain professional objectivity. She had so much to do now the arm was connected, wanting to record as much data as possible while the girl was still willing. 'Don't worry about it now. Just relax and make the hand work for you. That's what's important.'

Ingrid was a perfect test case, a healthy twelve-year-old who had lost her right arm from just above the elbow when she was four years old, the victim of a car crash, a rather catastrophic one in which she had also lost her mother and sister. Her father, Lars Neilson, a grey-haired thirty-six-year-old, was all she had left. He had described the accident to Nina when they first met. Although he had not been involved, from what he could gather the four-year-old Ingrid had her arm sticking out of the rear window as she was being driven to a lake in Sweden. Her English mother lost control of the car, no one ever discovered why, and it ploughed headlong into an approaching logging truck. The car was thrown aside like an empty soft drinks can and landed on its side, rapidly removing Ingrid's right forearm.

Nina smiled at Lars Neilson. He was a charming man, utterly devoted to his daughter, and rich enough to afford this groundbreaking treatment. When he had told her the story of Ingrid's accident, the account had struck a chord with Nina. She too had escaped serious injury as a young girl when her slightly drunken father had driven into a tree. No one was killed in Nina's crash, but she was reminded of the accident on meeting young Ingrid.

Professor Nina Nash was at the forefront of her speciality, although she would be the first to admit that she had not created the remarkable prosthetic limb single handed. A large team of chemists, microengineers, electricians and computer specialists had been involved in the project. They had been working on Ingrid's case from the time she was six, and since they'd taken the most recent measurements the girl had grown

2

considerably. Hence one of the problems they already faced was that the arm was slightly too short. For the time being this was only a problem of cosmetics, clearly not an issue for the girl or her father, but it wouldn't be long before an overly short prosthetic arm would draw more attention to the girl than the stump it replaced.

Nina had risen fast, achieving her professorship at the age of thirty-one. She had been running the cybernetics department at Coventon Research, Cambridge, for a little over a year. She was not working in an ivy-clad fifteen-century cloister, as many of her American guests expected, but in a very new, and in her eyes rather ugly building in an industrial park three miles outside the ancient university town.

Coventon Research was well funded, receiving grants from numerous foundations and global corporations, but even with all these generous resources the costs involved in Ingrid's new arm were being carefully watched by the management team. It had set them back well in excess of one million pounds – not the arm itself, although its costs ran into many hundreds of thousands, but the research into the technology behind it.

A microscopic computer chip and power storage system, only slightly larger than a match head, was lodged inside Ingrid's upper right arm. Inserting the chip had required a one-hour operation under local anaesthetic. However, the chip's only external sensor, a tiny electrical receiver, a tenth the thickness of a human hair, had to be wrapped around a group of very specific nerves in Ingrid's arm. Any mistake placing this sensor would not only have permanently damaged the nerve, but would have made all their work pointless. There would be no signal from brain to nerve, and through the nerve to the chip, and eventually from the chip to the control system in the prosthetic arm.

It was not just a case of inserting the chip and attaching the arm – the chip needed to know what the signals it was receiving were for. Almost a year earlier a recording chip had been inserted into Ingrid's left arm, and for ten days the girl lived with a small storage device strapped to her belt. This little box recorded the information that was streaming up and down her nerves. Every time Ingrid moved her arm, picked something up, drew a picture, scratched her head or picked her nose, the activity was recorded on a computer. This information was then used to 'train' the new arm long before it was attached to Ingrid. For several weeks the limb was mounted on a frame on a workbench in the main workshop, while Nina tested it with the signals she'd recorded from Ingrid's left hand in order to calibrate the movements the mechanical arm made. It was an odd sight – a very lifelike disembodied arm twitching, picking things up, pointing, making gestures, drumming its fingers on the table.

'Pretty amazing.'

Nina turned. Hugo Harwood, a research graduate and one of the junior team members, was standing beside her.

'Yes. Very special,' said Nina.

They stood side by side staring out of the large laboratory window, watching Lars and Ingrid walk across the rain-soaked carpark in front of the main building, Lars holding his daughter's left hand.

'You must be really proud,' said Hugo.

'Pretty proud. Yeah,' agreed Nina. 'But it's not just me.'

'Oh, I know, Professor. We all know. You're nothing if not fair, but it wouldn't have happened without you.'

She turned to look at him. He was a sweet young man, although she'd always had the feeling that he thought she had been over-promoted. Maybe it was just his manner. He was very bright, and without his help she wouldn't have been able to decode the mass of data they had recorded from Ingrid's chip.

Ingrid stopped, lifted her right arm and slowly pointed. Nina glanced in the direction she indicated. In the distance, catching a rare ray of bright spring sunshine, was the spire of All Souls Church. It was a wonderful sight, a wonderful moment.

'Bloody hell, who's that?' asked Hugo.

Nina looked around. There was no one else in the laboratory. She glanced at Hugo. 'Who?'

'Down there, in the carpark, where Ingrid is pointing.'

Nina looked down. She saw Lars walking with his daughter more swiftly now, then something awful caught her eye.

Ingrid hadn't been pointing at the church, but at something at the very opposite end of the moral spectrum, as far removed from a church spire bathed in spring sunlight as it was possible to be.

In the far corner of the carpark was the familiar, chilling sight of the filthy Saab convertible. Not only was the roof ripped and the wing even more badly damaged than the last time she'd seen it, but one tyre was completely flat and the wheel had gouged an ugly mark right across the new carpark. Looking as if it had been left in a pigeon coop for two years, the vehicle was parked in the managing director's private parking space, which a sign clearly marked as reserved.

Standing by the open driver's door, head thrown back, unshaven, scruffy and dishevelled, penis on display as he urinated with eye-catching force in full view of anyone unfortunate enough to be watching, was Nina's younger brother, Jason Nash.

2

Around the time John Nash and Val Beresford got married in the summer of 1972, they were talking about having children a great deal. It was what had originally brought them together, a quiet admission to each other that they wanted a family and wanted to be monogamous. They were both involved on the fringes of the radical politics of the time, and their decision to get married wouldn't exactly have raised their status among the gently Bohemian peer group they mixed with in London's Shepherd's Bush. Having children and getting married were not considered particularly hip in 1972, and John and Val kept these desires to themselves. Most of their friends wanted to live in communes or move to Paris and set fire to upturned Renaults. Most of their friends slept with each other in rapid succession. John and Val, as they were known to all their friends, kept to each other exclusively. In some ways the external pressure to behave otherwise was what brought them together. Even with shoulder-length hair and long sideburns, John Nash was a very responsible man, and he was hopelessly in love with his future wife.

John was a chef, a very hard-working and dedicated one. He'd started as a kitchen hand in a small hotel in Somerset. By the time he met Val he'd landed a job at the Dorchester in London. He didn't join in the rather sordid banter that flew around the kitchen, considering himself a modern and liberated man and believing woman's lib was a good thing and that women deserved respect.

This attitude was borne out by Val's career. She was doing very well in a postgraduate chemistry degree at Imperial College, London. She loved her work, she admired the people she worked with, and as the reality of the wedding crept up on her the idea of having children so soon started to become less attractive.

Like sixty per cent of the women of her generation, Val was on the Pill. She smiled as they made love, realising that John was convinced that he was, as he put it, 'having sex for the real reason – not for recreation, but for procreation'. As a chemist, Val knew that the Pill was not a hundred per cent effective against pregnancy, but she never worried about it. However, within ten months of their wedding, she was pregnant. She went to the doctor before she told John. He confirmed her fears and assured her there was no need to worry about the baby. Many women had become pregnant while on the Pill and had given birth to normal, happy children. He was an old man, and couldn't understand her obvious despair – she was married, she was healthy and young, what could be wrong with having a baby?

John was thrilled when she finally told him the news. So thrilled, in fact, that she kept her misery to herself and never expressed any of her fears to him. She told her mother, who had always quietly disapproved of her daughter's desire to become a scientist and said it was a good thing she was giving up the whole silly idea and settling down at last. So, after finishing her second year at Imperial College, she tearfully informed her tutor that she was leaving to start a family. The term 'start a family' sounded absurd to the young would-be scientist, but she swallowed her dignity and followed her fate.

Val settled down to a life of relative poverty and disappointment. Within weeks she found herself carrying shopping through the scruffy streets of Shepherd's Bush with an ever-growing belly and a faster-growing bitterness.

John Nash rose through the ranks at the Dorchester until, at the age of thirty, he was offered the chance to run his own restaurant at the King Charles at Cookham, a well-established hotel and eatery next to the Thames, in rural Berkshire.

Baby Nina was born in September 1973, three weeks before

he was due to start, so not only did Val have to deal with the baby, but she also had to pack up their meagre belongings and move house.

With a heavily loaded Ford Anglia, they drove out of London on a Saturday morning, baby Nina in a carry cot on her mother's lap, the back of the car stuffed with clothes, books and kitchen equipment.

John had always wanted four children, hoping for two boys and two girls. When Nina was born his life lit up with delight. Val seemed less excited by the whole affair, and when things got tough her first response was to attack John for forcing her into early motherhood. 'I should have had a bloody abortion,' she would say, a statement precisely designed to upset John, a lazy Catholic. However, Nina was a divine baby, everyone said so – pretty blonde hair in tight curls, a lovely disposition. She slept well, was rarely ill, teethed without problem, learned to talk at a very young age, walk at an even younger one, and by the time she was three could write her own name, swim and recite poetry.

Then along came baby number two.

'There's a baby growing in Mummy's tummy,' John Nash said to his daughter. 'Do you think it will be a boy baby or a girl baby?'

'A girl, a girl!' Nina squealed.

'It's a boy, Mrs Nash,' said the midwife at the maternity hospital.

'A boy!' said Val Nash. 'Are you sure?'

'Oh, I'm very sure, Mrs Nash. There's no doubting it with this little fellow.'

Val Nash burst into tears as soon as she saw the face of her son – very different from how she had reacted to the birth of her daughter. Maybe it was just that she had resigned herself to motherhood, or maybe it was that something special which often occurs between mother and son. Val Nash had a son, and she held him to her breast in a way she never had her daughter.

As an increasingly traditional man, John Nash stared into his son's face with tears running down his already slightly chubby cheeks. A son, a man, to carry on his name – someone he could talk to when he was older, someone on his side in the very feminine Nash household.

Jason's projectile vomiting started early. With roughly three hours' life under his belt, he directed the first salvo at his father, just as John Nash first picked up his son. This was greeted with great amusement by the rest of the family, who had gathered to welcome the new arrival.

A year later John Nash had a vasectomy operation at a private hospital. Always a staunch Labourite, he willingly broke his own ethical and religious diktat and paid for an operation he had always believed was intrinsically wrong.

Within another year he was a broken man. Baby Jason had turned the family's previously tranquil life into a hell on earth. They were living in an idyllic-looking two-bedroomed thatched cottage in the nearby village of Bourne End. A ten-minute cycle ride from the hotel, it was a beautiful little place. It was also damp, low lying and very small, and John Nash was working unspeakable hours. The restaurant was doing very well – it had been included in prestigious guides and had achieved four-star status, which meant there was a lot of cooking to do. Every night John rode back to the cottage exhausted, only to be greeted, even before he got through the door, by the wailing of his endlessly awkward son. When he braced himself and opened the tiny front door, he was greeted by a woman who had been going crazy all day, stuck in the middle of nowhere with a baby she obsessed over and a little girl who whined and whimpered almost non-stop.

John Nash would hold his daughter for hours, trying to stop her miserable sobs, but he generally fell asleep before she had settled, such was the level of his exhaustion.

Rarely sleeping for more than thirty minutes at a time, Jason screamed with a volume that was hard to credit, constant stomach and chest problems resulting in continuous coughing, diarrhoea and vomiting. Plus colic you could write a thesis on,

9

teething from hell, ear problems, infections everywhere a baby can get them, and more places besides, resulted in over seventy visits to the family GP in the first twelve months.

Nina's earliest memories, when she was aged around four, consisted of seeing her mother crying, her brother vomiting and her father sitting in the corner with his head in his hands. The house was in a terminal state, cramped and chronically untidy. She spent a lot of time alone in her bedroom – Jason had a cot stuffed into the corner of her parents' bedroom. However, by the age of five she had to unwillingly share her precious little corner with her already enormous and destructive brother.

Even when he was sleeping she had little respite – he kept her awake at night with his groaning, coughing and violent twitching. He broke her toys as he stormed around, grinning widely, his chin and clothes soaked in dribble from his teething, which seemed to last a decade.

By the time she went to school, Nina had already vowed that she would never have babies. Babies were something to be avoided. By the time she was ten she vowed never to have boyfriends. Boys were also something to be avoided because her brother, seven by this time, was still a constant thorn in her side. Her friends wouldn't come around to play because her little brother wouldn't leave them alone and either broke something, said rude words or obsessively showed them his willy.

And if there was an argument, which there often was, Nina would get the blame from her mother. She was always the one who started it, according to her mother. 'If you tease him, what do you expect, young lady,' she would spit, picking up the tearful Jason.

It seemed the wonderful Jason could do no wrong.

'Watcher, sis,' said the adult version of this phenomenon as he barged through the doors to Nina's laboratory. 'Christ alive, girl, you could do with putting on a bit of fat. Scrawny as a plucked GM chicken.'

Jason Nash was three years younger than his sister, a good

six inches taller, his clothes what can only be described as well worn. Soiled would be more accurate. He had mismatched socks, hair that looked as if he'd just been fished out of a sewer, and a strong, tangy smell that was discernible from two meters' distance.

'Thank you, Jason,' said Nina, her smile set at unpleasant, version 1 point 2. Her work colleagues, Hugo and Mandira, who had not previously had the pleasure of meeting brother Jason, looked on with a mixture of shock and amusement.

As Jason bent forward to kiss her, she reeled back instinctively. The smell on his breath was intolerable – vomit, smoke and alcohol, and something else she preferred to remain ignorant about.

'Sorry, haven't had a bath for a couple of days. Been really, really busy.' He leaned closer, mock-whispering in her ear. 'Actually I was, er . . . oh, never mind. Let's just say I got some.' He smiled at her lecherously, his once-perfect teeth stained and uncared for.

'Please, Jason.'

Jason finally cottoned on to the nods and nudges he was getting from his sister. He spun his head around dramatically and, Nina noticed, nearly lost his balance. He was obviously slightly drunk.

'Blimey! Didn't know anyone else was here.'

Without any hesitation, Jason moved towards the other people in the lab. Nina winced.

Mandira, a very bright but cripplingly shy Indian chemist, stood politely as he approached. Jason shook her hand vigorously.

'Sorry, love. Jason. Jason Nash. Nina's younger and, though I say it myself, far more attractive brother.' He was putting on a comic cheesy barfly voice, smarmy and creepy. Nina knew it was a joke, but it was clear Mandira was taking this awful sight at face value. She smiled and sat down, but Jason didn't let go of her hand.

'How long have you worked here?'

'Jason, they're busy,' Nina intervened. 'We have a lot on.' She could see the look of discomfort on Mandira's face.

'Hey, I'm only being friendly. Just thought I'd let them know I'm not another of the lecherous old married men who try to get in your pants, sis.'

Hugo laughed, but stopped as soon as he glanced at Nina, who felt great discomfort at this public reference to her private life. Hugo walked up to Jason, hand outstretched.

'Hi, I'm Hugo.'

'Hi there, Hugo, mate, how's it hanging?' said Jason as the two men shook hands vigorously.

'Very nicely, thank you.'

'Is sis being good to you?'

'She's wonderful, Jason, we couldn't ask for a better boss.'

'Yeah, I bet. She made my life a living hell when I was a kid,' said Jason with an explosive laugh.

It was the laugh Nina hated almost more than anything else. A defensive, showy and annoying laugh, at once to attract attention and repel anyone who tried to get close to him.

'Come into my office,' she said coldly.

She walked into her office. Her phone was ringing but she ignored it and turned to face Jason. He wasn't there. Nonplussed, she looked out of the door and saw that he was still talking to Hugo. The two men were standing close. She could see Hugo wasn't enjoying the interaction, but Jason had hold of his lab coat. He was whispering and gesturing in a manner that could only mean he was telling Hugo a joke or story with, as Jason would say, a high level of adult content.

'Jason, please!'

'Sorry, sis. Here I come.' As he said this he grunted and shuddered. Nina realised with repulsion that he was giving a crude rendition of a male orgasm. It was rounded off with a vulgar and very loud laugh. He nudged Hugo as he moved towards Nina, half trotting, half stumbling across the lab to her office.

'Very swish,' he said as he entered. Nina opened one of the

big windows, even though it wasn't warm outside. She needed fresh air if Jason was to be in the room.

'You could have rung.'

'Mobile's been cut off. That's why I'm here.'

'Jason!' said Nina. She had given him £1,000 a mere month before when he'd rung to explain that he was in a very dire situation and needed to borrow some money on what he described as a short-term fully repayable loan.

'I don't want any cash. Got any coffee, though? I could murder a cup. Only slept an hour last night.'

'I don't want to know what you were doing last night.'

'No, I was working. I've been busy-busy. Things are looking highly, highly positive. I mean capital H highly, capital P positive. Any chance of a coffee? I can make it.' He was walking around in circles as he spoke. She noticed that the sole on one of his battered low-heeled cowboy boots was hanging down like a dead pig's tongue.

'Look, Jason, I'm very busy. I've got a meeting with a new client in about ten minutes,' said Nina. She moved to the door and looked out. 'Hugo, could you make my dreadful brother a cup of coffee, please?'

She watched Hugo still smiling, get up.

'Milk and five sugars, please,' shouted Jason from within her office. Nina saw Hugo nod as he walked towards the canteen. Then she smelled something new. She turned to see Jason sitting back in her chair, feet on her desk, smoking a cigarette.

'Jason! This is a no-smoking building. For crying out loud.'

'Sorreeee,' said Jason annoyingly. He stood up and, after taking a few last puffs, flicked the cigarette out of the open window.

'There's a lot of very volatile material in the lab. You could blow us all up. There're huge notices everywhere.'

'Don't I know it. Bloody nanny state. Safety Nazis every-where. Anyway, lovely clever sis. I have a legit, top-drawer, kosher business proposition I'd like to slip between your legs and see if it makes you squirm. Sit yourself down and pin back the luggingtons.'

Nina sighed. He never gave up, any more than he ever did anything other than hassle innocent people, including Nina and her parents, for money.

'Jason, I can't get involved, I don't want to get involved. You already owe me more money than either of us can remember. This is ridiculous.'

'Wait, this is right up your street. I've met this bloke.'

'Oh, God.'

'Hear me out. Pretty please, sis.' Jason smiled. His smile was another of his disturbing aspects. Smiling looked as if it actually hurt his face. 'The man I met, he's different. He's government, not some fly-blown dot-commoner like me. He's legit. Serious budget, serious contacts, and he's very interested in your work.'

'What have you been telling him!' said Nina, a note of alarm in her voice. 'My work is very sensitive, you know that. There are a lot of influential corporations involved who have ploughed millions into what we are doing here.'

'Sure, sure. I know that. I was very discreet.'

'Jason!' she wailed. Discretion and Jason had never met, let alone communicated.

'Sure, sure.'

And she hated the way he always said 'sure, sure'. It was only just more polite than him saying 'I'm not listening to you anyway so you may as well shut up'. Which was clearly what he was thinking.

'The point is, I didn't need to tell him. As soon as he found out my name, he asked if I was related to you. My famous sister. I didn't have to tell him what you were doing. He already knew.'

'What did he say?'

'That you're top in your field . . . no, you're the only one in your damn field.'

'Well, he doesn't know what he's talking about. Who is he anyway?'

14

'Aha!' said Jason, tapping the side of his nose.

'What does that mean?'

'Here's your coffee,' said Hugo. He hadn't knocked, just walked straight in. Why, thought Nina, did her normal life collapse whenever her brother was present?

'Excellent. Is there somewhere we can go where I can smoke? I'm getting severe withdrawals now. I'll start scratching in a minute. You don't want me to do that.'

'There's the fire escape. That's where I go,' said Hugo.

'You don't smoke, do you?' asked Nina incredulously.

'Not tobacco.'

'Excellent,' said Jason. 'Man after my own heart. Lead on, McStoned.' He got up and followed Hugo through the lab.

Nina checked her watch. The man from the St Thomas' Hospital Trust was due any minute, but she felt duty bound to escort her brother. She followed Hugo and Jason down the brightly lit corridor and out on to the fire escape at the back of the building.

'Thanks, Hugo,' she said as he held the door open for her. 'Tell Amy I'll be down very soon.'

Hugo nodded and pulled a half-brick that was on the fire escape into the doorway, stopping the security door from shutting.

She watched Hugo depart, feeling lost and out of touch. She should be telling Amy herself, and she shouldn't be instructing one of her top data analysts to go and make coffee. Amy was the new department secretary, and she was alarmingly efficient. She had organised the meeting with the man from St Thomas', which was very important. It was Coventon's first brush with a major medical institution and could lead to a huge expansion.

'Aaaah, better now,' said Jason through a cloud of smoke. The day was cold and dull, typical for March, typical of the area in which the laboratory was situated. The distant hiss of the M11 was clearly audible, although it couldn't be seen from their vantage point. Nina felt tense and uncomfortable. She leaned against the safety rail and felt a damp patch seep through to her back. Everything was dripping wet and cold – the rain had only just stopped.

'Right, here's the gig,' said Jason. 'Mr X, as I shall now refer to him, has discussed various business propositions, one of which involves me recontextualising my present operations.'

'What, airline-food.com!' sneered Nina. 'I thought that had gone bankrupt.'

'In theory, yes, but as a business model it's cutting-edge, he really liked it. Anyway, the business is still in existence, virtually, and a radical recontextualisation at this stage of the game could send stocks off the scale. A lot of big investors are already sniffing around.'

'Jason, wake up. No one wants to buy airline food unless they're flying, and even then most people don't want it. It's a crap idea.'

A year previously, Jason had started up a top-flight dot-com start-up, as he described it, delivering top-drawer airline food to specifically targeted consumers from the A and B social groups. The food was to be delivered to the door within half an hour of the order being placed via the Internet. He had managed to do some dodgy deal with an airline catering company near Heathrow. Any excess meals they produced he would take off their hands at an enormous discount, then, using a network of equally dodgy pizza delivery firms working on a percentage, he would get the product to the customer in the allotted window. Nina had heard all about it at great and painful length. When she was staying with Sir Brian Coventon in his Kensington apartment she told him about it, and they ordered a first-class meal at a cost of £38 each, including delivery. Forty-eight minutes later a helmeted youth rang the elegant bell and delivered a lukewarm plastic meal platter which would have embarrassed the economy class cabin crew of even the most mealy-mouthed airline.

'Lucky I have a thick skin, courtesy of Mama and Papa,' said Jason. 'But anyway, it's all going to change. It's only the skeletal structure of the company that'll remain, and your share of company stock will be worth something again.'

'Again! When was it ever worth anything? I gave you ten grand to get off my back. What's that worth now?'

'Shares are currently trading at a little under point four of a cent, except they're not trading because of various misunderstandings with NASDAQ, but that's all being seen to. Mr X is sorting out the whole shebang.'

'Jason, listen. I have just fitted the first fully functional prosthetic arm to a twelve-year-old girl. She picked up a pencil with it. Do you understand how that might preoccupy me a little? It's something that will change her life, it's something that could help change the lives of millions of people throughout the world. It cost nearly a million pounds to develop and you want to waste my time talking about some sod-awful idea you've had with some drunk bloke you met in a cheesy hotel bar.'

'It was on a ship actually.'

'I don't care!' she shouted. 'I've had enough.'

'But you haven't heard what he wants to do.'

'Who?'

'Mr X. He wants to set up a company with over a billion dollars behind it. Not a million, Nina, a billion. He wants to employ the two of us, me as CEO and marketing manager, you as head of research, and, of course, you'd be a major, major shareholder in your own right. Which you already are because it's more or less airline-food.com under another name.'

'I have to go, Jason. And move your car. It's in Sir Brian's parking space.'

3

To look at him it would not be immediately apparent that an enormous amount of money had transferred through Jason Nash in his twenty-nine hectic years. Many hundreds of thousands of pounds, dollars and Euros had sluiced through his multiple bank, building society, trust fund and on-line bank accounts. However, none of it seemed to stay with him for any length of time.

Hence, when he needed some rainy-day money, he had nothing. Rain was pouring down as he sat in his Saab 900 convertible. He was barely aware of it, busy taking a series of deep gulps from a can of Carlsberg Special Brew. It was his last one – he'd been saving it up. He was shivering with cold, the roof of the car leaked, and a drip was running down his neck.

He wasn't that worried – he had managed to get the rather cute secretary in reception at the lab to call a recovery service to help him get moving again. He'd had to borrow Nina's membership card in order to make this feasible, and when he'd walked in on her meeting to hassle her for it, he got the distinct impression that she was very pissed off with him. Nothing new there, then.

He wound down the electric window – at least that worked – and spat a very impressive greenie on a high-lob trajectory. It landed right in the middle of the windscreen of the car next to him, a late-model BMW.

'Shit, that's a bit much,' he admitted, quickly opening the door and clambering out. He attempted to wipe the mess with the sleeve of his Prada jacket, making it much worse. He leaned on the car to give it a better wipe and the alarm started screaming immediately. All the lights started flashing. Jason lowered his head on to the rain-spattered bonnet.

'Shit,' he said.

He shook his head. It was always the way somehow – he tried to help people and everything got worse. He stood up and looked at his own car through the rain. It really was a pile of shit, no point arguing about it. A once prestigious motor, it was now a pile of mucky filth that would and regularly did disgrace even the most seedy of inner-city streets.

All the tyres on the Saab were bald enough to be actually dangerous, one of them had entirely disintegrated, and they'd all been illegal for months. He'd felt the car sliding all over the road as he'd driven up to Cambridge to pitch the new venture to his high-and-mighty sister. Luckily he hadn't been pulled over by the law. That would have been an extra load of hassle he didn't need – the car wasn't insured or taxed either. Not to mention he had lost his licence a year earlier, a totally fabricated drink-driving charge. He wasn't even driving – the car had been up a bank on the side of the M11, with Jason fast asleep.

Against all this, Jason was anything but depressed. He could sense that if he could just get past this last hurdle he'd be home free and driving a brand spanking new Mercedes CL500, fully kosher, with the built-in TV and GPS navigation system. He could pay off the various debts that had built up, come out of hiding in Tony's flat, start having a life again.

An hour and a half later a yellow van from the AA pulled up behind the Saab. A young man climbed out and walked towards the now silent BMW. He looked through the window and, seeing no one there, turned and noticed a man asleep in the filthy Saab. He tapped lightly on the window. Slowly the man came round and stared up at him, smiled and opened the door.

'Sorry, chief, must have nodded off there. Life in the fast lane can take it out of you.'

'Certainly seems to have taken it out of the vehicle, sir,' said the AA man dryly as he stood back and surveyed the damage. 'What seems to be the problem?'

'Oh, just a flat. Got no spare – it was nicked last week along with the radio and my laptop, and my phone and cheque book and wallet and about three grand in cash. Bit of a setback, but there we go.'

'I've got an emergency spare, sir, but it'll only get you to the nearest tyre dealers. Would it be better if I towed you? All the tyres are looking a bit . . . well, I suppose worn doesn't really do them justice.'

'Try seriously shagged.'

'Yeah.'

'Sure, sure, this is the problem,' said Jason without blanching. 'I guess the only option is to take the motor back to London and get a full service and valet there. It's booked in. I've been out of the country on business – all kinds of stuff's happened to it.'

Three hours later the patient AA man winched the car down on to Craven Hill Road in Bayswater. It was, he pointed out, a resident-only parking zone, but Jason assured him he had a permit in the house and would pop straight out and sort it.

He waved off the AA man and turned, bumping into something solid. He looked down. It was Costas.

'Hey, man, how's it going?' he asked with a nervous smile.

'Not good,' said Costas. 'If I told you I had a knife just under your balls, you wouldn't feel happy, would you?'

Costas was short and rather vicious looking with swept-back black hair. He was also standing very close, and although Jason couldn't actually feel a knife in the position Costas had described, he had seen enough of the diminutive Greek dealer to know he probably wasn't arseing about.

'No, that isn't a suggestion which fills me with calm and relaxing thoughts, Costas, my old pal,' said Jason as brightly as he could.

'Just like me and Michael,' said Costas. 'We are full of tense and depressed thoughts because you owe us around forty grand.'

'Forty is it now? Goodness me, I only remembering you

investing a mere thirty K in my venture, which, I can assure you, is about to go totally ballistic.'

'Yeah, well, we ain't interested in your dot-com crap, Jason. We want our money back, and we want it now.'

'Okay, Costas, I hear you, and here's the situation as I see it. You disembowel me here and now and you can wave bye-bye to any future share bonus, or you allow me time to set up my new venture, at no further cost to yourselves, and your minor investment will turn into a major, and I really mean major, revenue stream. You won't be wandering the streets looking for people who owe you at all times of the day and night. You will have other people to do that for you. You won't have time because you will be too busy perusing yacht catalogues and working out which colour to have the bathroom in your West Indian mansion.'

'Oh yeah, we heard it before.'

'No, you've never heard this before, Costas, because you have never been lucky enough to invest in a man who is destined to be the captain of one of the most exciting tech-no-breakthroughs of the last thousand years. You will be worth billions, and I'm not exaggerating – you and Michael will be praised as two of the canniest investors this century. There will be art galleries and shopping malls named after you. Two weeks, Costas. That's all I need, matey boy. Two diddly weeks and you can retire.'

Costas stepped back. Only then did Jason realise that Michael, his sidekick and an even more unsavoury-looking character, was standing right behind him.

'If you're bullshitting, Nash, we won't want our money back, we won't fucking need it. When they find your head in a litter bin it will tell everyone that they don't fuck with Costas.'

'Lanky cunt,' was all Michael could add to the threat. The two men sloped off down the street. Jason stood motionless for a moment, then breathed very deeply. He could feel his heart pounding in his chest. But at least it was still pounding.

'Haven't lost it yet, Jason, me old mucker,' he said quietly to himself as he climbed the rubbish-bestrewn steps and pressed on the buzzer of flat 14C. He waited. Eventually he heard someone pick up the receiver.

'It's Jase.'

'Where did you call from?' came the tinny voice.

'What? No, Tony, it's me, Jason.'

'Oh, bloody hell, thought you were a punter. What do you want, love?'

'I need a piss and a bath.'

The door buzzed open and Jason ran in. He climbed the three flights of stairs and pushed open the unlocked door.

'Jeeesus. I need a slash,' he said as he stormed through the tiny apartment and pushed back the beaded curtain hanging precariously in the bathroom doorway. He could sense Tony standing in the kitchen, which faced the bathroom. When Jason had relieved himself, he washed his hands and face messily in the cramped bathroom sink.

'Look at you, love. What have you been doing?' asked Tony, who, Jason noticed, was wearing an orange pair of Diesel underpants and white socks. 'You smell like an Egyptian brothel.'

'I *am* an Egyptian brothel,' said Jason as he dried his face on a towel printed with an explicit Tom of Finland cartoon. 'But I'm about to be a very flash, rich Egyptian brothel. Any calls?'

'Loads, love, I've been worked off my feet. Anyone would think you straight boys never got any.'

'No, I mean any calls for me?'

'Some Yank.'

'George. When did he call?'

'Woke me up at the crack of doom. Where've you been, then?'

'Met some totty last night, can't remember where we ended up. Must have shagged her, though, the old todger's sore as a raw stump. I shot up to Cambridge this morning to see big sis. I think she's very interested.'

'What's she interested in – your raw stump?'

'No, fuck off. We're not into that in my family.'

'That's what my Uncle Sid said to me when I was eleven,' said Tony. 'Well, you can't stay here, love. I've got customers coming any minute. They'll think you're a punter I can't get rid of.'

'Look, I'll stay in the back bedroom, you won't hear a thing. Just need a mobile.'

'You want to use my mobile? Oh, love, walk all over me. Why not just steal the telly and the stereo while you're at it?'

Jason smiled. 'Look, Tone, I'll make you a nice cup of tea. Put your feet up, relax. I'll clean up the kitchen. In a couple of weeks I'll buy you your own massage parlour. Okay?'

'Go on, then, you dreary old fuck,' snapped Tony. The phone rang. Tony dropped on the couch, which was covered in a red velvet throw, and languorously picked up the receiver.

'Hello . . . yes, that's right. Fees start at fifty pounds. Yes, full body-to-body and hand relief. Yes. Would you like to come and see Tony? He's twenty-two, dark haired, very tight, very trim and very hung. Yes.'

Jason watched Tony work the phone almost affectionately. They had met during Jason's brief time as an actor in America five years previously. Jason always described what he did as acting – it made life easier. He was actually appearing in adult films (he only made seven, but they were all big sellers) and he'd worked with the best – Jeanna Jameson, Tanya Murphy and Annabel Chong. All top women in the field, as he referred to them.

Tony, by contrast, had been working as a fluffer for gay movies, a job he enjoyed a great deal. It was his task to encourage the actors to 'get wood' on set.

Jason had decided to try the gay ones because he would be paid a great deal more money, but even with Tony's expert help he couldn't really do the business. 'Wood, as they say, could not be got,' Tony had commented at the time. Jason was very much heterosexual, and he never lost any sleep wondering why.

Entering the kitchen, Jason breathed a sigh of relief to find it tidy and clean. He wouldn't have to do anything after all – always the best option. He crept out, picked up Tony's mobile from the low coffee table, which was neatly displaying a pile of gay magazines, and entered the back bedroom. This was a tiny cubbyhole with a window looking out on to a damp brick wall – for the time being, Jason's home.

'Hello, can I speak to George Quinn?' he said quietly, cupping his hand over the tiny mobile. He could hear that someone had come to the apartment to be serviced by Tony, and he knew all hell would break loose if he made too much noise.

'May I ask who's speaking?' asked a woman's voice.

'Yeah, Jason Nash. I'm calling from England.'

'I'll check, see if he's available.'

Jason kicked off what remained of his shoes. He glanced at his socks. They were stiff and holed and even Jason, who had a well-developed degree of tolerance to human filth, didn't want them anywhere near him.

'Mr Nash, nice of you to call,' said the voice of George Quinn. 'How is everything?'

'It's all good,' replied Jason. 'I've been in deep discussions with my sister. I feel we've covered most of the vital areas. I have to remind you that she is a very sensitive individual.'

'Sure, I hear you.'

'And as her only brother I feel responsible for making sure she's not being exploited.'

'There's no question of that, Jason. Both of you will be very well looked after.'

Jason silently punched the air and felt his toes curl up tight with delight.

'Of course, I know that, but I have to convince her. She is very interested but, as you know, seriously committed to her work at Coventon Research. I'm working on convincing her, and I think I'm close, very, very close, to full closure. She's been ringing me hourly, which is a good sign.'

'Oh, really? Well now, that is good news. You know we've approached her boss, Sir Brian. He's been very unhelpful, really, which is a shame for him.'

'Sure, sure.'

'So we really are up against a brick wall here, Jason, and if there's any way you can help us, we would be very grateful. I think you know what I mean.'

'Sure, sure. Yeah, it's all as good as very sorted here. When are you due over?'

'I arrive in Europe next Tuesday. I'm in Zurich on Wednesday, Munich on Thursday.'

'Sure, sure,' said Jason, his mind spinning for a moment with the problem of getting his sister to do anything he actually wanted her to do, even when he knew it was a good thing for her. Then it hit him. He was a lucky guy – his birthday was the following Friday.

'Yeah, I've got a hell of a week and so has Nina. Now let me see,' he said, looking at his rather grey bed-sheet. 'I know Nina is free Friday night, and, yes, so am I. Friday is the only day – well, evening, I've got meetings all day.'

'Friday I can do.'

Jason again punched the air in silence. He wanted to sound cool – he really couldn't afford to blow it now. 'Okay. Let's meet at the Met Bar, Friday evening.'

'Maybe somewhere a little quieter. Do you know the Cobden Club?'

'No, but I can find it. What time?'

'Let's say seven-thirty. I'll see you then?'

'Sure, sure. Yeah, no probs. Great. Oh, and George . . .' Jason was thinking ahead, something he could do only when he was under severe pressure. 'I'm worried about her feeling put upon. What would be good would be to make it look like an informal gathering, like a low-key party. Can you, like, invite some people you know in London to come along, just to, you know, make the place seem easy and relaxed? I'll have loads of my work colleagues there, of course, but new faces could really help. To help Nina relax and not feel like the centre of attention – she's really not into that.'

'I understand.'

'I'll spin her a bit of a line about it being a party or something. Leave it with me.'

'No problem,' said George Quinn.

Jason could hear him smiling. He switched off the mobile and lay back on the tiny bed. 'Sorted,' he lied to himself. 'Absolutely a hundred per cent sorted.'

He smiled and allowed his very tired eyes to close. He imagined a car bomb going off outside the flat, the windows being blown in, glass flying everywhere. He imagined the screams of the injured as he rushed about trying to help people. Then he imagined looking up into the night sky as it became brighter than day. A huge meteor was heading for the middle of London. He imagined the impact, the shattering blast, the whole city flapping like a giant sheet, everything destroyed. He smiled as he imagined his body being smashed to pulp by vast chunks of flying building. He turned on one side and visualised the meteor hitting the sea and a vast tidal wave a mile and a half high approaching the city skyline. He could see individual people trying to swim up the inconceivable wall of water as it crushed everything in its path. There were tanks charging down the streets of West London, followed by hordes of murderous troops, killing everyone in their path. He slowly fell asleep.

4

Nina sat in her BMW in the carpark watching with annoyance as the wipers failed to clean a great big smear off her windscreen. She couldn't work out what it was. Not bird droppings, but something very sticky and unpleasant had been smeared all over the glass. She didn't need it – she'd been going flat out all day; all she wanted to do was drive home, have a bath, put her feet up and watch the telly.

Nina had grown into a very self-contained woman. Her new little house on River Lane in Cambridge was clean and tidy, some might even say a little spartan. She lived alone, although at times had taken in lodgers, Japanese students being the preferred type as they were not very demanding but were very tidy. She didn't have cats, dogs or pot plants. She didn't even have curtains – all the windows sported blinds. Nina had no longings for old country cottages. She'd grown up in one and knew what they were really like. Although not a radical woman in terms of her behaviour, she did tend to react against her parents' way of life. Cooking, gardening, country walks, dogs, children, piles of laundry and chaos were something she brutally banished from her life. She wanted none of it. When she had first walked into a laboratory at school she had felt her heart leap for joy – it was so tidy, so easy to understand, so sensible. She excelled at science and maths – she loved the logic, the predictable pattern of events, the clear thinking and, for her at least, the easy-to-achieve answers.

As she got older she found to her consternation that life became more complex. Interactions with other people seemed to bring chaos and disorder. Men in particular seemed so disorganised, messy, emotionally chaotic and alarming to be near – particularly men her own age. She lost her virginity when she was eighteen, during her first weeks at Corpus Christi College in Cambridge. The young man in question was a year older than her, wonderfully attractive and carefree. However, within hours of doing the deed, as they lay in bed together talking, she had proof positive that young men really were a bunch of losers. He managed to talk about himself and his mother and how lonely he was for most of the night, and then he asked her to masturbate him, something she had no desire to do at all. It was like listening to a spoilt child. In fact, that's what she decided as she left – she had been listening to a spoilt child, a six-foot-tall one.

Now she was on her way to a sort of romantic assignation with a man very nearly old enough to be her father. Older men had been Nina's only romantic interest for most of her adult life, and Sir Brian Coventon was far and away the best.

He was up from London to give a talk at the Cambridge Union, and their assignation had been arranged weeks before. Normally she would be thrilled to be seeing him; it was simply exhaustion which made her wish she could cancel.

She drove the short distance into Cambridge and found her way through the one-way system, turning into Magdalene Street and slowing down to a crawl. It was the start of the spring term, and a swirling mass of students filled her vision. She took a left into Thompsons Lane and, by a miracle, found somewhere to park. Cambridge was not a city that made a motorist's life easy. When she had been a student there herself she wouldn't have dreamed of having a car. Now she had been given one and found it very useful, although still felt a little uncomfortable about being in such a smart one. As she got out, she noticed young men looking at her, but also looking at the car. When she first took possession of it, she was immediately aware that it made men turn and stare. She had no idea what the car was – it was a car, like any other. New and clean, that was the main thing. When she had parked it on a street for the first time and watched men walk past looking at it, she was worried she had driven into the kerb and damaged it in some way. She had got out and walked around the car to see what everyone was looking at. She found nothing wrong.

She retrieved her bag from the back seat. As she walked away the card in her wallet sent a signal to the car and the doors locked, the lights flashed and the engine was immobilised.

She remembered how this was explained to her in great awe by the young man who had delivered the car, how important it was to him that the car had no key, that merely placing her hand on the gearshift would start the engine.

She knew it was simple engineering, and that in fact motor manufacturers were years behind in tech development. They could easily produce hybrid electric cars that ran for thousands of miles on one battery charge. Having a car that started when you put your hand on the gearshift was so mundane, but it pleased the boys, and the boys were the customers.

She walked into the Cambridge Union building. A smartly dressed young man standing by the door to the debating chamber smiled at her.

'Hello, I'm Professor Nash, a colleague of Sir Brian Coventon,' she said. 'I'd just like to watch from the gallery.'

'Oh, yeah, cool. Hello, Professor. Sir Brian said you'd be coming. D'you know where to go?'

'I certainly do. I was at Cambridge, not that long ago.'

'Oh, right. Cool. Sorry. Yeah.'

'Tell me,' said Nina, interrupting the man's babble, 'is this a debate or a talk?'

'It's a really intense debate,' said the young man. 'This house believes machines will destroy us. Wish I could see it. Got the old short straw tonight, doing security, et cetera. Place is heaving. I've had to turn hundreds away, but I've saved a seat for you, yeah.'

Nina made her way upstairs and into the chamber. Although she'd been warned of the size of the crowd it didn't really strike her until she saw the audience shoulder to shoulder in the old debating hall. When she had been a student the notion that a scientist might fill the Union building was a non-starter. A soap star, a comedian, a page-three girl maybe, but not a scientist. It only went to show what sort of man Sir Brian was, apart from being fiercely rich. He had a charming way of dealing with the world, at once enthusiastic and dry, knowledgeable but never patronising.

She smiled when she saw him standing in the centre of the chamber, looking rather dashing in his dinner jacket. Publicly this man was happily married – his wife was a doctor, a vivacious and well-respected public figure, appearing on TV news shows when the subject of the health service was on the agenda. They had three wonderfully clever children and a black Labrador dog.

However, all is often not as it seems. Sir Brian was conducting a furtive and long-term affair with Nina Nash, the most senior member of his research department.

'There are, of course, people who fear machines, fear where they are taking us, and that I can understand. New things can be scary – not everyone likes change.' He put on a funny voice and pulled a clown face. 'Oh, please, we were used to it the way it was, Sir Brian. Don't tell us something new – eeee.'

The audience erupted in delight. He looked around the packed chamber, his face alight with what he had to impart.

'There have been plenty of examples of how machines have been greeted with fear and misunderstanding in history, but, ladies and gentlemen, although they may have caused disturbance at their introduction, people very rapidly adapted to the advantages they had to offer. And if you think the development of internal combustion engines, rocket power or electricity made an impact, well, to use a phrase once admired by young people, bu-bu-bu-bu-baby, you ain't seen nothing yet.'

Another cheer and a round of hearty applause from the enraptured crowd.

'At our laboratories we are developing machines of such microscopic smallness that they can be injected into the human body to carry out remedial surgery. People are going to hate them – they will have religious reasons as to why it's wrong to send a mini-digger to excavate the blocked ventricles of someone's heart. We are developing microcomputers the size of a grain of sand that will enable the limbless to walk, the blind to see, the deaf to hear and the dumb to rabbit on like me. We are standing in the doorway of a new period of unfounded human development, where man and machine come together, not letting machine take over, but improving both. I plead with you to vote against this absurd and dated motion. We are not building machines so that they can take over the world, we are really building them so that we might better understand ourselves. The defence rests. I thank you.'

He sat down to thunderous applause and cheering. Nina noticed an old man sitting opposite him shake his head. It certainly looked as if Sir Brian had done it again.

She met him outside the members' area half an hour later, having dealt with more than one eager young lad who wanted to know whether she wanted to go for a drink. Nothing if not confident, Cambridge students.

'Well done,' she said as he approached her.

'Thank you. Hungry?' he asked. He didn't even give her a kiss on the cheek; his hand just gave the barest brush to her forearm. They were in public – even if they were only being observed by students, they had to be careful.

'Starving.'

'Me too.'

They left swiftly, Sir Brian signing two autographs as they walked out of the building.

Although the weather was cold, Nina found it refreshing to walk through the streets. It was as if she hadn't done it since her college days. Her work commitments meant that she rarely walked anywhere – she was always driving, being driven, riding in trains or planes. Just a simple walk was uplifting. After a while Sir Brian put his arm through hers, which surprised her – he was usually very discreet. She glanced at him and he smiled.

'We're colleagues, after all.'

'You were good tonight,' she said, inwardly cursing herself as she said it for sounding like an impressionable teenager.

'I was, wasn't I,' said Sir Brian with a big grin. 'Poor old McThirdle.'

'Who?'

'James McThirdle, the fellow at the debate. He's a philosophy don at Oxford. Funny old stick, but sweet chap.'

'Oh, I didn't hear him talk. He looked a bit downtrodden at the end.'

'Didn't he just.'

'Have you heard about the Neilson girl?'

'I spoke to her father this afternoon.'

'Was he impressed?'

'Ecstatic. He was in tears. She was clapping in the background, proper claps, both hands cupped.'

'I know. It's amazing. And you know something else?'

'Tell me, you gorgeous creature,' said Sir Brian, squeezing her arm.

'I went through the data with Hugo this afternoon. The stuff we recorded while she was trying out the arm. We were getting readings that had nothing to do with movement.'

'I'm sorry?'

'Well, we've got a huge database of movement readings from when she had the training chip inserted. We studied the data and removed everything that wasn't associated with actual movement.'

'This I know,' said Sir Brian, a slight snip in his delivery, very much the arrogant scientist having to listen to the greenhorn student.

'But today we did the opposite. Cleared out all the data we knew to be movement readings, and when we played back the videotape in time with the data we concluded there could only be one explanation.'

'Which is?'

'It's recording emotional response.'

'No, no, no. It's just static, outside interference.'

'It isn't, Brian. Not this time. It's absolutely clear. Big spikes just before tears, big spikes when her father reassured her. We recorded Ingrid Neilson's emotional responses, clear as day.'

Sir Brian stopped walking. He held Nina by the shoulders and looked into her eyes – not something he did very often.

'I don't want you to follow that line of research. Is that clear?'

'What d'you mean? This is earth-shattering.'

'Nina, listen to me. It's nothing new. Scientists discover things, all sorts of things. Some have a practical use, some don't. If we get diverted into some very dubious research cul-de-sac, we're going to lose out. The whole operation is running on a knife-edge as it is. We must stick to our primary goal of health-based cybernetic development. It's not as if we don't have enough to do already.'

'I don't believe this,' said Nina. She could feel a wave of anger washing over her as she looked at him. It was so out of character. This was the renegade, the maverick, the man who'd try anything and often ended up being pilloried by the scientific establishment for his efforts. Nina groped for the right words, trying not to sound too angry. 'How can you stand there and say, "You've discovered something, now just go home and forget it"?'

Sir Brian rubbed his face. He looked up and down the street. He looked scared.

'I didn't want to say anything, but I see I have no choice. I have to trust you on this.' He waited for her to respond. She wasn't sure she understood what he was saying. 'Nina, I need to trust you. Can I trust you?'

'Of course you can bloody trust me,' she snapped.

'I've known about this from day one. Because of the advances we've been able to make with chip design, I always knew we were going to have to confront this issue at some time. It's explosive, Nina, and it's too far too soon. No one is ready for what this could mean. The arm works, we can record and play back nervous responses and signals. We know we can do it. There is nothing to stop us recording and playing back emotional ones. Not only that, we could record them from one person and play them back in another. Do you understand the implications of such power?'

'I haven't really thought about it,' said Nina, feeling a sudden chill. 'I only worked it out this afternoon. I can't believe you knew. You've never said anything.'

'Of course not.' Sir Brian looked around almost furtively. They started walking again and he spoke in a hushed voice. 'If we record emotion – let's just say, for the sake of argument, aggression – and we play that back to another individual, who d'you think might be interested in such a system?'

'I don't bloody know,' said Nina, who was feeling confused.

'Well, it's not likely to be a hospital, is it?'

'The military,' said Nina.

Sir Brian nodded. 'I'm sure they're already doing it in some dreadful way. It's too awful. I refuse to go down in history as the next J. Robert Oppenheimer.'

'Who's he?' asked Nina.

'Oh, for goodness' sake, Nina. You're a scientist, how can you not know. He's the man who produced the atomic bomb.'

'Oh, sure, of course. The Manhattan project. Sorry, I just wasn't following your line of thought. I didn't study history.'

'That's a very poor excuse. Maybe you should before you dive headlong into territory that is very, very dangerous.'

'But you can't stop research, no one can. If we don't do it someone else, someone else with far less ethical sensitivity, will!'

'Dammit, I know I can't stop it!' he shouted.

Nina wasn't sure what to do. She'd never known Sir Brian like this before. They walked in silence for a while, soon approaching Browns restaurant on Keble Street.

They ate in virtual silence. Only after they'd eaten and the waiter bought them coffee did Sir Brian start speaking.

'I'm utterly stumped as to what to do. It's an ethical dilemma of the first order. I don't know what to do about the company.'

'What's wrong with the company?'

'Oh, nothing serious. It's just that we're out there, right at the front, and something this big would push us even farther into the lead. The pressures are enormous, Nina.'

'What are you talking about?'

'Let me just say that it's horrible, the pressure I am under from the trustees, from corporations, the government – they're all piling it on as we are starting to show real results, but they always want more. We've got to stay so far ahead to even hope to survive.'

'What about the Neilson girl? That's pretty leading edge, for crying out loud.'

'I know, but that's already in the public domain. Everyone knows about that, it's yesterday's news. What keeps Coventon Research funded is next week's news, or next year's news. The only news I've got is news I don't want to have.'

Sir Brian was well known for his ardent pacifist standpoint. Nina knew from first-hand experience that he had frequently turned down lucrative research fellowships and funding from corporations with military links.

'So what are you going to do?'

'I don't know. I really don't know. But if we can record and play back emotional responses using the same chip . . . well, where's the stop point? It's so explosive. Yes, there are possibly dozens of benign applications for such technology, but there are far more hostile ones. And hopefully, Nina, you and I are just about the only people who really know about this.'

She looked at him, the married man who had been her occasional lover for as long as she cared to remember. He was so lean and elegant, so wise, and now, for the first time she could remember, deeply troubled. Although she was developing reservations about him, she still found him oddly attractive.

'Poor darling,' she said softly. 'Let's go to the hotel. I'll give you one of my massages.'

Sir Brian slowly looked up. His face broke into a smile and he raised one eyebrow lasciviously. 'If I had a chip insert and we were recording my emotions and sensations now, I'd want to play this one back all the time.'

5

Jason mopped up the remains of his fried egg with a slice of white bread and folded his copy of the *Sun*. Breakfast at Luigi's café on Queensway was one of his big treats. It was only possible because Tony had loaned him £100, enabling him to enter a cash-based transaction mode. Jason didn't like to think of himself as a cash-based person. He'd been transmitting and receiving money via computer for as long as he could remember – the whole idea of cash was somehow grubby to him.

What Tony didn't know was that Jason had borrowed his mobile. Tony was still asleep. It was only 11.30 in the morning, after all, and he rarely got up before one. But Jason needed to talk to big sister Nina, needed to get her to meet with him. He didn't like doing it but he realised he was going to have to work a bit of subterfuge to get what he wanted.

'Good morning, Coventon Research Trust, can I help you?'

'Hello, yeah, sure, sure. This is Jason Nash calling.'

'Ah, good morning, Mr Nash. How are you? It's Amy speaking.'

Amy was the secretary at the lab Jason had hassled the previous day. He found her quite cute, but nothing special. However, now he could hear a distinct flirtatiousness in her tone he started to change his opinion. It had been a while since he'd heard that. In his youth he had become blasé about women flirting with him – it had happened all the time. He knew he was one hell of a good-looking guy; but he also knew he had been looking none too good of late. Times had been hard in many departments, including the shagging area. It was clearly worth a play.

'Sure, sure. Hi, Amy, of course, how are you?'

'I'm fine, thank you, Mr Nash.'

'Hey, call me Jason, please.'

'Okay, Jason. Are you coming to visit us again?'

'I'm sure I will be.' He was on a roll, he could feel it. 'Actually, now you're there, Amy, maybe I can have a discreet word.'

'Oh, please do.'

Oh yes – Jason's thoughts had already transferred the requisite signals to his nethers.

'Sure, sure. I'm actually starting up a company that really needs, like, a top-grade – I'm talking top of the range – secretary. Now clearly I've been headhunting through the on-line recruitment services, but there's nothing like one-to-one contact.'

'I know, you're right.'

'I'm talking a lot more responsibility than you've got work-ing there. D'you think you could handle it?'

'Well, it sounds very interesting.'

'Of course, the offices would be in central London, or maybe Cambridge, as it's all ultra hi-tech. We haven't decided on a location just yet – been to see a few places – but we're talking absolute top-flight stuff.'

'Well, yes, please keep me in mind.'

'Sure, sure. I will, Amy, don't you worry about it. Now, is that sister of mine around?'

'I'll put you through, Jason. One moment.'

Jason punched the air. He sighed as the line went quiet, then shook himself. This had to be good.

'What!' snapped Nina's voice on the phone.

'Hi, it's me.'

'I know it's you. What do you want?'

'Nothing. I'm inviting you to my birthday party.'

'Your birthday?'

'This Friday.'

'Oh God, Jason. You know I hate your parties.'

'Sure, sure, but I've turned over a new leaf.'

'Didn't know you had any more leaves to turn.'

'Oh, ha-de-ha,' said Jason. He took a big pull on his Marlboro. 'Look, it's different. It's at a nice club. There'll be no strippers. It's just me and a few friends, but not my old crowd – it's dot-commoners mostly. Geeks, nerds and their ilk.'

'Oh God . . . Jason.'

He could tell from her voice that she was malleable. Time for a trump card.

'I've asked Mum and Dad,' he lied, planning to ring them the moment he finished talking to Nina. 'They said they'd come, as long as . . . Well, same reasons you're reluctant, and I can understand that. I know I've been a prick in the past, but I'm thirty, for God's sake, or I will be on Friday. It's like a big turning point. Please, sis. It would really mean a lot to me.'

'Oh, I don't know. Where is it?'

'The party? Cobden Club. It's cool, not a strip joint. It's in Notting Hill, you know, Julia Roberts and all that – she might be there for all I know. I'll e-mail you the address. Great, see you Friday, and I don't even want a present.'

He hung up before she could say anything. 'Yes!' he shouted. He wasn't even aware that this made other customers in the steamy café jump in surprise. He'd started to pull a deal together again.

'Hi, Mum, it's Jase.'

'Hello, darling, I knew you'd call. You are a good boy.'

'Thanks, Mum, and before you start your worrying, it's all right, I don't want anything. I'm not broke or in prison or in Acapulco needing an air ticket. I was just ringing to see how you were.'

'That's kind, darling. Are you well?' asked his mother.

'I'm fine. Look, it's my birthday on Friday.'

'I know. I've knitted you a lovely jumper.'

'Sure, sure. Great, Mum, I love your jumpers, wear them all the time. But listen, I'm having a little celebration.' He waited for the response but his mother said nothing. Tough nut to crack with his track record.

'I'm having a party, Mum, a normal, pleasant party. Not with my old crowd, I've moved on. I've really cleaned up my act. Ask Nina, she's coming.'

'Is she? Well, we all know she'd go to the opening of an envelope, dear.'

'Yeah, but it should be a bit of a family celebration, shouldn't it. Thirty years old, turning point and all that.'

'What a lovely thought, darling, you're so kind. But you know what your father's like. Can't get him out of that sodding kitchen no matter what.'

'Well, you could come on your own, Mum. I'd lay on a taxi and everything.'

'Well, I'm not sure.'

'As I said, it's not some rave, it's in a nice discreet club in London, not a strip joint – there's not going to be any bare bosoms or pulsating buttocks.'

'Please, dear.'

'Just a little get-together with some of my business collea- gues, legitimate business people, Mum, not like before. I'd really like you and Dad to come. I am thirty, after all.'

'I don't know, dear. You know I'd love to come. See my big boy.'

'Sure, sure.'

'But your father's very busy, we've got a big wedding reception on Saturday. You know how he gets before a big do.'

'Sure, sure, well, maybe you could come. Please, Mum. Blimey, I haven't seen you in I don't know how long.'

'A month, when you came and borrowed the car.'

'Sure, sure.'

'Where is it, by the way, dear?'

'I'll get it back to you, it's all a bit complicated, but I've turned over a new leaf. I'm really sorted now, I know what I want to do, and I've been given a golden opportunity to do it. And it's not porn, Mum, it's a legitimate business, and I'll actually get paid big time, I'm talking shed-loads, and I'll buy you a new car if it comes to that.' He knew it would come to that – he'd sold his mother's nice little silver Golf and already somehow redistributed the resulting funds.

'I know dear. I'll have a word with John, but you know you're less than popular at home at the moment.'

'Sure, sure. I understand. I know I've been a burden.'

'You're not a burden, you know that, darling.'

'Sure, yeah, that's nice, Mum. Look, I'll send you a card with the address on. Please come.'

'Is there anywhere I can ring you, darling? I miss talking to you.'

'Well, it's complicated at the moment until we've decided on a suitable office. It's all going ahead a hundred per cent. Just a few more things to sort out then I'll let you know.'

'All right, dear, and where are you living now?'

'Really nice place in W2, really handy for Paddington. Just having it decorated at the moment so it's a bit of a mess, but when it's all done, I want to have you and Dad round for dinner. I'll cook. I've really changed, Mum. Honest.'

'All right, dear. Well, take care.'

'Sure, sure. See you Friday.'

He switched off the phone, pushed his chair back and lit up another Marlboro. He looked out of the window at the people rushing past in the heavy rain. It was all going to plan. Almost.

He sat up and tapped the ash off the end of his cigarette. No one else was coming to the party except his sister and his mum and dad, and even then his mum and dad probably wouldn't show. It would be obvious to Nina that she was being set up. He had to get some other people along.

The only problem was he owed money to most of the people he knew, and in some cases more than money. Some of them wanted to kill him, or so they had threatened. He took another long pull on the cigarette and stood up to leave.

'That's four pounds fifty,' said the eagle-eyed waitress, who was standing near the door. When he had arrived they had accused him of leaving without paying on a previous visit, an occurrence he could not recall.

'Don't worry, I'm going to pay,' said Jason, flashing his charming smile. 'It was a lovely breakfast, thank you.'

He gave her a five-pound note. 'Keep the change, Maria.'

'I'm not Maria,' said the waitress as she stuffed the money in her apron pocket.

6

It was Friday night, it was raining, and there were rumblings of yet another fuel shortage. Everyone knew that on Friday night getting into or out of London in a car was a bit of a non-starter. Nina knew this too but it didn't help – the annoying man on Capital Radio, 98.5 FM, was rubbing it in.

'Whatever you do, don't go on the M25!' he was screaming over the sound of the twin-engine plane he was supposedly buzzing around in, although Nina always imagined him sitting in a studio with a clever technician playing the soundtrack of a plane in the background. 'It's a total SWOT situation, yes indeed. Sheer Weight of Traffic. Clockwise near the M11 we're looking at fourteen-mile tailbacks – as far as the flying eye can see it's a total nose-to-tail horror show. I don't think I've ever seen it this bad. Lordy, lordy, if you're in that mess, you've got a long wait, baby.'

Nina tapped her fingers on the steering wheel as the car in front of her slowly moved another metre forward. She checked her watch. She was supposed to be in Notting Hill at a party she didn't want to go to. It was hopeless. She tried to resign herself to the fact that she was going to be very late. She tried not to remind herself that she had considered going by train. She tried not to worry that her brother was an incurable hopeless case who had spent his entire adult life making a mess of everything he came into contact with. Something happened whenever she had contact with him. Her life would be running smoothly, with very little stress outside work, and then he'd turn up and things would start to break, or go missing, or get lost for weeks, until he'd gone again, when they would suddenly turn up and life would return to its normal calm.

She couldn't remember him being born, but she knew her childhood had been affected by his arrival. Her parents changed – no longer happy and giggling, they were short tempered, tired, bored by what she had to say, her father always distant, her mother spiteful and resentful.

She could remember specific instances where everything had gone wrong and what had been enjoyable high jinks turned into distressing dramas. The bath of hell, as it had come to be known in the family, had started out so innocently.

It was very soon after her father had managed to raise the financial backing to buy the hotel he had been working in when the previous owners finally gave up. They moved from their cramped little cottage into the hotel. Nina remembered how exciting it was to live in such a huge building with so many rooms, even if they weren't allowed in most of them. Everything seemed to change for the better. Nina had her own room which Jason was not, under any circumstances, allowed to go into. Family life improved, there was more space, and her parents seemed happier.

One night she was sharing a bath with her little brother. He would have been about four. They were happy, frolicking under the foam of their scented bubble bath. Jason was laughing and giggling, and started to show off. He jumped out of the bath and picked up his clothes which their mother had neatly folded on the bathroom chair. He said he wanted to wash them. It seemed like fun, so Nina got her clothes – she was only seven, after all – and they too went in the bath. Nina could remember that this was enough for her, but not for Jason. He then pulled all the towels off the towel rail, and the dressing gowns off the peg on the bathroom door, and threw them in the bath, jumping on top of them to make sure they got wet. They were still giggling, although Nina could remember feeling alarmed, worrying how their mother would react. Then Jason disappeared and came back in carrying armfuls of his clothes – he'd pulled them out of his chest of drawers. As they jumped up and down on them in the bath, more and more water was ending up on the floor. The bathroom was directly above the public bar in the old hotel. There had already been strict rulings on spilling water on to the floor, as naturally it had happened before.

Somehow, and Nina could not remember how, within a few minutes virtually all the clothes the family owned were in the bath – suits, overcoats, smart dresses, underwear, the lot. The taps were full on, and Jason was in incredibly high spirits, his scrawny naked body jumping in and out of the bath, squealing with delight at the warm, soggy water bed he had made for himself.

By the time their mother walked in, Nina was standing by the wall, holding her own clothes which she had managed to snatch from Jason before they joined the now monstrous pile of sogginess that was pouring torrential amounts of water on to the floor.

Her mother smacked her hard on the legs.

'What have you done!' she shouted, seeming to ignore Jason.

'I didn't do anything, Jason did!'

'He's only a baby. You're old enough to know better. Go to your room!

Nina sighed and looked out of the window of the BMW. She didn't want to go back there – the distress, the tears and screaming, her responsibility for Jason, which never seemed to end.

She could remember shaking as her father, puce with rage, shouted into Jason's face that he'd had to clear the bar as water started gushing through the ceiling. Screaming at him that the building was four hundred years old, and in four short months Jason had nearly destroyed it. Then her mother screaming at her father that he was always picking on Jason and letting his temper get the better of him. Even then, Nina remembered, she had felt confused as to what was right and who was right – she could still feel the sting on her legs.

She also remembered, now with confusion as to how her seven-year-old self could have come up with such a feeling, that she actually felt sorry for her little brother – the look of pain on his face as he stood, clutching a pair of soggy pyjama trousers in front of his naked little body, his bottom lip quivering as he tried not to cry; her father, now hoarse with rage, somehow managing to contain himself and not hit the child.

And it only got worse.

She knew Jason wasn't evil, he wasn't mentally ill – or not seriously. He wasn't even a bad person; all he ever did was try to be good, in fact, but in doing so, he caused incalculable damage. Nina had been fascinated by her brother all her life. She had watched him and tried to understand what made him do what he did.

It could be said that her fascination for her younger sibling drove her to the decision to start her academic life by studying psychology at Warwick University, although it very soon became clear to her that this wasn't the area she was truly interested in. Psychology felt woolly and hard to grasp. She longed for something more concrete. The act of leaving university after less than a term had caused enormous stress at home. Nina and her mother fought night and day. She became even more determined to crush her mother's criticism under the sheer weight of her achievements.

Nina had been very good at mathematics and science at school, her teachers encouraging her to study physics and computer science, and when, after a year off and a world trip, she applied to Cambridge to do just that, she got a place with very little trouble.

She excelled in her field, easily getting her Bachelor of Science degree and securing a post as a research fellow. In her final year she met Sir Brian, then just plain Professor Coventon. His enthusiasm and imagination made him very popular with his students, and he was rapidly gaining public recognition for his work. Never once did she suspect he had feelings for her.

At this time Brian Coventon was fifty-two, easily old enough to be Nina's father, and yet very unlike her real father. Where

John Nash was a tightly packed, rotund man of five foot four, Sir Brian was a loose-limbed, slim man of six foot two. Her father was almost bald, and what was left was grey. Sir Brian was grey haired too, but his hair was still thick and lush, cut short like that of a 1960s American scientist. Consciously so – 1960s American scientists were a group much admired by Sir Brian.

Nina had spent quite a bit of time wondering why she was attracted to this man. Clearly any notion of having a relationship akin to a marriage with him was out of the question. He was already married, happily married, and he still had sex with his wife. She knew that, he had told her – he had always been scrupulously honest with her. He explained that he wanted to have sex with her because he was a man and that was what men were like.

He didn't expect anything and he didn't demand anything. He had just let her know that he found her very attractive and the rest was up to her. He even admitted to having had affairs with some of his students in the past. He assured her that he was very discreet and very generous – he was still in touch with the other students and they were still friends.

Somehow the way he presented this information wasn't seedy. As she thought about it later, it sounded as if it should have been, but it was so honest, so transparent, that it seemed to make sense.

Nina did nothing with this information for almost two years. She already had a boyfriend, Patrick, a biology postgraduate who was obsessed with photographing her. They had even discussed moving in together, but there was something about their relationship that she knew would never work. He was interesting, handsome even, but there was no spark there. He would spend longer looking at the pictures he'd taken of her than he ever spent talking to her. And she never forgot about Professor Coventon, who, she noticed, became Sir Brian one New Year's Day.

She only had a vague grasp of his rise to prominence.

He had been involved in many breakthroughs in the field of cybernetics and had formed a private research foundation when he had developed a hand-held scanner which, using a variety of cutting-edge techniques, allowed doctors to assess all a patient's vital functions within seconds. It sold in the millions, worldwide, and Sir Brian became a very rich man.

A few months after Nina and Patrick finally drifted apart, she met Sir Brian again when they both attended a conference on cybernetics at Lucerne in Switzerland. On the first night, they ended up in the same bed. It was incredibly exciting, romantic even, to be doing something so wicked – knowing this man was married was what actually made him attractive. She knew she shouldn't be doing it, but with very little effort she could drive him wild, make him beg her for more. He adored her passionately and poured flattery on her with the ferocity of a fire hose.

The phone rang in the car, just as the traffic started to move. Nina flicked the thumb switch.

'Where on earth are you?' said her mother. 'I've been trying to get hold of you all night.'

'Hello, Mum, nice of you to call.'

'I've rung you at home again and again. I just get the awful answer machine.'

'I'm stuck in traffic on the M25. Where are you?'

'At home. Where do you think? We're always here. We're not going to come.'

'Oh no! But Jason told me you were coming.'

'Oh, poor Jason. I know he was looking forward to seeing us. I would have, but your father's in a strop.'

'That's all I need. I was hoping I could put in an appearance and then go off with you and Dad and get something to eat. I haven't seen you in ages.'

'Oh, no, no. We couldn't have done that. It's his party. He's thirty, after all. I've sent him a lovely jumper.'

'He hates your jumpers, Mum.'

'Don't be so silly,' snapped her mother. 'And I suppose that awful old grandad is with you.'

'No, Sir Brian is not with me.'

'Ghastly man. Every time I see him on the television my skin crawls. How could you? It's bad enough with your father, but at least we're much the same age.'

'I'd better go before we have a row.'

'We're not having a row. Why does everything always have to be so dramatic with you?'

'Bye, Mum,' said Nina.

She flipped the phone toggle and cursed herself for agreeing to go to see her stupid brother, for having anything to do with her frightful family.

Capital Radio was now playing classics from the 1990s – George Michael. She liked it – it reminded her of her student days. She turned up the volume, found a gap in the nose-to-tail traffic and put her foot down. Although she was only moving at forty-five miles an hour, at least she was moving.

An hour later she pulled up outside the Cobden Club on Kensal Road, parked the car and breathed deeply. She found the present she had bought for her brother and walked in.

'Sis!' he said, looking well scrubbed and clean shaven. 'Blimey, I thought you were going to let me down. Brilliant.'

'Happy birthday, Jason,' she said, giving him a kiss on the cheek and handing him the small package. He ripped off the paper like a seven-year-old. It was a selection of exclusive shower gels and deodorants. 'Hey, get the message, sis. Cool. Helping me clean up my act. I like it.'

He gave her a hug and she felt cheap. It was a bit of an obvious dig at him, and life had treated him badly enough already without her kicking him. He would always take insults so well, never complaining. She pondered on how she would react if someone implied that she was a bit grubby. She would throw a mood for weeks. As she followed him to the bar, she decided to be a little more generous to her brother.

'What'll you have?'

'Just a white wine,' she said.

'There is champagne if you want it. I'm only on orange juice,' he said proudly, holding up a pint mug full of juice.

'Oh, okay, I'll have champagne.'

She took a quick glance around the bar. It was okay. Quite pleasant music but not too loud. Very trendy, Notting Hilly sort of décor. Slightly Gothic – plenty of richly coloured drapes, dark red walls, slightly battered but comfy-looking easy chairs. It reminded her of clubs in New York.

There were only twenty or so people present. They looked quite reasonable – no obvious sign of hard drug use, no stripper like the frightful one at his twenty-first bash. She eyed some of the women. They all looked very smart and professional, not the tarty sort with big hair Jason normally hung out with.

Her brother passed her a glass of champagne.

'So, nice crowd – who are all these people?'

'Oh, just various colleagues.' He pointed to a man in the crowd. 'That's Peter Clews, he's a bit of a dot-com diva. The woman next to him, Claire Bugden, she's just made about four mill on her IPO. They're just people I work with.'

Nina smiled at him. She couldn't help being slightly impressed by what seemed to have happened to her brother's life.

'And how's the new venture?' she asked.

Jason smiled at her. 'Do you really want to know?'

'Yes, sure.'

'Oh, that's brilliant,' said Jason. He embraced her warmly and stood back. She noticed he smelled a great deal better than on their previous meeting. 'It's so exciting, sis, I can barely talk about it. One of my new partners is here, I'd love you to meet him.'

Jason started to look around the room. He soon lost interest and turned back to her, taking alarming gulps from his pint of orange juice.

'He's here somewhere, anyway. He's called George Quinn. He's such a cool bloke, really knows his stuff. Meeting him has been a total godsend. Seriously. You see, what we're going to do is start running on-line experiments for research facilities. Sure, sure, I know that sounds like it could be dodgy and, believe me, I've been wary of the whole concept, but it's totally kosher. You see, I was barking up the wrong alley for so long, smashing my head against the brick wall of B2C sites.'

'Sorry, you've lost me.'

'It's no longer business to consumer – you know, what I tried to do with airline-food.com and discontinued-products.com. That's over, so totally over. So what we're doing now is called B2B, business to business. It's so obvious I feel like such a twat, all the years I've spent trying to get consumers to . . .'

'Consume?'

'Sure, sure. But this is different. You see, we not only do the experiments, but we run the software the research companies use, we run it for them so they don't need to worry about it. They outsource all their tech worries to us. They just use a remote terminal to get what they want. And there are real revenue streams with this model, real income. Actual money that we get paid for the vital service we provide. It's taken me years to work it all out, but I know I have finally reached pay dirt.'

'It sounds a lot more promising.'

'It is, sis, truly, and it's great you're interested. Shit, I wish I could find George. He'd explain the biotech side a lot better than I could. He talks your language.'

'Biotech? Is this what you're doing, then? Experiments for biotech companies?'

'Sure, sure, that's the basic idea.'

'That's a bit worrying, Jason. I mean, there are a lot of slightly shady companies in the field.'

'Sure, sure, and they have serious shed-loads of money to spend.'

'Yeah,' said Nina. The positive spin on anything – such a truly Jason-like response she felt a fool to have expected anything else. Never thrown by her criticism – just took it and ran with it as always.

51

A very sleek-looking young man made his way across the bar to them.

'Oh, hi, George,' said Jason.

Nina could tell by the way Jason twitched that he was a little nervous of this man. He was handsome enough, about the same height as her, very well turned out. He smiled at her; he had charming eyes.

'Nina, this is George, from the States,' said Jason, his hand resting slightly nervously on George's back. He stood a good four inches taller than George, but size isn't everything and George was clearly a man happily in control in the relationship.

'Hi, Nina, great to meet you.' he said. His voice was deeper than she had expected. Although he was not petit, he was also not a Clint Eastwood type, which is what he sounded like. His eyes were locked on hers, but it was only slightly disconcerting.

'How d'you do,' she said, hearing suddenly how English she sounded.

'I've heard a bit about you from Jason. He's very proud of you.'

'Oh, is he now, and what has he told you?' This time Nina worried that she sounded too flirtatious.

'Well, he told me you were highly skilled, a leader in the field of cybernetics. He told me you were a big sister who turned dull days in your childhood to afternoons of delight. He didn't, of course, tell me you were beautiful, but I guess he's your brother so I shouldn't be surprised.'

Nina breathed in and briefly smiled at George. She had been with him until he had started to pile on the cheese.

'Right, and what field are you in?' she asked politely.

'Hi-tech research, pretty close to yours, I guess. I work out of Stanford University, California.'

'Oh, really? I've visited many times,' said Nina. 'What are you doing there?'

'Oh, behavioural research mostly, at the Center for Advanced Study in Behavioral Sciences. Pretty basic stuff in comparison to you.'

'Sounds very interesting.'

'Hello, love, just escaped from hell on two twigs over there.' Nina stood back as a short man with a fierce flat-top haircut barged between her and the American. 'Where did you get these fucking awful people from? Rent-a-prick.com? Got any more gargle? I'm parched.'

Nina glanced at Jason, who looked a little uncomfortable. He smiled at her.

'Sorry, this is Tony,' he said. The man looked at her for a moment before saying. 'Who's she?' rather abruptly.

'This is my sister, Nina,' Jason said rather hurriedly. He handed Tony a bottle of champagne. 'Look, there you go, Tony. Get that down your neck.'

Tony smiled at her as he took the bottle without so much as a thank you. Nina could have sworn he'd had his teeth filed into sharklike points.

'So you're the famous sister. How did you put up with him when you was kiddies?'

'With difficulty,' she said with a laugh, hoping it was the right thing to say.

'Bloody hell, love. He's a total liability. If he wasn't hung like a baby's arm holding an apple he'd be out on his ear. Believe me.'

Tony walked away with a bit of a shimmy. He was wearing a pink cap-sleeved T-shirt and cripplingly tight white trousers which in turn were tucked into mid-calf-high red lace-up boots.

'Now, that's the sort of person I normally associate with you, Jason,' she said with a smile.

'Yeah, sorry about that. He's Tony, he's an old friend. I sort of had to invite him really. Hard to believe he's an expert in HTML code, isn't it? Still, it takes all sorts to build a web presence, doesn't it, George?'

'I guess so,' said George, who seemed to have pulled back a little from the two siblings. He checked to see where Tony had got to, then leaned forward and spoke directly to Nina.

'Did you ever have the feeling that you had just received a

little too much information about someone you know? I'm still thinking babies' arms and apples.'

'Yes, not terribly pleasant,' said Nina. She sipped her champagne and raised her eyebrows. As if he'd change. For a moment, when she walked in, she genuinely thought her brother had turned some corner in his life and was going to come out of it all right. But the arrival of the dreadful Tony soon put a dent in that fantasy.

'So, let's get back to where we were,' said George. 'What are you working on at the moment?'

'Well, it's complicated.'

'You mean it's sensitive?'

'Oh, some of it. But we're developing nerve-respondent chip control systems for artificial limbs. We've had an amazing breakthrough this week. Little twelve-year-old girl who lost her arm in a traffic accident. She's got a new one.'

'And we're talking functional?' asked George.

'Amazing amount of function. She can even write with it. Bit wobbly, but we'd recorded the nerve signals from her remaining arm, so when the prosthetic arm received the same signals, the arm just did as it was told. It was extraordinary.'

'And the recording chips? Are they working okay?'

'Yes. But . . .' Nina faltered. She knew she could say no more. Suddenly she was faced with the reality of what Sir Brian had been talking about in Cambridge. The chip design the company had developed was their main source of future income – it was what all the investors had paid for, and they were expecting some return for their risk. The success of their work had already reached the public domain, so it clearly had huge significance for their competitors. Nina had no idea who this man George was, but he obviously knew something about her work.

'You know about them, then?'

'Only what I've read in the scientific press. I met Sir Brian Coventon last year,' said George. 'He's an amazing guy.'

'Yes,' said Nina. 'He's one of a kind, all right.'

'You know him well, I guess.'

'We've worked closely together for a few years.'

'I guess you have,' George said. He looked at Jason, who was hovering over them like a nervous giraffe. 'Hey, Jason, could you see if they have any more of those dips? The really hot salsa one, and some more of the potato chips?'

'Sure, sure. Not a problem, George.'

Jason wandered off through the crowd, interestingly, as Nina noticed, more or less ignored by all the friends he had invited to his party. A man in the crowd was looking at her, a very handsome, possibly American man with wonderful eyes. Bit of a George Clooney, only taller. She didn't know whether George Clooney was short, but she assumed he must be. He turned away when she returned his gaze.

'Look, Nina,' said George Quinn, who was very not George Clooney material. 'I don't know what Jason has told you about this new venture, and I know he's not got what you could call a clean record when it comes to his business enterprises. But despite it all, that guy has got a head on his shoulders when it comes to finding a market and making something of it. When he pitched this to us, well, I left my safe research post and jumped at it. We've raised over two billion dollars in finance, we have some very serious backers, and we know we're going to make many billions of dollars out of this. I'd like to hire you.'

'Oh, I see.'

'I know you are very committed to Sir Brian. I know he means a lot to you, and I can understand your reticence. But with us, you would be the Sir Brian, it would be your show, Nina. I don't even want to go into what sort of salary I could offer you. I don't want to overdo the value of the share package I have been authorised to give you, but both are, even on a global level, extremely attractive.'

'Right,' said Nina. She was beginning to see what Jason's so-called birthday party was all about.

'Don't say anything now. I have arranged a late breakfast meeting tomorrow at the Hilton on Park Lane. I'd really like you to join us, just to talk through in more detail what we're doing.'

'Well, I was going to go back to Cambridge tonight and . . .'

'Yeah, I kind of planned ahead on this one. Don't feel in any way obliged, but . . .' He reached into his inside jacket pocket and produced a small plastic card. 'I've booked a room for you at the hotel. Save you having to schlep up and down from Cambridge tonight. Like I say, it's up to you.'

He held the card in front of him. She smiled. What was she going to do?

7

Jason fell through the door of Tony's tiny apartment. He wasn't overly drunk, he'd been talking too much to get seriously hammered, but Tony was in a state of semi-toxic shock.

'Fuck me, Mary, that was the most fucking awful party I've ever been to,' he screamed as he collapsed in a heap on the floor. 'And definitely the worst fucking party I've ever paid for. I need a drink!'

'Have a coffee,' said Jason. He knew that when Tony started to call everyone and everything Mary he was in a state of deep inebriation which demanded great sensitivity on the part of his carers. 'You need a coffee, Tone, I'll make you one.'

'Don't tell me what I need, Mary,' said Tony, crawling on his hands and knees towards the kitchen. 'I need a drink!'

Jason rubbed his face. 'Sure, sure, well, I need a bit of shut-eye, so I'm off to my bed.'

Tony stood up very slowly and looked at him through bleary bloodshot eyes.

'Don't leave now! I need someone to talk to. Bring that great big cock of yours over here, Mary.'

'Yeah, no, really, Tony. I need to get to sleep. I've got a really important meeting tomorrow. I've got to be on the case.'

'You're always having meetings. I let you stay here, walk all over me, and what do I get out of it? I'll tell you, Mary. Nothing.'

Tony put his hands on his hips and stared almost straight at Jason. He often found it hard to stare at anything for very long.

'Well, I need a bit of cock!'

Jason sighed. 'Look, you know I don't bat for your team, Tony. There's no point asking again.'

Tony flopped on to the messy couch. An empty can of Special Brew fell on the floor – seemingly Tony didn't notice. 'Don't you remember when I first saw you? In the lodge, darling. In the lodge.'

'Yes, I remember,' said Jason uncomfortably. The lodge was a house in the San Raphael mountains outside Los Angeles, where Jason went to record his one-and-only gay adult movie. He was to be paid $7,000 for the day, much better money than he got working on the straight films. He had spoken to the other guys, who all seemed to do it. The girls all did girl-on-girl movies – it seemed to be the thing to do. Jason had not found the experience easy, although he had always got on well with gay men socially.

'Oh, you looked gorgeous, Mary. Fucking gorgeous. I was happy then, that was a nice job, getting all you lovely boys ready. What do I get now, Mary? A string of fat suburban husbands, coming here and telling me they long for the feel of a man's hands. That's what they say to me. They leave their fucking awful wives and their tragic little lives and come here to be serviced by Tony. I'm sick of it, Mary! I need some decent cock. Is that so bad? I'm a fucking homosexual, darling!'

'I'd kind of worked that bit out,' said Jason.

'And you come here, all tall and hung like a baby's arm holding an apple, and it's "can I stay with you for a bit, Tony?" I was over the fucking moon. It's not often I get an offer of something I actually want. But what do I get? "I need a bit of shut-eye, Tony", "I've got a meeting, Tony", and "You know I don't bat for your team, Tony". I'm sick of it!'

It was true. Jason just wasn't wired that way.

Six months after his day at 'the lodge', when he had got back to London and everything collapsed in a heap of horror, Tony's address, scrawled in the back of his tattered Filofax, had been a salvation. Central location, no rent, and apart from Tony's drunken lunges late at night, there was very little hassle as long as he got out before Tony's punters started arriving at eleven each morning.

He turned and started walking towards the back bedroom, even though he was bursting for a pee. He knew than if he went into the bathroom Tony would be hanging around trying to get a bleary peek at his todger.

He shut the door and pushed the wardrobe across, blocking it off completely. He could hear Tony crashing about and screaming, but this was nothing new. He opened his window, climbed on to a very frail-looking Ikea stool and relieved himself on to the paved area below. There was no one about that he could see, although he did notice with slight alarm that when the torrent hit the pavement below it did make rather a lot of noise. He comforted himself by working out that people would probably think it was a bit of overflowing plumbing – that sort of thing happened all the time.

When he had finished he closed the window and fell on the bed. He lay back, hands cradling his head, happily ignoring the moaning and vomiting sounds coming from the corridor outside his room.

Soon all this would be in his past. He would be living in his own apartment somewhere like Mayfair, with a beautiful young woman to keep him company. He might, he pondered, even make the effort to fall in love and get married. He wanted to do things properly this time, show his parents that he really had changed. He was thirty, after all – it was time to grow up and join the real world. And from where Jason was lying, the real world looked terribly attractive.

He actually managed to get up early the following morning, and crept about the flat as he tried to tidy himself up a little. He really didn't want to see his landlord, although in fact he could have stamped, screamed and played Van Halen at full whack on the battered micro system Tony owned – after a night of super-heavy alcohol consumption, very little would rouse the sleeping masseuse.

Jason looked for something resembling a clean shirt. He could find nothing – his entire wardrobe filled one bin-bag. As he tipped the contents over the floor of his small room, he saw that they were in a truly terminal state. He could not go to the meeting in the same suit he had worn to the party, he had to have something new. He sat on the bed and scratched his head. He had five pounds in his pocket, and a couple of coppers in change. This called for radical action. He checked his watch – 8.30. Selfridges department store beckoned.

He put on the least cheesy shirt, his old suit, and a pair of socks whose stiffness just about outdid odour in terms of unpleasantness. This ensemble was rounded off by his trusty old black cowboy boots, the soles reattached with a strip of insulating tape. He crept out of the apartment and down the two flights of stairs to the street. He rubbed his eyes. He wasn't ready for sunshine – few people in London were – but it was a beautiful crisp spring morning. A good omen. A truck was making a noise near where he'd left the car. Then he saw what was happening – the car was being lifted on to the back of a removal vehicle. He started to move towards the lorry to remonstrate with the two swarthy-looking individuals who were taking his wheels, but then he stopped. There was no point. Anyway, they could keep the thing, it was shot to fuck. He would get a new one, a Porsche Boxter or one of its ilk. Not a problem.

He caught the Tube at Queensway, got off at Bond Street and made his way into Selfridges. It was early, but the place was already crawling with shoppers. He went to the men's department and tried on several suits, each time taking them from a different designer section in the store to the same changing room. He had been told how to do this by Tony, who had, for a time, worked as a professional shoplifter before turning his nimble hands to the subtle art of male massage, or, as he described it, 'rub and tug'.

He took one of the ensembles back to the desk and apologised for the fact that it wasn't quite 'him' and that he'd left some of the garments in the changing room. The place was busy, the assistants just smiled and nodded at him curtly, not noticing that he was actually wearing one of the pair of trousers and the shirt he'd taken in with him. His filthy old stained ones were folded neatly over a hanger in the changing room.

He left the shoes until last, trying a pair on, standing up, saying he thought they pinched his feet a little, and then just walking out wearing them.

After fifteen minutes of hustle, Jason Nash walked out with a brand new Jasper Conran jacket in black wool, a pair of black Church's brogues and a nice pair of trousers by Giorgio Armani. No one stopped him, and he didn't run; he even lingered a while in the perfume section and tried a little Calvin on his wrists.

What he'd do, he thought as he walked through the crowded street, was write Selfridges a letter, enclosing the cash for the clothing, explaining that on the day in question he had had no choice. However, the clothes had enabled him to secure a multibillion-dollar contract and he thought it only fair to make reparations. Jason knew he wasn't a criminal, and the main reason he wasn't was because he genuinely wanted to make amends for what was, in effect, a temporary sin. He really wanted to sort everything out once and for all.

He felt wonderful as he strolled back down Oxford Street. He bought ten cigarettes from a newsagent's, hassled a street dweller for a light, and made his way to the Hilton on Park Lane.

8

Nina woke late. She hadn't slept as well in months. The time leading up to the fitting of Ingrid Neilson's arm had been extremely busy – she'd put long hours in and hadn't realised how tired she was.

She took a shower, and only as she was drying herself realised she had no clothes to wear other than the smoke-infected dress-suit she had worn the night before. There was nothing for it. The whole venture was daft anyway, but she might as well have breakfast with the American. He was rather nice looking, she had to admit.

She checked herself in the mirror – not bad for thirty-three. She was tall, slim and had a neatly trimmed mop of dark hair. She'd tried many different styles over the years, but this one was the easiest to manage. Her hair was naturally curly, always had been. It came from her mother's side of the family, while Jason had taken after his father in the hair department – lank and greasy.

She took the lift down to the restaurant, feeling slightly odd being in this particular hotel. She had passed it dozens of times – the Hilton on Park Lane, a London landmark. She had even met one of the students who had paraglided off the roof in the 1980s; the other had died in the attempt. Now she was staying there, meeting some American for breakfast.

'Morning, sis,' said Jason as she stood at the entrance to the restaurant. She glanced at him. He looked smart – new suit, clean shaven; there was even a whiff of aftershave about him.

'Good morning, broth,' she said with a smile. 'How are you?'

'I'm good, very good.'

It was almost a pleasant surprise to see him. She didn't feel ashamed standing next to him; in fact, she almost felt proud. Her big younger brother, who could protect her.

'Nina, this is going to be the major, and I mean major, change point in your life. Okay, now bear with me on this. I truly know what I'm doing. I know how these people operate and I have the whole situation under complete and utter control from the ground up.'

Nina smiled. He was quite sweet when he was talking deadly serious rubbish.

'Okay, now I know you have reservations and I totally respect them, but just for now, for this meeting, just listen. I'll do the talking. I'll cut you a deal that will make you wince with the sheer scale of incoming fiscal muscle. Remember, this is our baby, this is the beginning of Nash as an international brand. Are you with me?'

'Not being a weency bit over the top, Jason?'

'No way. If anything I'm being conservative in my hyperbole. We are talking a life-changing, global-affecting, human-existence-modifying moment here, historic on a grand, and I mean globally grand, scale.'

'So you're saying I should shut up and listen.'

'Sis, you are psychic.'

'I was going to anyway, big dork.'

'Are you joining the Quinn table?' asked a waitress as she approached them.

'Sure, sure,' said Jason.

'Follow me, please.'

With an uncannily uncharacteristic gesture, Jason allowed Nina to walk in front of him. He smiled at her as he held out an arm to guide her. She shook her head. She couldn't recall him ever doing anything other than barge past her, especially if there was food in the direction they were travelling. She couldn't count the number of times she had tumbled down the stairs when they were kids, Jason charging past her when their mother had announced that a meal was ready.

Nina's eyes fell on the sight before her – a large table in a discreet corner of the restaurant that was already looking a little crowded. She couldn't take in all the faces at first, but there were at least five people present.

One of them stood up to greet her. It was George Quinn, the American she had met the night before.

'Good morning, Nina, great of you to join us. Please, sit down, and I'll introduce you to everyone.'

'Morning, George, mate,' said Jason.

'Good morning, Jason,' replied George with a smile. 'Great night last night. You never told me it was your birthday.'

'Sure, sure. It was cool. Yeah, I don't like to make a fuss, just a discreet group of close associates and I'm happy. Morning, everyone.'

Jason sat down and immediately started to pour himself a cup of coffee. The people around the table nodded and smiled. Nina couldn't work out from their reaction whether they had met Jason previously.

'Nina, this is Emen Trouville. He's our chief engineer.'

Nina looked at the man. His smile revealed perfect American teeth, but he looked European. He was lean and bright eyed. Nina smiled at him and glanced at his hands. They were exquisite. She had become a connoisseur of hands since working with young Ingrid Neilson.

'Cindy Volksmann, our CEO,' said George Quinn.

Nina smiled as she shook hands with the woman. She looked kind, fun even, with a bright face and closely cropped blonde hair – corporate-commercial hair, the sort businesswomen were meant to have. It was hard to put an age to these women, although Nina guessed Cindy was well into her forties.

'Michael Del Papa, chief programmer.'

Nina raised her eyebrows. She had heard of Del Papa, although she'd never met him. Now in his seventies, he had a very big reputation in virtual intelligence and advanced human–machine interface systems. He was on the original team that had designed the WYSIWYG screen at the Xerox Park research establishment in California.

64

'And Pete Van Missen. He's security, a very trustworthy man.'

The man she had seen looking at her at Jason's party stood up and offered his hand. He was, there was no point denying it, gorgeous, with thick dark eyebrows over deep blue eyes. Nina felt unsure as she shook his hand. He was looking at her very intensely and she couldn't hold his gaze.

George sat down beside her and took a sip of coffee. He looked at her and smiled. 'Hungry?'

'Ravenous,' said Jason.

'Great.' George raised his arm and gestured to a waiter.

Nina ordered a croissant with jam. Jason demanded the full English breakfast with fries and a chocolate milk-shake on the side.

'This is great,' said George. 'We've all wanted to meet you for so long. It's crazy that we've never bumped into you at any seminar or convention. Like I was saying, I think we've all met Sir Brian at some time or other.'

'Oh, he gets around a bit, doesn't he, Nina,' said Jason.

She smiled painfully at her brother, wondering whether she could cause actual injury if she kicked him under the table.

'Let me explain what's going on here,' said George. 'We're basically a collection of scientists and researchers who've struck out and formed our own company. It was really Emen's idea. He worked for ParkerSoft – you know, the iris-catcher, that was mostly Emen's work.'

Nina did know the iris-catcher; she used it every day – a complex combination of hard and software that followed a computer user's eye movements and did away with the mouse. The cursor on the screen was controlled by the eye – a blink instructed the computer to open or close documents or applications. It had become ubiquitous within months of its launch.

'That was eight years in development and put ParkerSoft in the multibillion bracket, and he got very little.'

'I'm not crying over it,' said Emen, without a trace of a

European accent. He was very American. 'I just thought it was a sucker's job doing all that work for someone else.'

'We have secured serious funding,' George continued. 'And we're looking at being the biggest mover in the cybernetics and behavioural field. As the Wall Street guys say, human machine interaction is the next step – we're here to put keyboards, mice and screens in the trash.'

'At least in a museum,' said Emen.

George smiled at him, then turned back to Nina. Clearly he didn't really want anyone else to talk.

'And what you are doing, Nina, is so extraordinary it can come as no surprise that we sought you out. You can cross us off as cheap headhunters if you like, but what we can offer you now, today, is control over your own work. We're not asking you to work for us, we're asking you to join the company. You'd head the research team, be on the board, help make the decisions that steer the company.'

'If I might add something here,' said Pete Van Missen.

'Sure, go ahead Pete.'

Pete Van Missen looked at the assembly as he spoke. 'I know how you guys get enthusiastic and all, which is fine.' With immaculate timing he turned to Nina and went on, 'But I'm sure you understand, Professor Nash, the offer we're making you is strictly confidential.'

Nina looked at Van Missen and smiled and nodded, still not having said a word.

'Sure, sure. She's cool,' said Jason. Everyone looked at him for a moment. He seemed unaware of this, but it was very clear to Nina immediately that already Jason was seen as something of a burden and clearly had been used only to get in contact with her. How, she pondered for a moment, could he not be aware of that?

'As long as that's understood, which I feel confident it is.' Pete Van Missen picked up his coffee cup and looked at Nina as he took a sip. She smiled at him, trying not to be transfixed by his wonderful gaze.

'And I know you people over here don't really like to talk about such things, but we're American and we talk about money,' said Cindy Volksmann. 'We're offering you $500,000 a year basic salary, plus a fifteen per cent share package, presently valued at a little over seven million US.'

Nina didn't move. She could feel her face fixed in a smile. With rapid mental calculations she transferred the figure into UK currency. Not bad. She slowly looked around the table. These people, she realised, were for real.

'Now I understand that you are very committed to Sir Brian Coventon and we totally respect that,' said Pete Van Missen. 'But you should understand that he is in no position to offer you this kind of equity. And although again I have to insert a confidentiality caveat, I know for a fact that Sir Brian's research facility is under grave financial constraints and may go to the wall at any time.'

'I think my sister is well aware of the grave state of Coventon's,' said Jason. Nina was about to say that the company was booming as far as she was concerned, but she kept quiet.

Jason sat back in his chair as his enormous breakfast plate was placed in front of him. 'Would you look at that. I've got to come here more often.'

'Have some breakfast,' said George Quinn to Nina. 'We'll keep filling you in.'

9

Office space – a huge expanse of office space, empty, slightly dusty, but ready for occupation. All the latest kit being delivered in large white vans, and when he said latest, Jason really did mean latest. As an avid reader of multiple PC magazines, even Jason had never seen some of this stuff.

Men in blue overalls wiring up the terminals, men in white overalls helping him decide on the lighting design, then there were the men who delivered the sound muffling boards, the men in black suits who brought in the security systems. Jason Nash was having a whale of a time.

It had been a mere two weeks since the Hilton breakfast. Jason had already started taking notes for a book about the early days of the company and had decided that *Breakfast at the Hilton* was a good working title.

In three days he turned an empty shell of a building into a bustling hub of activity. The company that held the previous lease on the building had gone bankrupt – they were an on-line retailer, B2C, so yesterday's news. He never met any of the people who had put heart and soul into the start-up only to founder two years later with monstrous debts all around, but he knew they were suckers.

And he, Jason Nash, had managed to find an escape route from the massive B2C plughole that had sucked down so many. Although airline-food.com was technically no more, it had been recoded and replaced by something far more volatile, far more exciting.

He was still theoretically negotiating his deal with Nash Systems, which is what the company had come to be called. He was pleased with himself about that; using his ever absent sister as leverage had become very useful.

'It's simple, George,' he had said over a lunch at Le Gavroche. 'For obvious reasons Nina wants the name Nash to be a major, and I mean major, component of the whole operation. She's been in touch with me on an hourly basis over this. Now, for me personally, I couldn't give a damn – the name means nothing to me. We could be called Quinn Systems for all I care.'

George had smiled. With very little resistance, the name Nash Systems was chosen, and when Jason first saw his new business card he felt a rush of pleasure. This was not any old business card, it was an absolute state-of-the-art micro data transfer system. A blank white plastic card with a hole in the centre, it doubled as either a mini-CD or a PC card, and when inserted into a computer held a huge amount of information on Nash Systems, on Jason, and on the work they were doing, including pictures and HTML links.

He was now Jason Nash, Deputy CEO, Nash Systems, Millford Business Park, Cambridgeshire. It sounded good. What was even more astounding and definitely cool was the location. The building Nash Systems had taken over was next door to the old Coventon Research building. There were barely five metres between them – it was incredible. George had actually located the building, although Jason did the deal and felt he had sourced at least 90 per cent of the whole thing. After all, sourcing wasn't just about finding, it was about actually getting, and Jason had managed to hammer the rent down to a very reasonable level.

If, as George predicted, Coventon's folded, they could simply take over the whole operation, which would not only reduce costs but also decrease their start-up time. George was very keen on the speed factor. 'This is not an industry that rewards those who sit on their ass' was how the confident Mr Quinn had described the situation.

'I like it,' Jason had responded.

Nonetheless, the speed of the whole operation had surprised him. He had never experienced so much sourcing, organisation and logistics compressed into such a short time. Not only had the office come together in a matter of days, but all his other problems seemed to have been solved overnight. His housing and car requirements were more than catered for. He was now the proud holder of the keys to apartment 14 in the Cadogan Mansion block in Audley Court, London, W1. That had taken some wangling, but he had convinced his business partners that if he was to be taken seriously he needed to be in London. Having a Cambridge address would just spell 'small-time hustler' to any prospective clients.

He had managed to source Audley Court at a reduced rent – reduced from £3,000 a week to £2,800. Each night when he arrived home, he would park his silver-grey Mercedes CL500 in his private underground carpark. He had sourced the car directly from the factory in Germany, saving Nash Systems over £7,000, although that was then reabsorbed in extras which he had fitted, like the ear-splitting stereo system. The amplifiers took up half the boot and required extra batteries. When he first hit the play button on the car's steering wheel, he shook with joyous laughter as the volume caused actual physical pain to his ears.

He would climb out of the car and simply walk away – no car keys for Mr Nash. He would hear its reassuring little beep as it locked itself, the signal from his wallet-based smart card instructing the self-locking and immobilising system to kick in.

It was all so much more civilised than illegally parking the battered old Saab outside Tony's gaff. He did visit his old haunt once, theoretically to pick up his stuff, but when he saw it, a plastic carrier bag full of broken shoes and dirty laundry, he dropped it in the communal waste bin. While he was there he gave Tony a cheque for £5,000, which was received with much delight and the opening of a fresh can of Tennents Extra. Jason had one can but then left Tony to his carousing, promising him a position with the new company as soon as something came up. He also stuffed an envelope with £500 in used twenties and posted it to the Selfridges store on Oxford Street. Along with the money was a handwritten explanatory note – he'd worn kitchen gloves for the whole operation just to be doubly safe. As he dropped the envelope in the postbox he experienced a very good feeling about himself. The Nash was back on top.

Jason loved his new car. He didn't even need to say top of the range to himself, let alone to anyone else.

He'd even, and this was definitely a first for him, taken it to a valet service on the A4 to have it cleaned. The vehicle was immaculate. He only ever smoked in it with the windows open, although the air-conditioning was easily powerful enough to remove any smoky residue. There wasn't a scratch on the bodywork – when he was parking, little sensors on the exterior of the car warned him with gentle beeps if he was getting too close to something.

There was, as always, one little fly in the vast vat of pleasure he found himself wallowing in; he wasn't exactly sure what he was meant to be doing. Sourcing the office and laboratory was fun, demanding, challenging even, but once the office was set up, it became less and less clear to him what he was supposed to do.

In the floor below the office the laboratory was being fitted out. He had walked around the area when the building crews were still there. The main effort seemed to be focused on constructing a concrete shell in the centre of the large open-plan area. This was to be a small chip-manufacturing plant, a hyper-clean dust-free area that would be out of bounds to all but the most senior engineers. Including, of course, his sister.

He hadn't heard from Nina since the whole thing started to roll. He'd rung her countless times but had only ever got her answer service. He had noticed a lot of people coming and going at the Coventon Research building, but Nina wasn't one of them. He saw the old man himself one day, Sir Brian, getting out of a rather battered-looking Jaguar and glancing in the direction of the Nash Systems building.

One bright, fresh-feeling morning, he pulled the Mercedes to a halt in the area designated for him, with his name on the sign, in the company carpark. Jason Nash, Deputy CEO. He looked at the sign as a Mos Def classic pounded out of the sound system. Why had he agreed so readily to be deputy CEO? Why was some uppity little bitch the CEO? Although he got on with Cindy Volksmann, he couldn't remember the reason they had given him as to why she needed to be CEO. It had something to do with encouraging big venture capitalists to risk serious sums in the project, and they assured him that Cindy would be very much in the background. Still, it didn't feel right. He needed to have a word with George about it.

He glanced out of the window and saw George talking to Pete Van Missen. He turned the stereo off. He was playing a compilation of heavy metal and rap music he had burned on to twelve CDs that were in the multi-player rack in the boot. Tracks from Puff Daddy's classic collection, a bit of Van Halen and some seriously awesome Run DMC had been thundering out of the very impressive system.

'Good morning, Jason. I see the stereo works, then,' said George with a smile. 'How's the car?'

'It's totally excellent,' responded Jason. 'Yeah, it's fantastic. So you're back. How's it all going?'

'It's all going real well,' said George. 'The lab should be on line in a matter of days, the office is up and running, and you look great.'

'Thanks,' said Jason. 'I feel great, but I've got one little problem that's kind of slowing my data processing.'

'Fire away.'

'What exactly am I supposed to be doing as deputy CEO?'

George smiled at him, then turned and smiled at Pete Van Missen, who smiled back at Jason.

'That is so English. I love it. No deputy CEO in the States would ever ask such a basic, fundamental and, dare I say it, fucking sensible question. Jason, you are a find.'

'Sure, sure,' said Jason.

'Doesn't really answer your question, though, does it?' said Van Missen.

'Not really, no.'

George put a gentle hand on Jason's back and started to guide him towards the building. 'Jason, you are already *so* doing what you should be doing. You've organised this office in record time, you've made sure everything is in its place, you've sourced some of the best equipment on the market ready for the company to go fully on line on Monday.'

'We're going on line that soon?'

'Sure, if all goes to plan. We're going to have a board meeting this afternoon, and we need you there, and I think the full company strategy will become a great deal clearer then.'

'Sure, sure, that's great. Is Cindy going to be there?'

'Cindy should be landing at London Heathrow right about now. She had to catch the red-eye but she's one hell of a lady. She'll be here. Any word from Nina?'

'She won't be present just yet,' said Jason, immediately on his guard.

'But is she going to join us?'

'The signs are good.' Jason looked across the carpark to the Coventon Research building. 'Things aren't going too well next door. I can guarantee she'll be with us in hours, not days.'

'That's good, Jason, very good,' said George.

They entered the building. It looked fabulous – a team of builders had been working through the night and transformed the place.

'Have you met Amy?' Van Missen asked as they approached the centrepiece of the entrance lobby.

Jason looked towards the Spitfire wing reception desk that he'd specifically asked for. Standing behind it, looking very pretty, although a little lost, was the young woman who had been in the same position at Coventon Research.

'I do believe I have,' said Jason. He walked over to her and they shook hands.

'Good morning, Mr Nash.' Her smile was beguiling.

'Jason, please,' he said quietly. 'Hey, how are you?'

'I'm fine, really excited I'm going to be working here. It's fantastic that you sorted this out for me. I can't believe my luck.'

Jason smiled at her. He had no idea she was coming to work for him.

'Hey, when I make a promise, I keep it,' he said with a broad smile.

'Listen, Jason,' said George, who was also smiling broadly. Everyone was smiling – it was the smile company, Jason thought. 'Pete and I have a couple of things to sort out. We'll let you and Amy familiarise yourselves with the operation here, okay? We'll catch up later.'

'Sure, sure. Board meeting at . . .?'

'Two-thirty sharp,' said Van Missen.

'I'll be there,' said Jason.

He watched the two men climb the broad stairs to the upper floors, then sat himself on the Spitfire wing reception desk and looked up at the Nash Systems logo, which had just been mounted on the wall.

'Not bad, is it?'

'It's fantastic. I love this desk. It's from an aeroplane, isn't it? It looks real.'

'Sure, sure. It's a hundred per cent real. It's from a Super-marine Spitfire. Battle of Britain and all that. I sourced it myself, on the Web.'

'Blimey, I wouldn't know where to start.'

'It's a doddle, especially here. We've got a two-gig connection – we are talking seriously fast data transfer.'

'So this is all yours, then?'

'What, Nash Systems? No, no. I'm just the boss. It's a huge multibillion-dollar concern. I'm just a small cog in a major, and I really mean major, global operation.'

'But it's named after you.'

'Sure, sure. The thing is, Amy, a man like me has an idea, but it's people like George and Cindy Volksmann, our CEO, who really make it happen. They're not ideas people, they're make-it-happen people, and that stimulates ideas from someone like me.'

'Sounds amazing.'

'It's like a . . . like a contained reactor of creativity, if you like,' said Jason. He couldn't take his eyes off this girl. She was hot. 'They give me the space to explore my ideas, but contain it within a working environment that supports me. My job at the moment is to recruit the very top people in the field, and that's where you come in. I could just tell, with one look, that you were good at your job. You wouldn't have worked for my sister if you weren't. She takes after me in that respect.'

'Oh, thanks.'

He was pretty sure Amy was blushing. This was excellent.

'It's magic that she's going to work here too. She's great,' said Amy, looking at him with her wondrous brown eyes. For Jason, mixed-race women were the crème de la crop, and Amy had the mix down to perfection.

'So she's decided to join us, then?' he asked discreetly.

'Oh, yes. Well, I think so,' said Amy. She looked a little confused. 'I thought you would have known that.'

'You know what it's like with brothers and sisters. She never tells me anything. What's going on next door, then?'

'Oh, it's been awful. Poor Sir Brian, he's in so much trouble. He's so upset about everything. It's a shame because he's such a nice old bloke. He was really upset when I left and I'm nobody.'

'Amy, let me tell you something, you are *so* not nobody. A company like Coventon's really needs someone like you. The fact that we've snatched you away in the night is just a sign of the times. I'm sorry, respect to Sir Brian and everything, but he's yesterday's news. He can't keep up. He's had a good run, he should go back to the good lady wife and grow his roses or whatever. The Nash is here and he ain't going away.'

'I know, but I still feel sorry for him. The research centre was everything to him, and now, with Nina leaving as well, I don't know how he's going to take it.'

'Yeah, she's a pretty special lady.' Jason looked around the reception area briefly. There was no one around, although he knew that the place was under constant surveillance because he'd been involved in installing the system with Pete Van Missen. He pondered for a moment and then smiled at Amy. She was very cute, petite and curvy in all the right places. He might as well take the chance.

'Sure, sure. It's all good, but . . .' He ran his hands through his hair. 'I don't know. I can't say I'm happy.'

'Oh dear. Why not?'

'Well . . . oh, I don't want to burden you with all my stuff.'

'You can, don't worry.'

Oh yes, she was being so receptive he couldn't stop now.

'Oh, well. It's nothing really, just loneliness. You see, when you're as successful as I am, you're torn in two ways. On the one hand people think you've got everything, you know, they're envious, so they stay away. Maybe they're even frightened. Women, I mean – I think they look at me and just say to themselves unattainable, beyond my reach, or whatever. They assume I'm married or something. Either that or they're suburban gold-diggers with all-over tans and too much jewellery. I have to watch out for them – only after the money, not the man, you know what I mean?'

'So are you single, Jason?'

'Very, I'm afraid. Just not had time, you know, to meet the right person, to really get to know someone and trust them. When you're in my line of work, well, you just don't meet anyone suitable.'

'That's a shame,' said Amy. She looked at him sympathetically. He assumed a position of being lost in reverie by leaning his head on the floor-to-ceiling window that ran down one wall. He concentrated on keeping his face glum but made sure he was at the right angle for her to be able to see him clearly. Then, without warning, he said, 'Have you seen the labs yet?'

Amy shook her head – she hadn't seen this coming.

'I only got here a few minutes ago,' she said. 'I haven't seen anything but this desk yet.'

'Look, don't tell anyone, because strictly speaking it's a security area, but I know we can trust you, and if you're with me, what harm can you do?'

'Oh, don't worry, I'm really up to speed on corporate security. We did it at college.'

'Sure, sure. This way.'

Although the final security systems check hadn't taken place and all the doors were still unlocked, Jason swiped his clearance card through the reader and pushed open the door to the labs.

'It's just basic common sense in the end. Nash Systems' wealth is going to be entirely tied up with ideas of value as opposed to actual physical product. If anyone could walk in here, they could walk out naked but with our ideas in their heads.'

They entered the inner sanctum of the lab, now fitted out with workbenches and some very impressive-looking computers. One wall of the room was entirely taken up with banks of servers and storage devices, as yet off line. Their footsteps echoed. The place was very quiet, smelling of fresh cement and paint, newly sawn wood and brand-new computer equipment.

Jason opened the huge steel door that led into the airtight chamber which in turn led into the clean room. It was already 'clean'. The massive air-conditioning system was in operation – he could just hear the humming. As yet no equipment had been installed, and the air felt dry and peculiar as they entered the inner sanctum.

'This, Amy, is the clean room, the area in which we will be manufacturing the smallest microprocessors on the planet. Only a few microns in diameter. You'd only just be able to see them with the naked eye.'

'Wow.'

'Small is beautiful,' Jason said, gently holding her hand. He moved it to his crotch. For a moment he felt her resist, and then, as he slowly let go, her hand stayed put.

'Wow,' she said.

'It's all yours. This is the one place with no security camera installed. We're perfectly alone and won't be interrupted.'

'Oh, Jason. That feels very big.'

'No nanotechnology down there, Amy,' he said with a smile. He undid his Cartier belt and let his trousers fall to the ground. He was already three-quarters erect, and in this situation was rapidly heading for a full hundred per cent engorgement. He found Amy very attractive. He hadn't felt this way about a lady in a long time, being sober and horny and not in front of a camera simultaneously. It was great.

Amy pulled his large penis from his Brass Monkey camouflage-printed butt floss pants and held it in her small hand.

'I know it's a cliché, but I've never seen one this big,' she said.

'Just put it in your mouth for a while,' he said as he looked down at her.

She held it and looked at it, and then, very slowly, she opened her mouth and moved her head toward's him. He did everything he could to resist thrusting forward. He didn't need to. She slowly engulfed the end of his now fully throbbing pego and, just as he'd wanted, looked up at him with her big brown eyes. The size of his member stretched her lips as she slid her mouth back and forth.

'Cup the balls, Amy, cup the balls,' he whispered hoarsely. 'You're blowing the Nash, baby, you're blowing the Nash. Easy. Easy.'

She moved slowly and deliciously. Her small hand cupped his heavy balls and the only sounds were his groans and Amy breathing deeply through her nose. After a while he pulled her up, held her face between his hands and kissed her, a lecherous, wet, tongue-ridden kiss of filthy lust. She responded magically, opening her mouth wide and letting him mash his tongue into it. He undid her blouse and pushed it off her slim shoulders.

He introduced his penis gently. He knew he was big – he didn't need to prove it. Amy gasped as he entered her. She looked at him, her face a mixture of shock and pleasure.

'Oh my God,' she said. 'Oh God, Jason, you are . . . here . . . in the lab . . . anyone could come in and see us. On the table, you big animal.'

Amy was lying on a large workbench in the clean room, now completely naked and prone, her legs spread wide, held in place by Jason's huge hands.

'Take the cock, baby, take it all,' said Jason, his hair falling over his face as he started to thrust. He pulled off the remainder of his clothes as he watched with timeless fascination the classic close-up – his glistening manhood moving in and out of Amy's wonderful body.

Jason fucked Amy in every position his considerable experience in the field had taught him. He fucked her from on top, to one side, the other side, from behind and, finally, after much coaxing and oral lubrication and stimulation, in the ass. She never complained, although she moaned and writhed under his oversized tutelage.

'I'm going to come for you, baby,' he said as he felt the start of his climax. 'The Nash is going to give you a pearl necklace.'

'Oh, baby.'

'Oh yes. The Nash . . . is going . . . to come.'

He was concentrating on her back, the brown skin glistening slightly, the wonderful shape of her buttocks, holding the moment for as long as he possibly could.

'Oh, yes, yes,' moaned Amy, looking around at him, her hair stuck to her face with perspiration.

He withdrew and moved her again. She lay on the bench looking up at him as he positioned himself to ejaculate over her breasts. She put her hand on his cock, but he gently brushed it away.

'The cock needs no help,' he said. He tensed and relaxed and it started. His plan was to come on her breasts in a gentlemanly way, a classic pearl necklace. But the force of his ejaculation surprised even him. It had been his stock-in-trade as a professional – he was blessed with some very powerful pelvic muscles – but this was a one-off. His sperm flew a good metre, hitting the wall behind them. Without any manual encouragement. Even in the midst of a mind-altering orgasm he had the presence of mind to manually aim the hose, but he was unable to deliver the full necklace. It all went in one place, just above her perfect left breast.

'It's a brooch,' he grunted, still mid-climax. 'It's a pearl brooch.'

The Nash had come. He couldn't speak, his mind a total blank, except for an amazing feeling of love for this gorgeous woman he was kissing.

She was a rare find, unique. She was smiling at him, her eyes full of kinky mischief.

'That's the most beautiful pearl brooch anyone has ever given me,' she said.

This little Amy was his kind of girl.

10

On the morning that Jason gave Amy a pearl brooch, Nina looked out at what had once been a large herb and vegetable patch at the rear of her parents' hotel in Cookham as she washed up the breakfast things.

It had been turned into a large carpark, and the space in front of the kitchen window, reserved for the family, contained a new-model Audi saloon with, Nina noticed, the plastic seat protectors still in place.

'Is that a new car, Mum?'

'Yes, it arrived this morning. Isn't it wonderful? It's from your brother.'

'You're kidding.'

'Brand new. Isn't he a good lad? He sent a note with it, apologising for losing the other one.'

'Oh, don't tell me you lent him your car,' said Nina incredulously. The history of Jason's abuse of his family was so long, any new chapter barely constituted family news.

'No, no. He borrowed it, it was fine. We did think it was stolen at first, but when we looked at the tapes we saw that it was Jason who had just borrowed it.'

'What tapes?'

'Oh, we had to have security cameras installed – so many cars being broken into in the carpark. Cost your father a fortune. I never hear the end of it.'

'So Jason took your car! Really, Mum.'

'What? We use your father's mostly anyway. This new one is so much nicer, though.'

'I can't believe he's done that. How does he get away with it!'

'Oh, he's so much better. He's set up this new company, he

81

told me all about it yesterday. He's got a lovely flat in Mayfair, imagine that. He's doing so well. I'm so pleased for him, he tries so hard.'

'Oh, yeah, he tries hard.'

'What?' snapped her mother. Nina grimaced. She had been trying extra hard to keep on a even keel with her mother, never an easy task.

'I mean he tries hard, Mum. I'm not having a go at him.'

'That'd make a change. The way you and your awful father go on, you'd think he was a criminal.'

'Well, he has got a criminal record, Mum.'

'Not really. Drunk-driving, silly lad,' her mother said with a smile. Nothing, thought Nina, probably up to and including his conviction for serial killing, could put a dent in Val Nash's adoration of her son.

'I have to admit it really does look like he's cleaned up his act,' Nina said as she put away a pile of plates.

'He's doing very well, *and* he isn't sleeping with his boss.'

Nina felt her hackles rise but again attempted to float over the insult.

'Has Dad seen the car?'

'He thinks it's stolen, of course, great oaf. He won't talk about it.'

'Oh, God. It's all so familiar.'

'Isn't it?' snipped her mother. 'Well, to what do we owe the privilege of your sudden arrival in the middle of the night with no warning?'

'Sorry about that.'

'I can never tell what you're going to do next,' her mother said with a sigh. 'You could at least have rung.'

'I didn't want to wake you up.'

'Well, you could have rung earlier.'

'I didn't know I was coming earlier.'

'I don't know.' Her mother opened the newspaper, resigned to the fact, as far as Nina could see, that she would never understand her perfectly straightforward daughter and yet utterly sympathised with her almost psychotically deranged son.

Nina had arrived late the night before. She wanted to get away from everyone – she needed time to think through what was happening; basically too much for her to take control of.

In the two weeks since her meeting with George Quinn and everybody at the Hilton Hotel, she had been in a spin dive. Her normally ordered life had turned into a chaotic struggle to maintain control.

She had done no work – the new chip she was supposed to be working on had lain dormant in its polyvinyl case on a shelf by her desk. All she did was listen to people cry, talk to people in corridors, try and reassure them that Coventon's would continue, that they would be paid and that Sir Brian was doing everything he could to protect them.

Of course, the staff and anyone else only had to read the papers to know that the research group was going down the pan at an almost impolite velocity. The staff were leaving in droves, even when Nina begged them not to, begged them to give the set-up another chance.

She had heard the day before that Hugo Harwood had found a post at Birmingham University and would be leaving at the end of the month. It was catastrophic.

The whole disaster had culminated the previous day when she had had a very heated discussion in public with Sir Brian, which later ended with a bitter row in private.

A crisis trustee meeting had been called at Coventon Research's headquarters in Percy Street, London. Nina was never normally summoned to such meetings, but this one was an exception.

The situation was terminal. There were stories in the tabloids about Sir Brian's large donations to the Labour Party, implying that he had bought his knighthood. Nina knew this wasn't true – he had been a leading light of British academia for years, and the New Year's honours list reflected this long-ignored achievement. He protested that he had supported the party since his

83

student days. This fact was ignored by journalists, who added with glee that now his business was on the rocks the government had washed their hands of him, another fact Nina knew to be wrong. The business would be booming, if only he'd exploit what he'd discovered – this was where the friction lay between them. The board of trustees was made up of a group of over-fifties academics with no idea about making a profit. In fact the word profit was almost taboo – it was all about helping develop the human race.

That morning Sir Brian told the trustees that Coventon Research had just lost a £3 million grant from the Department of Trade and Industry. 'The government is tightening its belt,' he said. 'Something has to go and research is always the first victim.'

Nothing was solved during the meeting. Nina got the distinct impression that everyone around the table was looking for a personal way out of the mess. Sir Brian put on a brave face and mumbled something about having charted a course across choppy waters in the past. It was pretty obvious to everyone present that the boat they were charting the course in was as seaworthy as a Greek ferry.

It was during the row after the meeting that Nina had let slip the information that she was thinking about leaving the company. That was how she liked to think of it.

In fact, what she actually said was, 'Fuck you. You two-faced bastard!'

This sort of outburst was unusual for Nina, but she was genuinely angry. Sir Brian was ducking and diving as he always had. Nina had finally lost her patience over the impossibility of getting him to commit to anything. It wasn't just the research set-up, it was the way he treated her. He would never actually come out and say, 'Look, I'm married and I will never leave my wife, I just want to have sex with you when it suits me with no strings.' She could suddenly see, now than he was under pressure from all sides, that this was what he really wanted, and she felt a fool for having hung around for so long nurturing the thought that he might one day, just possibly, be with her.

'Everything's fine. What's the problem?' he said. 'Look, we went into this with our eyes wide open.'

'Into what – Coventon Research or our farcical, so-called relationship.'

'I never lied to you,' he said, staring at her unwaveringly.

'No, but you've been economical with the truth, as your slimy politico mates would have it.'

'Sweetheart, I haven't.' Sir Brian sat on the side of the enormous bed and looked up at her pleadingly.

She wasn't having it. 'Oh, really! For a start you've kept me in the dark about the totally disastrous state the whole operation is in financially, and you've kept me in the dark about your feelings for me. I'm such a bloody fool to even think you had feelings for me.'

'I do, you know I do. All I'm saying is we need to take it easy for a while. Maybe see less of each other privately, just for a couple of weeks. Look, I didn't want to tell you, but life has got very complicated at home. Irene suspects something.'

'Oh, really, oh, boo-hoo, Irene.'

Nina wasn't close to tears; she was too angry for that. The force of her anger surprised even her. She had put up with so much from this man for so long. When she had first arrived at the meeting she felt guilty. She'd spent three days with George Quinn, meeting men in suits in offices in Mayfair, talking about her work with Coventon Research and what she knew they could achieve given the requisite backing. She had gone behind Sir Brian's back and she wasn't sure why. Standing in front of him now, she remembered the reason.

For years she went running to him whenever he had a free night away from his wife, sexually servicing him in hotel rooms all around the world. And it wasn't as if he was the world's greatest lover.

'And you are anything but the world's greatest lover, Brian. Jesus, I've been a fool.'

'Nina, please, you haven't been a fool. It's just been a very stressful period. I just need a little time with the family. I know it'll pass.'

'No it bloody won't, and anyway, I'm leaving!'

'Oh, please don't. I've ordered room service.'

They were staying at Home House, a private hotel on Portman Square, in a bedroom purportedly used by Madonna when she was house-hunting in London. The room was sumptuous, to say the least, but it wasn't having quite the effect on Nina that Sir Brian had clearly hoped.

'Fuck room service. I'm your fucking room service, Brian, at least I was. I've worked so hard for you for so long, in the lab and in your bed. I've developed things that could have made both of us multimillionaires without the need for some two-bit government grant. But no more. I'm leaving the whole thing!'

She picked up her coat, faltering for a moment as she saw the look of utter devastation on his face.

'Oh, God. Nina, if you leave Coventon Research now, I'm done for.'

'Too late.'

She walked to the door.

'What am I going to do?'

Nina turned and looked at him. 'Let me just say this. If you had asked me what *I* was going to do just then, I might have changed my mind.'

'What are you going to do?' he asked quickly. Pathetically.

'It has nothing whatever to do with you.'

And that was how she left it.

She drove straight out of London and arrived at her parents' hotel in Cookham at one in the morning. She didn't wake them, just crept to the spare room and fell asleep immediately.

'So, how are things at work, dear?' asked her mother with her lemon-in-the-mouth smile. Mother and daughter sat on either side of the huge old kitchen table that had once taken up virtually the whole room in the tiny cottage she had lived in as a child.

'I've just walked out. That's why I'm here.'

'Oh, goodness.' Her mother looked genuinely shocked. 'That's not like you, Nina.'

'I know, Mum.'

'No, no. You like the straight and narrow. You're not adventurous like Jason. What on earth has got into you?'

'I've quit Coventon Research.'

'What a silly thing to do. You've been very happy there. Is it the awful Conventon man?'

'Partly.'

Her mother put her hands up. 'Frankly I'd rather be left in the dark about the whole sordid affair.'

'It's not sordid.'

'Of course it is. He's a married man, for goodness' sake. Same age as your father. Imagine if Daddy started taking up with a girl your age.'

'A woman my age. Yes, it is hard to imagine. But Sir Brian is rather different.'

'Richer, you mean. Oh, it's awful. I don't want to think about it.'

Nina hadn't meant to bring Sir Brian into the conversation. She thought she'd throw a spanner in the works by telling her mother that she'd made her mind up about working with Jason, which she hadn't.

'I've got another job lined up. Better pay, and I'm not going to sleep with the boss.'

'Oh, for goodness' sake. You can't just up and leave. Surely Sir Brian will be disappointed.'

'But you were just saying he's a dirty old lech!' Nina squealed. She noted that she never squealed unless she was in the company of her mother. She cursed herself and vowed to lower her voice.

'He is, but you've had a very responsible position at that research station or whatever it is. He's been very good to you. Trust you to throw your weight around and flounce off like that.'

'I did not flounce off, Mother,' shouted Nina. 'And anyway, I'm joining with Jason's company.'

It worked. There was a silence. The occasions when Nina managed to stop her mother in her tracks were rare and deserved to be relished.

'I've decided to continue my work at this new organisation for so many reasons, none of which are to do with my relationship with Sir Brian.'

'Ghastly word.'

'What?'

'Relationship. It's your father's fault, he's always talking about relationships. His dreadful hippie ideas.'

'You were a hippie, Mum.'

'I was not, I was a scientist.'

'I'm a scientist.'

'Don't be so silly. You're a technician. Sir Brian is a scientist.'

Nina laughed. That was all she could do, other than stab her mother in the eye with a fork. It was all so predictable, and yet she still fell into it.

She had been through almost the exact same conversation with her mother countless times – 'I'm a scientist' followed by 'You're a technician'. It was all there, plain for anyone to see – her mother's jealousy of her success. The fact that she didn't have children when she was twenty-one and kept studying, unlike her mother. The fact that she had sex with a man twice her age and clearly enjoyed it, and didn't have to get married because he was already married. She could see it all, and yet her mother could still crush her with a look. Fight as she might, she lost, time and time again.

'Oh, goodness, what on earth are you going to do?'

'I've been approached by the people who set up Jason's company.'

'What people? Jason set it all up himself, he told me.'

'Oh, what's the point.'

'Why on earth should you cash in on all his hard work?'

'Mum, he owes me thousands of pounds!'

'More fool you.'

'Bloody hell,' said Nina, scratching her head furiously. She was lost in it now – there was nothing else for it. 'I'm not cashing in! How can you sit there and say that! You don't know anything about what he's really like. Listen, the only reason he's got the job is because I'm his stupid sister.'

'I'm sure not. It's his airline food thing. He told me all about it.'

'Mum! Airline-food.com is a bloody joke. Did you ever try it? It was inedible filth. He's cost you and Dad, God knows how much.'

'It doesn't seem fair than you should jump on his band-wagon. I know how you wrap him round your little finger, poor lad.'

'Poor lad! Poor lad! Mum, hello, wake-up time. He's a useless half-witted idiot. He can barely dress himself he's been so smothered by you.'

Her mother looked pained, but Nina was way beyond feeling guilty.

'Just to get back to me for a minute . . .'

'As usual.'

'My old job is finished anyway. The whole place looks like it's going to go down the plughole in the next year or so – people are leaving in droves. I had no idea before yesterday what a state Coventon Research was in. They'd never told me anything. At the moment it looks like all the work I've done for them will come to nothing. It's made me so angry because they didn't consult me earlier. I was just quietly beavering away, spending money, not knowing they didn't have any to spend. All the investors are getting nervous, all the government money is drying up.'

'Poor Sir Brian. He's worked so hard.'

'Mum! You hate Sir Brian. And you're right – he's a tosser, just like Dad, just like Jason.'

'Don't speak about your family like that, young lady.'

'Well, it's true. They're both like little babies.'

'They both work very hard, especially your father. They don't sleep around to try and get favours.'

'I'll ignore that,' said Nina, now breathing very deeply. 'Listen for once. For the first time it looks like your wonderful, faultless son has actually helped me, instead of the other way round. I'll grant you that.'

'I suppose we should be grateful for small mercies.'

Nina rubbed her face, trying to persuade herself not to be such a fool. She was sitting in the hotel kitchen doing the two things she had managed not to do for years – trying to communicate with her mother and starting to trust her brother and anything he was connected with. But she was going to be paid so much, she was going to be able to do so much with the new venture. It was all so tempting, and yet here, with her mother, she would so willingly have said she was going to live in a nunnery.

Her mother stood up and started to wipe the top of the Aga with a familiar tea towel Jason had given her as a Christmas present when he'd remembered it was Christmas. On it was printed 'The Rules of the House', and it probably came from a charity shop as it wasn't new when she'd received it. Her mother had her back to Nina as she spoke.

'And what on earth do Jason and his colleagues want you for?'

'Very much the same sort of thing as Coventon Research wanted me for, only we'll have a lot more money behind us.'

'Us?'

'Well, yes, I'm on the board too.'

'Oh, heaven protect us! What is Jason thinking of? He'd give away his right arm if he thought it would help someone.'

'Mum, please, this isn't Jason on his own. It's basically a group of American scientists very interested in what I've been doing. I don't want to tell you what I'll earn, but it's a hell of a lot more than I got at Coventon's. And I'll have the back-up and funding I need to carry on. We're right on the edge of some amazing new things. It's too exciting to stop now, and the new set-up is giving me the opportunity to really move ahead.'

Nina's father walked into the kitchen at that moment. He was in his white chef's overalls, his hands clean but his apron dusty with flour. He smiled when he saw Nina. She stood and they embraced briefly.

'What a lovely surprise! How are you, darling?' he said, his face beaming with obvious joy.

'Okay, thanks, Dad,' said Nina. She sat down again, feeling comforted by the presence of her father. It had only been since Jason finally left the family home for good four years previously that she had actually started to enjoy her visits. It was the first time she could remember having her father sane and to herself.

When Jason still lived at home, the place was always tense, her father was always in a bad mood, and Jason would be sulking somewhere in the hotel, causing trouble and running up huge phone bills. Her mother was always defending him, fighting with her father and generally making life behind the scenes at the King Charles pretty unbearable. Jason was always surfing the Net, claiming he was starting some great new scheme that was going to make them all millionaires.

At one time he set fire to his room in the middle of the night – a cigarette fell on the floor and started burning the clothes and bedding that were lying in heaps all around. Only rapid action from Jack Johnson, the hotel manager, had put the fire out. On another occasion Jason had fired his father's shotgun in an upstairs corridor when he thought there was an intruder in the building. There wasn't any sign of an intruder, but there was of course general panic among the guests and a huge hole in a wall, which thankfully only led into a bathroom. The blast did however split a water pipe; there was a flood, the ceiling in the dining room below fell in, and his father was up half the night trying to calm the guests, assure them that the police had been informed, although they hadn't been. He had to clean up the mess in the dining room and prepare it for breakfast the next morning.

There were plenty of reasons as to why John Nash should become tense if his son's name was mentioned, and it was therefore not surprising that there was a certain amount of tension in the kitchen when he walked in.

'Seen the car?' he asked.

Nina didn't want to talk about it. She didn't want to talk about anything to do with Jason. She wanted to explore her own feelings about joining Jason's new company, but the opportunity had been cut short. She didn't want to discuss it with her father, and she now realised she'd been stupid to think she could talk about it reasonably with her mother.

'Yeah.'

'Nice, isn't it?'

'Very. So how are you, Dad?'

'Worried, as usual. D'you know what's going on with him?'

She wasn't going to be able to get out of it. Here he was, affecting every aspect of her life as usual.

'I think Jason may possibly have finally grown up.'

'Hmm,' said her father.

'He's doing very well,' said Val Nash as she poured her husband a cup of coffee from the cafetière. 'Anyway, it's been so peaceful here recently.' She was clearly telling John to drop the subject of Jason, which he seemed willing to do.

John Nash stirred his coffee and sat in silence. Nina wasn't sure what to do, but she took his silence as a sign that he was prepared to listen.

'He's set up a company.'

Her father sighed very deliberately. Her mother picked up the newspaper and shook it rather violently.

'I'm thinking of joining him.'

Her father looked at her in alarm.

'He's only gone and got his odd sister a job,' said her mother from behind the *Daily Mail*. Her father sneered quietly at the newspaper.

'It's not quite that simple,' said Nina, glancing at her mother. 'He's not in total control. That's the important thing to remember. The people he's working with have seen that he is in fact, well, underneath it all a really talented person.'

'Mmm.' Her father's face showed no expression.

'I know that's hard for us to believe, but his renegade attitude can pay off, especially if it's reined in a bit by people who know what they're doing. If there's one thing we know about Jason, it's that he could sell shit to a sewer.'

'Please.'

'Sorry, Mum, but you know what I mean. And this new team are used to looking after and utilising people like Jase. These aren't his usual crowd. I've heard of some of them. I know their work and their backgrounds. It's quite extraordinary, I know, but it does look, well, quite hopeful.'

'Oh well,' said John Nash. 'I suppose that's good news.'

He managed to say it without conveying any emotion that Nina could detect. Only men could do that, she thought. No matter how hard she tried to remain neutral, she could sense she always gave herself away a little bit. Was it true that women exposed themselves emotionally more than men? It seemed like such an old cliché, and yet here was a perfect example. A man whose life had been virtually ruined by his son, a man who had screamed and shouted and threatened his offspring so often there was no telling the damage that had been done to both parties. How did men do that, and then in another moment not express any feelings about it?

Ever since she could remember Nina had watched her brother, and her father's reaction to her brother, with bewilderment. Her mother had just lived a life of utter denial as far as Jason was concerned, but her father had fought him every step of the way. Not a day passed in their childhood when their father didn't try to rein Jason in, to make him behave, to make him try to understand that what he did was destructive and hurtful to other people. John Nash was an incredibly decent man; although he had beaten Jason severely on several occasions, it was only after major provocation. But he had never thrown him out of the house or cut him off from the family.

Many times Nina had suggested that this was the only option left to them, but neither of her parents would hear of it. Nina looked at her father – slightly overweight, balding, his big clean hands nursing his coffee cup. He looked a picture of tranquillity, and yet he clearly had to have feelings. He just didn't display them.

How could he? More to the point, why did he? What was it about men that made them this way? What had her parents done to Jason to turn him into the nightmare he was – or rather, she hoped, then he had once been? What Sir Brian had told her when they met in Cambridge was still lingering in the back of her mind. It was just possible she would be able to find out.

'Is that all you're going to say?' her mother asked her father.

'Don't know what else to say. Thirty years of Jason have more or less done me in.'

In the afternoon, Nina walked along the banks of the Thames, which ran right past the old hotel. Although there were no leaves on the trees, it was still beautiful – a little corner of the world she knew so well. She felt relaxed, could sense the tension in her shoulders dropping away. She was carrying her mobile phone in the pocket of her windcheater, but it was switched off. As she stood on the bank of the river, just where it turned a sharp corner, she saw some swans gliding along midstream. It was here, many years ago, that she had experienced her first kiss. A boy called Peter Toft – she had been at school with him. He was a farmer's son and a bit of a ruffian, but a really nice boy underneath. She remembered it so clearly, how exciting it was, how new, how heart-stoopingly romantic. How unlike her life now. The drab sky loomed heavily above her – it felt very familiar and not in the least bit exciting.

What was she going to do? She had burst a bubble in her fight with Sir Brian, and he had revealed a weak side to himself than she could not tolerate. Why did men turn so readily into little boys? Just like Patrick, her old boyfriend, just like Peter Toft when she got a place at Cambridge and he got a place at

Reading. He sulked and threw himself around like a baby. And her brother, in fact, when she thought about it. She had yet to meet a man who didn't behave this way.

She carried on walking, thinking the problem through, considering the men she had known and trying to see a pattern. The only conclusion she could come to was that the exercise wasn't worth the bother. Unless, of course, it was her. Lateral thinking indicated that this could be the source of her problem, but then in every other aspect of her life she had more than enough proof that she wasn't doing the wrong thing. Far from it – she had really only ever experienced success. Her studies, her research, her experimentation had all come out well.

She climbed the old metal footbridge that crossed the river about a mile downstream from her parents' hotel. A pleasure cruiser chugged its way beneath her, a man alone at the wheel who didn't cast her a glance. The river could also be very lonely. Her hand went to her mobile phone. She pulled it out and switched it on.

It beeped as soon as it went on line. Messages.

'Nina, it's me,' said the voice of Sir Brian Coventon. 'Please let's talk this through. I don't think I can make it without you by my side. Everything's going wrong. Please call me. No, wait, don't call me, I'll try you again later. Don't call me. Oh God, Irene's seen the phone bill, it's very ugly here. I miss you. I'm at the garage getting some petrol, had to make an excuse to get out of the house. It's hell. Please ring me, darling.'

She erased the message. What more proof did she need? She couldn't call him because he was at home with his wife. She felt like throwing the phone in the river. He'd given it to her, after all.

11

Jason cursed himself. He would readily admit that he was slightly drunk, but all the same, the mess he'd made of the passenger door of the Mercedes was ridiculous, especially as the sensors on the car beeped at him when he drove too near something. They only beeped as he was pulling past the two large steel posts that marked the entrance to the carpark of Nash Systems' UK headquarters at the crack of 10.45 in the morning. They kept on beeping as the heart-rending sound of expensive metal and paintwork adjustment shuddered through the once immaculate vehicle. They carried on beeping even when he forced the car forward, scraping it against the unyielding post and inflicting a great deal more damage.

'Must be a short in the system somewhere,' he said without much thought, gunning the car across the carpark and screeching to a halt in his personal parking space.

Amy, sitting in the passenger seat and looking a little dishevelled, stared ahead in horror. She had not found the journey from the underground carpark in Mayfair to Cambridge a relaxing one. Never a big Wu Tang Clan fan or a keen supporter of high-speed motorway driving, she had had to put up with an ample supply of both on the way to work that morning.

Jason had planned to get there by nine but things had got on top of him, things in particular being Amy. There was something insatiable about the little lady – he had never known a woman who always wanted more, who always seemed ready for some top-grade adult action. Frankly, although he was always up for a session, she had completely knackered him.

The previous evening they had dropped in at the Met Bar for a quick drink. It turned into a bit of a session. Amy had never been there before, and Jason couldn't resist the temptation to show her around, and show her off. She was a foxy little thing – he noticed her getting scoped by a large proportion of the crowd. Even some famous faces gave her the second-glance special. Then back to his place for some serious shagging. He'd had a great time, but three hours' sleep was not enough. He was thirty, he was deputy CEO, and this was not a good moment.

'That is one hell of a mess,' said George as they surveyed the damage to the car together. George had appeared in the carpark worryingly fast, as if they knew he was coming, as if they knew everything already. Jason didn't like it – he was feeling prickly and ready for a scrap.

'I'm really sorry we're late,' said Amy. 'The traffic was terrible, and now this. I'm really sorry.'

'Hey, it's cool, it's only a car,' said Jason. 'We can have it fixed. No one's been hurt.'

'Good attitude, Jason,' said George flatly. 'Okay, the skeleton board are in the office at last. We need to get going.'

'Sure, sure. I'm on it,' said Jason. That was why he was there, he remembered now, a board meeting – the board meeting that had been cancelled the previous week owing to Cindy not being able to get to England. Something about meetings with vice-presidents of major US venture capital funds. He had worried that he should be in on those meetings. He wasn't sure Cindy Volksmann was truly up to the task, lovely lady though she might be.

But now, with the board finally convened, he had his chance to put his mark on the company, to guide it in the direction he wanted it to go in. He'd been in touch with every major research facility in the world over the previous week, put in many hundreds of hours' work. Although the initial reactions were muted, to say the least, he was beginning to get some feedback. The mere mention of the people in the company carried more weight than he had expected, most particularly dear sister Nina.

They walked briskly across the carpark; to be more precise, George and Amy walked briskly across the carpark, while Jason stumbled and trotted, dropping his cellular phone and later his coat, which spilled loose change in every direction. One shoelace was undone and he promptly tripped over it, saved from falling over only by George's rapid intervention.

'Good morning, Jason,' said Cindy Volksmann as he entered the corner of the open-plan office they had designated the boardroom. Jason looked around. It wasn't quite as crowded as he had expected. In fact it was virtually people free.

'Good morning, Cindy, you're looking radiant.'

'Why, thank you.'

'Slept well?' asked Pete Van Missen. The head of security at Nash Systems was beginning to get on Jason's nerves. He reacted in the only way he knew how under such circumstances, by delivering a data torrent.

'Got a bit of lower back pain, to be honest, Pete.'

'Oh, nothing serious, I hope,' said Cindy Volksmann.

'No, my fault,' said Jason 'Amy and I got up to some truly spectacular positions last night.'

'Oh, goodness,' muttered Volksmann, a blush already apparent on her neck.

'Thank God my apartment is soundproof, that's all I can say. She is an orgasm T1 line – she quite literally cannot get enough of my fat-pipe technology.'

Jason smiled as he looked around. Cindy Volksmann's face was a picture of displeasure, which made Jason feel good. He wasn't about to start being judged by these prickly Yanks. So he shagged the company secretary all night and trashed a car. He could afford it and so could they, and he hadn't committed a crime or damaged the company's reputation.

'Thank you, Jason,' said Pete Van Missen. He didn't seem at all fazed by what Jason had said. 'Okay, here's the problem as I see it . . .' he went on.

Jason interrupted. 'Where is everybody?'

Only George, Van Missen and Cindy Volksmann were present.

'Michael and Emen are very busy at the moment, buried in the clean room,' said Cindy. 'Any word from Nina?'

'Sure, sure,' lied Jason. 'I was talking to her only this morning. She's being very careful – there's a lot at stake. She is busy extricating herself from the whole Coventon débâcle with as much data as she can. I think it's imperative at this time than we allow her the space to do as she sees fit. She's a very sensitive and hyper-intelligent lady, and obviously, as her only blood relative, I feel very protective towards her.'

Jason hadn't actually seen or heard from Nina once since the breakfast meeting at the Hilton Hotel. He had no idea what she was doing; he hadn't even worried about it until now.

'So,' he said, cracking his knuckles, 'we're up and running. The clean room is on line, I take it.'

'It now has a security camera installed,' said Pete Van Missen. Jason smiled at him. How come this spook knew everything? He wasn't going to be intimidated by that.

'We need to have a skeletal board meeting to sort out some pretty basic problems we're facing,' said Cindy. 'You were saying, Pete.'

'Sure, okay,' said Van Missen. 'What we are embarking upon is not viewed by the medical establishment as totally acceptable. We clearly have to run a tight ship, Jason, and the merest glimpse of your records indicates to us that you are not really a tight ship type of guy.'

'What are you saying exactly, Pete? You mean Nash Systems can't trust its deputy CEO?'

'That's what we're worried about,' said Van Missen without hesitation. 'If any information about the company, or the work the company is involved in, is leaked out, either accidentally, or maliciously, it could cause extreme problems. It's my job to make sure that kind of thing doesn't happen.'

'So what are you telling me?'

'We need you, Jason. That's why we contacted you in the first place,' said George Quinn.

'Sure, sure. This is my baby, for fuck sake,' said Jason, now feeling even more unsure of himself and experiencing the awful sense of regret he had known all his life. If only he hadn't had that can of beer for breakfast, if only he hadn't damaged the car after spending the whole night rutting with Amy. It was a cold feeling – the realisation that once again he had convinced himself he'd finally got it together and was a new person, feeling good about himself and relaxing, and then celebrating, getting pissed, chasing girls and ending up back where he started. He clenched his fists tightly.

'Look, I know I screwed up with the car. I'm really sorry.'

'Don't worry about the car,' said George Quinn. 'The car is not an issue. Listen, Jason, when I met you on that god-awful cruise ship, I didn't know anything about you, other than airline-food.com. Okay, we can look back now and see that the B2C notion was bankrupt from day one. But to set up an intranet that tracked the catering capacity of fifteen in-flight food purveyors, which automatically updated an on-line menu for the consumer, that was a very cool idea. That's why we wanted you here, running the database of the research projects we want to undertake. What I didn't know about was the rest of your past, Jason. You know, the appearances in adult films, the minor thefts, the endless problems with drink-driving and borrowing money and avoiding bankruptcy by the skin of your laptop. These are problems that make us worry. We know you've turned over a new leaf, but surely you can understand our concern.'

They knew everything about him, and that made Jason feel even more uncomfortable. He was always running away from his past, but as he did so he always seemed to make more past to run away from. He had to change this time – he could sense it was his last chance. He was thirty, the chips were down.

'Okay, it's gauntlet time,' he said. 'I want to be put under twenty-four-hour surveillance, I want you guys to know what

100

I'm doing around the clock. I want to show you that I've changed. I've fucked up a little recently, I know. Amy and I have been pushing the envelope and that's not cool. I will stop all nefarious, alcohol-related and sexual activity. I will live like a monk. I will eat wholesome food and take copious exercise, work all the hours I possibly can. Okay?'

'That sounds kind of crazy,' said Cindy.

'It sounds kind of what we needed to hear,' said Pete Van Missen.

'Yeah, maybe,' agreed Cindy.

Jason looked at her. She seemed so calm, and he felt so utterly confused. He didn't really know these people, and he was angry that they had this much hold over him. It was a feeling he knew well, one he had always had to live with. One he was keen to avoid.

'It can all be arranged, and it would certainly make all the investors feel a lot more secure,' said Pete Van Missen.

'So, what d'you want me to do?' asked Jason rather snappily. 'D'you want me to fit myself up with surveillance equipment – flat, car, body?'

'You don't need to worry about all that,' said Pete calmly. 'We can have everything we need in place without a problem. I just need to know you are happy and there's nothing we need to change here.'

'Sure, sure,' said Jason. 'Look, all I want to change is the level of trust I know you can place in me. And that's my own particular mountain to climb.'

'That's good, Jason. I knew we could rely on you,' said Cindy.

'It's all going to be great,' said George. 'This is all shit. This will all be behind us really soon. You are really vital to the operation, Jason. Firstly as a grade-one conduit to your sister, who I know is not an easy person. Don't get me wrong, but she is vital to us at this time.'

'I know she's not easy – we're not an easy family,' said Jason. 'Very talented and complex but not easy. You should meet my mother if you want not easy. It's genetic.'

George smiled. 'Sure. But let me tell you we are really excited about all the contacts you've been making. I've been getting feedback from various academics and they are really impressed.'

'Sure, sure. I've been doing my job,' said Jason plaintively.

'Great. They're impressed, one, with the way we are approaching this whole research idea, which is essentially yours, Jason.'

Jason liked hearing that, even though it made no sense. He moved this worry into long-term storage.

'But,' continued George, 'they are also really impressed with you. I can see you've got a downer on yourself today, but I know you know why it is and I know you know how to debug the whole thing. We want to go on line with this project really soon, and I want to know I was right in choosing you to do it with.'

'I'd like to support those sentiments,' said Pete Van Missen.

'Sounds like we need a group hug,' said Cindy, standing up and holding her arms out. Jason stared in amazement as the two men joined her, leaving a space for him.

'When in Rome,' he said as he stood up to join them. They held him tight – it seemed they really wanted him there. He felt a little dizzy, a little sad, but very safe.

12

Nina had steadfastly refused contact with Sir Brian, who had gradually reduced the number of messages he left on her mobile as the weeks went by. Jason had left a torrent of panicky messages, but those gave her pleasure. She wanted them all to stew for a while – she needed to be sure what she was doing.

As she drove into the familiar carpark at Coventon Research, everything seemed normal, although it was eerily silent. There was no one at the reception desk when she entered the building – it looked as if the place had been gutted.

She heard a sound, someone talking. She walked into the lab, the door to which was held open by a pile of document boxes. Inside she saw Mandira, her chief chemist, sitting on the floor speaking on the phone. She gave her a wave and looked around. There was nothing there – the place had been stripped.

Mandira hung up the phone and looked at Nina.

'What are you doing here, Professor?'

'Well, I came to see what was happening,' said Nina. Her shoe crunched on some broken glass on the floor. 'I can't believe my eyes.'

'The last of the stuff was taken this morning.'

'Who by?'

'The receivers.'

'The what? You're kidding. What's happened?'

'You really don't know, do you?'

'Well, I knew when I was at the trustees' meeting in London two days ago that things were not looking good.'

'I think it all happened yesterday. Sir Brian is apparently bankrupt, the trust has folded, the lab has closed – it's all a little terminal, I'm afraid.'

'Oh my God. I can't believe it,' said Nina. 'How could I not have known?'

But she knew how. She hadn't spoken to anyone, hadn't even been home to get her messages, hadn't read any e-mails, even though she could easily retrieve them through her phone.

Mandira stood up and picked up a large canvas bag.

'So what are you doing?'

'Well, I came to get my things. I haven't got a job – that's why I was on the phone. I've got an interview in Inverness with a biotech company. I don't really want to go there but I haven't got much choice.'

'Oh, Mandira, I'm so sorry.'

Mandira looked at her with a hard smile. 'Well, you're all right.'

'Am I?'

'I thought you were working next door.'

'Next door?'

'At Nash Systems.'

'At what systems?' Nina walked to the window. She looked out at the Silicon Hammer building next to the lab. It looked the same.

Mandira joined her. 'No, the other way,' she said, pointing in the other direction.

Nina looked. She could see only a row of rather ugly conifer trees. But then something caught her eye through the foliage. It took a while for the sign on the front wall to come into focus, such was the shock.

'Fuck!' was all she could say.

'You didn't know?'

'No. I . . .' She looked at Mandira. She should know. It felt as if she were to blame. Nash Systems – how could it be called that?

'Hello there.'

Nina turned to see Jason at the door of the lab. He looked very elegant in an understated black suit, collar and tie. Every bit the sensitive corporate man. 'Wow, things are a bit different here,' he said with a big smile. 'Hi, Mandira, how are you?'

'I've been better.'

'Hey, why so glum?'

'You may have noticed,' she said with more confidence than Nina had ever seen her display previously, 'Than I don't have anywhere to work. I've lost my job.'

'Not an issue. Come and work for us,' said Jason with no discernible hesitation.

'Jason, please, this is really serious,' snapped Nina. 'I don't know what's happened here. This is all new to me, for crying out loud. What am I going to do?'

'Check out the clean room. Emen and Del Papa are already in there.'

Nina felt dizzy. It was all happening too quickly. She found herself actually wanting to talk to Sir Brian, to find out what was going on.

'Actually, before we go over, I need a quick word. Would you excuse us, Mandira? And drop your résumé off at Nash Systems reception. I'll see what I can do.'

Mandira nodded but looked rather confused as Nina followed Jason down the once familiar corridor. They went out of the fire door, where only three weeks earlier she had listened to Jason drivel on in his normal way. How things had changed.

'Okay, let me finally get you up to speed, oh sister of mine.'

'What the hell has been going on? Nash Systems – whose idea was that?'

'They insisted on it, trading on the family name and everything. You are one very famous lady, up there with Gates and Jobs. It will be reflected in your remuneration package, believe me. But listen, this is very important. The boardroom battles over there are really ugly. I have been fighting your corner for all I'm worth, but look at the state of me. Talk about workload – I haven't had a moment to myself for weeks. I don't want you to get caught up in all that. I want you where you belong, in that lab, working on the chips. Okay?'

'Jason.'

'I know, you've been burnt here, I know how you feel. Old man Coventon wasn't exactly liberal with the truth about the mess he'd got himself in, but this time it's different. There's the funding and anything you need in the lab. Come and see me and I'll source it for you.'

'You'll what?'

'I'll source it, find it, get it. Whatever. Now, your housing needs – d'you need somewhere bigger?'

'No.'

'Car?'

'What about it?'

'Well, yours is going to be impounded or whatever, I imagine. It's a Coventon's deal you got it with, isn't it?'

'I think so,' she said, feeling rapidly more unsure of herself. She had got used to her car.

'Well, I think a little Porsche Boxter would suit. Yellow okay? Consider it sourced.'

'Jason. Hello, it's me, your sister, living here in the real world.'

'No, the real world is next door, at Nash Systems.'

'Jason, it's all too easy. Don't you see? Something weird is happening here.'

'Yes, it's called life in the fast lane.'

'No, it's called spooky. Two weeks ago Coventon's were in a bit of financial trouble, then I meet your weird American mates who offer me an amazing job and suddenly the whole Coventon's operation folds overnight and your friends take over the building next door. Don't you think that's a little bit suspicious?'

'Not in the least, it's business. Coventon's was already yesterday's news. There's other companies doing better work, cheaper and faster, and we need to get in there pronto. Believe me. I just need you to get on with, with whatever it is you do. Chip development and its ilk. Leave the board and the running of the business to me. They'll try and get you involved because

106

they feel insecure, but let them suffer. They'll just confuse you with all the business plans, but I have it so under control it's not true.'

'Yes, I'm sure,' said Nina.

'Come on, let's hit the ground running. They are going to be so pleased to see you.'

Her arrival at Nash Systems was fairly tumultuous, overwhelming even. As she walked through the huge glass doors, she was greeted with a logo featuring her name that had to be at least two metres high, mounted on a grey wall above a reception desk that looked like the wing of a Spitfire. George Quinn was standing in front of the wing, wearing standard-issue khaki slacks and a light blue polo shirt.

'Nina, are we glad to see you,' he said, walking over and embracing her. 'I've just been talking to Michael and Emen. They're in the clean room right now and they really need your expert advice.'

'Oh, right,' said Nina. 'So I'm already working here, am I?'

'Sis,' said Jason with an embarrassed laugh. 'She's a one, isn't she, George.' He pulled her gently but firmly towards a set of double doors to the right of the Spitfire wing. It was then that Nina noticed Amy sitting behind the wing, looking a little the worse for wear.

'Oh, hi, Amy, you're here too.'

'Yes. How are you, Professor?'

'I've been less confused,' she said.

'Look, sis, catch up with Amy later. Please, just get your suit on and get in that clean room and sort those two bozos out, will you. We'll have plenty of time to get you up to speed on the personnel front later.'

As she walked through the door her brother was holding open for her, she was momentarily stunned. The laboratory was incredible – she had never seen anything like it. She had visited well-equipped labs in various universities and research facilities around the globe, but nothing on this scale. One whole wall of the room was taken up with servers and computer equipment. In the centre of the room a massive, humming dust extraction unit stood next to a newly built clean room. She could just see the two white-clad figures inside.

Within an hour of arriving at the laboratory, Nina was standing inside the clean room covered from head to foot in a white boiler suit. Michael Del Papa and Emen Trouville were likewise attired, breathing through a system of long tubes that were linked to nozzles in the wall. The air blowing over their faces was cool, but the suits could not be described as comfortable. If you wanted to scratch your face, you had to wait.

Working with Emen Trouville and Michael Del Papa was a very challenging experience for Nina – she was in charge of a team made up of two of the top people in the field of cybernetics. Both of the men she had working for her had enormous experience of microelectronics development – in Michael Del Papa's case since the mid-1960s, developing human–machine interfaces from the ground up. The computer screen that went on to be so familiar courtesy of Windows and Macintosh was initially developed by the team at Xerox Park, and Michael was one of the young guns then. Emen Trouville had concentrated on very refined experiments with virtual intelligence and neural networks from the beginning of this still-esoteric area of computer science. He had worked for IBM, on the team that had developed Deep Blue, the computer that beat Boris Spassky in a game of chess.

Nina had been in clean rooms before, but not as part of a team actually working on a project. She had always been present as an observer, merely seeing what was going on. Here she was present as the person who had to know what to do – not so much with the design and development of the chip, but with what it had to achieve.

'This is truly weird stuff,' said Michael Del Papa, his voice curiously muffled. Hearing him speak wasn't helped by the incessant rattle of the powerful air-conditioning system which fought day and night to kept the room dust free. 'I can barely see this shit, and look what it's doing.'

He pointed to a screen. Lines of code poured down it like rain on a windscreen, and all the code was coming from the tiny chip.

The reason the clean room needed to be so incredibly clean was obvious when a casual observer saw the scale of the technology being developed inside the brightly lit unit.

Centred on a small dish on a steel table in front of Del Papa was a speck of something looking very like a lice egg on a fine human hair. It was in fact a microprocessor, battery and sensor wire which had been engineered entirely by machine. The machine in question, a microchip fabricator, was only a little bigger than a domestic toaster, but considerably more expensive.

Nina had never seen one of the machines before she came into the clean room that morning. The chip fabricator that Coventon Research used was still, effectively, the human hand. Sir Brian and his team had made chips using their rubber-clad fingers, watching what they were doing under microscopes.

Casual observation of the machine told Nina that it was most likely manufactured in America, but it had no maker's name apparent on its shell – just a series of terminals on one side, wired to a computer outside the clean room.

'Where on earth does that come from?' she asked as Emen opened the side to reveal a densely packed mass of wires and circuit boards, stainless-steel gearing mechanisms and sophisticated sliding trays which gripped the minute objects it manufactured.

'You can't buy one of these babies down at Radio Shack. That's for sure. You are looking at seven million dollars sitting right there.'

The price astonished her. She was used to very expensive, one-off pieces of scientific equipment, but $7 million! How could Nash Systems afford such a thing?

'Is it from the States?'

'You betcha,' said Emen. 'That's a Sands Microtron. There's only three in the world, and we got us one.'

'It's a bitch to operate,' said Del Papa. 'System controls beyond any individual's understanding. We're talking billions of variables, and there's plenty of fuck-ups in the operating system.'

'Tell me about it,' said Emen.

'Will there ever come a day when an operating system does what it says it should do?'

'Operate,' said all three of them together. They laughed. Nina felt more comfortable – they were good people, a little blinkered about their work, a little talkative for her taste, but she liked them all the same.

'So how long before we know this is working?' she asked, looking closely at the tiny chip.

'It's working now. We're just testing battery life,' said Del Papa. 'Theoretically it should recharge through the sensor wire. The current running through human nerve fibre is what?'

'A hundred and fifty millivolts,' said Emen Trouville. It was something Nina already knew, but these two men relished their knowledge. 'And this chip is running at?'

'A hundred and fifty millivolts,' said Del Papa. 'At least, that's what it's meant to do.'

'How are you testing it?' asked Nina. She knew the theory. In order to make the chip run as long as its human host, it would receive the tiny amount of electricity it needed from the electrical nerve impulses that shot up and down the spinal cord.

'That's what I'm trying to set up. We'll kludge together an ultra-low-voltage unit to see if it's all working.'

'Kludge it?' queried Nina.

'Don't you guys kludge stuff here?' said Michael. 'We're always kludging stuff.'

'I think the British equivalent is "bodge", to bodge something,' said Emen.

'God, I hope we're not bodging anything,' said Nina. 'It seems a very expensive way of bodging.'

'You gotta kludge. Surely you've kludged, or bodged, or whatever?'

'I don't think so.'

'You mean to tell me when you work up a prototype for a prosthetic arm you don't kind of nip and tuck and tie the whole thing together with tape and cable grips?'

'No.'

'Weird. Okay, fair enough,' said Del Papa. 'Well, let me put it this way. I've constructed a state-of-the-art low-voltage unit which should charge the battery. We'll need to leave it to run for a couple of days and then run really sophisticated tests. How's that sound?'

'A lot better,' said Nina.

'Yeah, the really sophisticated tests are. If the thing is still working, it works.'

'Now that is sophisticated,' said Del Papa.

'Gentlemen, you seem to be very on the case here,' said Nina. 'I'm going to go into the lab and familiarise myself with the set-up here. It's been a hectic time for me, as you can probably imagine.'

'Sure thing, Professor. Me and Emen are happy as hogs in here,' said Michael Del Papa.

Nina unplugged her air supply and walked to the door, slid the key card Pete Van Missen had given her through it and was let into the outer chamber. The air hissed around her as high-pressure jets blew at her from all directions. Eventually the outer door opened and she walked back into the lab.

As she pulled the white suit off she checked the monitors and saw that the two men were still in the clean room, busy 'kludging' no doubt. She found her computer bag and lifted it on to a long workbench. As she booted up her laptop she stood in silence, listening to the room. How had she arrived in this amazing place; how could all this have happened so fast? She had never really looked at the building she was in before. It had been empty for quite a while, she knew that, and she never really knew what went on there. What she couldn't decide was whether Jason was a prime mover in all these events or merely a hanger-on. She could move her research forward at a dizzying

111

speed now, that much was obvious, but there was so much unexplained.

She opened her e-mail program, and Scrolled down the list of names in her address book until she fell upon Hugo Harwood. She had decided she needed a little outside help, a little information she clearly wasn't going to get from her new work colleagues.

She typed her message. She didn't want to dictate as she knew she could easily be seen and heard – according to Jason, Nash Systems was bristling with cameras and state-of-the-art surveillance equipment. She didn't want to surf – too many tracks, too easy to follow her trail. Encrypted e-mail was the safest bet, and she still had the encryption keys she had used at Coventon's; 128-bit encryption was still as good as impossible to break, which was why organisations like the CIA and MI6 really didn't like people using it. They could easily get hold of the e-mails in transit, but they couldn't read them.

She hoped the recipient had kept his own encryption keys.

> Hugo
> Too much to tell in e-mail. To précis, I've left Coventon's, which has disappeared anyway. Working in that weird building next door. Now Nash Systems HQ. Crazy but good so far. 1st day so what do I know. Brother in charge so expect chaos. Ever come across a 'Sands Microtron' chip fabricator? Been told they cost in the region of 7 million US. Size of a big cake tin. Can you find out for me? Hope Birmingham's okay. Heard from Sir Brian?
> Love Nina

She looked at the send icon and off it went.

She then checked her inbox – over fifty messages from Jason. She deleted them as a block, knowing they would all say the same thing. 'Where are you!' A dozen or so from Sir Brian – she would read those later – and several from old students who had done occasional work for Coventon Research, now wondering

112

whether there was an opening at Nash Systems. News had got out fast.

Then her inbox gave out its familiar chime. She had a new mail. From Hugo.

Nina

A Sands. Lucky bugger. Where from? Simple answer. Military.
Sands Microsystems work exclusively for Pentagon.
Wish I'd seen you before the big closedown.
Birmingham is a drag.
Sir Brian in court next week, yippee!
Keep me in mind if Nash expands.
Hugo

13

Jason sat at his desk, his eyes glazed. Great slews of text flew across the screen in front of him but he wasn't taking it in. He was thinking; he was thinking very hard. He had managed to get his sister into the clean room and close to starting work. At least he hoped she would start, there was no telling with her. She could blow the whole thing at any moment, walk out and leave him without a job, a car, a top apartment and a very high-quality adult action partner. It was too grim to contemplate.

He was trying to work out how, without raising too much suspicion, to keep her away from George and Pete Van Missen as much as possible. If she started to have an easy-going relationship with them he was going to be out of the picture before he knew it. In some ways it was great that she was so prickly and difficult. If he could keep pissing her off enough to make her annoyed, but not enough to make her leave, they would probably want to keep clear of her.

One of the reasons he was worried was that at the end of the meeting where he had willingly allowed himself to be put under twenty-four-hour surveillance George told him that Pete Van Missen had volunteered to be the first chip recipient. Jason didn't immediately catch on to what this meant, but friendly old Mr Van Missen had told him that he would have the first chip implant that Nina and the team produced. This was not good, and he was trying to work out how to avoid this.

There was a knock on his door. He turned and saw sister Nina looking a little icy, standing in his doorway. He engaged full chirpy mode.

'Aha, Professor, just the person I wanted to see,' he said.

'Good, because I wanted to talk to you very urgently.'

'What other way have you ever wanted to talk to me? It's always an urgent matter. What have I done now?'

'I don't know. That's what I want to talk to you about.'

'Okay, fire away,' said Jason. A glance at his screen saver icon dimmed the screen and then the saver came on. As soon as he saw it he knew it was a mistake. Flocks of flying erections took off from the base of the screen and circled around in amazing 3D reality.

Nina didn't seem to notice, or care. 'Can we go outside?' she said. 'I've got something personal to ask you.'

'Wey-hey,' said Jason with a big grin. 'Who are you shagging now, you dark old trollop? Not old tubby Del Papa, is it? He's nearly old enough for you.'

'Jason, come outside. Please.'

They walked down the stairs and through the reception area, where Jason winked discreetly at Amy, who was looking a little more cheerful than when he'd last bothered to look at her. He followed his sister out into the carpark and watched her stretch in a rather exaggerated style that annoyed him. She was so 'in tune' with herself, and yet still a total headcase as far as he was concerned. He took a large Cuban out of his top pocket and lit it with his gale-proof stainless-steel lighter.

'Jason, where did you actually meet George?'

'George Quinn?' asked Jason slightly too quickly. Dead giveaway – he should have been more cool, especially with the big sis. He could see her watching him think as he tried to obscure his face with cigar smoke. It wasn't working – it was too breezy.

'No, George Michael, who do you think? Of course George bloody Quinn.'

'George. Well, I met him on a cruise liner.'

'A what? What d'you mean?'

'I was working on a cruise liner, last year. Set off from Vancouver, up the coast of Alaska. It was a dedicated theme cruise, for failed dot-commoners. I was a speaker. Being a total fucking failure, I was just right for the job.'

'How on earth did you get involved in that?'

'Just hassled a few contacts. No big deal, sis. I'm on line, in tune with the zeitgeist and all that. Anyway, George was on the cruise, he was giving a talk too. He's not a failed dot-commoner, as you may have noticed, he's a bit of a hyper-successful one, so he was pointing the way forward and all that bull. We met up, and got talking. Why d'you ask?'

'Well, he seems to be the money man, or at least have the contacts. I'm just wondering where the money comes from, and who the contacts are. And don't answer because I know you'll just spin me a line, but the chip fabricator in the clean room . . .'

'The Sands. Little beauty, isn't it?'

'You know about it!'

'Of course I bloody know about it,' he said. He had known this would happen one day – she'd never let anything lie, she had to know everything all the bloody time.

'I sourced it, I ordered it. Fuck it, Nina, I helped carry the damn thing in. I am deputy CEO, you know.'

'Sorry, Jason. Yes, I know you are deputy CEO. I just didn't realise you were so hands-on. But d'you know where it came from?'

' 'Course I bloody know. Sands Technologies. Alamogordo, New Mexico.'

'Okay,' said Nina. She held her chin as she looked at him, just as she had done when she was the bigger girl and he had ripped her dolls to bits when his Action Man had somehow run amok in her bedroom.

'Okay, the Sands people. I've never heard of them before,' she said finally.

'Well, I'm standing here trying to work out whose fault that is, and at the moment the blame needle is pointing to you. Let's face it, they're a pretty big operation.'

'Have you visited the plant?'

'No, 'course not. No one has. I've seen the pictures, though.'

'What d'you mean?'

'There's pictures all over the Web. Satellite pictures of the plant.'

'Why are the pictures taken by a satellite, Jason?'

'I don't know, Nina,' said Jason impatiently. 'Maybe because the work that goes on at Sands is very sensitive.'

'Commercially sensitive.'

'Oh, bloody hello,' said Jason, walking in a circle. 'Here we go. Little Miss Ethics is about to throw a major wobbly. Okay, let's call in the lunatic fringe and start picketing Nash Systems, let's get a bunch of recently graduated film school students to do a shocking exposé of the links Nash Systems has with the fucking military.'

'Oh,' said Nina with a smile. 'So Sands are a military supplier.'

'Yes, they're a fucking military supplier, but they also happen to make the best nanochip fabricators around. And George had the contacts and we had the money. It's not stolen. I can show you the fucking invoice. I signed for it. It's the single most expensive thing I've ever bought.'

'Well, you didn't actually buy it yourself, did you?'

'Nash Systems bought it, and for the sake of argument I am Nash Systems. The way I see it, I bought it.'

'Okay. Okay,' said Nina. She walked away from Jason as he took another large pull on his cigar. He looked up when he heard a vehicle approaching.

'Shit. Timing,' he said to himself.

A low-loader truck pulled into the carpark. It juddered to a halt next to Nina and a young man jumped out of the cab.

'Looking for a party name of Nash,' he said.

'Yes, what can I do for you?' replied Nina.

'Come to pick up a trashed car.'

Nina shrugged and looked at Jason. He smiled, knowing he needed to be a bit nimble in the blame realignment department.

'Ah, yes, the little lady put a bit of a dint in the Merc,' he said, feeling a rush of pride at the sheer speed with which he had deflected a potentially ugly scenario.

The truck driver looked at Nina and grimaced. 'Oh dear, bet you're not too popular.'

'It's nothing to do with me,' she spat.

'Not that little lady. That's my sister. No, no. It was Amy, the little lady in the office. Best not make too much fuss about it, she's already a bit shaken up by the whole thing. She's not used to driving a large executive motor, poor lass. Engine's a bit much for her.'

Jason led the truck driver towards the Mercedes. From where they were standing everything looked fine. He awaited the inevitable reaction as the three of them reached the bad side.

'Jason! Look at the state of that!' said Nina. 'Did Amy do that?'

'Yeah, yeah. But keep it quiet, sis.'

'But she hasn't even got a driving licence.'

Jason faltered for a moment. There was a bit of a hole in the alibi there. He smiled, shrugged and said, 'It's all my fault. I encouraged her. I wanted to give her a taste of what true motoring can be. She only drove the last couple of hundred yards. Please don't say anything.'

'Jason!'

'Sorreeeeeeeee.'

The two of them watched the truck pull out once the car had been winched on board.

'Why does this sort of thing always happen to you?'

'It's my destiny, I suppose,' said Jason, feeling philosophical. 'I'm always pushing boundaries, always searching for the next big thing. Sometimes that's creative and beneficial, sometimes it's a fucking nightmare. The only talent I lack is to be able to see which is which.'

Nina looked at him with a strange smile. She punched him on the arm. 'God, you're a nightmare, but I have to say that laboratory is a dream. You know, for the first time in my life I'm really glad you're my brother.'

'Well, that's good, sis, because we've got a problem.'

'Have we?'

'Yes. Listen, the board want you to insert the first chip into Pete Van Missen.'

'Do they?' said Nina.

'Yes.'

'God, we haven't got that far yet. We've barely started making the first prototype. If it works it's going to be about a thousand times more sensitive than the one in Ingrid Neilson's arm.'

'Sure, sure, but when you do, Van Missen's going to be standing there with his sleeve rolled up.'

Nina stared at him with an odd smile, not fully comprehending when he was saying, he assumed. He needed to clarify.

'He's a spook, Nina, and I don't want you to get involved. Look, I'm expendable. If they take me out on a dark night somewhere, it's no great loss to the world, but you are vital. I don't want you getting tangled up with a psycho like Van Missen. Can you suggest that you use me as the guinea-pig?'

'I'm sorry.'

'Shove the chip in me. If the whole thing blows up, where's the damage?'

Nina scratched her head as she stared at him. 'What are you telling me? George wants me to put a chip in Pete Van Missen?'

'Yes. God, sis, get up to speed. Van Missen, the spook guy with the weird eyes.'

'Has he got weird eyes?'

'Sis! He's a murdering loony, anyone can see that.'

'Oh, right. I didn't know. He seems very polite.' She scratched her head again for a moment, then said, 'I don't think putting a chip in you would be much help, Jason. We're trying to get readings from, well, stable individuals.'

'Oh, thank you.'

'Sorry, but I think you're a bit of a . . . well, how should I put this . . . a one-off. Why not Pete?'

'I have my reasons,' said Jason, wishing he could tell her. If only he could explain in an honest way that if the board had

119

more direct communication with her he'd have less than a toe in the door of the company that bore his name. Of course, if he did tell her she would probably be glad to see him go. He had to try to dupe her.

'I don't trust anyone in the company. Especially Van Missen. He may just get the chip and leg it, sell it to someone for three bill, and that's the last we'll ever see of him. Plastic surgery, new identity created by the government, and Nash Systems is left high and dry.'

'Oh really, Jason,' Nina said almost kindly. 'Mr Van Missen seems like a very suitable test individual. I'm sure he's trust-worthy.' She turned and walked back into the building, which now, for the first time since Jason had been there, was bathed in bright sunlight.

'Shit,' he said, and stamped out the fat stub of his expensive Cuban cigar.

14

Jason was right, of course, Pete Van Missen was a peculiar man. Two days later Nina glanced at him as he sat in the lab with a wonderful air of calm about him. Professional calm, Nina thought. His hair was too neat, and it grew too thickly for a man his age, although his exact age was hard to guess. Nina thought he could be anywhere between twenty-five and forty. The telltale signs weren't there, certainly not on the face, which was lean and smooth, only some tiny wrinkles around the eyes revealing a lifetime living in bright sunlight. His hands were large, clearly strong, but the skin was very smooth, too smooth for a man in his forties.

Nina had spoken to Van Missen earlier in the week, asking whether he could find the time to join her in her lab when everyone had gone home. He had been very polite and obliging. She had thought about what Jason had said in the carpark and decided that it would be asking for trouble to put a chip into him.

The idea with the new chip, which they had only just created, was that it would record all the data that the brain sent the body, not just the data that went down one arm, as in young Ingrid. In order to be able to do this, the chip had to be a thousand times more powerful than the ones she had been using at Coventon's. Initially this had seemed like an impossible task, but her two associates had relished the challenge.

They'd had some setbacks – the first few chips they manufactured simply failed to function. Finding the cause of the problem required the purchase of an electron microscope. Nina knew that in her old world, the procedure to get such an expensive piece of equipment would have been long and arduous. Committees would have to convene to discuss it, funding would have to be sought, reports would have to be written.

At Nash Systems, Nina soon learned, it was fast track all the way.

'We need an electron microscope to really see where the malfunction in the design is,' said Emen Trouville when they sat in the boardroom one day.

'I can source that,' said Jason. That was all there was to it. Her little brother Jason was going to 'source it', which sounded alarmingly similar to the claim he had made when he was a kid that he could 'source pork' from the local pig farm for his dad. That episode ended with the family chasing after a living and very vocal pig in the carpark of the hotel, Nina getting blamed for leaving the gate open and allowing the animal to disappear up the main road to High Wycombe, never to be seen again.

Later that afternoon a large truck arrived in the Nash Systems carpark and four men manoeuvred the expensive equipment into the lab, set it up and left without saying a word.

The following week, after Nina had redesigned the chip's structure on the impressive computers the lab contained, they produced the first working chip. They ran tests on it, focusing mainly on power consumption. It was using such minute amounts it would, in theory, be able to take the necessary charge from the host body's electrical supply. Everything seemed to be functioning perfectly, and there was nothing to do but test it in the field. Hence Van Missen's quiet presence in the lab.

'I know you've said you're fine about this, Mr Van Missen,' said Nina softly as she sat in front of him. 'But just for my own peace of mind, and for the most basic ethical reasons, I want to know how you feel about the chip insertion.'

'I feel fine about it,' said Van Missen, not too hurriedly, not too slowly. His response was perfect.

'Nobody's put any pressure on you to do it?'

'Not at all. I'm quite aware of the risks, Professor. As long as it's the left one. I need the right one for weapon guidance.'

'I beg your pardon?' said Nina.

'For aiming a weapon,' he responded flatly. 'It's part of my job.'

Nina, who had grown up with Jason, immediately assumed that any sentence with the words weapon or guidance in it meant he was referring to his penis. In some ways she almost wished that was what he did mean – for all the obscenity that Jason came out with, he didn't use a gun.

'I see. Well, okay,' said Nina, deciding to try to elicit more information. 'But you know it's not going to be in your arm, don't you?'

'Not in my arm?' said Pete Van Missen, for the first time giving the slightest hint of alarm in his reaction.

'We're not going to put the chip in your arm. Hasn't anyone told you?'

'I guess not.'

Nina sat back and smiled. She had worked in the company that bore her name for four weeks and had felt she knew less and less about what was going on in that time.

'I don't believe this place. I always feel like I'm left behind when it comes to information, and then I discover the information isn't a hundred per cent accurate and it's my responsibility.'

'The only information I have received regarding this issue has been from your written reports, Professor,' said Pete Van Missen neutrally. 'I haven't been speaking to any of your colleagues behind your back, if that's what you're concerned about.'

'Oh, I see,' said Nina. The solid clarity of Pete Van Missen's speech was as disconcerting as what he actually said. She found it impossible to doubt anything he told her.

'Where is it going, then?' he asked finally.

'In your neck,' said Nina seriously. She reached around him and poked him gently in the back of the neck, just below the

hairline. 'About there.' The move felt peculiarly intimate, quite
pleasurably so. She found herself wanting to leave her finger
there, but she removed it and maintained her composure.

'Okay. That is news. Better remember to wash my neck come
Friday.' His smile was flat and without humour, but his eyes
were spectacular. Very blue but somehow not cold. She had to
shake off the desire to look into them in silence.

'Let me explain,' said Nina, spinning around on her chair
and opening her laptop. She looked at the screen as she spoke.
'You will be the first person who has ever had this chip inserted
in this position, Mr Van Missen.'

'Call me Pete.'

Again she was a little thrown. She looked around and smiled
at him, at his eyes, which were looking straight at hers without
threat or malice, just with clear focus.

'It's a very delicate operation.'

'Okay, but this chip – how big are we talking?'

'It's incredibly small considering what it does, a little larger
than a match head. It's completely safe in itself. It's encased in
bio-neutral plastic – your immune system will ignore it so we
don't have a problem with rejection. However, the danger lies
in where the connecting fibres go.'

She moved her eyes across the screen, opening a 3D animated image of the human spinal cord. The image expanded
until it showed a close-up of one vertebra.

'The receptor fibres have to feed directly into your spinal
column. Essentially we are going to insert two microscopically
fine wires into your central nervous system. There is a risk, and
it's a very serious risk, that these fibres could damage the tissue,
and if you damage tissue in your spinal column . . .'

'It can really put a crimp in your day.'

'To say the least, in the event of a catastrophic failure of the
chip you could be partially, or even completely, paralysed.'

'That would not be good.'

'No.' Nina looked at him for a moment. He was clearly
having second thoughts. Maybe she'd pushed it too far, made it

sound more likely than it was. The chances were infinitesimally small.

'I just wanted to explain the situation. I want you to take a few days to really think about it.'

'There's no need. I'm fully committed.'

'Okay, well, I just don't want you to feel like you're under pressure. I don't care what George or the board are saying. While you have the chip in you are my responsibility. I want to know it's okay with you.'

'That's very considerate and I appreciate it.'

'Anyway, I've been assured the surgeon is absolutely top of the league, and the insertion is the most dangerous part of the whole procedure. Once you've got the chip in place, it's not a problem. You have to be a bit careful, of course. A sudden jolt, any jarring to the spine, could also cause . . . well, problems. Do you understand?'

'I understand,' said Pete Van Missen.

'Good. So you feel you would still like to go ahead?'

'Certainly, Professor.'

'Call me Nina.'

'Sure.'

'Thank you. Well, I have to say you are a very brave man, Mr Van Missen. Sorry, Pete.' Nina smiled and stood up. Van Missen did the same, like a well-trained dog. He was so polite.

'Thank you, ma'am,' he said, his face placid and unreadable. They shook hands, and as their hands touched Nina felt a tingle run down one side of her body. Pete Van Missen smiled.

15

Jason had worked out before, he knew how to do it, and he certainly didn't need some poncified personal trainer in Lycra smelling of cheap aftershave shouting 'One more!' in his ear every five seconds. He'd had a discreet multigym installed in the spare bedroom of his apartment. He lay back on the bench pressing a bar-bell, looking all the time at the tiny camera that was fitted inconspicuously in the corner of the room.

He felt good. He wanted to show them that he had changed. True, he was a little eccentric, he was completely naked – not the normal dress code for working out – but there was no one else around so it could hardly be deemed a crime.

Considering the abuse it had received, the long periods of time without sleep, food or vitamin sustenance, Jason's six-foot-three body was in pretty good shape.

He carefully placed the bar-bell back on its support and slid out from underneath. He then moved to the chin bar he'd fitted into the doorway and did a series of pull-ups.

'Come on, you lazy bastard. Pull!' he said to himself. He managed six before he dropped to the floor, his arms feeling like two sacks of rock hanging from his shoulders.

'Oh yes, baby. That's good.'

He stretched his arms over his head as he walked into the main room of the spacious apartment and found his cigarettes. As he lit one, he glanced up at the camera that was placed above the door. He liked it being there. He felt much happier knowing that someone was probably watching him.

'Music,' he said to the desktop. It spun into life. An image of a young Japanese woman appeared on the screen. 'Aerosmith,

"Pink",' he said, and a moment later the familiar snare drums of the Aerosmith classic filled the room.

He started to gyrate to the sound, to luxuriate in the tingling feeling in his body. He knew he had released some serious endorphins which made him feel good. His whole body was tingling, life was good.

'Pink is my favourite colour.'

Something in his hearing alerted him, some note in the song that wasn't quite right. He paused for a moment, chose to ignore it and pranced around the room, always making sure he was in range of one of the many cameras.

Again there was a jarring note. A bell? In 'Pink'? Surely not.

'Cut music,' he shouted, and as soon as the music died he heard the sound. A buzzer. His door buzzer.

'Fuck,' he said. 'Who the fuck is that?' It was a Saturday afternoon. Amy had gone to some friend's wedding in Scotland; it couldn't be her.

He went to the entry panel and pressed the button. The image popped to life in full, disturbing colour.

'Fuck.'

It was his mother, wearing a headscarf, standing on his doorstep. He glanced around the room. It wasn't too bad, except for the clouds of cigarette smoke that hung in the air.

He picked up the phone. 'Hello?'

'Hello, dear, it's only me. I was just doing a bit of shopping with Alison – you remember, from the Mill. Are you busy?'

'No, not a problem, Mother, dear. Take the lift to the fifth floor.'

He buzzed her in.

'Shit,' he said. He was naked, smoking and dripping with sweat. The first two his mother could not deal with. The third was a problem because, although he'd had a shower when he got up at 11.30, he'd probably worked up a bit of a fug. He pushed open one of the sash windows at the front of the apartment, which immediately let in a gust of cold, but at least fresh, air. The sweat covering his body immediately seemed to freeze.

'Fucking hell!' he cried. 'Brass fucking monkeys!' He ran into the bedroom, rubbed himself frantically with a towel and pulled on clothes as fast as he could – jeans and a T-shirt. He glanced at the T-shirt. It was one he'd been given in America. It bore a screen print of a young woman performing fellatio, a present from a director he'd worked with. The penis in the picture, what could be seen of it, was in fact Jason's.

'Shit,' he said, pulling it off again. He heard a gentle knock on his door. He pulled the next T-shirt out of the drawer, a Microsoft one, dark blue with the corporate logo discreetly printed on the patch pocket.

'Naff as fuck,' he said. But it would have to do. He ran across the large reception room and opened the door.

'Hi, Mum, sorry about that, you caught me on the hop.'

'Hello, dear.' She embraced him warmly. 'Lovely to see you. We won't stop long. You remember Alison, don't you?'

'Sure, sure. Hi, Alison.'

He shook hands with the diminutive woman who stood by the door, looking quite nervous. He noticed her eyes dart around the room, and smiled at her.

'Egg on your face, darling,' said his mother. 'I'm busting for the loo. Where is it?'

'Oh, just down the corridor, third on the left.'

'What a place!' said his mother as she walked away. Jason turned to the Alison woman, who he could not for the life of him remember.

'Come in, Alison, sorry. Take a seat. Would you like a coffee?'

'Oh, I don't want to be any trouble.'

Jason smiled. 'Making people coffee isn't trouble, it's a pleasure, Alison. I love making coffee. I have a very cool new coffee machine. Would you like a latte?'

'Goodness, I don't even know what it is.'

'Big milky coffee that's very popular in America.'

'Lovely.'

Jason walked to the kitchen area. His mother returned. 'What a place!' she squeaked. 'You must be doing very well.'

'Can't complain,' said Jason. 'It's all going pretty well.'

'He's doing so well,' his mother said to the Alison woman. 'He's running his own company in Oxford.'

'Cambridge,' corrected Jason as he struggled with the coffee machine.

'Yes, it's wonderful. Such a clever lad.'

'Not really, Mum. Lucky maybe.'

'And what's going on, then? With your sister.' His mother stood looking at him, her face meant to convey volumes. It was lost on Jason.

'Sure, sure. She's good. Working very hard.'

'I was furious when I heard she was coming to work for you.'

'She's not working for me, we work together. She's on the board, Mum, a vital component in the whole operation.'

'But she had a job. Why did she have to throw everything away and start relying on you? I don't know what to think with that girl. And that dreadful man she worked for.'

Jason scratched his head. His mother always threw him into a state of utter confusion. 'Sorry, Mum, I'm not sure I'm with you. Didn't you know Sir Brian Coventon's gone bankrupt? The research institute has closed down.'

'Oh, I might have known he'd come to no good. Filthy old man. But she's always relied on you, always blamed you if things went wrong. She's such an odd girl.'

'Mum, we've barely had anything to do with each other since she went to university.'

'Waste of your father's money that was.'

Jason laughed. Although his sister was a pious, prissy, judgmental pain in the ass, the rest of the world was prepared to acknowledge that she was a pretty damned clever woman.

'She seems to have done very well, though, Val,' chipped in Alison with a nervous smile. 'I read about her in *marie claire* last year.'

129

'Oh, you don't know the half of it, Alison,' snapped his mother.

'Look, the thing with Sir Brian is over,' said Jason, puzzled as to why he was defending his sister in this way.

'It's disgraceful. She's been carrying on with a married man. Her boss. What am I supposed to think?' said Val. Jason handed her a coffee and shook his head.

'Well, we've both been in the wars a bit in our love lives, Mum. Comes with the territory, I suppose. Don't all parents despair over their children?'

Jason turned to Alison for help.

'Her children are angels,' said Val. 'You remember Toby – he's a dentist in America, doing very well.'

'I never see him,' said Alison rather sadly.

'Rubbish. He flew you to New York last year.'

Jason glanced at his watch. It wasn't that he had anything to do, just that his mother made him tense and he wanted to smoke, but he didn't dare in front of her. Thirty years old and he was still terrified of this bloody woman.

The door buzzer sounded, long and annoying.

'Oh, who's that?' said Val.

'Dunno.'

'Jason, please, you're not a Londoner. Don't know. Don't know.'

'Sure, sure. I don't know,' said Jason, walking to the door monitor and checking the screen. 'Shit,' he said under his breath. It was Tony.

'Hello.'

'It's me, love, come to see the new palace,' said Tony, holding up a shopping bag which was clearly full of cans of lager.

'Sure, sure,' said Jason. He thought quickly. Maybe he could avoid a problem. 'Come on up. Seventh floor.'

Tony – what the fuck did he want? At least he could piss about on the seventh floor for a bit, give him time to get rid of his mum. Jason's cosy Saturday was turning into a grade-one nightmare – his mother and a drunk rent boy in his house.

130

'Mum, sorry, I've got a meeting with one of my employees,' he said. 'Tony – he's a bit of an eccentric, but he's got a heart of gold.'

'Oh, sorry, dear, we should leave.'

'Sorry, Mum, it's just that, well, in the world of new media there's no such thing as a day off.'

'Oh, you poor thing. He works so hard,' Val said to Alison, who even in Jason's limited appreciation of such things was clearly desperate to leave.

There was a loud knock on the door. How could that be? How could the drunken old queen have worked it out that fast? Jason opened it and Tony walked in without invitation. It was worse than Jason feared – he was wearing a pink knitted top and a pair of yellow high-heeled fuck-me pumps.

'Daaarling, did you say fifth or seventh floor? Still, what the fuck, here I am and I am out of my fucking tits!' he screamed.

'Sure, sure,' muttered Jason. 'This is my mum.'

Tony staggered to a halt and stared at Jason's mother for a moment. 'Sorry, love. Tony. Lovely to meet you.'

'Hello,' said Val, her face frozen in horror. 'We were just leaving. You must have so much to do.'

His mother stood, followed swiftly by Alison. They picked up their shopping bags and headed for the door.

'Don't go on my account,' said Tony, flicking his doubtfully dyed hair out of his eyes. 'I'm just gutter trash, Mrs Nash. I'm a trollop of ill repute, darling.'

'See you, Mum. How's the car, by the way?'

'Heavenly, darling. Ring me,' she said as she kissed him on the cheek.

'Lovely to see you, Jason,' said the Alison woman. Both dressed head to toe in M&S, they looked strangely comforting when compared to the savagely pink Tony.

'Sure, sure. See you soon.'

He closed the door and slumped down on the floor.

'That bad, was it, darling? She looks like an absolute fucking dragon,' said Tony. He pulled a can of Tennents Extra from his coat pocket and opened it. 'Get that down your gullet, Mary. That'll sort you out.'

Jason took the can without thinking, then jumped with shock. He stood up and put it on the table and faced the mini-camera above the door with his arms outstretched.

'I'm not drinking,' he said. 'I didn't even have a sip.'

'Oh, love. What's happened to you?' said Tony, now flopped on the sofa and adjusting his nightmarishly tight sky-blue jeans. 'Seen God, have you, Mary?'

'No. Look, Tone, I'm under twenty-four-hour surveillance, I'm working in a high-security industry, I can't afford to fuck up. Sorry, mate, but it's new leaf city for me.'

'Don't be a cunt. I'm offering you a drink, that's all. What's the problem, Mary?' Tony stood up and started to walk around in a twitchy, agitated way. 'I've come all the way round here to see you, have a little chinwag. I'm not trying to get your cock out, love. Don't fucking flatter yourself!'

Tony was on a roll, and it was all highly irregular for Jason and his new regime. Having a drunk male prostitute ranting and swearing in his apartment was not in the remit.

'Sorry, Tone. Look, let's meet up for breakfast next week. It'd be great to see you. It's just not cool at the moment.'

'Why's that? Eh, Mary? 'Cos I'm a bit tipsy?' screamed Tony, collapsing again on the sofa and spilling beer all over the carpet. 'Listen, bollock boy. You've got a bit of trouble brewing with the Greek lads.'

'Yeah, sure, sure. That's all been sorted.'

'Has it buggery. They came round to my place last night looking for you. I've been scared out of my fucking tits, Mary!'

Jason sat down opposite Tony, making gestures as best he could to encourage him to reduce the volume a little.

'Which Greek boys?' he asked, knowing perfectly well who Tony was referring to.

'Fucking big bloke with a beer gut and some little horror with a ponytail. I don't know. Those horrors you used to borrow money off.'

'Right. Mr Andreou.'

'Forty grand. That's what they want.'

'There's obviously been a little confusion, which isn't surprising where Mr Andreou is concerned. It's all been sorted,' said Jason. He was anxious because he had dropped off a cheque for them at the café they frequented on Westbourne Grove. In fact he had got Amy to do it on the way to work as he didn't really want to see them. He'd paid them £30,000, which was what he owed them, and they'd cashed the cheque – he'd seen his bank statement on line. 'You didn't tell them about this place, did you?' he asked.

''Course I fucking didn't. What am I, a grass now as well as a sad old poof!' Tony took his glasses off and wiped them. Jason noticed a tear running down his face. 'Look, love. It's all well and good you coming and going as you please, but what am I supposed to do? Two ugly bastards turn up at my little pied-à-terre in the middle of the fucking night waving baseball bats. I don't need it, love. Wouldn't be so bad if they were like George Michael or someone, but this lot were total dogs, Mary.'

'I'm really sorry, Tony. D'you want a coffee?'

Tony stood up and threw a cushion at Jason. He was screaming hysterically. 'No I do not want a fucking coffee! You're always offering me coffee. Look . . .' He stood motionless for a moment, then grabbed his carrier bag and stormed out, slamming the door.

Jason sat still for a while. He didn't want to do anything. He wanted his past to fuck off and leave him alone. His mum, Tony, everyone. He wanted to change, but they kept finding him and giving him grief and dragging him back down. He was very aware of the camera pointing at the back of his head. There was no peace, anywhere, and now the Greeks. He knew he owed them, he just didn't want to see them again. He'd have to sort it out. Maybe Van Missen could do it on his behalf.

16

Seeing a light blue Rolls-Royce pull up outside the front door of Nash Systems was not what Nina expected to witness on a Tuesday morning. Nor was seeing an immaculately dressed man in his sixties emerge from the driver's seat, wearing a pin-stripe suit, exquisite black brogues and revealing a long grey ponytail neatly tied at the back of his head when he turned to retrieve his bag.

He turned and smiled at Nina when he saw her, and held out his hand.

'Professor Nash?'

'Yes.'

'Roger Turnpike.' His English accent was impeccable – he was clearly no American, which was what Nina had expected.

'Aha. How do you do,' said Nina as they shook hands. Turnpike was the surgeon who Nash Systems had engaged to carry out the chip insertion. Nina had also expected a younger man.

'Very exciting day.'

'Very.'

'Everything ready?'

'Seems to be. Would you like to follow me.'

Nina lead the way into the building. 'Emen Trouville and Michael Del Papa will be here shortly. We were working very late last night to make sure the chip was running correctly. I didn't know you were going to arrive so early.'

'I've just got off a flight from Atlanta,' said the surgeon. 'Came straight here. I barely see my wife anyway.'

Nina glanced at him. He spoke with no irony or bitterness; it was just a simple statement of fact.

'In theory I live in Surrey, but I have been so busy the past few weeks I never get there. I was supposed to be having this week off, then George rang me and, I have to say, the project was very hard to turn down.'

They entered the lab, a corner of which, Nina was relieved to see, had been cleared overnight and separated by surgical plastic curtains, an air-conditioning unit and tool sterilisation equipment. In the centre was a sophisticated operating table.

All the equipment had once again been sourced by Jason.

'Is everything in order?' Nina asked as she walked to her lab bench and checked her overnight e-mails.

'Fine, yes. This is great. I've never done this before, but then neither has anyone else. From what I understand it should be a fairly simple procedure, but then who knows. Where's the patient?'

'I'm right here,' said Pete Van Missen.

Nina turned sharply. She hated the way he did that. She hadn't even bothered to check whether anyone was in the lab, had just assumed it was empty. Van Missen had been waiting quietly at the far end, behind the centrally located clean room.

'Oh,' said Nina. 'I'm sorry. Yes. Mr Turnpike, this is Pete Van Missen.'

'Peter, how are you, old chap?'

'Very well, thank you, sir,' said Van Missen.

'I see you've met before,' said Nina. The two men were smiling and shaking hands.

'Yes, we have,' said Roger Turnpike. 'Not for a while, though. How is everything?'

'Very good, thank you, sir.'

'No aggravation, then?'

'None. You did a very good job.'

'Excellent. I take it you've been fully briefed?'

Van Missen nodded.

'This won't take quite as long as the last time I saw you. Slightly quicker procedure. I wouldn't say easier, as this is microsurgery of the highest order, but you know I'm the man for that.' He offered a well-dentured smile. 'Local anaesthetic and muscle relaxant only. I'll have to strap your head into position so you don't move, but we'll be done in half an hour. Let me have a quick look at you. Take your shirt off.'

Van Missen did as he was told, slipping his shirt off as Nina tried not to notice his very well-formed body. Then she saw the answer to the riddle the two men had spun before her. Van Missen had a scar on his chest, and a larger one on his back. Although she had never seen a scar quite like it, there was no doubt in her mind that it came from a bullet wound.

'Goodness, what's that?' she asked, deciding she would like some clarification.

'It's a bullet wound, ma'am,' said Van Missen as he lifted himself on to the operating couch.

'He is one very lucky young man,' said Roger Turnpike. 'An inch to the left and he wouldn't be here now.' The surgeon pointed to the small dent in Van Missen's chest. 'High-velocity round, luckily nearing the end of its trajectory, entered the body here and tore straight through. The exit wound looked very ugly, but as you can see, it was mostly tissue damage. It missed his heart, his lungs and his spine by a matter of millimetres.'

'I felt very blessed that day,' said Van Missen with a smile.

'Four-hour operation to sew him back together,' said Roger Turnpike. 'But look at him now.' He patted Van Missen on the back with a tenderness Nina didn't expect. He then pulled a stethoscope out of his bag and started to listen to Van Missen's chest.

'How are the flashbacks?' he asked.

'Still have them, but not so often,' said Van Missen flatly.

'What flashbacks?' asked Nina. The word struck an alarm bell in her.

'It's really nothing to be concerned about. I've had counselling,' said Van Missen between breaths. Roger Turnpike carried on listening to his chest, but Nina noticed him cast a glance at her.

136

'Oh, and is that supposed to make me feel better?' Nina failed to control the annoyance in her voice – this was big news.

Van Missen looked at her. 'Occasionally I still experience moments from traumatic events. Nothing dangerous. I don't act on them or anything.'

'He's an amazingly well-balanced young man,' said Turnpike. 'I doubt we'd be as sane if we'd been where he's been.'

'Where have you been?'

'Classified, I'm afraid, Professor.'

'What does that mean?' she asked, feeling annoyed.

'It means I can't tell you,' said Van Missen.

'I don't bloody believe it,' she snapped. 'This could be very important. We have no idea how the chip will be affected if you have a flashback. It could damage you, it's just such an unknown situation.'

'Please, Professor,' said Van Missen. 'Look at me.' She looked into his blue eyes. 'I won't let you down. I'm aware of the dangers. The flashbacks are very momentary and I have them very infrequently. Please don't concern yourself with them.'

'Lift your arms, please,' said Roger Turnpike.

Nina found herself watching as Van Missen raised his arms above his head. He wasn't heavily built, but he was very wiry, and Nina now realised she found him incredibly attractive.

Roger Turnpike felt the glands under Van Missen's arms. Nina was suddenly aware of a strong desire to bury her face in his armpits and feel the warmth, smell him. He was clean, he showered regularly, she knew it would be a wonderful smell. She felt herself flush and decided she should get out as soon as possible.

'I just need to check a couple of things,' she said to both of them.

Pete Van Missen nodded.

Nina left the laboratory feeling very shaken. She wasn't sure why. She knew Van Missen probably had a military or police background, but it seemed everything that happened at Nash Systems had been prearranged way before she had met anybody involved. Everybody seemed to know everybody else, and their shared history made her feel uncomfortable.

'Morning, Professor Nash,' said Amy, who had just arrived in the reception area. She was carrying glossy shopping bags which she put behind the reception desk.

'Been shopping already?' asked Nina, checking the digital read-out on the brushed-steel wall behind her.

'I wish,' said Amy with a smile. 'No, these are from your brother – lovely things from Prada and Agnès B.'

'That's very kind of him.'

'I know, he's so sweet. He really is.' Amy looked at Nina with doe eyes. She was besotted with Jason, that much was obvious.

'Amy, quick question,' said Nina, leaning on the reception desk and speaking quietly. 'Are most of the people who ring to speak to Van Missen or George Quinn Americans?'

'Um, I suppose so.'

'Right. And do they ever say where they're calling from?'

'Oh yeah, some of them, the ones from universities, but some of them just tell me that whoever it is they're calling will know who they are.'

'Right.'

'Why, is something wrong?'

'No, no. Is George here?'

Amy touched her keypad and Nina could see the light reflected on her face as her screen came on line. She glanced at the screen, bringing up the cameras.

'Yes, he's in his office.'

'Thanks.'

Nina climbed the steel stairs to the office floor and walked along the quiet corridor. She knocked discreetly on George Quinn's half-open office door.

'Hi, Nina, come in,' she heard him say. She walked in. George was on the phone.

'Yeah, they're about to do it right now. I'll get back to you with a report. Yeah. Okay.'

He hung up. 'Turnpike here already?'

'Yes, he's downstairs checking on Van Missen's vitals. George, can I ask you something?'

'Sure. Sit down. D'you want a coffee? I've got this great machine. Jason sourced it for me actually. It makes lattes. Can I tempt you?'

Nina smiled. 'No, thank you.' A latte would be good, but she didn't want to be distracted. 'It's about Van Missen. Well, actually, it's about everything. Turnpike is a military doctor, am I right?'

'No, he's a private surgeon.' George smiled as he spoke. 'He has a practice in Harley Street.'

'But he treated Van Missen for a bullet wound.'

Nina noticed George's eyebrows lift for a moment. 'Did he? Well, I didn't know that, but sure, it's very possible.'

'But Pete Van Missen, he's military.'

'Sure, he has a military background,' said George as his coffee machine hissed and gurgled. 'He's a very skilled guy, indispensable.'

'Okay, look, what worries me is . . .'

But George cut her off. 'What worries you is the fact that Nash Systems is a front for an NSA operation, doing highly unethical covert work for the US government and you and your brother have been duped into going along with it.'

Nina sat back in her chair.

'Oh my God.'

'Nina, I'm not telling you that this is what's happening,' said George with a loud laugh. 'I'm hypothesising your concerns. Nash Systems is funded by grants and loans from American, British and Israeli companies and universities. Pete Van Missen is a very necessary part of that operation. It just so happens that people with a military or covert background understand security issues better than anyone else. To be honest, I know nothing about his background, and I doubt that I would be able to find out even if I wanted to.'

'Okay, what about the Sands microprocessor fabricator.'

'Yes, it's military hardware. Pete Van Missen worked closely with your brother in the sourcing process on that one. It's not illegal to possess one, it's just very difficult to get.'

George handed her a large mug of café latte.

'Made you one anyway.' He smiled, then sat down and glanced at his screen for a split second. 'Has anyone been talking to you? Is this why you have these concerns?'

Nina stared at him for a moment. Why should it matter if someone had been talking to her? She felt a wave of annoyance pass through her. She could talk to who she damned well pleased. She breathed in, trying to deal with the emotions she was feeling.

'No, I haven't been talking to anyone, George, I don't need to. I just want to know who I'm working for.'

'You are working for Nash Systems. Look at this.' He handed her a page of share quotes which had been printed from a web page. 'Check three down from the top.'

She scanned down the confusing list of names and numbers. It read 'Nsys, +34.8'.

'What does that mean?'

'Right, you don't play the market,' said George. 'That's your choice.' He took the sheet of paper from her, pointing to the columns of numbers. 'It means that in the last twelve hours Nash System stocks have been revalued at thirty-four dollars and eight cents more than they were at close of trade yesterday, and Wall Street isn't even awake yet. By this time tonight you will be a multi, and I mean multi, millionaire. The *Wall Street Journal* is running a full-page feature on us. That's who you're working for, Nina. Yourself.'

She noticed a warm flush run through her body – a comforting warm feeling that reached all her extremities. Was she really as rich as he said? She wasn't sure what to believe, but it was a nice feeling.

'Why has this happened?' she asked.

'You mean why has the stock price shot off the scale?'

'Yes.'

'Because the market knows what we're doing is world-changing, that the technology is going to experience huge take-up, the demand is going to be Cisco or Sun Microsystems scaled. We're talking trillions in total value. No one else is anywhere near doing what we're doing.'

'I know that, but sometimes for good reason.'

'What good reason?'

'Well, it's still very dangerous. The potential damage to tissue, all the drawbacks that we've discussed. Van Missen could be crippled by what we do to him.'

'But those are minor technical issues. We'll work on ways around that, that's what we're here for, to overcome the obvious drawbacks. And Pete knows the risks, he's aware of what could go wrong, and he's cool with that. He's really proud to be in a position to help us, and believe me, he's being paid well. But he's also very discreet and trustworthy. We cannot allow any information about what we're doing to leave the confines of the company, not yet. That's why I got Pete involved.'

Nina smiled and tasted her latte. It was delicious. 'There's just a dash of almond essence in there,' said George. 'Good, huh?'

She nodded.

'Get used to it, Nina. You are one very rich lady.'

Nina took her latte back down the stairs and returned to the lab. As she walked in, she saw Pete Van Missen lying face down on the special operating couch that had been delivered, his head held in a special support that allowed him to face forward. His back was covered with a green cloth. An air-conditioning unit was humming away near him. A nurse had appeared from somewhere.

'I'm sorry, you can't drink coffee in here,' she said, revealing herself to be an American also.

'Oh, sorry.'

'It's okay, Fran,' said Roger Turnpike, his head jutting around the doorway of the shower area. 'That's Professor Nash. She's the brains behind this whole thing.'

'I beg your pardon, ma'am.'

'No, no, you were quite right. I'll go and scrub up.'

Nina put her coffee cup down on a workbench and joined Roger Turnpike in the shower area. He was now dressed in a green gown, his hands and arms covered in surgical soap.

'I've given him a local anaesthetic in the neck and shoulders,' said Roger. The nurse walked in and waited her turn at the sink. Roger turned around, his hands held high in front of him. The nurse expertly pulled a pair of thin rubber gloves over his fingers.

'And I've just got Fran, my favourite nurse in the whole world – he smiled at the nurse in a fairly obviously lecherous way – 'to administer some muscle relaxant. We're only using a minute amount, but, as you will know, there is a lot of muscular tension in the neck merely because of the job those muscles have to do.'

'Hold up your head,' said Nina. She started washing her hands.

'Precisely,' said Turnpike. 'Now, before we go any farther, I need the chip.'

'Of course. As soon as I've scrubbed up, I'll get it. It's sealed in the clean room.'

'Excellent,' said Roger Turnpike. He left the shower area as Nina pulled on a surgical gown. She then backed through the doors and moved towards the clean room. The door hissed open without her touching anything, activated by a signal chip in her security pass. She waited for the door to close and the airlock to operate, then pulled a mask over her mouth and entered the dry air of the clean room.

On a table was a small stainless-steel dish. Resting in the dish was a minute item that looked no bigger than a grain of grit. She covered it with plastic film and left.

Once outside the clean room, she placed the dish on the table next to Roger Turnpike's operating instruments.

'There it is,' she said, feeling rather proud.

'Goodness me, not a very big fellow, is it?' said Turnpike, bending down to take a closer look. He straightened and moved a large medical enlarger over Van Missen's neck. The machine, basically a sophisticated video camera, could focus on an area a surgeon was working on and enlarge the image many thousand of times. He prodded Van Missen's neck with his gloved fingers. 'Can you feel anything?'

'No,' said Van Missen, his voice affected by the muscle relaxant, which made him sound slightly drunk.

'Okay, well, I know you can't move very easily, but none the less I would ask you to remain as still as you can, Pete. Just relax and it'll all be over in a few moments.'

Nina closed her eyes for a second as she saw Turnpike's scalpel open the skin. She had witnessed operations in the past, and once the procedure was under way she was not in the least squeamish. It was only the initial cut which seemed to affect her.

The nurse applied suction and the blood disappeared, revealing underneath a clearly visible joint in Van Missen's vertebrae. Turnpike worked with eye-dazzling speed, picking up and putting down instruments before Nina could see what he'd done with them. It only seemed moments later that he carefully picked up the chip with a fine pair of tweezers and started to place it in position. It was intended that the chip would rest right against the bone of a vertebra; the connecting filament would then be secured to the spinal cord.

'Can you bring the screen a little closer please, Fran,' said Turnpike. Nurse Fran did as she was asked, and he studied the high-resolution image for a while.

'These flat screens are very good. We used to have to work with cathode ray monitors which weighed half a ton. I was always worried they were going to drop on my patients and crush them.' He moved his hand fractionally. 'Now, there we can actually see the spinal cord. Suction please, Fran.'

Nina looked up at the screen. At the edge of some white bone there was what looked like a grey shadow. The image was distorted for a moment, which Nina realised was caused by the tip of the suction tube. To the naked eye, no fatter than a drinking straw, but on the screen the size of a 747.

'Okay, I'm starting to feed the filament into the cord. There we go.'

Nina watched, fascinated, as Roger Turnpike's inhumanly steady hands gently inserted the micro-fine filament into the incredibly delicate tissue.

There was no sound other than the air-conditioning, the distant hum of the mainframe, the faint buzz of the medical screen Turnpike was looking at, and the rustle of surgical cloth as he made small movements.

'It's in place,' he said finally. He stood back and stretched his neck, relaxing his concentration for a moment. 'Now, before I close up the wound, d'you want to run your checks?'

'Yes. Straight away,' said Nina. She moved to her desk and booted up her screen. If everything was working, the chip would be sending out data at a dedicated frequency which the mainframe was linked to.

The monitor band on her desktop showed a flat blue line. The chip wasn't activated – she had to send it a signal which would set it to work, initially looking for a power source, the electrical power running up and down Van Missen's spinal cord. The chip operated at 120 microvolts, 30 microvolts less than the human body. They still didn't know how, or even if, this would affect the patient.

Nina moved her mouse, opened the setting dialogue box and clicked 'send'. The whole process had been tested before again and again, but this was the first time she had activated the chip in an operating environment.

The blue line on her monitor suddenly flicked into life, counting seconds off as it moved across the screen, renewing itself as it reached the far side.

'All systems are functioning,' said Nina flatly. 'As far as I'm concerned, you can close him up.'

Ten minutes later Pete Van Missen was sitting up, the only evidence that anything untoward had happened a small plaster on the back of his neck. The incision was so tiny it hadn't needed sutures.

'It's still numb, but as for the rest of my body, feels fine,' he said. 'Feels no different.'

Roger Turnpike ran his finger along the sole of Van Missen's foot.

Instantly the data flooded into the mainframe. 'Wow, that's pretty impressive,' said Nina. 'We are getting much stronger data than we ever did from an arm-located chip. Can you just tickle his shin very lightly with this?'

Nina handed Turnpike a long pheasant feather, one she had used to tickle her patients in the past. He took it and brushed Van Missen's shin. 'Can you feel that?'

'Just about.'

'Turnpike moved his head closer and ran the feather as lightly as he could across Van Missen's skin.

'Feel that?'

'Not really.'

'What about you, Ms Nash?'

'Looks like a bomb went off. Huge reading. That's amazing, we're getting signals even you are not aware of,' said Nina excitedly.

'It's pretty weird,' said Van Missen.

'It certainly is,' agreed Roger Turnpike.

Later that afternoon, Nina found herself alone with her new patient once again. They had spent the morning running tests. Nina watched in awe as Pete completed complex eye–hand co-ordination tasks using a computer and old-fashioned mouse. He was so controlled and self-contained. His concentration fascinated her, and being able to watch the data stream in on the lab monitors made the whole experience doubly exciting. Emen and Michael had gone out for lunch. Nina was eating a bag of crisps Amy had given her. She took a mouthful of water from a cup on her lab bench.

'How are you feeling?' she asked.

'Good,' he said, turning to smile at her. 'How about you?'

'Me?' She was taken aback.

'Sure, how are you? I have to say you look a little tired.'

'I am. I'm exhausted but I don't care. I don't think I've slept more than five hours at a stretch in a month. But I am just totally blown away.' She felt herself smile. 'I just wanted to thank you for offering to help in this way. Not many people would be prepared to take the risk.'

'It's a very interesting experiment,' said Van Missen. 'Plus, well, I don't wish to speak out of line, Professor, but I get the chance to spend time with you, which is a bonus.'

Nina stopped logging the inputs and glanced at the wall-mounted monitor. As he had spoken to her a very large data spike had jumped up the screen. Something, some emotion, had gone through Pete's body. It was exciting and intriguing – a man she found very attractive was flirting with her, and she could watch the effect that had on his body. Without turning, without taking her eye off the monitor, she said, 'I like spending time with you too, Pete.'

Another data spike, if anything bigger than the first. She smiled and turned to him.

'What?' he asked.

'Oh, nothing,' she said.

17

Jason was very happy, sitting at his workstation at Nash Systems, his browser on line. He was checking the corporate web page – low hits, but every one a top-quality visit. This wasn't some dozy consumer page, it was business to business; in fact, better than that, it was global corporation to global corporation. There was more and more interest in what Nash Systems were going to be offering, interest from big hitters, particularly in the IT field.

'There's a lot of interest in what we're doing, particularly in the IT field,' he said out loud. He was wearing headphones and tapping his foot, breathing deeply and making a lot of noise as he twitched and fidgeted in his chair. As he sent search engines spinning off to dig out competitors' sites, he was also designing a presentation using music, still images from his library and short video clips, imagining himself on a platform like Steve Jobs or Bill Gates, walking up and down a huge stage, a giant animated Nash Systems logo projected behind him. 'Nash Systems is not leader of the field, we created and nurtured the field; in fact, ladies and gentlemen, we are the fucking field. Yes, sir. Anyone even comes into our field and I will personally, and with extreme prejudice, take them the fuck out of our field.' He sat back, imagining the crowd cheering and whoop-ing.

Jason had possibly seen too many IT, Web and computer entrepreneurs doing their presentations. He was enthralled by them, even more than he had been on the one occasion he had actually seen Mos Def playing live when he was in Denver. That was good, but he didn't want to be a rap star. He wanted to wear the black corporate T-shirt, the roomy jeans and the white sneakers. He wanted to walk up to his lectern, press 'go' on the whizziest computer around which no one else had and take his enraptured audience through a dazzling presentation of the new product. He even toyed with growing the beard, but that would get too itchy.

A little clock on Jason's desktop pinged. He looked at it, trying to remember what it was there to remind him about. Then a small video image popped up beside it, his perfect Japanese woman composite. The music he was playing in his earphones, 'You Can't Always Get What You Want' by the Rolling Stones' faded and a perfect digital voice with a slight Japanese accent said, 'Jason, it's time for the board meeting. Please remember to take the print-outs you requested.'

'Shit,' said Jason.

He stood up, pulled off his headphones, stubbed out his cigar, sprayed some breath freshener into his mouth, and stretched.

'Let's kick it,' he said, then picked up the print-outs from his desk and walked across the large open-plan office towards the boardroom, now sectioned off from the rest of the space by large sheets of double glazing.

'Good morning,' said George Quinn. Somehow, even though Jason had done everything he could to arrange to be at the meeting on time, he was still late. Either that or everyone else was early. They must have walked past him when he was in full flow, the bastards. They must have seen him, sitting in his special chair, cigar billowing great plumes of smoke, head-phones on, delivering his fucking keynote. Bastards. A lesser man would have been embarrassed. He looked around the table. It seemed the whole board was there, including sister Nina.

'Morning, folks,' said Jason as he sat down.

'Well,' said George Quinn, 'I was going to present the latest news to you, but as we all heard Jason rehearsing, maybe we should sit back and let the Nash do his thang.'

There was general laughter and approval from around the

148

table, except of course from sister Nina, who looked like death on two twigs, skinny little cow. Jason stood, breathed deeply, coughed rather unpleasantly.

'Sorry about that. Sure, sure. Okay, well, I could just stand here like a div and do the presentation cold, but I really need to hook my laptop up to a projector to give you the full picture.'

'There's a projector in my office,' said George.

'Is it the Sony?'

'No, Nokia.'

'Shit, I'll need an RS232 connector.'

'I've got one in my drawer somewhere,' said Emen Trouville.

'It's not the 232-to-firewire is it?'

'Yes.'

'I'll need the firewire-to-USB connector.'

'Can't you use Ethernet?' asked Michael Del Papa.

'I'll need a hub.'

'The Nokia doesn't have Ethernet,' said George Quinn.

'Of course it doesn't,' said Jason, slapping his forehead. 'Haven't we got a Sony?'

'I don't know,' said Emen. 'I'll go and get the RS232.'

'Can you get the firewire USB port, on my desk,' said Jason.

'Can do,' confirmed Emen as he was leaving.

'I don't want to believe what I've just seen,' said Nina. 'What are you going to show us?'

'I've been working on a bit of a presentation for when we go public.'

'Are we going public?'

'Not just yet,' interjected George Quinn, trying to keep things calm. 'We've got a bit to accomplish before that.'

Emen ran back into the room carrying a projector and a handful of wires.

'Excellent,' said Jason. 'Can we close the blinds?' He set up the projector on the table as Emen started joining the RS232 to the USB connector.

'We need an extension cable,' said Jason as he stood holding the projector's power plug. The nearest wall socket was two metres away.

'There's one in the lab,' said Nina. 'But I'm buggered if I'm going to get it. Can't you just talk to us?'

'Look, would I ask you to carry out your experiments in a garden shed using a couple of old jam jars and a garden hose? If I am going to make a credible IT presentation, I need state-of-the-art visual back-up.'

'I'll get the extension cable,' said Emen. 'Before I go, is there anything else you need?'

'We've got to take that picture down,' said Jason, pointing to a large framed photo of a Californian sunset on the wall at the opposite end of the boardroom table. 'And I really need the speakers that are on my desk, and the power supply for the laptop. Actually, now that I think about it, the hard disk array, unless you can find a firewire cable we can run in here, then I can hook into the local interanet in case we need any data from the hub.'

'I guess I can take the picture down,' said Cindy Volksmann.

'Jesus,' said Nina.

Ten minutes later, an exhausted Emen Trouville took his place between Nina and Cindy as they turned to face Jason, who was standing by the far wall of the room. Beside him was a crisp blue square projected on to the wall. He had a small remote in his hand, and after he had pressed the button the wall screen slowly faded to black as the sound of the Rolling Stones classic 'You Can't Always Get What You Want' surged through the tiny but very powerful speakers.

On the screen appeared images of each of the board members – at work, laughing, leaning over each other's workstations as they discussed some complex technical problem. Even though Jason had seen the whole thing before many times as he put it together, it still made the hair on the back of his neck stand up.

Text appeared in time with the lyrics, and an image of the chip that had been inserted into Pete Van Missen's neck, enlarged many times, replaced it as the chorus reached its glorious climax: 'You can't always get what you want, but if you try sometimes, you get what you need.'

'Nash Systems, taking interaction between the human and the machine into a new galaxy of possibilities,' Jason said to his tiny audience as the music faded and the Nash Systems logo appeared. 'Are we living in some sort of fantasy land? I hear you ask. Well, if we are, there are a great many people out there who are happy to join us. As you may or may not know, Nash Systems stock is presently riding at $382 a unit. That's risen from a mere $27 a unit only one month ago. We are rapidly heading for an IPO, which, as we all know, we can't do until our initial tranche of research is completed. But once we are there, look at the host of possibilities this new technology could offer.'

Jason pressed the remote and the Louis Armstrong song, 'Wonderful World' started to play. An image of a blind man on a street, white cane in hand, appeared, then a series of images of where the chip would be placed in his neck, and how the chip would receive information from glasses worn by the man, and finally an image of the man smiling, 'looking' into the eyes of a child. Jason too smiled at his small audience – he could see they were utterly captivated by what he'd done, even Nina.

Then came an image of a child with a hearing aid, followed by the same series of images of the chip implant, and then pictures of the child laughing as she played a drum.

'Yo! Way to go,' shouted Michael Del Papa.

He had them, he was the king of presentation.

As the music continued, and the images cut in beautifully with every chord and beat, a picture came up of a young girl looking very forlorn, with her right forearm missing.

'How the hell did you get that?' Nina shouted over the music. The series of images showed the child being fitted with a prosthetic arm, then a picture of her waving with her new arm, writing with it, being held by her grey-haired father, who had tears in his eyes.

The music stopped. Jason didn't look at Nina, who he could

tell was extremely agitated. 'Nash Systems is set to change the world for good. Our competitors know they don't have a hope. We have jumped so far ahead we have created the field we lead. There is no one else. Our chief researcher and, I'm very proud to say, my sister will now fill us in on the details of the latest breakthrough. Ladies and gentlemen, will you please welcome Nina Nash.'

Everybody around the table clapped with wild enthusiasm. Nina looked around. She was very upset.

'Where did you get those pictures?' she asked when the clapping finally stopped.

'Yeah, sorry about that, sis,' said Jason with a smile. 'I hacked them out of your laptop, but they were so good.'

'Jason!'

'Maybe you should have asked first, Jason,' said George Quinn.

'It's so typical of you,' said Nina.

'Sure, sure. Well, kill me, but only after you've filled us in.'

Nina stood, shook her head and looked at the table.

'Well, I was quite enjoying that until the end. It is very exciting and we have achieved an incredible amount in a very short timeframe. As we can all see, contrary to popular prejudice Pete Van Missen is still alive.' There was a small and possibly nervous chuckle from around the table. Pete Van Missen smiled. 'We have been recording everything that Pete's done for the past week, and so far we have used two petabytes of data storage.'

'Fucking hell,' said Jason.

'Please forgive my tech ignorance, but what is a petabyte?' asked Cindy Volksmann.

'A billion gigabytes,' said Emen Trouville.

'Fucking hell, what have you been doing?' asked Jason. He was grinning wildly, enjoying the sheer scale of the data storage they were talking about. 'A fuck of a lot of wrist movement or what,' he said, making the classic male masturbatory hand dance.

Pete Van Missen didn't react in any way Jason could perceive, however. Nina sighed deeply and ran her hands through her hair. She shot him the look of death and carried on.

'Every movement, every reaction to stimulus, creates torrents of data. When Pete smiles, we fill about five hundred gigs. You see, the sensitivity of the chip means it's not the muscular movement in the face we're picking up – those messages don't go through the spinal cord at the point where the chip is placed. What we're picking up is the series of emotions which lead to that smile. We can't break down that data yet, but we know we're getting it. Obviously every movement of the body creates vast lakes of data, but even when he's sleeping, during rapid eye movement periods, we are getting serious amounts of information.'

'His dreams,' said Michael Del Papa. 'Pretty weird, huh, Pete?'

'I guess so, although I'm not aware of any intrusion into my inner world at this stage,' said Van Missen flatly.

'Fucking hell. We can sell dreams,' said Jason. 'Buy-dreams. com. Think of the revenue.'

'Thank you, Jason,' said Nina, her standard put-down. Jason didn't rise to the bait. He sat back quietly, enjoying the thrill of his involvement.

'We've started to number-crunch what we've got, but I have to admit we may have bitten off more than we can chew. I would like to ask the board if we can hire someone to deal with this data explosion. A young postgraduate I worked with at Coventon's, Hugo Harwood, is very good. He's working at a lab in Birmingham now, but I know he'd respond positively. He's one of the best data analysts I've ever worked with, and he has broad experience in cybernetics.'

'Sounds good,' said George Quinn. 'Would you check him out, Pete?'

'I'm on it,' said Pete. He wrote something in his small black notebook.

'We also need a great deal more computing power if we're to process this data in a short timeframe. We are seriously up against it.'

George Quinn glanced up at Jason.

'I'm on it,' said Jason without looking up. He scrawled something in his Palm Pilot. Actually what he wrote was, 'I'm sitting in a room with a bunch of cunts who want even more computers.'

'And how soon will we know of any practical applications we can supply from this information?' asked Cindy.

'It's impossible to say. I knew you'd ask, but it really is,' said Nina. 'But the speed we're working, it's going to be fast. Weeks, not months. We've been studying nerve blocking by causing pain and storing the recordings separately. Pete's been a very good patient as we stick pins in him.'

'Think nothing of it,' said Pete. The slimy bastard fancied his sister, Jason noticed for the first time. He ignored Nina as she carried on speaking.

'We are now working on a transponder chip of similar power and longevity to the one in Pete.' She turned to Cindy. 'This is a chip that can receive signals from outside the body, as well as send them. Well, in theory we could send messages to block pain, or even encourage healing. Clearly the implications of such a system, allowing the body to heal itself without the use of chemicals, are going to change the face of medicine.'

'What about disease – cancer, Aids, all that shit?' said Jason, now bouncing up and down on his chair.

'It's too early to say,' said Nina, to Jason's surprise taking his question seriously. 'I can't see how we could affect such occurrences in the body, but that doesn't mean a solution isn't there. What we are learning is the true depth and complexity of the human nervous system. This is a real monster of a job we've taken on.'

'Don't we fucking know it!' said Jason, standing again and walking around the room. 'And by the look of things, doesn't the market. With the minimum of information, the world has gone crazy at our door. I'm getting such serious, grade-one approaches from all the big financial institutions. They are desperate to swamp us with raw cash.'

'If I might just interrupt you, Jason,' said George calmly. 'This is a very important point for all of us. We are going to find ourselves under increasing pressure. Some very rich corporations and institutions are going to be very interested, not to say nervous, about what we've done here. We have to hold together now more than ever before. Is everybody with me on this?'

'I think we should all stand,' said Cindy. Everyone stood up, including Nina, although she looked a little sheepish. Emen Trouville took hold of Jason's hand on one side, Cindy held the other. Seven people stood around the board table, their hands stretched out.

'We have changed the world,' said Cindy. 'We are blessed, we have huge responsibilities, we must trust each other and know we are trusted. We are making history. We cannot go back, we have to enter the new.'

'Yo, way to go!' shouted Del Papa. Jason smiled. He kind of liked it, although it all felt a bit wanky. Nina was smiling too, but it looked a bit like she was going to burst out laughing rather than enter a state of spiritual rapture. All the Americans seemed to have been transported somewhere else. What a bunch of nutters – this was a business, not some spiritual counselling group.

Jason wriggled his hands free and sat down quickly. For a start his back ached, he had to stretch some distance to reach the little Volksmann woman's arms, and Emen Trouville had unpleasantly sweaty palms.

The Americans all embraced each other and patted each other's backs as Jason stared at them.

'Is that it, then?' he asked eventually.

George Quinn took his seat and smiled at him. 'No, clearly not, Jason. What else do you have to impart to us?'

'Well, fuck knows how we're supposed to do all this. Nina

155

looks utterly shagged, we're all hugging each other, but we've got one chip in one bloke's neck and shag-all to show for it. Pardon me for being a party pooper, but we ain't done nothing yet that I can see a way of seriously marketing. And as deputy CEO and head of marketing of this fine organisation, I say that unless we start delivering product we may as well cash in our share options now while the going is good and get the fuck out.'

'Good point, Jason,' said George Quinn. 'But we are heavily funded now, and we also know that for at least another month we're not really going to be able to market any specific product.'

'A month!' said Jason. 'What am I supposed to say to everyone? Yes, we've proved what we can do, but d'you mind waiting a month while we sort it all out? We're going to be burned off the map by some two-bit hungry start-up if we do that. Have you heard what they're doing at MIT, or Delhi, or even Sussex Uni here in England? Same stuff, maybe not as refined, but fuck, we haven't got long. I've been burned at the starting gates too many times. Just 'cos we are a commercial company and able to market our product, that's the only reason people are interested in us. But they'll soon lose patience if we arse around.'

'I don't know how to respond to that,' said Nina, a whiff of anger in her tone. 'I have worked so hard to get us to where we are now and, dear brother of mine, I haven't noticed you staying late, or losing much sleep in the past couple of weeks. Michael and Emen have barely seen their beds in the last few days. As for the sacrifice Pete has made, well, please, look up the word empathy in your dictionary.'

'Bollocks,' said Jason. 'You're all scientists, you know nothing of the real world. We've got to get the product to the marketplace and we've got to start seeing income or this is all a load of wank. Surely we can get a pain removal chip design out. We can flog it for a fortune. Chip manufacturers would wet themselves.'

Nina was about to speak when George Quinn raised his

hand. 'This is all very interesting and Jason is of course right. We have to start using the information we have been blessed with, and we need to hire more people and expand very fast. Jason, I want you to source a couple of million square metres of office and research facilities. Clearly the Coventon building next door is not going to be enough, in fact we will need to build our own centre soon, so it's worth checking out available land around the Cambridge area. Let's put a budget limit of say three hundred million US. Within that, I give you free rein.'

'Fucking hell. I'm on it,' said Jason. Three hundred million to spend. Dream-come-true.com, he thought to himself.

George continued, 'Meanwhile I'll hire some heavy-duty recruitment people, as we are going to be bringing in busloads of specialists. Let's get back to work, people.'

Jason walked with Nina through the office. He knew he had to say sorry, again, but at least this time it wasn't because he'd broken something or stolen her car or needed to borrow money. He was apologising for being a highly effective member of an international corporation, deputy CEO no less.

'Sorry, sis.'

'Big dunderhead. Mister fucking marketing man,' she said, gently shoulder-barging him as they walked along.

'Knowall arse-wipe,' he responded under his breath.

'Tossbag.'

'Uptight prissy queen of denial.'

'Jason, can I borrow you a moment,' said Pete Van Missen, gently touching him on the arm.

'Aha, the cyborg calls,' said Jason, turning to face Van Missen. 'Hey, Nina, check the reading from Van Missen's chip when I show him my knob.'

Nina laughed and shook her head as she walked away with Emen Trouville.

'I've already seen your "knob" more times than I care to remember,' said Van Missen. 'Can we go to your work area?'

'There was a time in the bad old days when a deputy CEO

would have had a fucking office, but not in this hippie set-up,' said Jason. 'Doesn't it get on your wick?'

'I'm not aware of any discomfort, no,' said Van Missen. 'I am a little concerned, however, about two Greek gentlemen who seem to think you owe them money.'

Jason turned sharply. Van Missen's face showed no emotion. 'Ah, the Greeks, you've been checking the vid files.'

'Believe me, Jason, I don't watch them all, but certain key words are picked up by the software. What's happening?'

'Well, I got into a bit of a bind. These two Greek geezers invested some cash in airline-food.com, and it all went a bit pear-shaped. I've already paid them back, but they've been hassling an old friend.'

'The homosexual prostitute?'

'Tony. Yeah, of course, I keep forgetting you know everything,' said Jason with a sigh. 'Look, they are a couple of crooks, they've got greedy. They keep going on about outstanding interest, which is bollocks. We never arranged any interest. It was a straightforward investment in a business which flat-lined. I've explained all this.'

'I know,' said Van Missen. 'But now they've been in touch with us here. They claim they own part of this company because we took over airline-food.com which they had an interest in.'

'Oh, bollocks.'

'I entirely agree, but it's not a healthy situation. At present this information is only in our immediate domain and I suggest we keep it that way.'

'Sure, sure.'

'Do you have any way of making contact with them?'

'Fuck, I suppose so,' said Jason. 'They often hang out in a café on Westbourne Grove.'

'Is that in Cambridge?'

'No, Pete. That's like asking if Time Square is in Boston. Okay?'

'Cool.'

158

'Sure, sure. Look, they're just a couple of local dealers really, but they've got a lot of cash swishing about and they were trying to go a bit more legit. Usual story.'

'It's not uncommon for drug money to find its way into legitimate business, but it's normally done a little more discreetly than this, Jason.'

'Sure, sure. So, what are we going to do?'

'I suggest we meet the gentlemen involved and put our case to them.'

'Um, Pete, these blokes,' said Jason, trying to work out a way of describing them. 'Well, gentlemen they are not. They are a couple of nasty little tykes. They're not used to doing meetings, they're used to having a word, using a shiv and then legging it when they see the police.'

'A shiv?'

'A knife.'

'Okay, well, what say we take a trip to Westbourne Grove now and see if we can find them. We don't want this kind of business in the background and it's my job to see it's cleared up.'

'What, now?'

'Sure. Why not?

'I don't know. I was going to. . . . Well, I don't know what I was going to do, but I bet it was important.'

'I think this problem takes precedence,' said Van Missen. 'I'll meet you in the carpark in five.'

Jason shrugged. 'Sure, sure.'

18

Nina sat at her desk with her head bowed low. She couldn't move. She knew the news was bad, there was nothing to say. After a long time lost in misery, she looked up and saw Emen Trouville, who seemed to be in a similar state. He was staring at a monitor screen which showed previous data displays from Pete Van Missen's chip.

'It's my fault,' said Nina eventually. 'I should have known. I can't believe I let Pete get caught up in Jason's stupid life.'

She looked at Trouville for some feedback. She got none. She needed to talk about it, she couldn't just sit there, but who else could she talk to? She had worked so hard, for so long, she had lost contact with her friends so long ago, it would be next to impossible to suddenly call them up and tell them. Emen Trouville was her only hope.

'Emen, you don't know what it's like having a brother like Jason.'

He looked up at her and eventually smiled, his face drawn and tired. 'It's not your fault, Nina. You are the best scientist I've ever worked with, and I've worked with a few. This is a crazy situation we're in.'

'I should have known that if Jason had anything to do with it everything would turn to crap.'

'Listen, it's not even Jason's fault,' said Emen. 'Van Missen should have known better. Now he's really landed us in the shit. The first X-ray they take of his neck they're going to see the chip.'

'That's probably a good thing. I'm sick of all this secrecy,' said Nina. 'I want to work without worrying if anyone's going to find out what I'm doing. I'm doing nothing wrong!'

'I know.'

'I just want to get the recording device back and see if we can download what's on there. Might give us a clue as to what happened to Pete.'

Trouville laughed. 'I like it,' he said. 'With your beloved guinea-pig in hospital, your brother God knows where, you still want to check data.'

He joined her at the workbench and watched her as she gingerly started to take the machine to pieces.

'I can't work out why you're holding a torch for that guy,' he said after a moment.

'What guy?'

'Van Missen. He's a goddam automaton. They're all the same.'

Nina looked around at Emen.

'Oh, come on, Professor. It's pretty plain you've got the hots for him.'

'I do not. I never have the hots for anyone.'

'That's a shame,' he said with a sad smile.

'What are you saying?'

'Well, I think, like, in terms of initial compatibility, we're kind of hot-pluggable.'

'I'm sorry?'

'Sorry. I shouldn't download.'

'Emen, what are you talking about?'

'I've got an advanced compatibility reaction which I'm not crunching in any viable way.'

Nina turned to look at the diminutive figure of the strange-looking scientist. She understood – he had the hots for her. Only someone who had spent time with scientists this esoteric would have understood what was coming from his small, goatee-bearded mouth. She smiled at him. She felt sorry for him but found him about as attractive as a dull weekend in Bognor Regis.

'Thank you,' she said. 'I had no idea.'

'Well, it's not appropriate, is it. And I knew there was no

161

point porting my feelings when Van Missen was around, but I thought, well, go for broke.'

'That's very kind of you.'

'I take it you don't . . .?'

Nina didn't know what to say. She smiled at him and hoped he would get the message. He did. He turned and went back to his bench.

'Sorry, Professor, forget it. Erase that data.'

'I'm sorry, Emen.'

'It's okay. I know I'm weird, nothing new from where I am. Where were we?'

Nina scratched her head.

'We were talking about Pete.'

'Of course.'

'Look, Emen, I'm worried about what's happened to him, that's all. I feel responsible. And anyway, you said they're all the same. Who's he the same as?'

'Spooks, covert operators.'

'How do you know that?'

'I'm just guessing like everyone. No one knows except other spooks. That's what's weird. A beautiful woman like you, and you fall for an emotional ice warrior like Van Missen. Why? Huh. Shit, man, if we could put chips in women and work out how they were wired . . . It's a total mystery to me.'

Nina laughed.

'What's so funny?' asked Trouville. 'I'm serious.'

'It's just that one of the reasons I'm so interested in this work is for much the same reason. When I look at men, I know all the obvious stuff is there, stuff women think they understand and, let me add, are usually proved right about. But when you've grown up with my brother, the mystery only deepens.'

'Believe me, your brother is the exception.'

'I'm not so sure,' said Nina. She was just thinking about going home when the door burst open and Jason the mystery man walked in.

'Oh my God!' said Nina. 'What happened?'

162

Jason didn't seem injured, but he did look very drawn. He was smoking and clearly highly agitated.

'I'm sorry, man, you really can't smoke in here,' said Trouville warily.

'Sure, sure. I'll wait in the lobby. No, scratch that, they might see me. I'll wait upstairs.' So saying, he left just as abruptly as he'd arrived, a haze of tobacco smoke in his wake.

'What an absolute arsehole,' said Nina. 'You don't know what it's like.'

'I'm kind of glad about that,' said Trouville. Nina noticed he was looking at her.

'What?' she asked.

'Aren't you going up to hear what he has to say?'

'I've heard it all before.'

The door opened again. This time it was Amy. 'Jason's back, he's in a right state.'

'I know, I saw him.'

'He said he's waiting for you upstairs and I've got to hold all his calls.'

'Fascinating,' said Nina. She started to take off her lab coat.

'George is up there too. They're waiting for you as well, Emen, everyone is there. Cindy's on her way even though she's supposed to be on a flight to New York. Even I've got to go up to take minutes.'

'Well, I'm going home,' said Nina.

Emen stood up. 'This takes precedence, Nina, really.'

'Shit! Fuck! Bollocks!' screamed Nina. 'I hate my fucking brother with every ounce of my being!' She stood up, clenching her fists in fury. She could feel the tears welling up, the years and years of mental abuse she had suffered from her mother, all from her very firm standpoint caused by the arrival of her screaming, bawling baby brother.

She stormed up the stairs and barged open the doors into the main office, utterly unaware of the eyes that were on her. She saw Jason sitting down at the far end of the long room and went straight for him. She stood in front of him, her face contorted in sheer pent-up frustration.

'Hi, sis,' he said flatly.

'I am no longer your sister, you no-hoper. I am going to change my name and become someone else. I am finished with you.'

He sat before her, motionless. She couldn't believe he could really be this stupid, this oafish and destructive. She wanted to kill him. Her vision and sense of surroundings diminished until all that was in her world was this great lazy stupid nightmare of her sibling.

'You stupid lanky twat, you've screwed up one last time, you piece of dog dirt. Fuck you for ever and ever in hell.'

'Sure, sure,' said Jason under his breath.

He'd said it again. The 'sure, sure' thing had got on her nerves for so long, and she never reacted to it, but this was too much. She looked about. A phone lay on the desk beside Jason. She picked it up with both hands and brought it down on his head as hard as she could.

Jason fell to one side with barely a moan as she felt people grab her and pull her away. All the while she was screaming, spitting and swearing at her cursed brother.

'Let's everybody cool it,' said George Quinn. He held Nina in an uncomfortable armlock. 'Let's everybody think this through, okay?' He was breathing deeply. Nina could feel him shaking. She wanted to leave, didn't want to have to go through all this again. It was just like being at home, having to sit through the post-mortem of another of Jason's big screw-ups.

'Nina, sit down, please. Someone get us some coffee. We have to sort this out and we have to do it fast,' said George. The door at the far end of the office burst open and Cindy Volksmann ran in, her hair in a mess, her bag swinging by her side.

'I've just heard. What's going on?'

'Cool your jets, Cindy,' said George. 'Everything is under control, but we have a lot of clearing up to do.'

164

Nina felt herself being guided towards a chair. She sat down.

'I resign,' she said. 'I want to leave now.'

'Nina, please. Don't do anything for a second,' pleaded Cindy. 'This is terrible, I know, but we can sort it out. Well, hopefully George can sort it out.'

'I just need to know what happened,' said George, looking at Jason.

'Heavy, heavy shit,' said Jason eventually. There was some blood trickling from between Jason's fingers where he was holding his head, Nina felt a momentary pulse of concern for him, but it soon passed. Jason pulled himself back on to the chair, not looking at anyone, not making a sound.

'I just got back from the hospital,' said George. 'According to the chief surgeon, Van Missen seems to be paralysed. Here, I got this for you.' He passed Nina the small recording device. It contained up to six hours of Pete Van Missen's data, allowing them to monitor him almost around the clock. She looked at it and shook her head. She felt bitter tears fill her eyes. It was true, of course, she had grown increasingly fond of Pete Van Missen. Nothing had been said between them, nothing had taken place, but she felt enormous warmth between them. It was unmistakable.

'Jesus,' said Emen Trouville.

Jason adjusted his position in his seat and lit a cigarette he pulled out of a badly crushed pack.

'What the hell happened, Jason?' asked George.

Jason squirmed, a reaction Nina had seen so many times before. It was as if he were blind to what might happen ten seconds in the future, as if he'd never learned that if you put your hand on something hot it would hurt. He'd do it once, cry, look at the blister and still not make the connection. Ten seconds later he'd do the same thing again and not even remember that he'd repeated the same mistake.

'Sure, sure, here's how it is. Some of the investors that put money into airline-food.com were possibly not the most reputable of people.'

'Airline fucking food,' hissed Nina.

'Please, people, let him talk,' said George Quinn.

'Okay, sure, sure, I saw it as a long-term investment, they saw it as a short-term loan. They have been putting pressure on me to repay, and I did. I paid them back every penny, but then they started reading the financial pages of various periodicals – well, one of them did, I don't think the other one can read. So then they thought they should have some share action in Nash Systems because they saw themselves as founding investors, which in some ways they were. But they'd cashed in their stake and I said, 'Too bad, chummy.' Well, Pete became involved when they got in touch with the company direct, demanding some dividends or something – as I say, their grasp of corporate affairs is a little loose. So this morning I took Pete to meet with them, not something they're used to. A meeting, that is. Pete put it to them that they had no claim on the company, and any further contact between them and me or Nash Systems would be dealt with through the courts. Well, Costas, that's the one who can read, didn't react to this well. He's got a long history of being a little unstable in social situations, so he took a swing at Pete. I've got to hand it to Van Missen, he was pretty quick off the old mark – blocked the punch and delivered three pretty impressive blows to Costas, who just disappeared under the table.'

'What table?' asked George.

'Oh, didn't I say? We were in this café on Westbourne Grove,' said Jason, standing now and beginning to enthuse about his subject. 'I think Costas's dad owns it, or maybe it's his uncle – whatever, it's a family connection. So there's Pete, bing, bang, wallop, down goes Costas, then his big brother Michael, who's usually the one who does the violence, throws himself at Pete. Smash goes the table. Michael's a pretty big lad but he just seemed to slide off Pete Van Missen. Where did he learn that shit? I mean, he's no spring chicken but he seriously fucked those guys up. He just twisted around, grabbed Michael's arm and did some weird grip thing and there was this horrible sound and . . . well, I don't really know what happened. I suppose he broke his arm.'

'What were you doing during all this?' asked Cindy.

'Me?' said Jason, as though it were an odd question. 'I was trying not to spill my coffee. It was very hot, and I'd just lit a fag and I didn't want to drop it.'

Nina noticed the looks of disbelief on the faces of the people listening to Jason. It came as no surprise to her.

'Anyway, Costas got up, and bish, Pete bopped him right in the mush. God, that must have hurt. His face was really messed up, teeth missing and everything. Blood everywhere. It was seriously mashed. He just flopped over and that was it. Then Pete started to pull me out of the café and push me towards the car. It was all pretty sick, to be honest.'

'But I take it there were other people in the café at the time?'

'Sure, sure. But they all cleared out pretty fast when the rumble started. I mean, the whole thing was over in about three seconds – that's what it felt like. But once we got outside I could see Pete wasn't okay. He started falling over. He said he couldn't feel anything, and in the end he just . . . well, he kind of collapsed in a heap. He told me clear off.'

'And did you?' asked Cindy.

'Well, I wanted to, believe me, but he was just lying there on the pavement. I know you think I'm a selfish cunt, sis, but I'm not that bad. The poor guy couldn't seem to breathe.'

'Could it be the chip?' asked Cindy.

'We don't know yet,' said George.

Nina looked like death, her face as white as the wall she was standing in front of.

'Anyway, I couldn't just leave him,' said Jason. 'I dialled 999 on my mobile, then this ambulance arrived and the police and it all got really weird. I just stood in the crowd, and as the paramedics were loading Pete into the back of the meat wagon, I asked where they were taking him.'

The small gathering of people around Jason stood in silence

for a moment. Then George Quinn said, 'Okay, this is all in hand, people. Everybody stay calm.'

'What are you going to do?' asked Nina.

'I've already done it. I've made damn sure no one finds out what's in Pete Van Missen's neck,' said George as he picked up his jacket.

'But the chip is so near being in the public domain already. Surely that's not an issue,' said Cindy.

'It would become an issue very fast if it turns out the chip caused the paralysis. I don't think it would exactly help sales and boost the share price, do you?' said George, and he left the room.

Cindy bit her lip and grimaced. 'Sorry, obvious. I guess this has just thrown everyone.'

Nina looked at Jason as he pulled hard on his cigarette. 'I hope they kill you,' she said as she walked away.

19

'I'd never met either of them before,' said Jason. He was sitting on a plastic chair in the interview room at Paddington Green police station in central London. The view out of the window was not pleasant – the grey concrete side of the M40 flyover, a stretch of road Jason had been known to travel along at well over a hundred miles an hour. He had no idea it was so close to a bastion of law enforcement.

Lord Preston, QC, hired for the occasion by Nash Systems, was sitting beside him. Jason was wearing an immaculate Charlie Allen blue suit, Thomas Pink cream shirt and silk tie. He looked every inch the responsible executive; he even felt like a pretty important type of guy, and certainly not someone who would consort with low-life scum like Costas and Michael.

'So you stopped off for a coffee at this café, and the two men approached you,' said the inspector.

'Absolutely. Very brave-faced little chap. Just came up and demanded money, in broad daylight, and used some pretty strong language to boot.'

'Then Mr Van . . .'

'Missen, Van Missen,' said Jason helpfully.

'Yes. He took umbrage at this, I take it.'

'Not at all. Far from it. He was very calm and polite. He's American, a charming man. Wouldn't hurt a fly, but then this little fellow pulled a bloody great big hunting knife out of his pocket. I couldn't believe my eyes, and old Van Missen sprang into action. Military background and everything.'

'Ah, so he does have military training?'

'As far as I know. I've only employed him for the past couple of months, but he's proved himself more than reliable. You see, Officer, my company is doing research in a very commercially volatile area. For us, security is vital, which is why we hired Van Missen.'

'I see,' said the inspector. 'And what happened to you after the incident? Judging from the report of the officer in charge, you were nowhere to be seen.'

'I am entirely culpable, Officer. I ran away like a frightened chicken,' said Jason, hands in front of his face to underline his feeling of remorse. 'I have never been in a situation like that before, and until you have, it's very hard to know how you'll react. Well, I have discovered. I react stupidly.'

'It was you who called the police and ambulance, though.'

'Absolutely,' said Jason. 'Immediately we were outside the wretched café, Mr Van Missen collapsed and, well, I can't honestly say I remember what happened next, but I know I dialled 999.'

'Very commendable, sir, but then you left the scene.'

'Yes. Guilty on all charges, Officer.'

'And where did you go?'

'I sat in my car and just shook like a leaf. Then drove back to our headquarters.'

'I see. And you have witnesses who will corroborate this?'

'Oh, too many,' said Jason. 'As you can imagine, when I arrived, I was not Mr Popular Trousers, having caused the company so much trouble.'

'Well, from what you said, you hardly caused it, sir, or am I incorrect?'

Jason smiled – not very clever of the inspector, and not hard to deal with.

'No, you're quite correct, Officer, I certainly didn't cause the incident, but this sort of trouble is never popular in corporate circles. Van Missen is a very valued employee, and although he was in theory there to look after me, well, he's . . .'

'Fine. Now, what have you done with Van Missen?'

'I'm sorry?' said Jason. Although he knew this was coming, he hadn't seen it coming quite then.

'He was taken to University College Hospital yesterday afternoon, and he isn't there any longer. I was wondering what you'd done with him.'

'Goodness me, I didn't do anything!' said Jason. 'This is the first I've heard about it. I was on my way to visit him after leaving here.'

'You see,' said the inspector, making it clear he didn't really buy Jason's surprise, 'from where I'm standing, I have a violent incident take place in broad daylight, and suddenly one of my chief suspects . . .'

'I hardly think he's a suspect. He's a victim of a common street assault. Or café assault, at the very least,' said Jason, feeling rather proud of his little quip.

'Whatever, sir, but a man who initially appears to be very severely injured just ups and disappears in the night. It's hard for me not to presume that you are involved in some way, Mr Nash. Not too crazy of me to suspect that, is it?'

'My client clearly has no involvement in this,' said Lord Preston.

The inspector looked at the lawyer with what could only be described as disgust. 'Yeah. Thank you, your Lordship. I imagine that one sentence will cost Mr Nash about five grand. So, Mr Nash, you're not going to suddenly disappear, are you?'

'Of course not, Officer, I'm as keen to get to the bottom of this as you are, and I'll certainly put my feelers out and see where the hell Van Missen has gone. He seemed utterly incapacitated when I last saw him.'

'He was completely paralysed, according to the hospital authorities,' said the Inspector. 'So someone had to have carried him.'

'Surely there are security cameras at the hospital?' asked Jason.

'Place is bristling with them, but they all failed at about the time he disappeared. It's kind of suspicious, don't you think, Mr Nash?'

'Incredibly dubious,' said Jason. 'There's something going on here, that's for sure.' He turned to Lord Preston. 'Maybe Mr Van Missen was working for someone else, you know, sent to spy on what we're doing.'

'I think if that's all, Officer, my client is a very busy man.' Lord Preston ignored Jason's comment with such smooth professionalism that Jason couldn't take offence. With a tight smile, the diminutive lord stood and picked up his beautiful leather briefcase.

'I'll be in touch,' said the inspector.

In the car on the way back to Nash Systems, Jason lit up a cigar. He didn't feel good, although he'd tried to make himself feel good about the fact that the last remnants of his old life, in the form of Costas and Michael, were well and truly sorted. They wouldn't dare hassle him again. But it was such a mess, and clearly not what Van Missen had intended. The plan had been to lure the two men into the car where Van Missen would deal with them out of the public eye, but Jason had screwed it up by being too boisterous. It had been just too tempting after all the threats they'd made to him to have a go when he knew he was safe. If only he'd done as Van Missen had instructed, none of the mess need have happened.

'Shit!' he shouted as he roared along the M11. 'Shit, shit, shit!'

He pulled into the carpark at Nash Systems fifty minutes later and noticed that his old car was back in his parking space, looking completely new. He parked the replacement Audi TT in Van Missen's space and went to look at the Mercedes.

It was only when he tried to open the door that he realised it wasn't his old car, but a brand-new one. His key card didn't pop the locks. Amazing – a brand new car. All this, all the opportunities he'd been given, and he'd screwed up again. He had to make amends. He'd been doing so well – no booze or sex for five weeks. Amy sitting there in reception day after day, looking dolefully at him as he arrived for work or left in the evening. Not so much as a blowjob. He'd made all that effort, and then in trying to clear up the last of the mess he'd left behind everything had fallen about him once more. It was the first time he could remember since making his vow that he really felt like getting hammered, shagging Amy and smashing all the cameras in his apartment.

He stood still and breathed deeply, then turned and walked into the building.

Amy was sitting behind the reception desk. She looked up and smiled at him as he approached her.

'Amy, I'm so sorry. I've been a complete twat. You know I still want you, don't you? I think about you all the time, but I'm really trying hard to make this work. You understand that, don't you?'

'Of course I do, Jason,' said Amy. 'And you keep buying me lovely presents. I'm okay. You come and see me when you're ready.'

'Jesus,' said Jason. 'I'm always ready for you, Amy. Believe me.'

'Sweet,' said Amy.

'Is anyone here or has everyone fucked off?'

'Nina is in the lab with George and the rest of them.'

'I'll take a look-see.'

'Good luck.'

Jason walked towards the lab door, slid his card through the security device and watched the door spring open. He liked the fact that it opened with a little hiss; he liked the superb quality of the fittings at Nash Systems. He really didn't want to blow it any more.

George, Emen Trouville and Nina were studying a monitor on the wall.

'Jason, come and look at this. It's total grade-A hard-core science, man,' said Emen.

Jason moved in behind them, making sure he kept his distance from his sister. He looked up at the screen – a beauty, a forty-eight-inch flat-panel from Sony, well into the seven-grand bracket from what he remembered. Beyond the make and model, nothing he could see made any sense. Some kind of bar graph was moving from left to right across the screen, with a bunch of huge jumps suddenly appearing.

'What time did the fight take place?' asked Nina without looking at him.

'I dunno,' said Jason. Nina looked at him sharply, her eyes brimming with hatred. 'Um, sorry, about two, maybe two-fifteen,' he said quickly.

Nina pointed at the screen with her pen. 'Look, two-twenty-three. It's got to be,' she said.

'What?' asked Jason. He'd seen a lot of software in his time, but this brightly coloured graph was a newie.

'Nina has managed to extract the data from Van Missen's recorder, even though it was seriously damaged,' said George.

'What does it mean?'

'We don't really know,' said Nina.

'But we can make a pretty good guess,' added Emen Trouville. 'Welcome to the future, everybody.'

20

Nina sat back in the chair opposite George Quinn's desk. It was 9.30 in the morning. The office outside was busy – new people had arrived at Nash Systems, people she had never met before, young, eager people who talked among themselves excitedly; many of them male, but dough-faced and spotty, the sort of people who didn't get out much.

'It's really exciting to meet you, Professor Nash,' had said one bespectacled lad who had stood in her way in the corridor.

'Thank you,' she had replied. She knew she should ask what he was doing in the company, she knew she should try to get to know all of them, but she had an overriding problem that needed solving.

'I'm sorry, I really must get on,' she had said when the young man didn't move out of her way.

'Oh, yeah, yeah, sorry,' he had responded, blushing profusely.

Nina had slid past the young man and barged into George Quinn's office. She had found something out that was too alarming to ignore. She felt she had been ignoring everything that was going on in her life too long. Her nails were a symptom of that, chipped and bitten down, the result of blinkered concentration on the new chip implant and the technical difficulties associated with it.

George Quinn's computer made a delicate and melodious ting, the sign of incoming e-mail. He glanced up at her.

'Won't be a moment, Nina.'

He hadn't offered her coffee yet, which was good. She was in no mood for coffee. She looked at her hands instead as George turned to his monitor and checked his mail. One further glance at her damaged nails and she clenched her fists – they didn't bear close inspection.

Earlier in the day Nina had managed to get in touch with a postgraduate who had worked for Coventon Research the year before, a young doctor who was now doing an internship at University College Hospital in London – the hospital Pete Van Missen had been taken to after the incident with Jason. The student, Helen Jameson, whom Nina knew to be very knowledgeable about databases and hospital management systems, could find no trace of him on the computerised records.

Nina glanced at George. He was still engrossed in his screen, and started to deftly touch-type a reply. The news was carrying the story of the incident Jason had described, but the details were scant, to say the least. Two men seriously injured in a café in West London, an incident thought to be drug or gang related, was what it had said on Radio 4 as she drove to the lab that morning.

'George, what's happened to Pete?' she asked as lightly as possible. 'He was never at the hospital, was he?'

'Nina,' said George, looking around his screen at her, 'Van Missen is safe and as well as can be expected.' He smiled at her. She assumed this was supposed to be enough. It wasn't.

'And?'

'That's it,' said George pleasantly.

'What d'you mean, that's it?'

'Do you need me to spell it out for you?' he asked, still smiling in much the same way he did when he offered her coffee from his machine.

'Clearly I do. I regard Mr Van Missen as my responsibility. What am I supposed to do? Just forget him?'

'Well, at the present time, that would seem to be the best option,' said George, more flatly.

'You can't be serious,' she said gravely.

'Never more so, Professor.'

'Well, I can't,' said Nina. 'I can't just forget the only man on earth who had the first successful neck implant. I want to know what happened. No, sod it, George, I need and have a right to know what happened to him.'

'It's very simple,' said George. 'You do not need to know. You are not in a position to know.'

'What are you talking about?' squealed Nina. She could sense her voice becoming shrill, and could immediately hear her mother criticising her for it. 'You'll never get anything if you use that shrill tone of voice, young lady.' She hated it when her voice became shrill, but this was outrageous. She stood up and paced the room.

'What's going on?' she shouted. 'What is going on here? What is this place? I feel like I'm ninety per cent in the dark working here. I get on with everybody, I have the best facilities any scientist could ask for.' She could hear her mother pointing out that she was a mere 'technician'. She had never felt comfortable describing herself as a scientist, even though it was obvious to everyone else in the world that she was one. 'But I walk in the lab in the morning with the feeling that there is an enormous amount going on that I know nothing about. Who Pete really is, how you got me and Jason involved. Who you are. Minor stuff. I imagine I don't know the half of it because you think I don't need to know. Well, now hear this, good buddy.' She leaned over his desk. 'I need to fucking know.'

George leaned back in his ample executive chair, put his hands behind his head and sighed. 'Nina, I'm sure I don't need to tell you that the area we are working in is very specialised and very sensitive. Any unwarranted information about our work would not only cause trouble with our competitors, but could cause a huge amount of public concern. The general population could so easily be sent off-message with this technology – computer chips in the brain, control by Big Brother, all that sort of bull. The last thing in the world we need right now is some ignorant journalist blowing the lid on what, let's face it, we're only halfway through doing here.'

'I still don't understand why I can't know what happened to Pete. Has he been killed?'

'Of course he hasn't been killed. Jesus, Nina!'

'Well, how do I know? All I've heard is what my stupid brother told us. He fell over. Why? Is he paralysed and was this paralysis caused by the chip, or some injury he received during the fight with the two men?'

'We don't know.'

'Oh, come on. I never believe anything my brother says, but there was a report on the telly last night about two known criminals being brutally beaten up in broad daylight, and the story matched up with Jason's in an alarmingly unfamiliar way. Unfamiliar in that what he said was clearly close to the truth. Now, if Pete's chip has caused some sort of spinal injury, George, that is something I really need to know, that's vital to the project.' She knew she was raising her voice and was aware that he was reacting badly. She took a deep breath and started again, trying to keep the volume down. 'I really don't think I'm being unreasonable, and why, for goodness' sake, can't you tell me? Is someone telling you not to tell me? Who the hell am I working for?' She held his gaze and gave him her fiercest look.

'You're working for Nash Systems,' said George with equal fervour. 'Which, as you know, is an entirely independent research facility funded by a variety of international bodies.'

'Yeah, none of which I have actually heard of before.'

'They're mainly US-based!' said George, as though this were an answer.

'I've been to America,' she retorted. 'I've been to seminars and conferences on every aspect of cybernetics. I've developed microchips using commercially available technology, and I come here and find a microprocessor fabricator of ground-breaking complexity which it turns out is produced solely for military use.' Nina was on a roll – all this had been stewing away and now the Van Missen incident had blown the lid. She felt as if she'd just woken up.

'I've explained all that to you.'

'Oh, yeah, I'm sure. And who is Pete Van Missen and where does he come from? Is he married, does he have children?'

'Why do you want to know that?'

'Because . . . Jesus!' Nina felt caught out. She wanted to know more about the man because she couldn't stop thinking about him. 'Because if he is,' she said, thinking quickly, 'he can't support them any longer if he's paralysed. What are we here, animals? He's a human being and we've done something that has ruined his life.'

'Professor, I really think you need to get a grip here. Please make sure you're not allowing your personal feelings to cloud your judgment.'

Nina sat with her mouth open. 'What did you say?'

'I just want you to be clear about why you're so upset about Mr Van Missen. I understand why you should be anxious about the scientific and medical aspects of the case, but beyond that I'm concerned that your personal involvement with Mr Van Missen could cloud the issue.'

'I won't dignify that slur with a response, Mr Quinn,' she spat. 'Just watch your step, okay. When it comes to my personal life, back right off.' She held his gaze, and he looked away first. She felt a surge of strength run through her. She had beaten a very confident, very rich man with pure anger and righteousness. Now the tables had turned a full 180 degrees.

'Now explain this to me,' she said calmly. 'Why can't I know where he's gone, and who the hell are you? I have to know what's going on or I can't work here any more.'

George sighed again and sat forward in his chair.

'We could not afford to allow the local authorities access to Van Missen. I called some people that he knew, people Pete Van Missen had worked with. They removed him.'

'Some people he knew?'

'I don't know who they were and I don't want to know. People.'

'People,' said Nina incredulously.

'People.'

'Not aliens, then,' said Nina with a laugh. 'That's a relief.'

George smiled, a smile that suggested he thought he'd got away with something. Nina didn't like it.

'So you called some people and they came and not only managed to get past the security at the hospital, not only managed to hack into the hospital data records and remove all traces, but managed to take a completely paralysed man out of the building and put him on a plane to America.'

'I guess so. Yes. He's been taken to a hospital in Virginia.'

'Oh, Virginia, is it. So you know that much.'

'That's all I know, and more than you need to know. The whole issue is still red hot. Van Missen is a witness to a serious assault, along with your brother. The police are going to be coming here and asking questions, and the more you know the more you're going to have to lie. I don't want to put you, or anyone else in the company, in that position. I don't know how I can make it clearer. If we are to succeed, we have to be very careful and release the information about our research when we know we can back it up with solid results. You know how it goes, Nina, it was the same at Coventon's, for Christ sake.'

'It was not!' she snapped. 'I knew where the funding came from, I'd heard of the companies and trusts and hospitals involved. In our labs, it was . . . well, not like this. We had the same kit as everyone else.'

'Well, that's good, then, isn't it? We've got the best equipment and the best scientists and the best research facilities, and we're way ahead of the field. That's what we went to all this trouble for. I can't tell you anything else. You know everything I do.'

'It's so weird,' said Nina. For some reason she was beginning to feel better. 'In any other circumstances, say you'd fitted a prosthetic leg to someone and the leg failed in some way, the first thing that would happen would be that you'd go and see the person to find out what happened. But with this stuff . . . well, it's all so covert.'

'It has to be for the time being, Nina.'

'Nash Systems. What a joke. Jason and I are barely a part of this. You only got him so you could have me. Now you're lumbered with him and I want to leave. Bit of a mess, isn't it, Georgie boy.'

'There's no point me denying that your loss at this time would be extremely detrimental to the whole project. We both know that basically you and Sir Brian Coventon are the only people who know how to do this.'

'True, and long may that remain so.'

'Well, sure, I understand how you feel, but it's not over, Nina, it's only just starting. True, we don't have anyone we can test the new chip on right now . . . well, other than Jason.'

'What?'

'No, it's okay. I was joking. Van Missen's replacement is coming here this afternoon.'

'What?'

'He's called . . .' George looked at his screen. 'Frank Garfelli.'

'What d'you mean, Van Missen's replacement? What are you talking about? It's all too much. I used to feel embarrassed when I couldn't keep up, but here I feel quite normal. Who could keep up with this level of subterfuge? Run it all by me again, slowly,' she demanded.

'Well, we need someone to run the security operation here. Pete Van Missen is clearly out of the picture but the show goes on. We could insert the chip into this Garfelli guy or we could ask Jason. That's all I'm saying.'

'I do not believe I am hearing this. The show cannot go on. We can't shove another chip into someone's neck until we know what happened the first time. Who the hell is Frank Garfelli anyway?'

'He's an associate of Van Missen's.'

'That doesn't exactly fill my databanks, George. I still don't have a clue who Van Missen was, so Garfelli's a bit of a dark horse on the other side of a big hill in the middle of the blasted night.'

'I can assure you that before we proceed with any further

chip insertions we will have a full medical breakdown on what happened to Van Missen.'

'Oh, we will, will we? Well, why didn't you tell me that earlier?'

'You didn't . . .'

'Don't tell me I didn't ask. What are you? I'm talking to you, but you're not talking back. You're revealing certain bits of information, but just enough to keep me here. Is that it?'

George nodded.

'I'm answering all my own questions, aren't I?'

George nodded again.

'Well, here's one that'll throw you. I won't take part in the project until I know for certain what happened to Van Missen. And also, just to try and take a little more control over what I'm doing here, I won't insert a chip into another clean-cut member of the American military in civilian clothes.'

'I see.'

She'd never thought about using Jason before, but it was a very interesting notion. She could study what was going on inside that bizarre creature for the first time, take her time to try to understand him.

'Jason, on the other hand . . .'

'Well, it is a possibility,' said George carefully.

Nina thought about it, thought about the dreadful mess he would make, about his utter inability to keep quiet about what was going on. There was one possible way around that problem.

'But I don't want him to know about it.'

'I'm sorry?'

'He mustn't know he's got the chip in him. I don't trust him. I want to find out about the true Jason John Nash. The only way of doing that is a covert insertion. That should be right up your street, George.' She smiled.

George stared at her with a peculiarly blank expression, as if he wasn't even thinking.

'Aha. Closure,' said Nina. 'Got you at last.'

She continued to smile at him. She had spent a long night thinking, going through all the possibilities regarding what could have happened to Pete Van Missen. She wanted to see him desperately. She wanted to hold him and reassure him; she felt even more out of control without him there. She was torn between jacking the whole thing in and pressing on regardless. It was so tempting not to ask any questions, just to accept that she found herself in a strange situation which allowed her to press ahead with the work she was so passionately dedicated to.

But what was emerging slowly was that the technology was so important, so revolutionary, that it would change everything about the way people operated in the world. It had so many possible applications – she had only ever seen the medical ones, that being the main thrust of the work she had been doing for Sir Brian Coventon. But at Nash Systems the applications seemed to come a poor second – it was the raw research which drove the small group of scientists. They didn't discuss what could be done with what they were discovering, they just worked to improve the way they were doing it.

When George had suggested the idea of inserting the new chip into Jason, suddenly the whole thing had fallen into place. It was perfect – she would be in control, she would be calling the shots. For a start, she would know the subject well and be able to predict exactly what he was likely to do. No longer studying the graphs of some distant and highly secretive individual with alarmingly clear blue eyes, but studying her own brother, her own flesh and blood.

'You are telling me you want to use your brother as the test individual without him being aware of it?'

'I'm not telling you I want to. I'm telling you I shall, or I leave.'

'Covertly insert the chip into Jason?'

'Yes, with extreme prejudice if I had my way,' she said with a laugh. George looked shocked and confused. 'I quite fancy hammering it into his skull, but that might damage the chip.'

She smiled at George's shocked expression. Surely he had lived in England long enough to have grasped the rudiments of British irony?

'I'm not serious about the hammer, George,' she explained. 'I would just feel a great deal more commitment to the project if I knew something about the test individual, as you put it. And I know Jason just about as well as I want to know anybody.'

'Nina, I don't know that I can sanction this. I was merely suggesting that we approach Jason, talk through the benefits and dangers of the operation.'

'Waste of time. He'd do it anyway, he's mad enough, but he'd do it for all the wrong reasons. He would not be able to keep quiet about it either. He'd be in some club one night, pissed, and he'd tell some poor cokehead model girl that he was the Terminator or something dreadful. The story would get out in hours, I can assure you.'

'I understand what you're saying, but to covertly carry out a chip implant has a great many ethical problems attached to it.'

Nina noticed he was smiling broadly as he spoke, and assumed he was just covering himself. George Quinn was a real mystery to her – even after working with him for three months she had no idea who he really was. She had made vague attempts to find out, but all had led to nothing. He claimed to have worked at Stanford University in California, but no one she knew there had ever heard of him. Of course, it was a very big university, so that wasn't entirely surprising, but George Quinn didn't strike her as the scientist type. A bureaucrat maybe, an office manager who'd clearly had experience of the hi-tech field. Where she could just say one word to Emen Trouville and know he understood what she was talking about, whenever she raised a technical aspect with George Quinn he managed to change to subject to the daily workings of the project rather than specific technicalities. Whoever he was, though, he made her life at Nash Systems much easier.

She smiled back. 'I'm not worried about ethical questions when it comes to my brother. He is a being without an ethical dimension. He is incapable of any political or ethical analysis of what he does. He's an emotional amoeba, a sort of turd on legs.'

'Nina, please,' said George with obvious distaste.

She ignored him; she was enjoying herself. 'Ethics? Bollocks is all I can say to that where he's concerned. I'd be more worried about a monkey, George. Jason Nash is a totally unethical, politically irrelevant unit as far as I'm concerned. Whatever happens to him is not an issue.'

'Well, I feel I have to be the voice of caution here. We don't actually know how he's going to react, do we?'

'No, of course we don't, that's why we need to try so we can find out,' said Nina. She knew that inserting the new chip could wreak havoc with Jason's life. But she was beyond caring about him. He had always been a prick and always would be. Why worry?

'The point is, Nina,' said George, looking at her intently, 'I don't want your emotional history with Jason to cloud your judgment. We are in such a delicate breakthrough area here. We've already had a very serious upset with Van Missen – you know what I'm saying.'

'It won't cloud my judgment. In fact, if anything, the opposite will happen. I'll be completely objective about it.'

21

A constantly recurring theme in Jason's life, which he had recently become aware of, was that when things got bad he somehow made an extra effort to make them worse. It wasn't a conscious decision – he didn't say to himself, 'Let's really screw things up now' – but that's just what he did. And he did it in a rush.

When airline-food.com was in its last death throes, he didn't back off and try to clear up the mess. He didn't go into his offices in Shoreditch in East London and explain to the handful of people working for him that they might lose their jobs. He didn't go and talk to the slightly dubious venture capitalists, among their ranks Costas and Michael, the crack cocaine dealers who had backed him, and explain what was going on. He withdrew what remaining resources he had and set up another e-business. This one was called discontinued-products.com, a simple idea and, to Jason's mind, a rock-solid certainty as the ultimate winning business plan and a top-drawer dot-com.

He had met a man at a party thrown by his solicitors who worked for a warehousing company that held vast stocks of assorted products from failed launches. Things like spreadable lard in a can, bottled dog food, washing-up liquid that removed the glaze from plates and the skin from hands. Products with badly thought-up names like 'Shite', a very successful window-cleaning gel from Poland which someone thought would sell well in the UK, importing thousands of bottles of the stuff, and 'Mayk-mipook' noodles from Singapore – over seventy thousand packets in stock. Jason could get hold of these items at nearly zero cost, use clever ironic advertising to shift them, and make a mint overnight.

It all went hideously wrong. The site, although launched, was lost in a sea of B2C chaos. No one wanted to buy well-made clothes or furniture over the Web, let alone bottles of 'Shite'. He lost what remained of his capital in a matter of days. He got drunk and went to the Shoreditch offices of airline-food.com and discontinued-products.com and told everyone to take what they wanted and leg it before the bailiffs arrived. His last memory of being a stand-alone start-up king was seeing a bunch of itinerant programmers staggering out of the building carrying IBM servers, Cisco routers and iMacs by the armload.

He'd blown it again. All that work, all that manic effort – management meetings, late-night page design sessions – had ended in utter failure. There was one computer left in the Shoreditch building. He picked it up and was about to carry it out to sell it when something stopped him. It was these moments which kept Jason Nash from going right over the edge. He didn't know what it was that stopped him, but some feeling made him sit down and boot the machine into action – one last browse before their line was cut off. He'd had plenty of rows on the phone with their fat-pipe provider. He owed £70,000 and there was no way they could begin to pay it, but Jason had somehow managed to string them out, week after week.

After typing 'dot-com failure' into the Google search engine, he came across a cruise that was due to travel up the Alaskan coast. It was a themed cruise, a floating convention focusing on dot-com failures. He noticed with a shout of glee that it was being organised by an individual who Jason knew as Derek Leahy, but who also went by the name of Frank Dobkitch, Marvil Giuseppi III and Howard S. Rawstone. Whoever he was, he had made a name for himself as the man who had really screwed up in e-business on a global scale. Hailed by one business journal as 'The Man Who Lost the Most Money in History', Leahy was a dot-com legend.

One phone call later, which happened to wake Leahy in

the middle of the night, Jason had hassled himself a job on the cruise, provided he could get to the Vancouver docks in time.

Using a Chase Manhattan credit card he'd ordered via the Net, he used the last of his borrowing margin and bought a one-way ticket to Vancouver. By seven that evening he was flying high, sitting in business class and leaving below him a financial mess of, even by his terminally optimistic assessment, very ugly proportions.

It was on the cruise that he met George Quinn, and within two hours, all his financial concerns were solved. George dug him out of debt and even bought him a first-class ticket back to London. George wanted Jason more than Jason wanted George – not an experience he was used to, but a very comforting one. At the eleventh hour Jason has managed to save himself and, it seemed, save the vital search code which had so nearly worked – the code which could, when linked to the right hardware, source an overproduction of duck in orange sauce in a catering company at Heathrow or Gatwick and immediately list it on his menu page. George claimed this was just what he was looking for.

Jason returned to England feeling like a king. He had pulled himself out of the pit of failure at the eleventh hour. He'd done it again and again throughout his life – that was what made it so hard to stop being impulsive. But since he had helped start Nash Systems he had begun to feel an enormous force making him curb his impulsive behaviour. It must be growing up, he thought, coming to terms with his history, realising that Nash Systems was an opportunity he'd been given.

But even with this obvious pressure, the desire to really screw up was turned up to eleven. He had to resist it. He squeezed the steering wheel of the Mercedes harder as he crawled through the streets of London, fighting his way through the absurd traffic to get up to Cambridge, to get to Nash Systems, the only place he felt safe. He was sitting in silence, not something he was comfortable with. A bit of Wu Tang Clan at max volume would have cleared the cobwebs, but he felt he had to be considerate.

He had already blown it a bit, but he kept trying to reassure himself that it was only a little bit. Sleeping in the passenger seat next to him was Amy, young Amy, the innocent girl who'd do anything in the sack. Jason pondered the whole sex thing. Was it a diversion for him? Did he really enjoy sex? He wondered whether doing sex as a job had affected him. He had been pounding away on top of Amy the night before and yet had been aware that his mind was on other things. Worries, mostly – they were seeping in even when he was fully involved in the hottest adult action he had experienced without a minicam aimed between his legs.

Maybe sex was just something he used to remain in denial about all his problems, whatever they were. He'd never had time to think about them before. Denial seemed to be a big thing in his family – his sister was certainly a degree-holder in the art. Maybe it was a Nash thing. His mother had trained them well. His mother – yes, his mother. Jason realised he hadn't spoken to her for too long. In fact, she hadn't called him either. His name had been in the papers – 'Business Man Attacked in Café Brawl,' it had said in the *Guardian*, but she didn't read the *Guardian*, so that was okay. The other papers hadn't picked up on it yet. They might, though.

'Mum, hi, it's Jase.'

His mother's voice came over the speaker system louder than he had imagined possible.

'Hello, dear, so nice to hear from you!'

The noise woke Amy with a start.

'What the fuck was that?' she screamed.

'Hello, dear, are you all right?' his mother's voice boomed from the crystal-clear speakers. The volume was preset to heavy metal, full bore. He panicked, trying to remember which way the volume preset went. He adjusted the controls as quickly as he could, using the buttons on the steering wheel. He put one hand over Amy's mouth and glared at her.

'I'm fine, Mum, stuck in traffic as per usual.'

'Oh dear, you poor thing.'

'Sure, sure. So how's things at Nash Central?'

'Fine, dear. We're all fine.'

'Great, sure. Great. Good.' He couldn't think of anything else to say.

'Your father comes out today.'

'Right, yeah. Of course.' He had been in this position before – not having a clue what she was talking about, but managing to sound as if he did.

'He's got to take it easy for a bit, but he seems fine.'

So he'd obviously been ill, but how to find out what exactly was wrong? He needed time.

'Sorry, Mum, going to put you on hold for a second, got another call coming in from America.'

He pressed 'mute' and turned to Amy.

'How do I find out what's wrong?'

'Who is it?' she asked, her eyes red rimmed. Young people – they just couldn't take it. He'd had an hour's sleep and felt fine. They'd been rutting like hogs all night and he felt great. She looked like a Hiroshima survivor.

'My mum. Obviously my dad's been in hospital. I don't know anything about it. It's probably in one of those letters she sends, but with my work commitments I really don't have time to take in that sort of data.'

'I don't know,' said Amy. 'Just ask what's wrong.'

'No can do, not with my mum.'

'Mums understand their sons.'

'Yeah, tell me about it,' said Jason, his finger rubbing the mute button.

'I know,' said Amy. 'Is their bedroom upstairs?'

'Yeah, they run a hotel. It's on the third floor.'

'Okay. Ask if he's going to sleep downstairs.'

'Sure, sure. Why?'

'Well, if it's incapacitated him, he won't be able to go upstairs, silly.'

'Sure, sure. Good one, Amy, remind me to give you a sixty-eight.'

'What's that?'

'Where I go down on you and you don't owe me one.'

Amy sat in silence for a moment as she worked it out, then screamed with laughter just as he pressed the mute button.

'Sorry, Mum, had to sort that out. Are you still there?'

'Yes, dear. What's that awful noise?'

'Oh, I'm giving a bunch of students a lift,' he said. 'They looked so bedraggled by the side of the road.'

'Oh, you are a good lad. You're always helping other people.'

'Sure, sure. Steady, Mum, they might hear you. Now, I'm worried about Dad. Is he going to be sleeping downstairs?'

'Why would he want to do that, dear?'

'Just thought he might not want to deal with all the stairs.'

'That's very considerate of you, dear. Your sister hasn't shown the slightest interest, even after all he's done for her. I don't think a fractured collarbone is going to stop him sleeping in his own bed.'

'Right, sure, sure, stupid of me,' said Jason. He smiled at Amy, who was looking at him lasciviously.

'I told you all about it in the last letter.'

'Yeah, yeah, I read it all, Mum, sure, sure.'

'Terrible to-do here, darling. We're very pushed, of course. I've been rushed off my feet trying to get someone to replace him in the kitchen. We're booked up solid and he's worried to death about the quality of the meals we're serving. Mark is very good, but he's not your father.'

'No, sure, sure. I'll see what I can do, Mum.'

'Oh, don't you worry about it, dear, you've got enough on your plate.'

'Sure, sure. I am pretty pushed,' said Jason as he watched Amy's hand slide over his thigh. 'But I'll get my people on to it. I don't want you and Dad to worry.'

'That's very kind, dear. And how's it all going at Nash Systems?'

'Amazing, Mum. We are industry leaders beyond question. Major, major breakthroughs in the cybernetics field. It's all going very, very smoothly with a capital Vee.'

Amy was now massaging his erection through his brand-new Prada trousers. The little lady was insatiable, although they had forgone their early-morning session as they hadn't woken up till after ten.

The great side effect of Pete Van Missen's sudden disappearance was that there was no one checking up on him. He had been shagging for England since he'd slapped masking tape over all the cameras in the flat just to make sure he wasn't being watched. He noticed that the little camera in the car was still operational, but he decided it didn't matter. Who'll see, he thought, as he carefully pulled down his fly.

'Mum, got another call coming in. I'll bell you later. Say get well soon to Dad.'

'All right, darling,' said his mother. 'Look after yourself, Jason, d'you hear what Mummy is saying? Think about yourself once in a while, don't just help other people.'

'I'll do my best, Mum,' said Jason as he gently guided Amy's head towards his now exposed member. He switched the phone off and howled as he felt Amy's wonderful mouth encompass everything.

An hour later Jason drove very carefully through the gates at the entrance to the Nash Systems compound. He didn't hit anything; he wasn't drunk, although he was feeling a bit woozy.

'Amy, you know I totally respect you,' he said as they pulled to a halt in his parking space. 'But I have to be careful in the corporate world.'

'It's all right, Jason baby,' said Amy, putting a gentle hand on his cheek. 'I know you can't admit to anything publicly at the moment.'

She was heaven on two slightly shorter legs than he truly

fancied, and she accepted and accommodated his various complexities. She was too good to be true. That thought made him stop and think for a moment.

She really was too good to be true.

Which could only mean that she wasn't true, which could only mean that she was there for his benefit, which could only mean that her job was to keep him occupied. Which in turn meant that someone had decided to put her in his orbit, which meant that someone had thought about it all in advance. He looked past Amy at the Nash Systems building. He knew that although it bore his name he was involved only on the periphery. His sister was the one in charge – he was just a figurehead. He looked at Amy again! She just didn't have that professional chrome-plated heart look – she wasn't a pro, he was sure. He was being paranoid.

'Look,' he said, 'I'm not a fool, Amy. I really, really like you. Totally. But I can't help wondering if you like me. I mean, you know. It's all too easy. You wait when I can't see you, you don't give me a hard time like a lot of ladies would. And when I can see you, you are happy again. I mean, I'm no spring chicken. I've been around a good many ladies, and let me tell you for starters, I've never met one like you. You are a red-blooded male's dream ticket to pussy heaven.'

'That's the nicest thing anyone's ever said to me,' said Amy, giving him an affectionate kiss on the cheek.

'Now, sure, sure. I hear what you're saying but, Amy, what gives? I mean, no lady ever behaves like you. You're too nice to me. I'm an arsehole, everyone tells me that.'

'I don't think you are,' she said. 'You are the best lover I've ever had, you have the biggest cock I have ever seen. You drive me crazy in bed and I'm a horny girl. You buy me lovely presents, you've got a lovely car and a lovely flat. I can't help it. I love you, Jason. I can wait until you're ready for me. Doesn't matter how long.'

'Sure, sure,' said Jason with a slight shake of his head. He glanced at her. She was looking at the building. Was it all an act? Only one way to find out.

'Maybe we could get married.'

'Oh, Jason.' Amy sat back in the leather seat and stared out of the window for a moment. 'That's amazing.'

He looked at her again. She was now staring at him with those wonderful, emotionally open eyes. How could he doubt her? She was the special lady he had always wanted to meet. She was there, in his luxury executive car, right beside him.

'You're a really special lady and I want to do the right thing,' he said, wondering what he was doing. 'No, I really mean it.'

They walked into Nash Systems together and he felt wonderful. Legitimate. For the first time he could remember in his life, he didn't have the niggling worry that someone was about to come up behind him and start hassling him for something he'd done and forgotten about. Like his dad used to, like his sister, like all the ladies he'd been with – hassling him because he'd forgotten something. Like all the people he'd allowed to invest in his ventures. He could walk around with Amy as his good lady wife, he could introduce her to people without worrying, he could take her home and with the full weight of the law behind him, and with the full acceptance of all authorities, he could fuck her stupid day and night for the rest of his natural life. It was all beginning to make sense. He wondered only why it had taken him so long to sort it out.

He opened the door and held it for Amy. She smiled at him, her delicious little smile that sent him crazy.

'Thank you,' she said.

'Mr Nash,' said a large, suited man standing in the middle of the reception area in front of him. 'I am going to personally and with great pleasure kick your ass.'

Jason felt his body snap into a defensive posture before he'd even had time to take in what was going on. The man was American, judging by his accent. His voice was peculiar, muffled with sloppy diction. A jock type and possibly a bit thick, with cropped hair, about the same age as Jason, but dangerous looking. He was sure he'd never seen the man before.

'What seems to be the problem, chief?' he asked, feeling enormous tension in his shoulders.

'You are going to take a grade-one beating, good buddy,' said the man.

Jason glanced at Amy.

'I'll call the police,' she said.

'Sure, sure. Maybe not,' said Jason. 'I'm sure whatever the problem is we can sort this out in a gentlemanly sort of way.' He tried to smile at the man, but his face didn't seem to want to smile.

The man walked towards Jason in a very threatening way.

'Help, someone, Jason's being attacked,' screamed Amy.

Everything inside Jason's head was screaming 'run', 'dive to one side', 'get the fuck out of the way', but his arm snapped up and caught the man's fist. Before he knew it he had twisted the fist and somehow blocked another blow from the man's other hand.

What happened next was essentially a blur of movement, very rapid close combat, as the cropped-headed man tried in every way he could to strike Jason. During the whole scuffle, Jason was fully in the experience, but there was still a small voice inside which kept trying to remind him that he didn't do this sort of shit.

Suddenly the man was lying on the floor, a trickle of blood coming out of his mouth. He put a hand up as a signal of surrender. Jason was standing over him, his hands up in some sort of weird praying-mantis posture, a position he had never once put himself in before. Amy was still screaming. Jason glanced up for a second. Emen Trouville and Michael Del Papa ran into the reception area, shortly followed by George Quinn.

'You are one hardassed motherfucker,' said the man on the floor after he had spat out a gum shield. 'Where did you train? The fucking SAS?'

'It's okay, it's okay, everyone,' said George, running up to Jason. 'It's okay, Jason. Are you okay?'

'Sure, sure. No. Well, it's hard to tell right now,' said Jason. 'Um, I think I hurt my hand a bit.' He held one hand up. A nasty gash on the knuckles was bleeding a little.

'What's happening?' said Amy. 'Who is this?'

The man who had attacked Jason sprang to his feet and held out his hand.

'Good to meet you, Jason. My name's Frank Garfelli. I'm the new head of security. I'm taking over from Pete Van Missen.'

Jason shook his hand. 'Sure, sure,' he said, feeling as confused as it was possible for him to feel, which for Jason was on the very cutting edge of human confusion. 'Yeah. Nice to meet you, Frank.'

22

Nina felt like a disused washcloth. She had been in bed all day after spending half the night vomiting. She couldn't even find the energy to get up and clean the house. As she had stumbled through it back and forth to the bathroom, it had looked very messy to her. In fact the mess she observed was caused by a pair of shoes on the floor and two unopened envelopes sitting on the table in the kitchen.

As she scrunched up in her bed, her stomach ached and she sensed she was running a temperature. By about eleven she had managed to rouse herself enough to call the lab and tell them she wasn't going to make it.

'Must have been something I ate,' she said to Emen Trouville, who'd answered the phone.

'Oh my God, Nina. Are you okay?'

'I think so. I feel pretty lousy but at least I've stopped throwing up.'

'D'you want me to get a doctor to come see you?'

'No. It's just mild food poisoning,' she said. Even talking to Emen made her head ache. 'I'll be okay. I'm drinking water and sleeping, that's all I want to do.'

'I can come round and see you after work if you like.'

'No, please don't. I don't want anyone to see me like this.'

'Jesus, Nina, you sound really bad. Let me get a doctor to come and see you.'

'Okay, maybe you should. I'm sure it's nothing, though.'

An hour later a very young female doctor came around and talked to Nina. She agreed it was probably mild food poisoning. After a brief examination she gave Nina some painkillers and told her to keep drinking – it would pass through her system in twenty-four hours.

As Nina lay in bed, she had time to think. Only twenty-four hours earlier she had taken part in the operation to insert the new chip in her brother's neck. At 3,000 microns, it was the smallest transponder chip ever produced. The size of a grain of sand, the whole thing was encased in a tiny bioneutral plastic bead.

Roger Turnpike had again carried out the operation, this time under a general anaesthetic, which had been administered to Jason when Nina was absent. She had asked how this was done. As usual all the answers were a little evasive.

'Jason was already sleeping,' said George as they brought his sleeping form into the lab on a gurney. 'Frank administered some mild relaxant. We brought him through the back office and the service lift. No need to raise the gossip level.'

'Need to know?' Nina asked.

'You got it, Professor. We've closed down the surveillance system for the time being.'

'We don't want records of this operation,' said Frank Garfelli.

'I'm just glad I'm here,' said Nina, looking at Frank with barely hidden dislike.

Roger Turnpike had brought Jackie Morris, an anaesthetist, along with him. She seemed like a nice woman, and more than a little shocked by her environment. She clearly wasn't used to working in the corner of a messy laboratory, even if it had been turned into a makeshift operating theatre.

She checked Jason's vitals as soon as he was on the operating table. Frank removed Jason's jacket and shirt and then turned him over so that he was face down on the table.

Nina really didn't like Frank Garfelli. He wasn't the same sort of man as Pete Van Missen. He was far more brusque, and really looked like a soldier, with cold blue killer's eyes and a dreadful cropped haircut. She didn't like the way he manhandled Jason's sleeping body – he was too abrupt. Van Missen would have been methodical but a great deal more caring.

When she first met Frank Garfelli he handed her a document which he pulled out of a sealed black canvas bag. She didn't get a good look at the bag, but it was clearly an official US government diplomatic bag, the sort of thing a courier was allowed to carry through customs without inspection.

The document turned out to be a closely typed ten-page breakdown of Pete Van Missen's medical condition. The theory the surgeons who had written it had come up with was that owing to a sudden jolt to the neck the chip had been crushed by the second and third vertebrae, which had caused it to short. They assumed there had been a massive voltage surge as the circuitry was damaged and the resulting electric charge went straight into his spinal column, damaging two-thirds of the nerve tissue. He wasn't totally paralysed, still having some movement in his right leg and arm, but he was unable to walk or move unassisted.

There was nothing in the report about his state of mind or his family, or where he was, or whether there was any way she could get in touch with him. She had never seen a document like it before. It had 'Highly Confidential – Property of US Government' printed on the front in big letters. There was no indication as to who had written the report or where it came from.

Frank Garfelli had been standing by her bench in the lab the entire time she was reading it. As soon as she closed the document he took it from her and replaced it in the bag.

'Can't I keep it?'

'I'm afraid that's not possible at this time, Professor,' said Garfelli. 'If for some reason in the future you need to check something, I suggest you contact me and I will endeavour to furnish access for you. It's my job to look after it.'

'Weird,' said Nina.

She missed Pete; she worried about him and what on earth might happen to him. She had been so busy she hadn't had time to really allow herself to dream about him, but reading the report had made her suddenly more aware of her feelings for him. They were big – they were a data spike in her existence. Now he was gone, paralysed, and even if it wasn't directly her fault, she was implicated. She didn't feel comfortable with the way serious problems like the assault and Van Missen's disappearance were just made to go away by Nash Systems. The police hadn't even been to visit the labs; she had heard nothing more about it.

None the less, the chip insertion was very exciting. If she had doubts about other aspects of her work, as she watched Jason being prepared for the operation she felt completely sure she was doing the right thing regarding her brother.

He would actually be doing something useful with his life for once, even though he didn't know it. If the chip worked, and all the signs said it would, they would be able to record and transmit from the same chip. That meant they could analyse and respond to the messages the brain sent out to the body, and if, as in the case of spinal injury or cerebral palsy, those messages were not getting through or were garbled, the chip could sort them out.

One minor operation like this could help millions of people. It was, after all, what she had been working towards for the best part of eight years. It was what Sir Brian had struggled to achieve, only half succeeding after twenty years. In three short months Nina had managed to create the technology that would, beyond doubt, change the world for ever.

Roger Turnpike worked with great speed and dexterity. The incision in Jason's skin was less than the width of a little fingernail. He was working with tiny remote-operated tools on the end of short steel cables. The operational area was lit very brightly, but all that could be seen with the naked eye was two thin wire-like utensils going into a tiny cut in Jason's neck.

'I'm getting better at this,' he said as he peered into the powerful electron microscope that was mounted directly above Jason's neck. 'This is an amazing little fellow, isn't it? Can't believe it'll work, but there we go.'

Nina watched the large screen mounted on the wall as the

camera built into the microscope sent the pictures around the lab. She could make out the chip, being held in a pair of steel claws that looked, in scale, to be about the same size as the bow of a cargo ship. Roger Turnpike manoeuvred the sensor filament between the vertebrae with incredibly steady hands – the whole thing was done in three minutes. He stitched the cut with two tiny internal stitches.

'This stuff dissolves in about a week,' he said. 'Plastic surgery does have some useful spin-offs. It's what I use when I'm doing breast enhancement.'

Nina noticed Roger looking at her chest as he spoke. She couldn't make out his expression under his surgeon's mask, but she could guess what it would be.

An hour later, after the initial tests had been done and the chip was on line, Nina and Frank Garfelli took Jason back up to his office on the gurney. They used the service lift, which Nina had never been in before. She felt very uncomfortable in Garfelli's company – he was so cold and stony faced. They pushed Jason along the wide concrete corridor of the upper level and into his office.

She watched in discomfort as Garfelli half threw Jason back into his office chair.

'Please be careful,' she said.

'Sorry, Professor, but he's a pretty big guy,' said Garfelli.

'I know, but he is a human being, not a slab of meat.'

'Yes, ma'am,' he said with a slightly more surly manner than she had come to expect from her American colleagues.

Once Jason was settled, she and Garfelli left the office. He walked, or rather marched, down the hall to his office. Nina went across the hall to George Quinn's office.

'Who is this guy?' she asked as she walked in. George turned sharply and smiled at her.

'Nina, great, just making you and Jason a coffee. He may feel a little rough when he wakes up and we've got to make sure we maintain our cover.'

'Yeah, sure, good idea,' said Nina. 'But George, who is

Garfelli? He's awful. He's not like Van Missen, he's so obvious. I mean, he looks like a thug. Couldn't we get anyone else?'

'I'm afraid not.'

'Well, didn't you interview him or something?'

'No time. It was a bit of an emergency.'

'So who sent him?'

'The agency.'

'The agency? What agency?'

'The security agency where he works.'

'Oh, great, we're in another need-to-know situation here, aren't we?'

George smiled. He handed her two cups of coffee, freshly made by his beloved machine.

'Take this into Jason's office,' he said. 'Just act like he's fallen asleep. His is the blue mug. Five sugars as usual.'

Nina went into the office and put the coffee down on Jason's desk. His screen saver was on, and a series of flying erections flapped their tumescent way across the screen.

'Jason, what are you doing?' she said close to his ear.

'Sure, sure, I'm on it,' he said groggily. He sat forward and looked around. 'Fuck, did I fall asleep again? This is really not good. Sorry, supreme sis. I'm on the case now.'

'It's okay, don't worry about it. I brought you some coffee.'

'Aha. Excellent. Just what I need.' He scratched his close-cropped hair, yawned and smiled at her. 'I also need a cigar, Nina. You may want to stand back as I light one of these babies up.' He stood and his hand instinctively went to his neck. 'Shit, done something to my neck.'

'I think it's called sleeping in your office chair, Jason,' said Nina, trying to smile. Guilt was beginning to creep up on her. Unproven technology inserted right into the spinal cord of her brother. It would be frowned upon by just about any medical authority she could imagine, especially as it had been done without the consent or knowledge of the patient.

She watched Jason puff on an enormous cigar and felt the guilt slip away. She glanced at her watch and made a mental note to check the readings from when Jason inhaled. Playing back that data could be a sure-fire way to help people stop smoking.

'Ah, that's more like it,' he said. 'What have you been up to?'

'Mainly trying to sort out the mess you've made.'

'Yes, I know I've really screwed up.'

'Again.'

'Sure, sure. Again. I always have, haven't I.' He inhaled a killer lungful of super-thick cigar smoke. 'But I was actually trying to sort out the mess I'd made before we started this. It hasn't been too bad, though, has it? Working here, I mean. I know they're Yanks, but they're not too bad, are they?'

'They're all very nice,' said Nina with a smile.

'And you'd never have got this far with old Droopy Balls Coventon, would you?'

'No. That's true. He seems to have really screwed up. I haven't heard a peep from him.'

'Well, I would imagine he's a bit busy at the moment,' said Jason, taking another luxurious pull on his cigar. 'He's in front of some House of Commons committee.'

'Is he?' Nina hadn't been keeping up with the news. Then she remembered Hugo mentioning something about it in his e-mail.

'Oh, Nina, talk about a blinkered existence. You bloody scientists. It's been all over the papers.'

'I knew something was going on, I was just too busy. I've been a bit preoccupied in case you hadn't noticed, Jason.'

'Sorreeee,' he said annoyingly. She wondered why she had even toyed with the notion of guilt as far as Jason was concerned.

'There's a lot of trouble about some sort of donation he made to the party,' he said with a big grin. 'It all looks well dodgy, buying a knighthood and all the usual stuff. It's probably bullshit, but the papers love it. I got you out just in time, sis.'

'I think I'm going mad,' she said without looking up. She was surprised to feel Jason's hand on her shoulder, touching her quite tenderly.

'No you're not. Everything's fine. What is there to worry about? I'm the one with major problems.' She felt Jason remove his hand. 'The police will probably turn up at any minute and drag me off as an accomplice to a violent assault.'

'But this is just it. None of it makes sense, but I've got this sick feeling that it all should. Jason, listen for a minute.' She sat down on a small office chair opposite him. 'Does it ever cross your mind that everything we've done here, and how we got here, has been a bit straightforward? It's all been a bit . . . well, it's almost as if it's been organised for us. Don't you think?'

'Have you been smoking dope?' he asked.

'No, I have not.'

'You just sound a little bit paranoid, sis. It all seems very straightforward to me. As deputy CEO of Nash Systems, I know exactly what is going on with the company.'

'What is going on?'

'Well, at the moment, nothing. It's lie-low time. We have to wait for the whole Van Missen thing to calm down. Have you met his replacement, Arnolfini or whatever his name is?'

'Frank Garfelli, yes, he's around somewhere,' said Nina. Thankfully he clearly had no recollection of the operation.

'Right, well, that's the next step, isn't it?' said Jason.

'How d'you mean?'

'We'll slip a chip in him and continue testing.' He blew out a perfect smoke ring. 'That's what George's been telling me, anyway.'

'Oh, I see, yes,' said Nina, thrown by the complex levels of duplicity she was navigating. The guilt returned and she experienced a very strong desire to tell Jason about the implant. It made her twitch.

'What's up?' asked her brother.

'Nothing. Yes, you're right, as soon as we've got the new chip on line and we've run all the necessary tests we'll . . .'

'Oh, sure, sure. But Michael Del Papa told me the new chip is ready to rock,' said Jason with a furrowed brow.

'He would say that. He's always jumping the gun,' countered Nina, thinking fast. 'We've got loads of tests to do first. Plus I don't want to do anything before I find out what really happened to Pete.'

As she spoke, the full enormity of what she'd done started to flood over her. Although the new chip was smaller, with a less powerful battery, whatever had happened to Van Missen could easily happen again. Van Missen was a soldier, of sorts, so he was clearly being looked after in some military hospital, but if Jason was suddenly paralysed, who'd look after him? He'd essentially be her responsibility, even more than he had been all her life. The prospect of that was too appalling to contemplate.

'What really happened to Pete was he was in a fight with two very violent little arseholes,' said Jason. He started to pace around his office, gesticulating with his cigar. 'I didn't really see exactly what happened, but they were both trying to kill him, so they're bound to have whacked him a couple of times. I don't think it had anything to do with the chip, and even if it did, it doesn't mean what we're doing isn't valid, does it?'

Nina was about to respond. She knew that Van Missen's paralysis was directly caused by the chip, but it appeared from what Jason was saying that he knew nothing of this. It was so hard to work out who had said what to whom. But Jason was on a roll.

'There's going to be so much interest in chip insertion technology when we can finally release it. That's all I'm waiting for. The shit is really going to hit the fan then. I've been working out roughs for the initial press releases. I've got a web page design worked out. Every computer software and hardware manufacturer on earth is going to be beating the proverbial path to the door of Nash.com. Oh, yes. I can feel it, sister of mine. Microsoft and Cisco Systems will be shagged into the dirt by the giant knob of Nash. They'll be looked on in the same way we look at steel manufacturers now, yesterday's industries. Lay the bastards off, close the units, bye-bye, every-one. Oh, sorry, didn't anyone tell you, you're out of fucking date, pal. We've moved on, big time.'

He paused, clearly in ecstasy, and drew on the cigar with renewed enthusiasm. He smiled at her. She realised she prob-ably looked deeply troubled.

'Don't worry about anything, Nina, we'll sort it out. All this stuff with Van Missen is nothing, a tiny glitch. You told me how much data you were getting off his chip. Once the new one is in Garfelli it's going to be streaming again. And that data is a gold mine. George has explained the whole thing to me. It's going to be brilliant. I've sourced some fantastic new premises down over the other side of town, nine hundred thousand square metres of prime development. The beginning of the Nash campus, Nina. I'm totally dedicated to this project, and the rewards are just incredible. I predict that by year's end you will be among the top five richest women on earth.'

Nina sat and watched her brother pace around. She was wondering what sort of readings they would get from him as he ranted on. She doubted they would be very useful – the only thing you could do with them was feed them into someone who didn't like public speaking, press 'go' and then sit back and be bored to death.

'I don't think I'm doing this for the money,' she said eventually.

'Sure, sure. It's a side issue for you which I totally respect,' said Jason without hesitation. 'But it means you won't really have to work again if you don't want to. You could devote a bit of time to yourself. Get your tits done or something so you can pull a man your own age.'

'Jason!' Nina squealed.

'Oh, come on, you're as flat as a teenage boy. Only poofs fancy you. I'm not saying get some great silicon bags shoved behind your tits, just a subtle amount of augmentation. Isn't that what they call it? A bit of roundness would work wonders

206

with you. You're so skinny, you never eat, you look like death warmed up half the time.'

'I do not.'

'You bloody do. Look in the mirror – you make a thread of cotton look fat. Mind you, it's no wonder old Sir Brian wanted to hump you. Have you seen pictures of his wife?'

'Yes, of course I have.'

'Well, she's the bloody opposite of you, isn't she. Great uncooked dumpling of a woman. Makes Barbara Bush look tasty in comparison. If you want to pull a decent bloke who isn't married to some great beached whale, some tragic old tosser who wants to mount a sack of sticks as a bit of light relief, get your tits done and eat some more meat pies and potatoes. That's all I'm saying.'

'Thank you, Jason, I think I've had enough advice.' Nina stood up. She wanted to leave, but she also wanted to sound out her demented brother a little more. 'Does it ever worry you that what we're doing could have, well, other uses?'

'What d'you mean?'

'I don't know. No one does. But it's possible some of what we have been discovering could be used for negative purposes. I mean, if we discover we can decode the signals we've recorded, well, it could be used to modify behaviour – you know, control people.'

'Oh, excellent,' said Jason. 'I hadn't even thought of that. Imagine the marketing possibilities. Oh, yes, yes, this is too good to be true.' He sat at his desk and stubbed the cigar out in his coffee. 'You could insert a chip into a top-level call-girl, or a porn actress. I know some who'd help. Then you sell a chip pre-programmed with this data, and anyone can turn their wife into a total whore in the bedroom. I mean, you're looking at a multibillion-dollar industry in that one application alone. Fucking hell, Nina.' He held her by the shoulders and shook her. 'We're making history here. The whore chip.' He finally registered the look of horror on Nina's face. 'Okay, sure, sure. You could also do the same with a really sensitive man who was very good at oral sex on the ladies and made breakfast without moaning, then you ladies could insert that chip in your fellas. The possibilities are endless.'

She left him then. It was pointless trying to have a dialogue about her concerns with him, but she didn't feel comfortable discussing them with anyone else in the company.

She went down the main stairs and past Amy on the reception desk. She didn't want to talk to her either, but Amy's expression indicated that it was going to happen.

'What's wrong?' Amy asked as she passed.

'I don't know. What is wrong?' Nina responded.

'My screen's dead. I've got no pictures so I don't know where anyone is.'

'Oh, right, Mr Garfelli told me they were patching in new cameras in the big office. It'll be back on in a minute.'

'Oh, right,' said Amy. 'Are you okay, Professor?'

'Yes, I'm fine,' responded Nina as she slid her card through the security scanner.

'You just look a bit tired.'

Nina stopped, felt her brow furrow. 'That's just what Jason said to me.'

'Well, he cares about you.'

'Does he?' said Nina incredulously. 'I don't think so, Amy. There's only one person he cares about.' She watched Amy blush. 'No, I mean he only cares about himself.'

Amy looked disappointed. Nina shook her head. Had she really become that insensitive? 'No, I'm sorry, Amy, I don't mean that. I mean . . . oh, look, it's a sibling thing. We've never really got on.'

'It's okay. I've got a sister and I hate her guts.'

'Do you?'

'Oh God, yes. She's awful. She's much taller than me. Men always go gaga over her – legs up to here.' She pointed to her throat. 'But she's such a cow, so I understand.'

'Oh. Right,' said Nina. She hesitated a moment and then added, 'I'd better get back to work.'

When she entered the lab she discovered Emen Trouville and Michael Del Papa in fits of laughter.

'You gotta hand it to the guy, he's got a special way of talking to his sister,' said Michael.

'Have you been listening to us?' asked Nina with a note of alarm.

'Hey, only a bit,' said Emen. 'Frank Garfelli patched the signal through a couple of minutes ago.'

'Did he? Amy's monitor still isn't on.'

'I would suspect he isolated it. We had no picture, just sound, but it was the best, was it not, Emen?' said Del Papa. 'Nothing that takes place in this fucking place is exactly clandestine. They can hear what we're saying in here, everywhere.'

'Even the john,' said Emen.

'Let 'em listen,' said Nina. She checked the computer screens. Michael and Emen were rebooting the whole system, which was an essential part of the process – backing up the vast data glut and making sure the complex array of computer memory wasn't getting buggy. A fatal system error on an array this complex could be disastrous.

'Are we getting good readings?' she asked as she sat at her bench.

'Sure. The signal seems fine while he's here,' said Emen. 'The problem is what we do when he's not here. We can only get a clear signal while he's in the building. It's not like with Van Missen when we could ask him to carry a portable storage device.'

'Yes, I know,' said Nina. 'But I'm not so worried about recording from Jason. You know what he's like – anything we record from his nervous system is going to be of very limited use to the rest of the human race. I want to try to play back.'

The two scientists stared at her in silence. She looked up when she felt their stare.

'You do,' said Emen Trouville.

'Yes, of course. That's what we're doing, isn't it?'

'I guess so. But, well, like you were saying to Jason just now, there's, well, a lot of issues here.'

Michael Del Papa got out of his chair. The bunch of keys attached to the belt loop of his chinos jangled as he walked.

'Oh boy, are there issues. We are totally living in a world of issues here, people. But, and I say this with certain reservations, we're in a unique position.' Del Papa spoke as rapidly as always. 'We're essentially doing covert research with no watch-dog breathing down our neck. We can do what the hell we like, with certain caveats of course, Professor. But what we've set up here is the libertarian scientist's dream. There's nothing to stop us experimenting, no fuck-awful committee pondering on what we're doing who don't make a decision for ten years and when they finally do make entirely the wrong one based on some fucking myth that's been spread around by organic potato-eating morons.' He glanced at the screens. 'Okay, we're back up.'

Nina shook her head. She had never met anyone before who could speak so fast, and expound so much bitterness.

'I guess you've had quite a lot to do with committees, then, Michael,' said Emen with a grin.

'Don't start me, man. Don't start me,' Del Papa said as he typed furiously. 'Jesus, look at all this shit. More fucking data. I thought we were bringing in someone to help with the data load.'

'We are, he starts next week,' said Nina. 'I think he had a bit of trouble with his contract, so he's had to wait.'

'He's not a committee type of guy, is he?' asked Emen.

'No, he worked with me at Coventon's. Hugo's very fast. He'll rip through this stuff in no time.'

'That's good, that's all good,' said Del Papa. 'Yes, looky here, people. Jason Nash, we are receiving you.'

Nina rolled her lab stool nearer the screen. On it was the now familiar scrolling bar graph that she had watched for hours when the previous chip was inserted into Van Missen. It was impossible for the human eye to distinguish any difference in

210

Jason's input, there was so much data. Behind the screens, racks of hard disks were spinning at 20,000 RPM, storing endless gigabytes of information. At last, thought his sister, Jason Nash was doing something useful with his existence.

23

In the early evening of the day following his clandestine and still, to him, unknown chip insertion, Jason pulled the Mercedes to a halt outside Nina's house and killed the engine. Amy was sitting beside him, and it all felt right.

'I have to admit, I'm kind of nervous about this,' he said after the rap blast of Biggy Smalls finally died. He had wanted to try listening to the entire track, but when it was blasting out he found it slightly disturbing for the first time in his life. An age thing, he was sure. He might even have to browse the easy-listening section of his massive MP3 collection.

'It's okay,' said Amy. 'Nina's really lovely. She'll be fine.'

Jason had never been to Nina's house before. It was an odd little place, a nondescript modern terraced house on a narrow street. The front door was next to a garage. It was all very neat. He imagined himself well able to walk past it and not even notice its existence.

Amy pressed the bell. After a moment Nina's voice came over the door security speaker.

'It's Amy, and Jason.'

There was another pause. Nina said nothing, but the front door buzzed.

There was a flight of stairs directly in front of them. Jason looked up. His death's-head sister was leaning over the banisters.

'Oh Lord, look at you,' he said. 'You look rougher than a camel's ball sack.'

'Thank you,' said Nina. 'I haven't been feeling too good.'

'George told me you'd been sick as a dog. Did the doc come?'

'Yeah, this morning.'

'What did he say?'

'She. She said it was food poisoning.'

'Oh, right. Lady doctor,' said Jason. Even though he felt different about a lot of things, he still felt like winding his sister up. 'Maybe you should get a second opinion. You know what some of these lady doctors are like. Might have been her time of the month.'

'Jason, that's sexist. Isn't it, Nina?' said Amy.

'With anyone else it would be, with Jason it's horribly normal. Anyway, it's not serious. Believe it or not I feel better. I'll be fine.'

'We've bought you some soup and special drink,' said Amy. 'With mineral salts and trace elements in it. It's organic.'

'Come on up,' Nina said wearily. By the time Jason and Amy entered the spartan room at the top of the stairs, Nina was already on the single piece of furniture, a long red sofa. She was wrapped in a red duvet with only her blue socks and the top of her head visible.

'Bit of Delhi belly, then, sis,' said Jason joyfully.

'Please don't smoke, Jason, or I'll vomit on your head,' responded Nina.

'Don't worry. I'm not going to. I've got one arm covered in patches.'

Nina's head came farther out of her duvet cocoon. 'Did I hear right or am I hallucinating?'

'No, he hasn't smoked today,' said Amy. 'I've been watching him on the security cameras. He really hasn't.'

'You're looking at the new-model Nash. Same knob, same creative ability when it comes to marketing, but totally new attitude towards health. I've even tried some camomile tea today.'

'I made it for him,' Amy chirped.

'Did you actually drink it?' asked Nina.

'Well, I tasted it. It wasn't easy. I'll have to work up to herb teas as I ease off the old six-sugared coffee. So, it's you who needs serious help now, sis. Look at me. I've changed and I'm a Nash, so it is possible.'

He sat on the arm of the sofa and looked down at his minuscule sister. He smiled at her and continued, 'If I had to sit next to you at a public release of our product, pundits would think we were some kind of fucking freak show. They'd think Nash Systems had been starving you to death. You'd scare off the punters. So Amy and I will make you some soup and toast just to start the old weight-gain ball rolling.'

'That's not really why we're here, though, is it, Jason?' said Amy teasingly.

'No, sweetmeat, it isn't.'

'What's going on?' asked Nina.

'Sister of mine, I have news to impart. The lovely Amy and I are going to tie the knot. I wanted you to be the first to know.'

'I'm sorry?'

'We're going to get married.'

Nina looked at them for a moment.

'Isn't it wonderful news!' squealed Amy.

'Oh, yes. Sorry. Of course. It's just a bit of a shock,' said Nina eventually. 'What made you decide to do it?'

Amy spoke, but even Jason noticed the question was aimed at him.

'We're in love. We want to be together.'

'Yeah. I want to make an honest lady out of little Amy here.'

'Well, congratulations,' said Nina. 'It's a bit of a shock, though. I mean, I don't want to be rude about your fiancé, Amy, but I've never had Jason down as the marrying type.'

'Neither did I, but he asked. I didn't.'

'I haven't done it very well,' said Jason. 'I didn't do the old down-on-one-knee thing. We haven't even got a ring, although I think I've sourced one.'

'And you haven't told Mum or Dad?' asked Nina.

'No, not yet. That's what I wanted to talk to you about. You know them so much better than me.'

'I do not!' snapped Nina, showing her true colours again, Jason noticed.

'Anyway,' he said, deciding to ignore her little snip, 'I'm a bit tense about it. I've got a lot of tension in my neck and shoulders.'

'Oh, poor monster,' said Amy. She reached up and tried to massage his shoulders. Jason smiled down at her. He was feeling less and less embarrassed by her lack of stature.

'What's that on the back of your neck?' said Amy as she moved behind him. Jason put his hand up and felt a small lump. It was sore.

'Dunno. Must have scratched myself this morning.'

'Oh God, yeah. We haven't told you. It was awful,' said Amy, sitting on the sofa next to Nina. 'The new security man attacked Jason this morning.'

'What?' said Nina.

'Yeah. I think it was some sort of misunderstanding,' explained Jason. 'He seems like a nice enough chap. I don't know what I'd done to upset him.'

'Was it Garfelli?' asked Nina.

'Yes, it was awful, but Jason was amazing. He knocked him on the floor. He's so strong.'

Nina was staring at Jason, her face even whiter than when they'd first seen her.

'Well, I was protecting the little lady,' said Jason. He still hadn't worked out quite what had happened or how he had managed to disable the man. 'I think it was a joke, because you know I'm crap at all the fighting stuff.'

'You fought him off?' asked Nina.

'Well, I sort of stopped him hitting me, I think.'

'Oh, you didn't,' said Amy. 'Mr Garfelli's mouth was bleeding afterwards, and he had one of those boxer things in.'

'Yeah, I thought he was a nutter because he had blue teeth when I first saw him, but it was a gum shield. He'd obviously been set up. It must have been George's practical joke or something. Anyway, it's all fine now.'

'Jesus,' said Nina. She buried her head in the duvet. After a while she looked up at him again. 'Are you feeling okay now?'

'Yeah, never better. I think the old lungs are freaking out a bit, massive carbon withdrawals. My hand hurts. I think I must have caught his head with it by mistake.'

'Take me through what happened slowly. This is really important, Jason. I really don't like Garfelli anyway, and if he's attacking people I want him out.'

'Sure, sure. Calm down, sis. It's all sorted now. He's fine, very efficient. George apologised. It was all some sort of mistake. Anyway, I just walked in this morning with Amy, just after we'd decided to get married, and this bloke with the blue teeth started to have a go at me.'

'Were you inside the building?'

'What?'

'Were you inside the building, or outside?'

'I don't remember. Inside, wasn't I?' he said, looking at Amy.

'Yeah, in the reception area, silly.'

'So we had a scuffle, he fell over, then he got up and shook my hand.'

'Was anyone else there?'

'Oh yeah, everyone came rushing in when it was over. George was pretty shaken up. But we had a really good meeting and everything's going really well. Del Papa told me the chip would be ready on Monday, so everything's fine. Just a bit weird.'

'What's a bit weird?'

'Well, everything. But it's cool.'

'Come on,' said Amy. 'Let's warm up the soup.'

'Kitchen's through there,' said Nina, pointing to a doorway.

Amy and Jason entered the kitchen, which, to Jason's eye, looked unlived in. Nina really didn't go for trinkets. As Amy reached up to open a cupboard, he slid his arm around her waist and pulled her close.

'Hello, wife figure,' he whispered into her ear.

'Hello, husband,' she said. She took out a bowl, the only one on the shelf, then turned within his grasp and pulled his face towards hers. He bent down and they kissed with some sort of new passion. Not an acting porn star kiss – something else, tender. It must be a loving kiss, he thought, he must be in love with the little creature. His hand went to her breast, small but firm, and even through her clothes he could feel her nipple.

'I need to fuck you,' he heard himself saying. 'I need to now.'

'Can you find everything?' Nina called from the other room.

'Yes, it's fine,' said Amy. She was smiling up at Jason as she got hold of his cock. As the soup boiled on the stove, Jason experienced the first truly loving fuck of his life. It was silent, careful and incredibly sexy, even though both of them were still almost fully dressed.

24

When they are alone and surrounded by the consequences of their actions, some people thrash around looking for someone to blame, or they turn to drink, sex or drugs to temporarily obliterate the mountain of awfulness that they perceive their life to have become.

Nina Nash didn't smoke or drink – she liked to organise. She would sort and tidy things even more than they were already sorted and tidied in her obsessively well-ordered personal life. But now there was nothing to do – no bills to pay, no laundry to iron and put away, no baths to clean or cupboards to tidy. Besides, she felt so weak she couldn't have done anything even if it needed doing.

There were always tears and wailing, but Nina hadn't cried since . . . she couldn't remember when. She didn't really know how to. She had cried as a little girl, but her tears had only brought scorn and reprimands from her mother and an exhausted sigh from her father. She assumed she must have decided to stop. She didn't remember the decision being taken, she just remembered a numbness that overcame her when she was the recipient of her mother's constant criticism.

She looked at the tray on the low table in front of her, with the half-empty bowl of soup that Amy had given her, the piece of toast with two bites taken out of it on a plate beside it.

It was their visit which had pushed her over the edge – hearing them screwing in her kitchen, seeing their flushed and happy faces when they walked back into the room. Did they really think she didn't know what they had been doing, or had they done it to get at her? She wouldn't put it past Jason, although he was looking and behaving very differently from normal. For a start he had been to visit her, hadn't hustled her for money, hadn't even smoked. Nina knew it would have been Amy who made him turn up, but the fact that he did it was a major revision of standard Nash junior behaviour.

She lay back on the sofa with a groan. Some time later – she wasn't sure how much later; time seemed to have stretched rather unpleasantly – she found herself looking at her ceiling, something she had never done before. It was ugly, stuccoed plaster with a badly rendered circle around the central light fitting. The lampshade was okay, she liked that – a steel fitting of the sort that used to adorn warehouses. She had bought it in a shop in London when she was attending a conference there about four years previously. It was a shop on Upper Street in Islington, a sort of trendy junk emporium; she couldn't remember the name. Something to do with Noah.

She remembered going to the shop with Sir Brian during their lunch break. It had been a moment in their strange relationship which almost felt normal – walking along a street together, arm in arm, talking excitedly about the conference. They were like a couple, like people who were meant to spend time together. As she was paying for the lampshade for what was then her new house, Sir Brian had bought a stainless-steel set of drawers for his eldest child. She stood next to him as he arranged for delivery; hearing his home address just erected a huge wall of distance between them. He had another life, an all-encompassing life, with a house and kids and birthdays, weekend visits from relatives, holidays cooking in the kitchen with his wife, Christmas trees, noise, arrangements, rows, shared history, security.

Nina never had anything like that with Sir Brian. She had sex, secret phone calls, stolen moments here and there. This had been going on for years. It suited her, or so she told herself. And it was all over after one row. She hadn't seen him for months. He hadn't even tried to get in touch with her.

She looked around the room. It was so cold and dull looking. She had one bookshelf against the wall, packed with books, all in order of size and author. On the wall beside it were three awards in rather ugly gold-plated frames. They were commendations for breakthroughs in research which she had been awarded with Sir Brian. They weren't for her personally, she was just part of the Coventon Research team, but looking at the awards took her back to the feeling of being in the team.

There had been responsibilities, but not of the sort she was presently experiencing at Nash Systems. She had been responsible only for specific areas of development at Coventon's, and that was as far as it went. Now she had got into a mess of horrendous proportions. Her own brother was a guinea-pig in an experiment that she was responsible for, and as soon as she was off the scene for a day all hell had broken loose. There was only one explanation for the fight Jason had described; Del Papa and Trouville must have sent signals to the chip, using the recordings made during Van Missen's fight. It was obvious than Jason didn't have a clue about anything. He was walking around in blissful ignorance. Who knew what those signals would do to his central nervous system, to his brain? To make it worse, she was the one who had suggested they start to send the signals. It was, without doubt, all her fault.

She had to stop them, she had to call a halt. But how? She hardly knew what was going on anywhere but in the lab. Clearly George Quinn had some pretty heavyweight contacts. If she just ran in there and confronted him, he would find a way of dissuading her, of misdirecting her, throwing her off whatever path she wanted to pursue.

She hauled herself off the sofa, noticing when she stood that she felt a little bit better. She walked into the kitchen, and her spirits lifted further. Amy and Jason hadn't cleared up. There was an open soup container, a saucepan half destroyed by heavily burned soup, a dirty spoon on the counter. It was a mess, which meant she could clear it up.

She turned on her Roberts radio, another gift from Sir Brian. Tuned to the BBC World Service as usual. She checked her watch – 3.30 a.m. She sighed and filled the sink, listening to a report about Eritrea as she wiped the soup off her immaculate counter top. It reminded her of having jet-lag, coming home in the middle of the night and feeling good to be back home where everything was in the right place.

The next item on the news was a report on British parliamentary committees. She raised her eyebrows when Sir Brian Coventon's name was mentioned.

As the report continued, she took a ready meal out of the freezer, put it in the microwave and turned up the volume on the radio as the microwave fan started to whir.

'Sir Brian is appearing before the Commons ethics committee. Ministers are trying to ascertain exactly how much money he donated to the Labour Party and when he did so,' said the female reporter. 'Sir Brian, fifty-eight, who was knighted three years ago, has been the target of much press attention of late, after the sudden demise of his privately funded research organisation. He claims that the government has been running a smear campaign against him and his company. According to Sir Brian, the Department of Trade and Industry was influenced in its decision to cut grant aid to the organisation because the research he was carrying out, into the medical applications of silicon chip implants in the human nervous system, was seen as highly controversial. He stated that influential groups both inside and outside the UK had put pressure on the government to stop his work, even though remarkable breakthroughs had been made. He cited the case of a twelve-year-old girl whose artificial arm was functional enough for her to write her name with it within ten minutes of its attachment. He said this was entirely due to the tiny computer chip embedded in her upper arm, a development that had, according to Sir Brian, huge potential benefits for millions of people throughout the world. He further stated that the press interest in his donations to the Labour Party was a smokescreen organised by the Ministry of Defence. When asked why the MOD would do such a thing, Sir Brian said he had information which pointed to the MOD being behind the decision to cut funding. The corruption allegations were merely to hide the fact that resources were being channelled into research for military uses of the technology. And now, sport . . .'

Nina sat on the stool in her kitchen eating her chicken chow mein as fast as she could. She was ravenous. When the report finished she put the carton in the bin and looked at the radio. Just suppose Sir Brian hadn't lost it; just suppose that such ludicrous claims were actually true.

If it were true, she and Nash Systems were part of the conspiracy.

She picked up her phone and dialled Sir Brian's mobile number. What if it was the middle of the night? What if he was in bed with his wife? He was in so much trouble already, Lady Coventon wasn't going to worry about some sordid little affair her husband once had with one of his ex-students.

The answer service came on immediately. She pondered for a moment, then thought better of it. What could she say in a message, anyway? 'Hello, Brian, I think I'm working for the military.'

She went into the living room and picked up her bag from the small table where she always left it. She retrieved her Palm Pilot and found Hugo Harwood's number.

'Hello?'

He had clearly been deeply asleep – it was the classic sound of a fumbled phone and a groggy voice.

'Hugo, it's Nina.'

'Oh, hi. Where are you?'

'At home.'

'What? You mean you're not in Australia? What the fuck are you doing ringing up at this time?' He was saying angry words, but he wasn't sounding angry.

'I need to talk.'

'I'm seeing you on Monday. What is the time, anyway?'

'It's Three-Thirty or something. I know I'm seeing you on Monday, but I need to talk now.'

'Three bloody thirty. Nina, what's going on? Are you okay?'

'Just had a bad dose of food poisoning. I'm fine, but I need to speak to you before you arrive at Nash Systems on Monday. Like, supremely importantly.'

'Oh, brilliant. That makes life really easy. I have about eleven million things to do between now and Monday morning, so another one can't possibly make my life any harder.'

'It's vitally important, Hugo.'

'Everything's always vitally important with you. Where shall we meet?'

She felt comforted by the sound of his voice. Someone she knew was just talking to her, with no other agendas. She didn't know how long that would last once he entered the doors at Nash Systems. She needed to speak with him alone.

'Come to my house.'

'Your house!' said Hugo with a cough. He cleared his throat. 'Sorry, but is this Professor Nina Nash I'm talking to?'

'Yes.'

'You want me to come to your house? What's going on? No one ever goes to your house! Even Sir Brian. What's been happening?'

'I can't think of anywhere else,' she said without resentment. She faltered for a moment, wondering how he knew Sir Brian had never been there. 'When can you get here?'

'Well, I've got to be at my final session tomorrow, Friday. I mean today. Shit. I even bothered to go to bed early. I was planning on getting to Cambridge on Sunday.'

'Come on Saturday.'

'Oh, what the hell. I'll see you at your place on Saturday morning.'

She bade him farewell and switched the phone off. She felt tired, but her stomach was warm and wasn't hurting for the first time that long, lonely day. She felt better than she'd felt in a while. She was doing something positive about her situation, after spending the whole day worrying about it and doing nothing.

As her head hit the pillow, she sank into sleep immediately.

The following morning a new Nina Nash emerged from her house. She had eaten a whole apple, then made toast and coffee but only managed to drink the coffee. Still, it was a start. She had looked at her face in the mirror and decided that, yes, it was actually a bit thin. Gaunt looking. She had never deliberately starved herself, she just never had that much of an appetite, but that was all going to change. She was really going to make an effort to eat and enjoy food, get back in touch with her body, and she wanted to try to stop worrying that everything was getting out of control. She had even left the dirty dishes in her sink as she had slept late.

She drove out to Millford Business Park feeling very confident. She hadn't felt so clear headed and rested in weeks.

She parked her car next to Jason's and walked through the crisp morning air towards the front entrance. She stopped for a while and took in the view. A great expanse of open land lay before the Nash Systems building; she could hear a skylark somewhere in the distance. The clouds were perfectly shaped and stood out beautifully against the deep blue sky. It didn't look like England, it was too pure and clean. Not grey and dull as normal. This was a special morning.

Amy was already behind her peculiar reception desk, smiling as usual.

'Morning, Professor. Goodness, my soup must have helped, you look miles better.'

'I am, thank you, Amy. I feel excellent this morning. Slept like a log last night. How about you?'

'Oh, we were so excited, making plans and talking until the small hours. I feel pretty exhausted but I don't care.'

'Come here,' said Nina. Amy stood and walked around the aircraft wing towards her. The two women embraced. 'I'm really happy for you. I think it's brilliant,' said Nina.

'Do you? I was so nervous last night.'

'Well, don't be on my account. I think it's great. You're the best thing that's happened to Jason ever. If he blows it with you, I'll kill him.'

'He won't. He's been so nice,' said Amy. 'I'm a bit worried about your mum and dad, though. We're going to see them this weekend.'

'Are you? Oh, they'll be fine. My mum adores Jason in a very unhealthy way. She's a pain, but my dad's great, he'll really love you, I'm sure. Don't listen to my mum. She'll say all the wrong things in the first five minutes, but if she sees Jason's happy, she'll be fine.'

'He's a bit scared of your dad, I think.'

'Yeah, well, he has good reason to be. He hasn't exactly been the ideal son,' said Nina. She glanced at her watch. 'Well, I suppose I'd better go and do some work.'

She entered the lab and smiled at everyone. Michael and Emen were standing next to Cindy Volksmann and George Quinn. They all looked just a little guilty. Possibly she was projecting, but it certainly felt as if they were waiting for her to appear. She knew they would have been able to see her on the security monitors.

'Morning, Nina,' said George. 'You didn't need to come in today. How are you feeling?'

'I'm fine. Had a bit of a rough day yesterday, but I slept very well and I'm raring to go.'

'Great,' said George with his best corporate smile. 'We were just talking about what sort of tests we could run today. We've checked out the system and everything seems to be running to plan.'

'Good,' said Nina. 'Where is the patient?'

'In his office,' said Frank Garfelli. Nina spun on her heel. Garfelli was right behind her. How he had got there she could not imagine. She hadn't seen him when she walked in, hadn't heard the lab door open. He was doing it to spook her, and she was determined not to show she was spooked.

'Good morning, Mr Garfelli,' she said with a broad smile.

'Good morning, Professor. Good to see you back. What was the medical diagnosis of your condition?'

'Food poisoning,' said Nina chirpily. She turned to look at

George. 'Which is weird because I didn't eat anything. Your coffee was the last thing I had, George.' Nina smiled as she spoke. She was having fun.

'Oh, no. I'm really sorry,' said George. 'I had some from the same batch, so did Jason. No ill effects. Maybe it was what you ate for breakfast.'

'Yes, probably,' said Nina. Bored now, she wanted to get on with something. 'So, what's the score with the brother?'

'He's great. He's sending us bulk data and everything is on line,' said Del Papa as speedily as usual. 'As long as he stays in the building, we can record everything he does.'

'And what about sending signals, have you tried that?' asked Nina, trying to bury the weight of the question by looking as if she were very busy, taking her coat off, switching on her laptop and picking up her white lab coat in quick succession.

'No, no, we haven't tried that,' said Emen Trouville. 'We wanted to wait till you got back before we tried, you know, to transmit.'

'Yeah, sure, we didn't try transmitting yet. As leader of the team, you should be here for the first transmission. We all agreed that, didn't we, guys?' said Del Papa, looking around the small group. 'Like we really discussed it this morning, not thinking you were coming in, due to you being kinda sick.'

'Sure, that's right, Michael,' said George.

'We're basically waiting on your input, Nina,' added Cindy.

They were nervous, they really were. Nina was feeling better and better.

'Good idea,' she said. 'It's a leap in the dark. We've no idea what will happen, so it should be very interesting.'

'What could possibly go wrong?' asked Cindy.

Nina turned and smiled at her. She shrugged. 'I've no idea, Cindy. Anything. A major nervous breakdown, or he could go stark raving mad, although with Jason that could be hard to judge based on previous behaviour.'

'You think it could be that serious?' asked George. 'This is what we were discussing before you came in.'

'Oh, right,' said Nina, as if she had just understood something. 'Well, no, I don't think so, but then, as we've never done it before, we really don't know. I suggest we run a simple test under controlled circumstances. If we find a bit of low-level data from when Pete was sleeping, and play that back while one of us is holding a conversation with Jason, we could see what happens.'

'Sure, yeah, great idea,' said Del Papa. 'At least we know Van Missen wasn't beating some poor criminal half to death while he was asleep.'

Nina smiled at Michael. In the world of loose cannons, Del Papa could always be relied on.

25

Jason was sitting in his office, eyes glued to his forty-four-inch LCD, on line as always. He applied more and more nicotine patches to his upper left arm, his desk littered with their thick plastic wrappers. He was scouring the Net for news leaks about Nash Systems and the incident involving him and the Greek boys. The chat groups were full of speculation but no concrete information. It was speculation city, as if the global scientific community knew that something was going on, could smell it, but couldn't get to the end source.

There had also been much fevered interest in Sir Brian Coventon's evidence to the House of Commons ethics committee. Jason scratched as he read them, and kept reaching for where his cigars normally lay. There was nothing there. It seemed Sir Brian was claiming he had been brought down by bodies outside the financial and academic communities. Jason loved it. The old man had probably stepped on too many toes and the nasty boys at MI5 had pulled the plug. He didn't know, of course, but it was fun to speculate. He left a couple of cryptic messages to that end on a chat forum that was raging about the once popular scientist.

He read on as he pressed the auto-dial on his land-line. He slipped on the hands-free unit and waited as the phone rang for what seemed an age.

'Good morning, King Charles Hotel, Cookham.'

'Hi, Harriet, it's Jason. Is Mum there?'

'Good morning, Jason. I'll put you through.'

The old biddy was still on reception. Jason smiled. He couldn't remember anyone else ever doing the job. She must be getting on for ninety.

He checked his screen. The idle ramblings of hapless nerds were getting a little close for comfort. It was only a matter of time before his piece of the jigsaw was fitted into the picture. More and more accusing fingers were being pointed at Nash Systems, and by default at the ex-CEO of airline-food.com, a site which had once featured heavily on www.worlds-dumbest-websites.org.

'Hello, darling, where are you? I've been worried sick!' said his mother suddenly.

'Sure, sure. Sorry I haven't got back to you. Been a bit busy.' Jason had blocked all calls from his mother for three days. He didn't need the hassle. 'I'm at work, Mum, where I should be.'

'I thought you might be in prison. I told your father, but he's so busy he didn't want to hear. The lovely new people you got for him, that was so kind, darling.'

'Sure, sure. How are they getting on?'

'Oh, they seemed so nice but they've gone. Your father's arm is still in a sling but he started shouting at them, you know how he is. I don't know. So how are you, darling?'

'I'm fine, Mum. The papers got it all wrong.'

Jason had surmised from the very short messages that she'd left that she had finally heard about the Van Missen incident.

'Oh, thank heavens for that. I said to Vera that it was rubbish. She brought the cutting round. I don't read the *Guardian*.'

'Sure, sure. No. It's all fine, it was just a little incident, but because I'm deputy CEO of a major global company, you know, the snoops get interested. How's the car, Mum?'

'The car, oh, it's fine, darling. Very nice. And thank you for all the petrol.'

'Not a problem,' said Jason. He'd stumbled on another chat room as he was speaking. He read as she talked to him.

'I said to Vera that you were a businessman and she said her son, you remember, Richard, he was in the year below you in school . . .'

'Sure, sure,' said Jason. He could recall no one from school, let alone someone called Richard. He was busy scrolling through reams of postings.

'She said he'd seen you on the Internet, in some dreadful pornography thing. I've got no idea what he was talking about and I'm sure I don't want to know. Why he'd want to look at that sort of thing says a lot about him. Anyway, I said it was rubbish.'

'It's amazing what people will say when you start to be seriously successful,' said Jason. 'But Mum, how's the bookings for the weekend?'

'This weekend?'

'Sure, sure. I'd like to come and stay if that's poss. I'd like to bring someone with me. I really want you to meet them.'

'Oh, wonderful, darling. I'm sure we can find room. That sounds heavenly.'

'Great. Look, I've got to go. Meetings, and top-level corporate decisions need to be made.'

'Goodness, what a life you have.'

'Sure, sure. We'll come up Friday evening. I'll bell you when we're on our way.'

'It'll be so nice to see you. It's been ages.'

'Sure, sure. Sorry, Mum. Got to go.'

'Bye, darling.'

He terminated the connection, pulled off the headset and moved himself closer to the screen. He'd found something.

A rather enterprising nethead who claimed to be in New York had picked up the story about Jason and Van Missen and the assault on two low-life drug dealers in London. He was adding two and two and unfortunately getting close to four.

Jason started typing furiously. He had taken on the job of flooding the chat rooms with heavy-duty scent-thrower.

Jason Nash was attacked by members of a CIA hit squad fearful of powerful new computer technology that would allow members of public easy access to most secret CIA files.

He wrote under the pseudonym maxmaxdorf. He sat back and watched the response. It was rapid and dizzying in its stupidity. He replied to his own posting.

> jason nash is claiming that the cia are trying to kill him because he knows too much. more like they're trying to kill him koz he knows too little. i've worked with him. he's dumber than he looks.

This insert carried the name she_bitch_queen/88. He smiled as he saw other people in the chat room respond and start to spin off into ever more weird and unlikely hypotheses.

Jason fidgeted in his chair as he read, then started typing again.

> I know for a fact that jason nash is making killer cyborgs in an underground factory in scotland. he's obsessed with the terminator movie and he's perfected the design of the death chip. he's a sick genius, in fact he's not a he, he's an it. it can't be bargained with. it can't be reasoned with. it doesn't feel pity, or remorse, or fear. and it absolutely WILL NOT STOP!

He laughed again as the responses to this absurdity flooded in from around the globe. He stretched his arms above his head, checked the time on the monitor, and yawned. He felt very tired, which didn't make sense as he'd slept much better than normal the previous night. He'd woken up feeling amazing, breathed in deeply and felt his lungs expand with none of the tight pain he normally experienced before he lit up the first cigar of the day. He rolled his head around. His neck felt stiff and he rubbed it. The sleepy feeling wouldn't go away. His body felt heavy and fuzzy.

'Jason, there you are,' said his sister. She was right behind him, bending over and looking him right in the eye.

'Morning, sis. You look one hell of a lot better.'

'Thank you. How are you feeling, husband to be?'

'Never better. Bit sleepy, but that's probably the effect all this

231

bloody healthy living is having on me. I even ate some of that rabbit food you eat for breakfast.'

'You had muesli!' said Nina with that annoying screech she sometimes came up with.

'Yes, I ate bloody measly, with yoghurt and freshly cut-up bits of actual fruit.'

'Actual fruit.'

'Sure, sure. I mean, I have to allow Amy some kudos here, she knew where to source fruit. You know me – the whole fresh fruit thing has always been a bit of a mystery.'

'It's great, Jason. I thought about you last night and I didn't come out in a rash,' said Nina. She smiled at him as though she actually meant it. She looked healthier than she'd looked in a long while. 'I'm really pleased for you and Amy. She's just right for you.'

'What, meaning she's an airhead who lets me do what the fuck I like?'

'No, I don't mean that at all.'

'Oh, right,' said Jason, slightly surprised. 'Well, she is a bit of an airhead, but such a well-meaning one, and she does let me do what I like within the bedroom scenario, which I know is an area you don't wish to download.'

'No thank you,' said Nina.

'But she's really good, and I think it'll really help me if I settle down now, stop trying to play the field and just bunk up with one very extra-special lady.'

'Good. Now, Jase, I want to ask you a favour.'

Jason felt a yawn coming on. He rubbed his eyes. It was ludicrous how sleepy he felt.

'I donate my entire run time to you, sister supreme.'

'Well, I'm trying to decode all the data we've got and it's proving very difficult. We need some simple behavioural responses from someone outside the test group, so I'd like to run a few tests with you.'

'Oh, wow. Do I have to sit in a room and get electric shocks if I get a hard-on when you show me great swathes of adult images?'

'No, for goodness' sake.'

'Pity.'

'It's very simple, just a series of simple tasks on a computer that we'll calibrate and use as a basic rate indicator. We've all been doing it. We just need more samples.'

'I'll do it,' he said, adopting the odd, slightly Scottish accent recognisable only to those who had played the computer game Myth II Soulblighter for rather too long.

Jason followed Nina downstairs, past Amy.

'I'm going to be a guinea-pig,' he said to her as he passed.

'Oh, what are they going to do to you?' asked Amy.

'I think they're going to do some weird experiment that shrinks my penis and turns me into a zombie flesh-eater.'

'Oh, no. I hope not,' said Amy without much thought – she was taking calls – and she returned to her work.

Michael and Emen were in the lab setting up a little iMac on a steel table when Jason entered.

'Computer games. I love 'em,' said Jason, sitting on a stool in front of the computer. 'Okay, what do I do?'

'It's fairly straightforward,' said Del Papa. 'You look at the screen, and every time you see the blue circle cover the red one, you press the mouse button once. If the red one goes over the blue one, you press it twice.'

'Doh,' said Jason.

'Are you comfortable?' asked Emen.

'As I'll ever be,' replied Jason, moving his head in a circle. His neck still felt very stiff and he was still sleepy. He stared at the screen. A blue circle appeared. He pressed the mouse button twice.

'We haven't started yet,' said Nina.

'Oh, right, I was jumping ahead. I assumed because the blue appeared first the red one would naturally appear over it, hence the two mouse clicks.'

'He's good,' said Michael.

'Okay, we're starting now, Jason,' said Nina. He glanced around at her. She was sitting at her bench with a huge bunch of computer equipment before her. The bar graph on that showed Van Missen's nerve data was streaming across the plasma screens at speed.

'Jason, concentrate, please.'

'I'm on it!' said Jason with the same Scottish accent.

'Myth II,' said Emen Trouville, immediately recognising the source.

'Make way for the dwarf,' grunted Jason.

'Incoming!' shouted Emen.

'Yes, sir, right away, sir,' said Del Papa.

'We're moving!' said Emen, trying to re-create the same accent.

'Have you two quite finished?' asked Nina.

'Sorry, Professor,' said Emen. 'It's not often you meet another Myth II aficionado. Such a classic game.'

'They don't make 'em like that any more.'

'Jason, the screen!' snapped Nina.

'Sure, sure.'

Jason looked at the screen. The blue circle appeared again, and a red circle started to slide in from the left. It moved beneath the blue circle and Jason clicked the mouse once. Immediately the circles disappeared and another red circle appeared. Jason felt his eyes go heavy. He screwed them up as a huge wave of tiredness engulfed him.

He suddenly felt himself snap awake and realised that he had actually dozed off, which considering he was in the middle of carrying out tests for the big sister was a little embarrassing.

'Sorry, sorry. I'm okay.'

'It's fine, don't worry,' said Nina. He glanced at her. She would normally have flipped, his falling asleep when he was supposed to be doing something for her. Tantamount to murder in Nina's book.

'Just carry on.'

Jason sat up straight and breathed in. He felt good, wide awake now, clicking the mouse as the circles appeared. They came faster and faster but he had no problem keeping up. He felt his heart rate rise a little, but put it down to nicotine withdrawal. He didn't take his eyes off the screen. The circles were appearing and disappearing at a blinding rate, but he kept up.

'Hey, cool,' said Emen, who was sitting right beside him. 'You must be lethal when you're playing Quake.'

'Deadly,' said Jason, clicking the mouse so fast now it sounded like a deranged cricket.

'That is fast,' said Del Papa from somewhere behind him.

'Okay, Jason, keep going,' said Nina. 'But try and answer these questions while you're doing it. What's your name?'

'Jason John Nash.'

'How old are you?'

'Thirty.'

'Who's your favourite band?'

'Wu Tang Clan.'

'Favourite computer?'

'Quad processor Mac G7.'

'What's the capital of New Zealand?'

'Wellington.'

'How much are Nash Systems shares trading for today?'

'Four thousand five hundred dollars.'

'What did you get for your tenth birthday?'

'Apricot PC with two meg of RAM and a five meg hard drive. No sound, fourteen-inch colour monitor and no printer.'

'Okay. That's enough,' said Nina.

The screen went blank. Jason blinked and let go of the mouse. His body felt rigid with tension. His neck hurt like hell; it was hot and very sore.

'How did I do?' he said as he stood up. He stretched and tried to loosen his neck by rubbing it. Nina walked towards him and grabbed his hands, holding them in front of her.

'You did really well. How d'you feel?'

'Fine. Why? Did I screw up?'

'Believe me, Jason, you did real good,' said Del Papa.

'No, you didn't screw up, you did better than any of us,' said

Nina. She looked at her two scientist colleagues. 'Except Pete. He was pretty good, wasn't he?'

'It would be very hard to beat Van Missen, but you got close,' said Emen.

'Cool,' said Jason. 'So is that it?'

'Yeah, that'll do for now.'

'Okay, because for once I've got my work cut out. I'm spreading misinformation about Nash Systems on the Web. There's a lot of rubbish going around and it takes a true expert to add to it.'

'You're the guy,' said Emen.

26

'Well, it works,' said Nina.

'It sure as hell does,' said George. 'The difference was truly awesome.'

'You could even say frightening,' said Cindy, who along with Frank Garfelli and George had been watching Jason perform on a monitor from one of the offices above the lab. Nina had asked them to keep out of the action and not confuse the patient.

'I used three phases,' said Nina. 'At the start I used nothing, that was just Jason with no input. Then I transmitted the sequence we had from when Van Missen was asleep, and you saw what happened.'

'That was amazing. It was like we'd given him knock-out drops,' said Emen.

'Then I just used a clump of data that we recorded when Pete did the same test. I had no idea what would happen, but as you saw, it seems to have worked rather well.'

'How many tasks did he perform?' asked George.

Emen checked a screen. 'Looks like over three hundred and fifty in, like, one and a half minutes. It was incredible.'

'And you don't think he would normally be able to achieve that kind of score?' asked George.

Nina smiled. 'Admittedly, you are looking at an individual who wasted an enormous amount of his youth playing complex computer games, but his pre-test score would be in the low two hundreds.'

'And did he make any errors?'

'Not one,' said Nina. 'The program stops running the minute you make a mistake.'

'Wow,' said George. 'This is incredible. This is the proof we need. And what's even more amazing is that he doesn't seem to have a clue what's happening.'

'I know,' said Nina. She was feeling more and more guilty about what they were doing. 'Did you see the way he rubbed his neck after we'd finished?'

'Yeah. Well done for stopping him,' said Cindy.

'I'm very worried about that aspect. He is clearly feeling some discomfort there. There's no obvious sign from outside, but there could be a minor infection around the chip. I think maybe we should take it out, just to be safe. There's no way of asking him about it.'

Nina noticed Frank Garfelli looking at the others. She wasn't sure why he was there; he certainly had no need to be from a technical standpoint. She resented it, and was constantly reminded of Pete's absence by his presence.

'I think we should leave it in for the time being,' he said.

'And why is that?' snapped Nina. She hadn't wanted to show her resentment so obviously, but she couldn't help it. Garfelli put his hands up in mock surrender. Everything he did was annoying.

'Okay, I admit I'm new on the scene and all, but it looks to me that we are in a vital stage of development here. I think to engineer a chip removal now would be very counterproductive.'

'Frank's right, Nina,' said Del Papa.

Nina looked at him. They were all in it, no doubt about that. But quite what they were all 'in' was not clear.

'I'm not happy about it,' she said. 'We still only have the vaguest idea of what happened to Pete. It's such a new area it would have been very easy for the medical team in America to have missed something.'

'I think they're up to speed,' said Garfelli flatly. 'I say we leave the chip in over the weekend.'

'Why over the weekend?' asked Nina.

'What do you think, Michael?' said George after a short silence.

'Well, we know that Pete had the chip in for twelve days before we had a problem,' said Del Papa. 'Jason has only had the chip in for three days. I feel confident we are not putting him at risk, although obviously, Professor, I quite understand your concern.'

'Another problem we have,' said Frank, 'is that Mr Turnpike is in Virginia at the moment. He's actually checking up on Van Missen.'

'Very convenient,' said Nina.

'Why do you say that?' asked Frank.

'You tell me.'

'I'm sorry, I'm not with you.' Frank looked at her blankly.

'Well, here I am, with my reputation on the line, a piece of untried technology buried in my brother's neck, and by chance the only surgeon on earth who we can ask to remove it is in America.'

'I don't think this can be described as a conspiracy, Nina. It's just the way things are,' said Frank. 'We don't have Roger Turnpike under contract. He's a freelance surgeon – he goes where the work is.'

'Okay,' said Nina, clasping her hands together tightly. 'We'll wait until after the weekend, but can we get Turnpike back by then?'

'I'll make sure we can,' said George.

27

'Are you ready to go?' asked Amy. She had come up to Jason's office without him noticing. It was hardly surprising – he was playing a Wu Tang Clan MP3 at full volume over his headphones as he typed into chat rooms like a man possessed.

'Amy, sweet precious dumpling lady. What a lovely surprise,' he said, pulling the headphones down. 'What are you doing up here?'

'I've been waiting for you.'

'Have you?' He glanced at the clock on his screen – 7.30, and he had promised his mother he'd get there that evening. 'Shit oh Lord,' he said. 'We're late.' He looked out of the window. 'Blimey, it's dark. We have to go.'

'I know, silly,' said Amy.

'Okay, have you got everything?'

'Yes. I've been waiting since six. Everyone else has gone home.'

'What a bunch of slackers,' he said as he frantically closed down programs and prepared to go off line. 'I've turned the whole gossip shop around up here. It's been an amazing day. I think I've posted something like four hundred messages and the results have been great.'

'I won't pretend to know what you're talking about.'

'I'll tell you in the car,' he said as the computer shut down. He stood up and found himself needing to stretch again. He rolled his head around – his neck was still feeling very stiff.

'God, I feel good,' he said as he embraced her, grabbing her arse immediately.

'Jason, not now, we're not married. What will people think?'

He smiled, held her face in his hands and kissed her.

'I love you,' he said. He felt his heart skip a beat. This really was very different. He'd certainly never said that to a lady before, and now he knew why it was seen as such a special thing. He felt amazing, warm and secure and sure of himself.

'I love you too,' she said. She kissed him and they stood together in silence, another thing he'd never done before. Always in the past, if he was getting passionate with a lady, it was straight down to adult activities or straight out on the town. With Amy he was amazed at how good it felt to do nothing, just to hold her small body in his arms.

He breathed in deeply. His lungs didn't hurt; they felt huge and healthy.

'Not one cigar, not one cigarette, and look at the time. I've done over twenty-four hours without a smoke.'

'You deserve a reward,' she said with a wicked glint in her eye.

'Oh, yes. The Nash is pleased to hear that,' he said, feeling himself stiffen in the trouser area. 'But let's wait until we're at the hotel. I've asked my mum to save us a room. If we get one of the posh ones they have four-poster beds. I could tie you up and fuck you.'

'Oh God, Jason. Would you?'

'You'd like that, huh?'

'Yes,' she said as she melted once again in his arms. 'I want you to do all that stuff to me. I love it.'

He shook his head and smiled as he held her. She was an angel, his special lady, someone who not only understood the needs of her man, but positively enjoyed them. She was a cyberbabe, a virtual whore – do anything to her and she still loves you. He could not believe his luck.

Jason felt better still as he gave the Mercedes its head and let the engine rip the car along at high speed down the M11. All was quiet in the passenger compartment – Amy had begged him to keep the noise down as she wanted to have a nap before meeting his parents. She wanted to look her best. He glanced at her every now and then. She looked beautiful, lying back on the large beige seat. He didn't want to be anywhere else. This was good. This was the best.

He arrived in the cramped carpark of the King Charles Hotel at ten, and drove very slowly and carefully through the rows of parked cars until he found a space near the back of the kitchens. He managed to park next to his mother's new Audi, the one he had bought her, without scratching it. The little warning sensors pinged gently as he manoeuvred.

'We're here, darling,' he said softly into her ear when the engine had died.

'Okay,' she said, yawning and stretching. 'Let me do my face.'

She pulled down the vanity mirror and he watched her apply a little make-up and lipstick. It was fascinating. He'd seen it before, of course, but he'd never just sat and watched a lady do her essentials. The way her lovely fingers held the eyeliner brush, the wonderful way she pursed and folded her lips as she applied the red lipstick.

She turned and smiled at him. 'How do I look?'

'Incredible. Just perfect.'

They walked arm in arm to the front entrance of the hotel. It was all very familiar to Jason, but he wanted to try to see it through Amy's eyes.

He had to bend down as he entered the busy bar. He glanced at the staff – no one he knew. They changed so often it was rare to find the same people there two visits running.

'It's a lovely old place,' said Amy. 'How long have your parents owned it?'

'For ever,' he said. 'Well, since I was about four. My dad sank everything he had into it. Must be worth a mint now, but he got it for a snip back then. It was a tip when they bought it.' He swept his arm around. 'This is where I grew up,' he said proudly.

'God, you were so lucky. What an amazing place to be when you're a kid. I lived in a tiny flat in London with my mum. I never even dreamed about places like this when I was a little girl.'

'It has its drawbacks,' said Jason. 'Like your mum and dad are always busy. It never stops, there's always something to be done, day or night. I couldn't hack it in the catering industry.'

He led Amy to the hotel reception desk.

'Hello, Jason, how are you?' said Harriet Marshall, the now seriously ancient receptionist. She sat in a tiny cubicle in the hallway, surrounded by big ledgers. Jason had suggested on his previous visit that they might benefit from some IT equipment in their booking system, but it was pretty obvious to anyone that Harriet wasn't about to dive into the hi-tech world with any confidence.

'Good, thanks, Harriet. I'm looking for Mum. I assume Dad's in the kitchen.'

'Yes, he is. We're full up tonight. Very busy weekend ahead of us.'

'Right. I asked Mum if we could have a room. What's available?'

'Ooh dear,' said Harriet slowly. 'I think we're pretty much jam packed, love.' She ran a gnarled finger down a page of her booking ledger, then looked up at him with a nervous grin. 'You'd better go and see your mum.'

'Sure, sure,' said Jason. 'This is Amy, by the way. My fiancée.'

'Oh, goodness me. Nice to meet you,' said Harriet, offering her hand over the counter.

'Nice to meet you too,' said Amy sweetly. Jason looked at her and smiled a soppy smile.

'Harriet, don't say anything to Mum yet. It's a surprise.'

'Don't worry, I'll keep mum, love,' said Harriet with a bright smile.

Holding Amy's hand, Jason led the way into the private quarters at the back of the hotel. He could hear a television on in the sitting room and pushed the door open slowly. He glanced inside. His mother was sitting in her old chair with a book on her lap, fast asleep.

'That's my mum,' he whispered. 'You've got a big advantage

at the moment 'cos she's sleeping. When she wakes up, she's a whole different experience.'

He beckoned Amy out of the room and walked down the corridor towards the hotel kitchen. Even before they got to the door the shouting could be heard. Jason stopped.

'My father's a chef,' he said. 'What that basically means is he's a bad-tempered bully.'

'I'm sure he isn't,' said Amy, looking slightly nervous.

'Hear that?' asked Jason. They stood in silence for a moment as the sound of a pan slamming on a cooker came rattling through the door. 'That means he's in a good mood, because there isn't some young sous-chef running out in tears.'

Jason breathed in deeply and walked into the kitchen. It was a big room, a very hot room, and a very, very noisy room. He felt Amy clinging to his sleeve as they moved past the central cooker and the young sweating men in chefs' white coats who were frantically busy at their labours.

'Hi, Dad, how's it going?'

John Nash was sitting at a low desk which was covered in papers. He was on the phone, one arm in a sling. He held the receiver against his chest for a moment and half turned towards Jason.

'Oh, bloody hell, look what the cat dragged in,' he said. 'Hang on a minute.'

He turned his back on them and continued to shout at the man on the phone. 'Yes, I'm here. Of course I'm bloody here, where else am I going to be! I have to work even if I'm ill. I've got a broken collarbone and I'm here. What's up with you?' He paused for a moment, then said, 'A bloody cold. We all have colds, matey boy. You've dropped us right in it. We've got a party booking for forty, and you decide you've got a bloody cold. Yes, of course you're fired.'

John Nash slammed the phone down and stood up. Jason looked down at his diminutive father and smiled.

'Nice to see you, Dad. How's the collarbone?'

'What the bloody hell do you want?' John said as he walked past Jason and looked in a large pot on the stove. 'Who's looking after this sauce?' he shouted. 'Is it stirring itself? Let me look. No, the spoon isn't moving. How very odd.'

'Sorry, Chef,' said a young and very nervous-looking kitchen hand with close-cropped red hair. He rushed across the kitchen and started stirring the sauce.

'Sorry, Chef. Oh, that's good,' said John, snatching the spoon from the pathetic creature beside him. He put on a wimpy voice. 'I've screwed up the sauce, sorry, Chef. What the bloody use is that, you plonker, Damien?' He tasted the sauce with an enormous steel spoon. 'You are one lucky little rusty-headed plonker. Now keep a bloody eye on it or you can follow William.'

'How's his cold, Chef?'

'I don't give a damn about his cold, he's fired,' said John, seemingly unaware of the fact that the information temporarily froze activity in the kitchen.

A waiter burst through the swing-doors at the far end of the kitchen. 'Three pork specials, two beef, one rare, one cooked to fuck, and I'm still waiting for soup for table thirteen.'

'Where's the bloody soup?' shouted John.

'It's ready,' came a shout from somewhere behind a cloud of steam. Jason moved towards his father again, Amy hanging on his arm.

'Maybe we should leave him to it,' said Amy softly.

Jason ignored her and stood in front of his father by the big cooker.

'Dad, there's someone I want you to meet.'

'Yes. What?' snapped his father.

'Dad, this is Amy, she's my fiancée.'

'What?'

'Amy and I are getting married, Dad.'

For the first time since they'd been in the kitchen, John Nash turned his angry gaze on Amy.

'You're doing what?'

'Getting married. I wanted you and Mum to be the first to know.'

'You, getting married! Ha. Jason, as you may or may not have noticed, I am just a tad busy at the moment.'

'I know. We'll leave you to it. We're staying the weekend.'

'Oh, that's nice for you.'

'I rang Mum and told her.'

'She never tells me anything, you know that.' John glanced at a pile of dirty plates balanced on the end of a steel table. 'Who's left these bloody plates here!'

'Sorry, Chef,' said the red-haired Damien.

'What are you Damien?'

'Plonker, Chef,' said the young man with a smile.

John took a deep breath and turned to Amy. 'How do you do, Amy,' he said, finally offering her his hand. She shook it. 'I'm John Nash, the very unfortunate and hard-done-by father of this lanky plonker.'

'How d'you do,' she said with a smile.

'You'll have to forgive me being a little confused, Amy. I'm just not sure what to make of this information. You look like a relatively intelligent young woman. You're willingly marrying this nutcase, are you?'

'Very willingly, Mr Nash.'

'Well, wonders will clearly never cease. If you can possibly make your way out of the kitchen, though, I may not have a cardiac tonight, then I may be able to do the catering for your wedding.'

'Hey, would you, Dad? That'd be totally cool,' said Jason. He grinned at Amy. 'Dad's a brilliant cook.'

'Go and annoy your mother. I'll see you later.'

'Sure, sure,' said Jason. He smiled and nodded to the kitchen staff, who had been watching the brief meeting with obvious interest.

'Okay, everybody, back to work!' shouted his father as they left the kitchen.

'He liked you!' said Jason. 'I can't believe it. He spoke to you, and he liked you. This is in the realms of the historic.'

'He seems really nice,' said Amy.

'Oh, yeah, he's a really really sensitive guy, like an alligator. But he liked you. Well done, sweet fuck cushion.' Jason kissed her passionately on the lips.

'Oh, goodness me,' said his mother. Jason broke off the kiss abruptly and looked around. His mother was standing in the corridor outside their sitting room, cup and saucer in hand.

'Hi, Mum. You've woken up!'

'I haven't been asleep, have I?'

'Yeah. We put our heads around the door just now. You were out like a baby. We didn't want to wake you.'

'That's very sweet of you, dear.' She walked up to him and kissed him lightly on the cheek. 'It's so nice to see you, darling. It's been months. You look very well.'

'I am very well,' said Jason.

He noticed that his mother had still not looked at Amy directly. He had to do something fast.

'Mum, this is Amy.'

'Hello,' she said with a tight smile. 'I've just got to pop this in the kitchen. I'll be with you in a minute.'

She walked off down the corridor. Jason looked at Amy with a grimace. 'She'll thaw. You watch the Nash at work.'

They entered the sitting room. Jason turned off the TV and they sat together on the sofa, Jason feeling slightly too teenaged for comfort.

'That was a classic moment, being caught snogging by your mum,' he said. 'Took me right back.'

'This is a lovely room,' commented Amy, looking around, sitting very still and clearly quite nervous.

'Sure, sure. Save it for the mother,' he said. He heard a creak from outside the door. 'Here she comes. Batten down.'

Jason turned around and saw his mother standing at the door.

'Hey, Mum, I've got some really important news to tell you.'

'Have you, dear? That's nice,' she said. She hadn't moved from the door.

'Aren't you going to come in and meet Amy?'

'Well, I should be helping your father. He's rushed off his feet as always.'

'Mum, please,' said Jason, standing up. 'This is really important to me. Come into the bloody room, for God's sake. You're hanging around the door like a visitor.'

Val Nash walked into the room with a very tight smile on her face, a smile that she had worn a great deal, judging by the deeply etched lines around it. She glanced at Amy.

'Hello, dear, I'm Val.'

'It's lovely to meet you,' said Amy, who was still sitting on the sofa.

'Mum, Amy and I have decided to get married.'

'Oh dear. Are you sure, dear? This is all rather sudden, isn't it? Don't you think you should think about it for a while?'

Jason laughed very loudly. 'That is totally classic, Mum. We come all the way here to tell you the great news, and there's me in my usual dream world thinking you and Dad would say, you know, kind of, "Congratulations" and "We're so happy for you, darling", and you do a number about not rushing into things.'

'Well, I know what you're like, darling,' she said, her smile even tighter than usual. She turned to Amy. 'I'm sorry, Amy, you must think me terribly rude.'

'Not at all, Mrs Nash.'

'It's just that Jason has always been so kind to people, and looked after them, and I worry that people will abuse his generosity.'

'Mum!' said Jason. 'Are you saying Amy is some kind of gold-digger?'

'Not at all, darling,' said his mother, putting her hand over her mouth in mock horror. 'I'm sure she's a very nice girl.'

'She's a lady, Mum. A really proper lady and I love her.'

'Goodness,' said Val Nash. She clearly didn't know where to

look. 'Well, this has all come as a bit of a surprise. Are you going to stay?'

'Sure, sure. Which room can we have?'

'Oh.' Val stood frozen to the spot. 'You want a hotel room.'

'That would be cool, yes. The King Charles suite?'

'Oh, sorry, dear. All the rooms are booked. We're packed solid the whole weekend.'

'Mum!' wailed Jason.

'Sorry, dear. I thought you'd just be staying in your room.'

'Mum, it's only got a single bed in it.'

'Well, can't Amy sleep in Nina's old room?'

'Mum, we're two fully grown adults. We're about to enter fully legit status through the whole marriage shebang.'

'Oh dear, this is all very difficult.'

Jason paced around the room. He glanced at Amy, who was sitting very forlornly on the sofa. The whole thing had somehow gone wrong again, after all the effort he'd been making to get things right.

'Look, Mum, leave it with me. You go and help Dad and I'll sort out the sleeping arrangements. Okay? It's all fine. I'll source another mattress and we'll hunker down with no problem.'

'Oh, you are a good lad,' his mother said, scooting towards the door. 'You know where everything is, don't you.'

'Sure, sure. We'll see you when things have calmed down a bit.'

His mother left. He heard her almost pelt down the corridor. He shook his head and looked at Amy.

'Never easy with the old folks, is it? I feel like getting in the fucking car and driving home. What a total fuck-up!'

'Oh, I feel so sorry for your mum. She's obviously upset. She just cares about you, Jason. It's only natural she's going to be put out.'

'Is it? Why? I thought she'd be totally pleased.'

'Jason, she's your mum. You're her only son, you're obviously really special to her.'

'Tell me about it.'

'Well, silly,' she said, 'give her a bit of time. She'll come round to the idea.'

Amy stood up, put her arms around Jason and looked up at him. 'Anyway, none of it matters. We love each other, that's what's important. My mum is going to freak when she finds out. We've got to go and see her next.'

'I bet she won't be as rude as my bloody awful parents.'

Amy was silent for a moment. She kissed him lightly. 'No, she probably won't, but she'll be ever so upset. I know she will.'

Jason sighed. 'Christ, I need a fag. I'm really worked up.'

'Let's go up to your room. Have you still got your teddy?'

'My teddy! No, I don't think so.'

'Oh, that's a shame. I'd love to have seen your stuff from when you were little.'

'Sure, sure. There's some old stuff stashed away in cupboards probably. I blew my teddy up when I was about twelve.'

'Blew him up!'

'Yeah. I strapped a load of bangers to him, out in the greenhouse, you know, around November the fifth and all that. Blew the poor thing to bits. Smashed a lot of glass in the greenhouse too. Got a right thrashing for that from the old bully.'

'Oh, you poor thing,' said Amy. 'My parents never hit me.'

'You didn't blow up your teddy, though, did you,' said Jason. He held her hand and led her out of the sitting room. 'Let's go and make our bed up. Actually, come to think of it, it's quite kinky. I've never shagged in my old bedroom before. Dreamed about it often enough, but never actually did it in there.'

'Then it's time we blessed it,' said Amy with a cheeky grin.

28

'Hi, Nina, I know you won't pick up, but I just wanted to say I hope you're okay. I've heard you've had a bit of trouble with your brother. I hope everything's oka . . .'

'Hello, Brian.'

'Oh, you're there!'

'Yes, I'm here.' Nina sat down on her sofa, she'd just finished vacuuming the house. She hadn't actually heard the phone ring; it was only as the powerful electric motor died down that she caught the sound of the voice on the answer machine. Nina had an industrial vacuum cleaner, a great big stainless-steel affair with five times the suction of a normal domestic machine. The house was beyond immaculate – it was surgically clean.

She hadn't reacted overly strongly to hearing Sir Brian's voice, although he hadn't rung her for a long time. She had stared at the phone as he spoke – his voice was familiar and reassuring. She pondered for a moment as to why she would want something familiar and reassuring; the answer was pretty obvious. She was feeling extremely insecure about everything that was taking place at Nash Systems.

'How are you?' she asked.

'As well as can be expected,' he said. 'It's been a pretty grim few weeks, I have to say.'

'I've not really followed things. Jason has. He seems to know all about what's been going on.'

'Does he now.'

'Why do you say that?'

'Well, I have an uncomfortable feeling Nash Systems had a role to play in the whole thing.'

'Oh, don't be so silly,' snapped Nina. Whenever Sir Brian whined like a little boy it immediately annoyed her. Then she felt odd, suddenly realising the reaction as being typical of her mother.

'Sorry.' She didn't like apologising either. She breathed deeply. 'Look, Brian, the only connection between the two companies is me. I know what we're doing, and it's very different from Coventon's, let me tell you. All the money is coming in from America. We're not getting any funding from the UK government.'

'Not directly. No, of course not.'

'What are you implying?'

'Look, I didn't call you to talk about this, and anyway, I'm not going to talk about it over the phone.'

'Why did you call me, then?' asked Nina. She felt like putting the phone down.

'I just wanted to talk, to try and explain my side of things and beg you to explain why you did what you did.'

'I got tired of the whole thing, Brian. I woke up. I thought I loved you, I thought one day you'd leave your wife and live with me, even though you told me that would never happen. You knew I would live in some sort of pathetic hope and you took advantage of that. I'm as mad at myself as I am with you. That's how stupid I was.'

'You're not stupid.'

'Oh, come on. I had to be a fool to believe all that.'

'Irene has left me.'

There was a long silence. Nina said nothing. She felt a smile creep across her face.

'She found out about you and she threw me out. I live in my London flat now. I'm an old divorcee with nothing to live for, my company's in the hands of the receivers, everything has gone. Most of my old friends and colleagues express concern but it's pretty obvious they feel uncomfortable in my presence. I'm not going to lie to you by saying you're top of my list of people to call to try and talk things through. I've hit rock bottom, Nina. I have nothing left.'

Nina sat down on the sofa and thought for a moment. If this had happened six months before, she would have gone running to him. But everything had changed, and she started thinking about Pete Van Missen. Whatever hadn't happened on the surface, she knew something had happened somewhere. 'I'm sorry.'

'Have you met someone else?' he asked plaintively.

Nina smiled. He was approaching sixty and he was still a little boy. 'I don't want to be your lover any more, Brian, whatever happens. I don't want to be your new wife either. But I do need to talk to you. Come up to Cambridge.'

'I'm on my way.'

He hung up, which really wasn't like him. She had always been the one who had hung up, with him always whispering how much he loved her. She put the phone down on the couch beside her, then jumped as the door buzzer sounded. He must have been outside all along. She didn't like it, she needed time to prepare. She felt angry to have been duped in this way.

She got up and walked to the entryphone.

'You creep,' she shouted.

'Oh, um, hello, is that Nina?' said a voice than clearly wasn't Sir Brian.

'Who's this?' demanded Nina.

'It's Hugo. Have I come at a bad time?'

'Hugo!' The arrangements flooded back. 'Oh, blimey. Sorry, come in,' said Nina. She pressed the button and heard the door open. She looked down the stairwell as Hugo lumbered through the door carrying a large bag and a laptop in a carry-case. He glanced up at her.

'Morning, Professor,' he said with a smile.

'I'm really sorry about that. I thought you were Sir Brian.'

'Oh, right. He's due, then, is he?'

'Well, sort of. Come on up.'

Nina put the phone back in its charger and checked the room as Hugo clambered up the stairs.

'I haven't heard from him in weeks,' she said as Hugo dropped his bags on the parquet floor. They looked a little untidy, but she could sort that out later. 'He's just rung. He wants to talk.'

'Oh, right,' said Hugo. He was standing awkwardly.

'Sorry, can I get you something – a coffee?'

'That would be very nice, Nina. Thank you. I came by train so it's been a bit of a schlep.'

'Oh, you poor thing.'

Nina went into the kitchen and put the kettle on. She still wasn't used to people in her house.

'Nice place,' said Hugo.

'Please, sit down,' she shouted over her shoulder. 'Sugar?'

'No thanks. Black with none for me.'

'Fine. And how are you?'

'Well, a little confused. A little in the dark. Hearing all sorts of nonsense about Nash Systems and not knowing what to believe.'

'Okay, let me get you up to speed,' said Nina as she filled the cafetière. 'Something very ugly is going on and I don't know what it is.'

'Ugly?'

'Yes. I was approached through my brother, as you know, and I met a group of scientists, including Michael Del Papa.'

'I'd heard he was working with you. What's he like?'

'Very nice. Incredibly experienced, never gives up, but that's become so unimportant. As a company, Nash Systems must have got through millions of dollars in the last three months. I mean many millions, perhaps even hundreds, and we haven't created any income. There seem to be limitless funds. I told you about the Sands chip fabricator – that's in the region of seven million dollars alone. But we've got electron microscopes, more computers than I've ever seen before, surgeons that turn up in Rolls-Royces – unlimited resources basically.'

'But that's good, isn't it?' said Hugo as they moved into Nina's sitting room. 'It sounds brilliant. I can't wait to start.'

She sat opposite him on a hard chair. He was so uninvolved in the whole business, so charming and innocent. Having Hugo to talk to was much better than she'd dared expect.

'Okay, here's where we are at the moment. My brother has a chip implanted in his neck at . . .'

'His neck! What's it doing in his neck?'

'Well, there's very a good reason. Just the sheer mass of electronic data that is shooting up and down the spinal cord, thousands of times more than in the arm.'

'Yeah, but the neck, Nina. Jesus.'

'Listen, we've been getting incredible data from both the neck implants we've used.'

'Wait! There's someone else with a neck implant?'

'Yes, Pete Van Missen.'

'My God, what have you been doing?'

'He's the one that beat up the two criminals in London. Anyway . . .'

'Wait. Wait a minute, Nina. He's the one that beat up the two criminals in London. You said that so easily, like it was nothing.'

'Did I? Sorry, of course it's a massive . . .'

'I mean, let's get real here. You've planted a chip in some man's neck and then he beats up two people. Do you think there just might be a connection here?'

'No, of course not,' snapped Nina. 'His chip was a record-only device.'

'Record-only. Okay. So, you've now got a recording of nerve impulses during an act of violence. Very useful,' said Hugo.

'I know, I've been through it thousands of times, believe me. It's so complicated.'

'Really,' said Hugo with a dash of rich irony. 'You don't say.'

'The other day our new head of security, Frank Garfelli, tried to beat Jason up.'

Nina sat in silence for a moment as the haze she'd been living in started to lift. The problem was that this haze she had been existing in was a very comfortable and well-paid one. What was revealed when it started to lift was very unpleasant.

'And I was sick, laid up with food poisoning. But I hadn't eaten anything. It's bloody obvious now – they wanted me out of the way. George must have spiked my coffee.'

'Okay, overload, overload. Who the hell is George, who is Frank Garibaldi?'

'Garfelli. Ex-military security guy. Not very nice.'

'Okay, ex-military, okay, I'll deal with that later, but why did he beat up Jason?'

'No, he didn't beat him up . . .'

'But you said . . .'

'He tried to, but Jason, who is crap at fighting – even I used to win fights when we were kids – Jason fought him off, with, judging from what Amy said, a high degree of skill.'

'Amy?'

'Company secretary, Jason's fiancée.'

'Okay, so what we have is a company which is developing chip insert technology of a very sophisticated type, with no supervision from any government body, and it seems that some of the people in control are American.'

'More or less all of them. Only administrative staff are from here. They're hiring people very fast, and moving to a huge new set-up the other side of Cambridge, from what Jason tells me.'

'Okay, so what you're saying is, even though you are right at the centre of the whole thing, you think work is going on there that you are not party to and have no control over.'

'Yes. I think that's what I'm saying,' said Nina.

'But you have nothing to go on. I mean, you've had a recording chip in the neck of a bloke who beat up two people. Now you have a recording chip in your brother's neck.'

'No, it's a transponder chip. It can send and receive signals.'

256

'What? You can send pre-recorded nerve impulse signals into the human central nervous system?'

'Yes, very successfully. We did it yesterday.'

'Jesus, Nina!'

'What?'

'Well, this is heavy stuff you're telling me. I mean, if what you're telling me is true, and this sort of stuff fell into the wrong hands . . . It's just world-changing.'

'I know. It is true and it is amazing. Listen, Jason did a controlled test – you know, the blue–red circle test we run on a Mac. He scored up to ten times higher when we played back a recording of Van Missen doing the same test. This is why I need you. At the moment the only way we can tell what the recordings mean is to use the time code. We knew when Van Missen did the test, so I just extracted that data and played it to Jason. Same with sleep. I copied a bit of data from Van Missen's sleep period, clicked "go" and Jason fell asleep instantly. As soon as I started playing the section where he had been doing the test Jason woke up and performed with in-credible speed.'

'So you're telling me it works.'

'Yes. It works very well.'

'And what are the side effects?'

'Well, Van Missen, the first patient we put a chip in, is paralysed.'

Hugo flopped back into the sofa, nursing his cup of coffee on his chest.

'I really don't think I want to hear any more,' he said. 'I'm feeling very depressed already and I was happy a moment ago.'

'Why?' asked Nina. Her head was spinning. She needed Hugo to help her work it all out.

'I've just jacked in a really steady, plodding job at Birmingham Uni to come and join an exciting new company in Cambridge for five times the money. I want to live here, my family live here, I know people and I feel at home here. It's all looking very good. And what do I find out when I get here? Nash Systems is a bloody front for the CIA or something. It's packed full of nutters and unstable people with chips buried in their spinal cords that tend to paralyse them for no apparent reason.'

'I know why Van Missen was paralysed. I'm not allowed to tell you, but I know. It wasn't just the chip, that much I can tell you.'

'Oh, make it worse, why don't you,' said Hugo. Now he buried his face in his hands. 'You can't tell me.'

'It's a need-to-know thing.'

'What is?'

'The information about Van Missen's paralysis. He's in a hospital in Virginia.'

'Oh, that's fine, then.'

'Look, I've been worried sick about all this. Don't try and make it sound like I don't care. That's why I need you. I need help, I need to work out the meaning of all this information I've recorded so I can fight back. Yes, it looks like they played back the recording of the fight that Van Missen had into Jason's chip while I was busy throwing up here. It seems to have worked. Jason seems to have turned into an instant SAS killer or something, so obviously they're doing something for the military using me. But that doesn't mean what I've discovered is invalid. GPS navigation, computers, satellite communications, Velcro, the blasted Internet – all of them were developed by the military in the first place. Doesn't make them not worth using. Yes, they are doing things behind my back, but I am really the only person who knows how to make these things work. They are very reliant on me. The only thing I can't do is crunch the fucking data, Hugo. That's why I need you to start work really bloody fast.'

'You're fucking mad, Nina. You know that, don't you? God, I have been such a bloody idiot.'

'You haven't. I need you here.'

'Look, ninety per cent of the reason I wanted to work here was because I'd be near you. Not that I'd expect you to be aware of it, but I have . . . well, fancied is such a crap word, but I have. Okay? I thought this might be a chance to get to know you better.' He laughed and looked up at Nina's ceiling. 'What a pillock.'

Nina felt uncomfortable. She had spent years with Hugo in the laboratory at Coventon's. It had never occurred to her that his dislike of Sir Brian was based on anything other than professional jealousy.

'Oh,' she said. 'You're right. I didn't know.'

'Well, there's no harm in telling you now,' said Hugo, standing up. 'Because there is no way on earth I am setting foot inside that research facility, no matter how much I'd be paid.'

'Hugo, what is it?' asked Nina. He really did look as if he meant it. He picked up his computer bag. 'Where are you going?'

'I'm going to my parents' house, where I'll ring my boss at Birmingham and beg for my dull old research post back.'

'Hugo, please. I need you.'

'Nina, you need a lot more than me. You need a team of top-flight therapists, and probably a private army to get you out of this one. What the fuck could I do to help?'

'Nina stood. She felt an incredible need to keep Hugo involved. 'I have forty petabytes of raw data which means fuck-all without someone we can trust to crunch it.'

'Forty petabytes,' said Hugo, his mouth hanging open, which made him look stupid.

'And counting.'

'Where's it all come from?'

'From Jason, and Van Missen. That's the quantity we've been getting. It's vast, Hugo. Listen to me. It's the raw code for the human operating system.'

Hugo stared at her with a look of genuine horror on his face. 'Nina, that is insane.'

She frowned and shook her head. 'No, it's not. I've seen it. We've had to buy racks and racks of servers and hard disks, hundreds of them, just to store it. We need someone who can handle that much code. You can't go all woosie on me now, you can't back out. This is truly groundbreaking, Hugo. We could understand what makes people do anything, what their true motivations are. We could treat depression, we could make the blind see . . .'

'Nina!'

She couldn't hear him. She was looking at him, her salvation, but she couldn't hear what he was saying, so convinced was she that she was right. If only she could tell him.

'We could do all the things Sir Brian droned on about, cure so many disorders, learn so much. Please, Hugo, please. I don't know anyone else I can trust who can do the job.'

Hugo looked at her for a long time. She held her hand out and smiled at him as an immense sense of wellbeing swept over her. She wanted this man in every way there was to want a man. She needed him, wanted to be with him, to share her life with him. He had beautiful eyes behind his glasses, and an appealing little lick of dark hair which fell over his proud forehead. He was Hugo, the best computer coder she had ever known, the man who solved problems without making a fuss. The man who had been in her lab all those years and who had fancied her and she'd never known. She'd been such a fool, but here he was, right in front of her. Torn, unsure. She wanted to embrace him, take him in, reassure him that he was okay.

With no change in his expression he turned towards the stairs.

'Hugo.' Nina merely whispered his name. He didn't turn around, but slowly went down the stairs.

'Hugo,' she whispered.

She heard the front door open, the rustle of his windproof coat, then the door closing.

'Hugo?'

Nina was frozen. He had left, had refused her so absolutely. She didn't cry, although her nose started running. She just couldn't seem to move. Hugo had thought what she was doing was insane. Insane enough for him to turn down a £100,000-a-year job and a nice car. A job in his home town, near his friends and family.

Slowly the tears started to form. They built up in the lower part of her eyes, distorting her vision, making her blink. Then she felt her mouth change shape and a sob erupted. She wasn't used to the whole crying thing – it didn't sit well on her shoulders.

The sound of the doorbell made her jump.

'Hugo!' she shouted. She found herself running down the stairs. 'Hugo!'

She saw the door in front of her. Never in the four years she had lived in the house had her front door seemed so significant. Every other day of her life it was just a door, a thing that sometimes made her feel safe when she closed it from the inside. But nothing more. Now it was glowing with the certainty of salvation. She reached out and released the lock, pulled the door towards her.

'Professor Nash?'

A policewoman.

A policewoman with a police hat on, in uniform. A policewoman carrying a neat black folder under her arm, standing on Nina's little step.

'Are you Professor Nash?' the woman asked.

Nina looked out of the door, up the short street. There was no one there but the woman and her police car parked in front of Nina's garage doors.

'Yes,' she said eventually.

'My name is Detective Constable Wendy Jones. Is it possible to come inside?'

'Sorry?'

'I'd like to come inside to talk to you, Professor. Is that possible?'

'What is it?'

'I'd like to talk about it inside. If that's possible.'

'I don't understand. What have I done?'

'Nothing. Please, Professor.'

The policewoman smiled gently. Nina wiped away her tears. She wasn't used to them. She stood to one side and Detective Constable Wendy Jones entered her house.

29

Detective Constable Wendy Jones's visit to Nina's house had been caused by what had happened in the King Charles Hotel in the middle of the previous night.

Jason found himself standing naked in the kitchen, clutching a fearsome-looking kitchen knife. It was quite dark – the only illumination was coming through the kitchen window from the external hotel lights. He was naked and covered in a weird cold sweat that he'd never experienced before. Except for a rather unpleasant burning sensation in his neck, he felt completely numb. He knew he had run into the kitchen, but he wasn't breathing deeply.

On the floor in front of him, pushed up against the wall and looking none too well, was his father, John Nash.

John wasn't injured, although he was in pain owing to the fact that he had run into the kitchen at quite a lick for a man his age, and had fallen on his side as his son had tried to grab him.

He had fallen on the same side he had fallen on two weeks previously – judging by what he was saying, the fall that had resulted in a broken collarbone. He was moaning in pain, breathing very fast, but looking at Jason with a fearsome intensity. His expression was one Jason had never seen on his father before. Jason assumed it was abject terror, but it didn't really communicate itself to him in any way he understood.

'Dad, I'm sorry,' said Jason eventually. He could talk quite easily, so maybe he hadn't gone completely barking mad after all. He breathed in deeply. 'I can honestly say I don't really know what's happened.'

'Put the knife down, Jason,' said his father between grunts. 'Just put the knife down. There's a good lad.'

Jason looked down at his hand. His father was right, he was indeed holding a knife. A very large kitchen knife which was covered in blood.

'I've just killed Mum, haven't I?' he asked calmly.

'Put the knife down, Jason,' his father grunted.

Jason put the knife on the counter top beside him. Then he noticed than his hand was covered in blood as well.

'Bloody hell,' he said, holding his hand in front of his face. 'I think this may be rather terminal, don't you, Dad?'

'Just stay there,' said his father, his face momentarily crumbling in pain. 'Just stay where you are.'

'Sure, sure. Okay, Dad,' said Jason. He did as he was told, looking up only when the trees outside the kitchen window started to flash with blue.

'That'll be the police,' he said.

'It's okay, Jason. Just stay where you are,' repeated his father, his eyes now closing. His breathing remained heavy. He tried to move but just groaned instead.

'I imagine Harriet called them. She's very good like that. Reliable. We could do with some of the older folk at Nash Systems. Sorry, I'm wittering. Like I say, sorry, Dad. I know it's a bit late, but I really don't know how all this happened. I'll naturally take full responsibility for my actions, whatever they were.'

'Jason!' screamed Amy as she entered the kitchen. Jason turned slowly. Silhouetted in the doorway was the woman he loved, looking very dishevelled, wrapped in a duvet that had special significance for him. It was a Buzz Lightyear duvet, very faded, one he had been given at Christmas by a girlfriend who knew how obsessed he was with the whole Pixar animation thing.

'Hi, Amy, are you okay?' he asked calmly.

'What . . . what have you done?' she said, sobbing. He pursed his lips. The little lady was very upset, and understandably. He knew there wasn't much he could do. He sighed deeply, feeling a little tired.

'Not too sure, but as I just said to my dad, I'm afraid it's a tad on the terminal side. You're okay, though, baby?'

'Yes, well, no.' Amy started to cry again. She held her hand to her mouth, staring at him from behind her messed-up hair. 'What happened?'

'It looks a bit like I may have stabbed my mother.'

'Okay, don't move! Police!' said a very loud male voice. Amy jumped and then saw a figure behind her holding a torch. Jason smiled.

'It's okay, fellers. I'm here. I'm not going anywhere.'

A bright light was shone in Jason's face.

'Don't move,' shouted the male voice. He almost spelled out each word as he barked them at Jason. 'The building is surrounded by armed police. Put your hands on your head.'

Jason smiled and did as he was told.

'Is there anyone else with you?' asked the police officer.

'My dad is here. He's hurt a bit, I think. His collarbone. He needs some medical attention pretty fast, I think.'

The police officer moved to one side as another entered the room, this one clearly armed with a revolver, which was pointed very accurately at Jason's head.

'Stay very still,' said the second officer.

'I will. Don't worry,' said Jason. He smiled. 'Really, guys, I'm very happy to co-operate.'

The lights suddenly came on, flashing a couple of times as the neon tubes pulsed into life. Jason then saw that the doorway was crammed with police officers, three of them in flak jackets, one with a submachine-gun. All the weapons were pointed at him.

The officer with the torch moved very slowly around the bench to where Jason was standing.

'Keep your hands on your head,' he said gruffly. 'Don't move a muscle until I tell you to.'

'Sure, sure,' said Jason.

The man moved up behind him and with amazing speed slipped a handcuff around his left wrist.

'You do not have to say anything,' he said as he worked, 'but it may harm your defence if you do not mention, when questioned, something which you later rely on in court. Anything you do say may be given in evidence.'

'Okay.'

'Do you understand?'

'Sure, sure.'

'Hands down, really slowly,' the officer barked.

Jason did as he was told. The officer turned him around. Jason could sense the other officers moving in very rapidly behind him.

'Easy, fellers. I'm naked, unarmed and I'm doing everything you say,' said Jason quickly.

He felt the cuff snap shut on his right wrist. He was then turned and pushed forward quite roughly towards the other officers. One of them covered his shoulders with a rough brown blanket and they walked him through the door and down the corridor, away from the kitchen. Amy was nowhere to be seen, but he noticed two men in paramedic outfits rush past him into the kitchen. He realised with relief that they were going to attend to his dad.

'I'm really sorry, Dad,' said Jason over his shoulder, slowly feeling his senses return. He was conscious of a lump in his throat, and his eyes started to well up with tears.

'Shit, what have I done?' he asked himself. No one answered him. He was marched past the family sitting room. The lights were on inside and he could see people in white coats kneeling on the floor. He could make out his mum's legs but nothing else.

'Mum. Mum, are you okay?' he said, his face now streaming with tears. 'What have I done?'

The carpark was very cold underfoot. Jason was completely naked save for the blanket. He was ushered into the back of a police van and sat on one of the seats. One of the armed officers stood at the door while a great deal of discussion took place. There was a lot of noise, and then Jason realised that the very bright light that was flooding the carpark was coming from a helicopter which seemed to be hovering just feet above their heads. He could see the trees whipping about in its down-draught. He shook his head. It didn't seem five minutes since he had been shagging Amy in his old bed. It had been so warm and nice and special, somehow linking his past with his present. He felt he was almost showing the young Jason how he had grown up, how he wasn't shagging for any reason other than that he loved the lady concerned, and that was a very grown-up thing to do. And then it all went red and weird and his heart rate went off the scale. He felt so sick. His muscles shook and he just couldn't keep still. He kept breaking things and shouting at Amy to get away and his mum had come in and then something really heavy happened. He stopped thinking about it quite deliberately – he didn't want to go back there.

Two police officers got in the back of the van with him and the doors were slammed shut. He looked at them. They stared back with fairly unpleasant expressions.

'Sorry about all this,' said Jason. He wiped the tears from his face with the blanket.

'Bit late for that, isn't it,' said the older of the two officers, a mean-looking man with close-cropped grey hair.

'Sure, sure,' said Jason. No point looking for sympathy in that particular quarter.

The van started to move off. Jason turned and looked out of the rear window. The scene was unreal – what seemed like dozens of police cars parked every which way, their lights flashing, the powerful beam from the helicopter playing on the whole scene.

'Amazing,' said Jason. 'Did I cause all that?'

'Looks that way, mate,' said the younger of the two officers. 'Best not say anything till we get to the station.'

'Where's that?' asked Jason.

'High Wycombe,' said the older officer.

Jason let his head rest against the side of the van as it drove along the familiar road from Cookham to High Wycombe, the road his old school bus used to follow every day. He looked down at his hands. They were clutching the blanket around him, and he could see blood on both of them. His mother's blood. Every now and then an image would flash before him – his mother's look of utter disbelief as he plunged a knife into her.

'Oh God. What did I do?' he said out loud. It was possible the police officers said something, but he was oblivious to them as he felt himself slip down into the hell he had somehow created for himself. He had killed his own mother. Much as she was a pain in the arse, he didn't want her dead, and he certainly didn't want to kill her. She had freaked when she found him making the old two-backed beast with Amy, but stuff like that had happened before. She was always freaking out when it came to his involvement with ladies. He had learned not to introduce them to her – it made life easier for everyone. But this time was different. Amy was the special one for him. He had wanted to introduce her to his family, as people did in the normal world. He just wanted to live in the normal world with Amy, and now, somehow, he had so utterly destroyed any hope of having any normal-world experiences ever again.

'I'm fucking sure I didn't do it.' He squeezed his fists together, pulling on the handcuffs in order to feel something. He wanted the numbness to leave, wanted to feel what he had done in his body. The only thing he could feel was the pain in his neck. Everything in his world started to crumble as he sat in the slow-moving police van – Nash Systems, Amy, his future which had looked so bright, his wonderful apartment, his big penis, his fantastic car that was sitting in the carpark. Everything started to fall down and break apart. Not like in a computer-animated vision of a crumbling world; not in some tidy, clever way timed to go with a suitable piece of music; not like in a movie – everything started to fall apart in a very real, messy, non-digitised way.

He jolted as the van came to a halt suddenly, and looked around. The older of the officers was standing up and moving towards the door.

'Stay where you are,' he said sternly. The rear doors opened and the van was flooded with bright light. Jason blinked a couple of times, his eyes stinging with tears.

'Okay, get out,' said the officer.

Jason stood up and bashed his head on the roof of the vehicle, which caused his neck to hurt again.

'Watch out, you long streak of piss,' said the older officer.

Jason looked around as he was helped out of the van and realised he was in the carpark of what he assumed to be High Wycombe police station.

'This way,' said the officer, moving him swiftly up two steps, then into a corridor with a security door. The door buzzed, and Jason was relieved to find himself in a much warmer room. Only then did he realise he was shivering with cold, or fear, or both – he couldn't be sure.

He was led to a low table behind which a very weary-looking police officer was sitting.

'This is the PQMS suspect Sarge,' said the older officer.

'From the King Charles?' queried the desk sergeant.

'Yep. He's not causing trouble.'

'Can I just ask what PQMS means?' said Jason as politely as he could.

'Person of Questionable Mental State,' said the desk sergeant without looking up.

Jason stood in front of the desk and answered the simple set of questions that were put to him. Name, age, address, reason he was staying at the hotel.

'My parents own it,' he said.

'Seems he knifed his mum,' said the policeman who had brought him in.

'Blimey,' said the desk sergeant. He looked at Jason for a while, then shook his head in the special 'seen it all before' way that some police officers adopted, to keep their sanity, Jason assumed. He had to admit it must look pretty weird – a naked man who'd just murdered his own mother.

'Put him in Cell fourteen,' said the sergeant. 'DS Cummins will be here in a minute. We've had a bit of a night of it what with the crash on the M40.'

Jason was led along another corridor to where a police-woman was holding a cell door open. He walked in and the older officer undid his handcuffs.

'D'you want a cup of tea?' asked the policewoman.

'Am I allowed?'

The policewoman smiled. 'Yes, you're allowed tea, and I'll try and find something for you to wear.'

'Thanks, that'd be great,' said Jason. The door was closed and bolted and he stood in the centre of the cell. He didn't really know what to do. He didn't want to see anyone, even Amy. He didn't want to do anything, so he just stood where he was. It didn't hurt to stand up – his neck felt a bit better. He didn't look at his hands, although he could feel that they were sticky. He tried to ignore them. He wanted to wash but he knew he'd have to wait. He knew he'd have to wait for a lot of things now. It was all going to be about waiting.

30

'I'm very sorry, Professor Nash, but we do need you to identify the body,' said the policewoman, who was sitting on her sofa. The same sofa that Hugo had been sitting on only a few moments earlier.

'Why? How can you not know who she is?' said Nina, desperately trying to understand what she had been told. Her brother had stabbed her mother in the sitting room of the hotel.

'It's a formality, I'm afraid. The situation at the hotel was fairly chaotic, as you can imagine. Your father can't do it as he is in High Wycombe general hospital.'

'Oh my God. Did Jason stab him too?'

'No. He seems to have fallen during the struggle and broken his collarbone. Apparently it had already been broken.'

Nina nodded, and felt further waves of guilt – she hadn't rung since she'd heard the news.

'So there have been some complications,' continued the policewoman. 'But he's as well as can be expected. I'm afraid you're the only family member we can find who can do an official identification.'

'I see,' said Nina. She was sitting in her armchair, wishing she had a cat. She had no idea why she suddenly wanted a cat, but she wished she had one curled up on her lap, purring. She needed something – anything was better than what she was going through.

When the policewoman had first, and very slowly, told her what had taken place the previous night, Nina's mind had raced with possible explanations. She felt no sadness, only fascination. Her brother had killed her mother, something she knew was utterly out of character. The one thing she knew about Jason was that he wasn't a violent person. She had known him all her life, had watched him grow from an annoying little boy into a lanky, smelly adolescent and eventually into an even taller and still occasionally pungent adult. Never at any time had she felt physically in danger in his presence. He was clumsy, stupid, ignorant and selfish, but never violent. She knew he couldn't just have upped and done it, even if he was drunk or strung out on cocaine, and she had seen him under the influence of both, sometimes at the same time, and still he never exhibited any signs of violent behaviour.

Everything pointed to one thing – a very small thing that she had buried in his neck. She knew that, but if there was one piece of information she couldn't give the police officer sitting in front of her it was that.

It was only as she tried to work out how to get to the mortuary in High Wycombe that the full implications of what she had just been told started to dawn on her. Her mother – somehow the very fact that she was dead had already changed something dramatically. She wasn't sure what, but she knew that one of the things that had made her miserable if she had any time to herself, one of the things that made her so driven to work longer, to achieve more and deny everything that might be wrong with what she was doing, had just disappeared.

'I can arrange transportation,' said the policewoman.

'No, it's okay. I'll drive myself,' said Nina.

'Are you sure?'

'Yep. Don't worry. I'm fine at the moment. I need the time to think.'

'Of course,' said the policewoman. 'I just need to ask one question at this stage, Professor.'

'Yes?'

'Have you any idea why your brother might have done this?'

'No,' said Nina rather too quickly. She blinked. It was going to be impossible to carry on. How could she not tell the authorities?

'It's . . . how shall I put it?' She stared at the sympathetic face of the policewoman. 'Very out of character. Very. He's not a violent man, and his relationship with our mother was very close. She was his favourite.'

'Why do you say that?'

'Oh, well, it was obvious, really. She was obsessed with her Jason. I was always a thorn in her side. That's what I mean. Doesn't make sense. If anyone was going to kill her, it would be me.' She smiled, suddenly feeling she might be incriminating herself.

'I see. So you didn't get on with her, then?'

'Oh, it's complicated. Families, mothers and daughters – you know how they are.'

The policewoman smiled. She knew, Nina could tell – it was a mother–daughter thing. She could see it in her eyes.

A few minutes later Nina backed her BMW out of the garage, got out and closed the up-and-over door.

'You sure you'll be all right?' asked the nice officer, now wearing her hat and looking more official than she had in Nina's house.

'Yes.' Nina had swapped mobile numbers with her. She was to call if it got too much and a police car would take her. But she knew she'd be all right.

'Please take care, Professor.'

Nina smiled weakly at the officer, got back in the car and put her seat belt on. She pulled slowly out of her narrow driveway, checking in the rear-view mirror. The policewoman was standing watching her.

She drove out of Cambridge easily. It was Saturday and the M11 wasn't too busy. Once she had settled down to a steady speed, she flicked on the cruise control, put in her earpiece and called Sir Brian.

'Where are you?' she asked as soon as he answered.

'Outside your house. I was just about to call you. Where are you?'

'Going to High Wycombe. Jason's murdered my mother.'

'What? Nina, what are you saying?'

'The chip. They used the chip.'

'Who did?' asked Sir Brain. 'Your brother?'

'Yes. Last night my brother murdered my mother. I am on my way to identify the body. He's in custody. Apparently he admits doing it.'

'Nina.'

'Sorry I'm not there.'

'For goodness' sake.'

'Not bad as far as excuses go, is it?' she said, feeling a smile creep across her face. She could picture Sir Brian standing outside her house, annoyed until he heard her story.

'Oh, Nina,' he said again.

'Pretty shit, isn't it?'

'Yes. Oh, my poor sweet girl. What can I do to help?'

She smiled again 'Don't know,' she said.

'I could come to High Wycombe.'

'Could you?' Nina thought for a moment. Did she want him there? 'There could be press interest once the story gets out.' She wanted to test him.

'Yes,' he said after a moment's thought. 'That's a good point. Look, as soon as you know what's happened, call me. I'll do anything to help, you know that.'

Nothing new there. Nina didn't want to hear any more whingeing from the grey-haired old bastard. She terminated the connection and flicked on the stereo. As soon as the music engulfed her the phone rang again. Without checking the screen, she answered.

'What?' she shouted, still picturing the cringeing Brian Coventon standing outside her house.

'Nina, I just heard.'

'Who's this?' She took a look at the screen – restricted number was all it told her.

'It's George. What the hell has been going on?'

'Jason killed my mum. I'm going to identify the body.'

'Shit, this is terrible.'

'Yes, it is rather bad, isn't it. What d'you know about it, George?' Her voice conveyed no emotion.

'I've just heard from Del Papa.'

'Oh, and where did he hear from?'

'Search me. Has it been on the news?'

'I don't know. Not as far as I know.'

There was a silence. George was thinking fast; she could almost hear him.

'Nina, you sound kinda calm. Are you okay?'

'That's a bit confusing, George. If I sound calm then I should be okay, shouldn't I?'

'I don't know. I'm totally confused. If I just discovered my mom had been murdered by my brother, I guess I would be kinda upset.'

'Oh, I'm very upset, George, don't worry,' she said with a certain amount of enjoyment.

'But this is very serious, Nina. I mean, I don't want to trouble you with extra worries, but Jason . . .'

'What about him?'

'Where is he?'

'I would imagine he's rather under arrest at the moment.'

'But the chip, Nina.'

'Yes, George, the chip,' repeated Nina with a grin. 'Bit of a mess, isn't it. I don't suppose your friends can get him out of a police station quite as easily as they got Van Missen out of the hospital, can they?'

'I guess not. But we could all be in serious trouble if someone discovers the chip.'

'I'm sorry, George, but that is at the very bottom of a very long list of concerns I have at the moment.'

'Sure, I understand. But I may have to act to protect the company.'

'What are you going to do now? Kill Jason?'

'Nina. Please. No, but we may have to bring in some heavyweight legal representation to get him bailed out so we can remove the chip.'

'Then you can kill him?'

'No, of course not. I'll do everything I can to look after Jason, but the company's responsibility has to end somewhere, Nina. If he has murdered his own mother he has kinda torn up our contract with him. I mean, although it doesn't say "Mr Nash promises not to bring the company's name into ill repute by murdering his mother" it's kinda implied.'

'George, tell me one thing,' said Nina, deciding that bridges had already been burned to such an extent that there was nothing to lose. 'Did you set this up? Is this a further test of the software that I didn't know about?'

'What are you talking about?'

'George, you spiked my coffee to keep me out of the lab so you and your fuckwit cronies could carry out a half-baked test on my stupid brother.'

'I'm really not with you here,' said George carefully. Typical of the man – don't give anything away, wait until your opponent shows their hand before you move. She was learning. Well, she would throw the whole deck of cards at him.

'Garfelli attacked Jason on the morning I was ill in bed, the only day's work I've missed in ten years, George. Very convenient. Did you really think I wouldn't find out?'

'Nina, I . . .'

'No, shut up and listen. I don't want to waste time. You got me out of the way, played the data we got from the assault in London back to Jason, and suddenly he could fight, couldn't he, George? He was really good, like when he could do the tests the next day. But you knew that by then, didn't you? You were just humouring me. So now you've played back some other piece of data and Jason's flipped his lid. Blown the whole thing.'

'No, this . . .'

'Has it ever occurred to you, George,' continued Nina, now almost shouting into the phone, 'that the reason I am in the position I am with you and the whole field of cybernetics is that I don't do stupid things like that?'

'I know, Nina, I really know that, but this isn't what's happened.'

'Oh, isn't it. What has happened, then?'

'I don't know, Nina. I honestly don't. But you sure have got me worried.'

'Oh, have I?' said Nina. 'Good!' she shouted.

'Nina, I know nothing of this.'

'Well now, judging from what happened to my mother, we know what happens if you play back untested data to an unknowing individual, you bastard.'

'Nina, this is not true. Jason was a hundred miles from the lab. I thought we could only play data to him if he was here.'

'Who knows,' she said, aware that he had a point.

'I know nothing about what happened with Jason and your mother, Nina. I want you to know that.' Nina could tell from his voice than he was angry, upset, all things that made her feel just a little better.

'We'll see,' she said. She switched the phone off and then with one deft hand flipped the battery off the back. No one could ring her or track her with the damn thing dead.

Nina arrived at the mortuary within two hours of leaving her house. There was no one around – no hordes of journalists trying to get stories, no paparazzi trying to get pictures.

The building was new and discreet, situated behind the general hospital. She had never been to a mortuary before, and as she entered the building she realised it hadn't been something she had been desperate to do.

'Good afternoon. Can I help you?' a very overweight man asked her as she entered the building.

'My name is Professor Nash. I've come to identify my mother.'

'Ah yes. There's a couple of police officers here waiting for you,' he said. He pressed a buzzer and an inner door opened. Nina followed him along a wide white corridor. A couple of rather chilling-looking stainless-steel gurneys were parked along one side. She was shown into a small office, where she was confronted with two police officers, one a grey-haired man, the other a very young-looking blonde woman.

'Professor Nash, thank you very much for coming so quickly,' said the male officer. 'My name is Detective Sergeant Millroyd. This is Constable Peters.'

Nina shook hands with them both.

'Now all I can tell you at this stage is that your mother died very quickly. One of the first wounds was directly into her heart. Not that it's much of a consolation, but it would appear she didn't suffer too greatly.'

Nina nodded. She didn't want to say anything, didn't want to talk at all, but above everything didn't want to see her mother.

The older officer rubbed his very clean, well-manicured hands together.

'Shall we get it over with, then?'

Nina nodded and followed the officers through another door. This room was very brightly lit, with high narrow windows along one side, huge sinks and three large tables in the centre. Along one wall was a series of stainless-steel doors. One of these was open, and a woman in a white lab coat was standing next to it. On a steel shelf extending out of the door was a body covered in a white sheet.

Nina felt nauseous. The smell in the room was very peculiar, a thick, chemical odour. The whole experience was unreal. She couldn't be sure exactly what was affecting her.

The woman in the white coat slowly pulled back the top of the sheet and revealed Nina's mother's face. Her skin was the most odd thing and immediately struck Nina – it was very white, waxy and clearly very dead. But she looked peaceful. Nina wondered whether it was possible to change someone's expression with a bit of deft manipulation after they died. Her mother's hair was neatly brushed back, not at all in the style she wore it in when she was alive.

'Can you identify the body, Professor?' asked the male police officer after a few moments.

'It's my mother,' said Nina immediately. She looked down at the face and found herself smiling. She loved her mother – how could she not? But something had changed. She reflected for a moment; for once she had the time to allow her life to come into focus. She experienced an immense feeling of peace and relaxation. Her own mother was dead. She didn't feel sad; in fact she felt more love for her mother now than she could remember, and no hostility.

She stared at the face, so like her own and now gone, dead, made of wax. She was like her mother, there was no denying it, but now, she realised, she was like no one. She felt light-headed, but she knew it wasn't a physiological response – she wasn't going to faint. She felt light-headed because the heavy cloak her mother had placed around her shoulders as a baby had been lifted for the first time.

'No doubt about it, that is my mother.'

'Thank you, Professor,' said the police officer. 'We'll leave you now.'

Nina nodded silently. She heard them leave the room and felt uncomfortable. She didn't know what she was meant to do. The woman in the white coat said nothing, but Nina could tell she was looking at her. It was part of the job – having relatives of people who had died suddenly coming in to identify bodies.

'There's an irony, eh, Mum,' she said suddenly. She hadn't thought anything before she said it; it just came out. She smiled at herself, then looked up at the woman in the white coat.

'We didn't really get on,' she said. 'She adored my brother, and look what happened.'

The woman said nothing. Her expression was professionally blank.

'Is it okay if I go now?'

The woman nodded and gently pulled the sheet back over her mother's face.

She walked out of the room and down the corridor, where two paramedics were wheeling in another body under a sheet.

Nina stood to one side as they passed. The overweight man was waiting at the end of the corridor.

'Not much fun, is it,' he said kindly.

'Oh, I don't know. It has a certain something,' replied Nina with a smile.

She didn't wait for a response, but walked straight through the entrance door and out into the carpark.

The change in the weather had a significant effect on her. The sun was out, the sky had cleared, and it was actually warm for the first time she could remember.

Nina started walking around the mortuary building towards the main entrance of the hospital. The sun felt good on her skin; even the air seemed finally to have thawed.

She found her father fairly quickly. He was in a public ward, in a bed next to a window and looking very pale.

'Hi, Dad,' she said, reaching out to hold his hand. He moved a little when he saw her, although his expression didn't change.

'Sorry, darling,' he said eventually. She looked at him in silence for a moment. Of all the possible things he could have said to her, this made the least sense. She expected a string of bitter words about Jason, she expected him to vent his fury about 'the boy', but all he said was 'sorry'.

'Dad, it's not your fault.'

He lay looking at the ceiling, saying nothing.

'Dad, it's my fault, if you want to know the truth.'

Even as she spoke she regretted it, but she had too much information to contain; she felt she had to tell everyone.

'Nina, you are an angel. If it wasn't for you I would have finished myself off long ago.' He sighed and slowly turned his head to look at her. 'It's all my fault, of course it is. I didn't bring Jason up properly. I hit him too many times when he was a kid. It all goes in, doesn't it? Everything you do to your kids, it all goes in and stays there, and then one day it comes out. But who would have thought . . .'

Nina gently stroked his brow. It felt hot and slightly damp.

'Are you in a lot of pain?'

'I'm barely awake. They've pumped me full of something, can't feel a damn thing.'

'Dad, I need to know something.'

'What is it?' he asked in a tired voice, as he used to respond to her when she asked for more sweets when they were on a long journey.

'Well, have the police been asking you questions?'

'Yes, lots.'

'Okay, well, I need to know one thing. Jason . . . I'm sorry, but this is very important. Did Jason try to . . . well, stab you as well as Mum?'

John Nash looked at her. She could see that through the fug of drugs something had registered with him.

'How do you mean? He was running around the hotel, stark naked, with a bloody great kitchen knife.'

'I know, Dad, but did he actually try and stab you?'

'No, I don't suppose he did. He stopped all of a sudden when he ran after me into the kitchen.'

'How d'you mean, he stopped?'

'He just stopped. I don't know. He just stood there, didn't do anything.'

'Like he'd just woken up?'

'I suppose so. What are you saying? He went mad, is that it?'

'No, Dad, I'm not saying that at all. He didn't go mad, he didn't want to murder anyone. If you think about it, if he responded like you suggest – you know, the fact that you hit him when he was a kid, the fact that you and he didn't really get on – well, who would you expect him to kill? Mum couldn't see past her own obsession with him. He could do no wrong in her eyes. Why would he kill her?'

Her father sighed, closed his eyes and slowly shrugged his shoulders. She sat with him for a while, then quietly took her leave. She couldn't stay. She had a lot to sort out.

31

Lord Preston, QC, entered the cell when Jason was still fast asleep. He sat at the small table without any hesitation. He was clearly a man who felt quite at ease walking into a cell and making himself at home.

Jason stirred slowly and opened one eye as his lawyer opened his briefcase.

'Oh, shit,' were the first words to leave his dry throat. He curled up on the hard bed, trying to find some part of his brain that didn't feel that it had to deal with what was before him. He had been trying all night, and found none.

'Good morning, Jason,' said his Lordship with a brief smile. 'We have rather a lot to do.'

'I'm really here, aren't I?' said Jason, covering his face with his large hands.

'Yes, you are, I'm afraid. Now, I've asked an officer to bring your breakfast in, but I'd like to start as soon as possible.'

'I need to take a leak,' said Jason. He sat up in bed, pulling the rough blanket about his groin. 'I've got serious wood, I'm afraid, but that's nothing to do with you your Lordness. Don't worry.'

The lawyer didn't react in any way as Jason relieved himself into the stainless-steel toilet in the corner of the cell.

'It's funny, isn't it,' he said. 'I saw one of these bogs in a brochure and thought I might have one fitted in the apartment. I thought it looked very hi-tech, but it's what they use in police stations. Kind of takes the edge off the product desire some-what.'

'So, tell me what happened,' said Lord Preston when Jason finally sat on the small stool opposite him. His pen was poised above a sheet of foolscap paper.

'It's very simple. For some reason which is utterly beyond my comprehension I . . .' Jason felt his eyes fill with tears. The last thing he remembered before he eventually fell asleep in the cell the night before was the hot tears streaming down his cheeks. There was nowhere he could go, nothing he could do to get out of this one.

'I stabbed my mum,' he finished eventually. He wiped his eyes on the T-shirt one of the policemen had given him the night before. It was printed with a football team logo which, for some reason, had made Jason feel even sadder.

'So you admit that you did it, Jason. As you can imagine, this does have a very serious bearing on the matter.'

'Yes, of course I bloody did it. Talk about red handed.'

'I'm sorry, I'm not with you.'

'My hands. They were covered in my mother's blood.' As he spoke his throat started to tighten. He hadn't wanted to do it, hadn't wanted to kill his mother. The confusion was all-encompassing.

'Okay,' said Lord Preston. 'At least this keeps things simple. It's really just a matter of proving diminished responsibility.'

'How do we do that?'

'It's not going to be a simple matter. Tell me, Jason, have you received any medical attention?'

'No. Why? Do I need some?'

'You haven't been seen by a doctor or a psychiatrist?'

'No.'

'No one has taken an X-ray?'

'No.'

'Fine, okay.'

'Why does that matter?'

'No reason. I'm just collecting all the facts.'

'Is that what you suggest, though? A shrink? I go for the nutter option?'

Lord Preston nodded slowly. Jason rubbed his face. It felt different – wrinkled, old and dirty. His eyes hurt. They were bloodshot, and although he had woken up feeling rough in the past, this particular morning took the biscuit.

'Okay, so what do I say to the shrink?'

'I don't think you have to make anything up, Jason,' said Lord Preston with a gentle smile. 'What you did last night constitutes insane behaviour in most people's books. Just explain what happened – that should be enough. I will work on getting you bailed out as soon as possible.'

'Does everyone know?' asked Jason.

Lord Preston started to put his pad away in his briefcase. 'I would imagine so. It's in the papers this morning.'

'Oh God, no.'

'I've spoken with Mr Quinn at Nash Systems. He obviously knows as he asked me to come and see you.'

'Shit. What's going to happen?' Jason pleaded.

'Well, my primary concern is to get you out of here as soon as possible. We'll have to work on the case once we've done that.'

He stood up and knocked on the door. After a moment it was unlocked and a police officer stood in the doorway.

'All finished, thank you,' said Lord Preston. 'Is that breakfast on its way?'

'Yes, sir, it'll be here in a minute,' said the officer. Jason looked up as Lord Preston left the cell. He didn't even cast a backward glance or say goodbye. He just left.

The cell door slammed shut and the bolt was slid across.

That was it. Jason Nash was alone again. No one to help him share the horror of what he'd done. The lawyer was so cold and businesslike. Jason wanted someone who would hold him, tell him it was okay and that he wasn't really a murderer. He wanted to see Amy. He thought about her, and then another thought entered his head which was too awful to deal with alone.

It made his whole body jump in shock. He wanted to be with his mum. He wanted her to come and see him and cuddle him and tell him everything was okay.

'Mum!' he cried out, the noise of his own voice coming as a shock. He wanted his mum badly – he needed her. The sting of the tears in his eyes rocketed him back to his childhood.

He was five years old, alone in his little wooden bed, suddenly awake and scared.

'Mum, I want my mum!' he shouted out. His body broke into sobs. That was how it felt, as if it were in different places, all of them sobbing independently. There was no part of his body he could hide in to get away from the sobbing. Not even his cock, which felt small and scared.

'Where's my mum?' he cried out.

He lay back on his bed, feeling an immense tiredness. The sobbing continued. He curled up into a ball, pressed his legs against his chest as hard as he could, trying to control the feeling of being blown to bits. He needed to hold on somehow. He didn't know how he was going to do it.

The next thing he was aware of was a gentle hand on his neck and a voice he recognised.

'Jason.' It was Nina. 'Jason, wake up.'

He turned over and saw the scrawny form of his sister leaning over him. She looked pretty rough, wearing a black dress-suit with a black polo-neck sweater.

All black. It must be true. He'd offed his mum. 'Oh, God,' he said, and turned back to the wall.

'Jason, we have to talk,' she said.

'I did it, Nina. Just leave me, I can't face you. I did it and that's all there is to it. You never have to see me again.'

'Jason, you didn't do it.'

'I'm a grade-one murderer. I killed Mum. I've got to do my bird.'

'Jason, did you hear what I said?'

'Leave me, Nina. I'm shit.'

'You didn't do it.'

Nothing registered in Jason's head for a moment. Slowly what Nina had just said started to create a chink of light in the layers of brown shit that seemed to have filled his world. But it didn't make sense – he could still remembers the feeling of the knife handle as he plunged it with so much force into his mother.

'Nina, I did it.'

'I know your body did it, but not your mind.'

'What?' said Jason. 'Look, I know I've got to claim I'm a nutter, but I did kill Mum.' Again, and without warning, the tears flowed and he started sobbing uncontrollably. Through the wails that racked his entire body he felt Nina, of all people, scrawny, bony-armed Nina, hold him and reassure him.

'It's okay, Jase. It's okay. You didn't do it. It's not your fault. It's all my fault.'

After a while he lay still in Nina's arms, the sobs coming only every second breath. He wiped his eyes again and looked up at her face. She did have a nice face really. She looked a bit like his mum, but nicer. She had nicer eyes.

'You have a chip insert,' she said softly.

Jason looked at her for a while longer as this information started to gel with his slightly less confused vision of his life.

'I have a . . .'

'I organised it. You've had it in for four days.'

'What d'you mean?'

'You've got a transponder chip inserted into your spinal cord.'

Nina looked at him with a very serious face. It was all too weird, it must be a dream, but there was a lot more real-time information coming in than he would expect in a dream. The smell – he could smell Nina's perfume, could feel the warmth of her arms on his shoulders.

'I don't know what you're trying to do, and I know I'm a bit confused at the moment, but having a chip inserted into my neck isn't the sort of thing I would forget, is it, sis.'

He tried to smile as he spoke, but he couldn't. His mouth was set in a quivering, downward position he just couldn't shift.

'We did it while you were asleep.'

'What? When?'

'At the office, when you fell asleep.'

'You put a chip in my neck?' said Jason. 'Where?' He put his hand up to his neck. 'The burning,' he said almost to himself.

'Have you noticed a burning sensation?'

'There's a fucking chip in my neck!' shouted Jason.

'Yes. The latest version.' Nina started to wring her hands in a way that Jason found acutely annoying. She spoke fast, staring into his eyes. 'It was meant to go in Frank Garfelli, but I hated the way George and everyone seemed to be controlling everything, so I thought if I put it in you, it would be my experiment again.'

'Nina,' said Jason. He shook his head and rubbed his neck. 'Take it out. Take the fucking thing out!'

'Please be careful, Jase,' she said: She held his hands, trying to stop him probing the back of his neck. 'Please, Jase. Remember what happened to Van Missen. Please, we will take it out.'

'Take it out now!' Jason shouted. He sat up and pushed her away. His sister had done this to him. His fucking stupid, scrawny sister had made him kill his own mother.

'How the fuck!' he shouted.

'Please, Jason,' she wailed. 'As soon as you're out on bail we'll take it out. It has to be done really carefully. You know how experimental this stuff is.'

'Oh, thank you,' he snapped bitterly. 'Shit! You put a chip in my neck! How could you!'

He held his head in his hands. It felt as if it was going to explode. 'If you'd asked me I would have done it, you know that. But at least I would have known.'

'I know. I know that now. I was crazy.' Now Nina was hiding her face in her hands.

Jason stood up and tried to pace up and down the cell, but he couldn't – there wasn't enough room.

'If I don't go clinically insane now, then that just proves what a well-balanced individual I am,' he hissed. He was breathing deeply, clenching his fists and doing everything he could to stop himself strangling his stupid sister.

'Hey, wait,' he said, standing still. 'Is it on now?'

'What?'

'The chip. Is it receiving signals now?'

'No, of course not,' she said quickly in the way he had known all his life – when he asked something that he felt was quite reasonable but which she obviously thought of as a subhuman request. 'It only works in the wiring loop at Nash Systems.' She said it as though she thought he was a moron, but she was being a moron.

'Like at Mum and Dad's,' he said with an exaggerated nod.

'Oh,' said Nina. What colour remained in her face fled south.

'Nina, what are you saying to me? I've got a chip in my neck which only works when I'm at the office, and then I go to visit Mum and Dad to introduce Amy to them, and everything at home is as uncomfortable as usual. Dad was in a stinking mood and Mum was prickly as fuck – she hated Amy. It was shit. She looked at her like she was trailer trash. You know that lemon face she pulls?'

Nina nodded slowly.

'And to top the whole thing off there was no room booked even though I'd phoned in the week to ask, so we had to stay in my old bedroom.'

'Right,' said Nina. 'So you were angry with Mum.'

'Spitting chips. We had to sleep in my old room with a single bed, but I thought "fuck 'em", and Amy and I started a major session on my old bed and it was really special.' He felt himself starting to cry again. 'It was really special, I am really in love for the first time, and then Mum bursts in.'

'Oh God, Jason.'

His eyes stinging again, he wiped the tears away with his forearm. He could smell the awful cheap soap he had been given in the little shower room they had put him in when he arrived at the police station.

'I don't know how it happened. I found a knife in the kitchen and I went into the old sitting room and stabbed her. It wasn't the chip, Nina. Fuck the chip. I'm a murderer, a crazy madman with a knife. So Nash Systems and most of all you can fuck right off.'

The last phrase came out so loud it almost hurt his own ears. The cell door burst open and three police officers came in and pushed Jason against the end wall.

'It's okay, it's okay!' screamed Nina. 'He's not doing anything. Please be careful with him. Please. He didn't do it! He didn't do it!'

Jason saw a policewoman pull Nina out of the cell. He could hear her screaming as she was dragged down the corridor.

'He didn't do it! Be gentle with him, please!'

Jason stood motionless, pinned against the wall by the burly and not terribly pleasant-smelling police officers.

'Are you going to cause trouble?' one asked.

Jason shook his head.

'Are you going to stop shouting?'

Jason nodded.

Slowly the officers released their grip and walked backwards out of the cell. One lingered in the doorway.

'One more outburst like that and we come in here and beat the living shit out of you. Okay, Mr Nash?'

Jason nodded again. Another officer leaned over the shoulder of the first.

'We don't mince words here, all right, son?'

The cell door slammed and Jason sat down on the bed very slowly. He put his hand to his neck and rubbed the skin gently. With the tip of his index finger he thought he could feel a tiny lump just below the hairline.

32

The King Charles Hotel in Cookham exuded an eerie feeling as Nina stepped through the front door. It was completely empty – for probably the first time in a few hundred years, Nina thought. As she shut the front door, everything was familiar except the sound. It was so quiet her footsteps echoed through the building.

There was a police officer stationed outside the hotel, and Nina had talked to him for some time. She explained that she was a member of the family and had come to pick up some things for her father. The whole building was still being treated as a crime scene but, as the officer explained, as there was no doubt about the identity of the culprit, it was considered a low-priority one. He was just on duty to protect the premises. He divulged that all sorts of weird people crawled out of the woodwork when there'd been a murder.

She walked through the reception area and into the staff area at the back of the building. She opened a door that led into a small office. Inside, the walls were crammed with file boxes, the windows virtually blacked out with piles of toilet rolls. An old grey PC, switched off and dusty, rested under a stack of unsorted papers and catering magazines. In theory her mother had done all the paperwork, but it wasn't something she had ever enjoyed, and there had always been rows about unpaid bills and unanswered letters.

Up on a high shelf was the security camera equipment. It was still running. On the little black-and-white screen were images from four points around the exterior of the hotel. She stood on a battered swivel chair and pressed the eject button.

She went back into the corridor and opened the door to the

sitting room. It was very warm – she assumed the heating was still on. The furniture was pushed to the side of the room; white dustsheets covered the floor.

She slid the cassette into the slim video machine and picked up the remote, which was on the mantelpiece, where it always was. Then she saw some marks up the wall – dark spots. It could only be one thing. She froze for a moment. It was her mother's blood, no doubt about that. It was horrible, the worst thing she had ever seen, but it didn't make her break down. There were so many more important things she needed to do. Wallowing in distress wasn't going to make anything better.

An image appeared on the screen – four grainy black-and-white pictures. She pressed 'rewind', keeping an eye on the date and time at the top of the screen. The security machine ran at a very slow speed. An ordinary three-hour videocassette lasted twenty-four hours when used this way, but the quality was poor.

'Right. I knew it,' she said after she'd pressed the 'play' button. There on the screen was an image of a white van in the carpark. The time was 11.32 on Friday evening.

No one got out of the van. There was only one explanation for what had happened. Somehow, someone from Nash Systems had rigged up a transmission device and sent signals to Jason's chip.

From what she could recall, the murder was believed to have taken place at about half past midnight. The little digital counter above the images raced towards 12.30, and soon after this the van shot out of the picture at comic speed.

'I rest my case,' said Nina to herself. She pressed the eject button and took the tape, slipping it into her leather bag.

She knew what she had to do. She had no choice, but she also knew it wasn't going to be easy.

She got back into her car and left the Crown Hotel carpark. She started the drive back to Cambridge, her mind fixed on the battle ahead. Then, without warning, she began to cry. It was the glimpse she caught of the hotel in the rear-view mirror – it struck right to the very centre of her being. Her home, smashed to bits by her brother. Her whole life, her history, taken away. It would never be the same, no matter what happened. Her stupid brother had managed to destroy her life for ever.

She drove slowly as the sobs flowed through her. She couldn't help imagining what it must have been like for her poor mum, to have her wonderful son attack her like that. To feel the knife enter her body. She put her fist to her mouth – the image was too much. She pulled over in a small bus stop and let herself give way to it.

Her mobile rang. At first she ignored it, assuming it to be Sir Brian. Then she glanced at the screen briefly. It was George Quinn, on the land-line from the office. She bit her lip, picked up the phone and clicked the 'yes' button.

'Hello, George.'

'Nina, hey. How's it hanging?'

'Not so good, George.'

'Where are you?'

'Driving back to Cambridge.'

'Good. Been thinking about what you said earlier.'

'Have you?'

'You bet. I'm on it, Nina. I'm on your side. I want you to know that.'

'I don't know what to think,' she said. She wasn't about to trust him, but she needed someone. 'I'm pretty blasted by everything.'

'I'll be here if you need to be with people.'

'Okay. I might take you up on that.'

'It would be great if you could. Obviously, on top of your own personal grief, this is a pretty dire situation for all of us.'

'I understand,' said Nina. As soon as her hopes that she was working with genuine concerned people were raised, those hopes where brutally shot down. 'The company.'

'It's going to be a rough ride,' said George.

'Sounds like you're almost looking forward to it,' responded Nina.

'Believe me, this is one crisis I could really do without managing. How long d'you think you'll be?'

Nina checked the time on her dash. 'Not more than an hour – the roads are pretty clear.'

'Okay. And Nina, anything I can do, give the word.'

'I will,' she said. She switched off the phone. George sounded oddly reassuring, and she did want to be with people. She shook her head as she pulled back out into the traffic.

33

'I have a transponder microchip inserted into my neck which controls my actions.'

Detective Inspector Morris stopped writing with his little blue pen for a moment. He didn't look up at Jason, just held the pen still, then sighed.

'Sorry, sir, I didn't quite catch that.'

'Nash Systems is involved in developing microchip technology which bypasses the need for external human–machine interfaces and will one day transform the way we live. I have become an unwitting guinea-pig in this development, and as the systems involved are still in their pre-release beta phase of development, things can obviously go wrong.'

The inspector did eventually look up at him only to Jason's dismay he was smiling. The smile very rapidly turned into a laugh.

'I have to hand it to you, sir, I've experienced a few excuses in my time, but this one is a scorcher.'

'It's not an excuse, it's an explanation. I have never had any desire to kill my mother. I was visiting to introduce her to my fiancée. Murder was not on my must-do list, Detective.'

The inspector dropped the pen and sat back in his chair. He sighed very slowly, rubbed his tired eyes and looked at Jason.

'The way I see it, sir, is that your mother interrupted you during a session of lovemaking which was just one intrusion too many into your life. It's understandable that you should be annoyed at such circumstances, but to murder your mother seems a bit over the top. Now this is a deeply traumatic event and I'm not even blaming you for trying to find a way out of it. It's pretty obvious to me that you are a well-educated individual with no previous record of violence, except the incident in London a few weeks back.'

'Yes, but that wasn't me.'

'Well, as far as we can ascertain it wasn't you, but our other chief witness to the event is still missing.'

'Yes. I know. Old Van Missen really landed me in it.'

'That was your accomplice on that mission, was it?'

'It wasn't a mission.'

'Whatever. Anyway, you've admitted that you killed your mother. At the end of the day, the whys and wherefors of the whole thing are more or less irrelevant to me. Once you've seen the psychiatrist, she can make a better judgment as to your sanity. I've got everything I need, Mr Nash. I'll get an officer to take you back to your cell.'

'If you get an X-ray of my neck, you'll see that I'm not telling stories. I didn't know I had the chip until my sister came in this morning. She did it. I'm not saying it's her fault, and I'm not saying I didn't kill my mother.'

The inspector had stood up and opened the door.

'Robinson, can you sort this one out, please?' he called down the corridor.

'I'm just pointing out some fairly groundbreaking extenuating circumstances here. It should make for an interesting court case if nothing else.'

Jason had been watching the detective inspector as he spoke. It was only as the door of the interview room closed that he realised nothing he said was going to make any difference. However, his mood had lightened since Nina had told him what was going on. It wasn't entirely his fault, although there was still a lingering doubt. Since the sobbing had stopped, he had managed to think about the horrific events without slipping into despair. He had felt an enormous hatred for his mother as he plunged the knife into her; he knew that there was something inside him that hated her. He had never been particularly conscious of it before – he hated his father, certainly, but that was for very obvious reasons. Even as an adolescent he'd got on okay with his mother – she had never scolded him, had always defended him, but on the other hand she hadn't let go.

'Come with me, sir, please,' said a uniformed officer. Jason stood and followed him back to the cell. As the door closed he felt a sense of relief. There was something deeply relaxing about being incarcerated. There was nothing he could do – no calls to answer, no e-mails to respond to, no meetings to attend. There was also no chance of any adult action, but as he lay back on his bed with his hands behind his head he was aware that adult action wasn't something he was craving. Possibly for the first time in his memory.

He had reached the age of thirty without ever really thinking about his mother – until she was dead. He wondered whether that was normal. As he waded through the dense thicket of his thoughts, he pondered on the possibility that his mother had done all the thinking for him. Maybe the chip had nothing to do with it, maybe he had actually wanted to kill her. Perhaps, hidden away in the depths of his utterly uninspected subconscious, there was a huge desire to off the old biddy. She was a total pain, he accepted that. It was the way she always assumed she knew everything about his life and what his motives were when in fact it was bloody obvious she hadn't got a clue.

He sighed. There was going to be a lot of sighing going on. This time he had so completely blown it there was no point trying to do something about it. Jason Nash felt a huge weight lifted from his shoulders. He didn't need to do anything about it. He'd murdered his mum, that was all there was to it. After a history of blowing it in a more or less non-criminal way, he had blown it in just about the most ultimate way any individual could. He had pushed the envelope to bursting and it had burst. He didn't want to go back and try and fix it. He had no desire to wriggle out of it. Claiming he had a chip in the neck was just a bad habit. He'd never mention it again, even if it was actually true.

34

'Nina, please forgive the panic here,' said George Quinn as they walked along the concrete corridor together. He had been waiting for her in the entrance lobby, Amy was not present, but it was a Saturday evening and she had been witness to a murder, so that wasn't totally surprising.

'It's okay,' said Nina. 'I don't really want to talk about my mother, if that's okay.'

'Of course,' said George. He looked pretty wired – his forehead was tight and she noticed that his fists were clenched.

As they approached his office, she saw that everyone else she worked with at Nash Systems seemed to be present.

'Nina.' Cindy Volksmann stood up and walked to the door. She took Nina's hands in her own, looking right into her eyes. 'How are you?'

'I'm fine,' said Nina. Frank Garfelli pushed a chair towards her. Nina sat down, aware that the room was very crowded.

Cindy Volksmann sat behind the desk next to George. As far as Nina could remember she had been in the States for some time. Del Papa and Trouville were sitting by the window next to Roger Turnpike, the surgeon.

A very smart-looking man was sitting in the far corner. Nina stared at him.

'Nina, this is Lord Preston, QC. He is representing Jason,' said George. Nina nodded. Nothing but the best, as usual. 'We all know that anything discussed here is in the absolute strictest confidence, don't we.'

Nina found herself nodding. She felt removed from her body, but thankfully this made her very calm. She glanced around the room at the small head movements of assent that were being sent George's way.

'This is, of course, a major crisis for the company. We seem to be back in the same position as when Pete Van Missen was in hospital. Clearly we have to get Jason out as soon as we can and remove the chip. We cannot allow the chip to play a part in the case.'

Nina's eyebrows went up.

'What is it, Nina?' said George. He didn't miss much, she had to give him that.

'I was just wondering what you meant,' she said after a short pause.

'I mean that if the authorities find the chip, Nash Systems could be in serious trouble.'

'I'm sorry, I don't really follow you.'

'Nina, surely it's obvious,' said Cindy Volksmann. 'The chip is what this whole company's future rests on. If the first one to be publicly released happens to be discovered in the neck of a murderer . . .'

'Cindy, please,' interrupted George. 'Let's all take it easy.'

'Sorry. I'm really sorry, Nina, but you know what I'm saying. It isn't going to be an easy sell. Is it?'

'What, because people will assume that the chip had some effect on Jason which made him kill his own mother?'

'Yes,' said Cindy.

'But we know that can't happen,' said Nina, casting a glance in the direction of Del Papa and Trouville. 'Don't we?'

'Yeah, sure,' said Michael Del Papa. 'The only area from where we can transmit signals to Jason's chip is here in the building.'

Nina nodded and said nothing else. Everyone waited. Trouville sneezed very loudly.

'Sorry,' he said as he blew his nose. 'Got one hell of a cold.'

'Okay, so what's the latest?' George asked the very well-dressed brief.

'Everything is fairly straightforward as far as the authorities are concerned. I'm going back to High Wycombe, where Jason has been arraigned first thing Monday morning. There will then be a preliminary hearing. I think we can get Jason out at than point.' Lord Preston spoke with an immaculate, cultured voice.

'Great,' said Cindy.

'He's been very co-operative with the police,' Lord Preston went on. 'So they're very happy. No case to solve. From what I can tell, the Crown Prosecution Service are not going to oppose bail. It's going to be set at a fairly hefty rate, though.'

'No problem,' said George. 'And from what we know, there's been no medical examination?'

'No. He wasn't injured in the incident so there's been no need. I take it you want to bring him back here?'

'Yes. Frank will arrange the transportation. We have to get him back here and then, using whatever we can improvise, we have to remove the chip.'

'I suggest we wait until Monday night, when he's asleep,' said Roger Turnpike.

George nodded. 'Good idea. Poor guy has got enough on his plate. How is the rest of your family, Nina?'

She smiled. 'There's only me and my father left, but we're fine. All things considered.'

'When is your mother's funeral?' asked Cindy Volksmann.

'Not till next week. They need to keep her body in the freezer for a while. Evidence and all that.'

'Oh, Nina, I am so sorry,' said Cindy, the sympathy as badly fitting on her face as a bikini on a statue of the Virgin Mary.

'Okay, well, I guess we should all go home and rest. I have a feeling the next few weeks are going to be a bit of a roller-coaster ride,' said George Quinn as he stood up. Everybody else started to shuffle around.

'Frank, you can organise everything okay?' George asked the replacement ice warrior. Nina noticed a tone in his voice she hadn't heard before. What was it? Hostility? Barely suppressed anger? Maybe.

'Everything is ready,' said Garfelli. 'We'll see you all back here Monday.'

Nina stayed seated as everyone filed out of the room, watching them carefully. She could see that George was fully occupied with the task ahead. Emen Trouville, the last to leave, paused at the door.

'You okay, Professor?'

'What d'you think, Emen?' she said with a sad chuckle.

'Must be a pretty shit time.'

'Yes. It is. You're not having much of a weekend, are you?'

'Hey, I'm a scientist, I don't have a life.'

Nina stood up and accompanied Emen out of the room. She felt very clear headed and strong. She knew she could use Emen – he was the weak link.

'What are you doing now?' she asked.

'I was going down to the labs. I've been working on a data management system. I know it feels kind of pointless now, after what's happened, but you know . . .'

Nina smiled at him and put her arm around his waist.

'Of course I know. I'm glad you're here, Emen. I'm sorry to be a pain, but I suppose I just need someone to be with.'

She noticed Emen's face twitch a little. He smiled at her. 'Hey, don't you worry about it,' he said.

Once they were in the lab, Nina sat down at her bench and watched Emen take up his position at his workstation.

'So tell me about the data management thing.'

'I think I've really cracked it, Professor.'

'Call me Nina,' she said, and made her eyes twinkle a little. It wasn't hard.

'Okay, thanks. But look, here you can see Van Missen's data.' Emen the scientist was still unaware of what she was trying to do, but she would get through eventually. Without looking at her, he continued, 'I've compressed it, and we're not losing vital information. I've managed to condense a days' data down to under a hundred gigs. But what's really good is that

I'm starting to make sense of what we've got. Look at this, this is so weird. Okay.'

He pointed at the screen. 'Right here, the time, look – eleven-forty-five at night. Van Missen is just about to go to sleep. Look at that data spike.'

On the screen, the bar graph showing the data input went into the red.

'What d'you think caused it?'

'Well, this is kind of embarrassing, but . . .'

'You mean, it's a masturbation session?'

'Huh,' said Emen. Nina glanced at him and saw clear signs of a blush on his pasty face. 'Yeah, well, that's what I thought, but then we have these very similar data events which I reckon are, as you say, masturbation sessions. Van Missen was an early-morning kind of guy. Look at this. Six-thirty-two in the morning. These slow build-ups here.'

He pointed to another graph which depicted a steady increase in activity, culminating in a large data spike.

'But look at this. It's sudden, total trauma, massive activity with no build-up.'

'Flashback,' said Nina, now lost in the information she was receiving.

'Yeah. You know about it, then.'

'Yes. Roger Turnpike talked about it the day we inserted the chip. I never thought, though. God. It's obvious.'

She walked away from Emen, held her head in her hands. Suddenly a thought hit her, and she spun on her heel. Trouville was watching her.

'When did you extract this data?'

'Yesterday,' he said. He was nervous, and she had to be careful. 'I wanted to show you, but there was so much going on, and we were all busy monitoring Jason.'

'Yeah, but you managed to create a transportable file with this data on it.'

Trouville faltered for a moment. 'Well, I guess you could, but . . .'

'So let's just say Emen,' she said as she walked up to him, standing very close, 'let's just say this was loaded on to a hard-disk array and run through a laptop, maybe connected to a directional transmitter, like one of those brilliant little Porrazzo Advanced Membrane Transducers we were trying here. They can transmit enough data, can't they, over a short distance? Now that wouldn't be hard to fit it into the back of a vehicle. Let's say, just for the sake of argument, a white VW van.'

'Oh, Nina. What are you saying?' asked Trouville. He was looking up at her, his head level with her stomach. He wasn't trying to move. She had never been this physically close to him before.

'I'm not saying anything, Emen. I'm standing very near you, I can feel your heat. I'm just standing here wondering if it was possible to do that. Just as an idea.'

'Please, Nina. I don't know.'

Nina smiled gently. 'Oh, you don't need to be scared of me, Emen. Tell me anything you like.'

'Well, you know I'm kind of in love with you.'

'Oh dear,' she said. As nerds went, Emen Trouville was in the top three per cent. This technical eminence required a condensed skillset that did not include the subtle arts of seduction, let alone much in the way of basic social ability. 'Oh, Emen. I had no idea you felt that way about me. I know you said we had advanced compatibility and you wondered if we were hot-pluggable, that was sweet, but I thought you were teasing me. There I was, standing near you, day after day, totally innocent. There's so much I don't know about you. You're so multi-skilled, and I like that. I admire that, Emen. I mean, whatever gave you the idea to isolate Van Missen's flashbacks? That was inspired.'

'Oh, I, well, it wasn't just me. It was Michael and Frank Garfelli, it was kind of their idea.'

'Oh, was it. And did you go with them in the van, Emen?'

'No, I don't . . . No, there is no van. It's gone. I . . . Nina, I'm not sure we should . . .'

'Should what, Emen? Should be this close, physically close like we are? Is my body disturbing you?'

'I guess I'm a bit thrown by you. I really do actually love you, Nina. I wouldn't do anything to harm you. I didn't.'

'You didn't do anything, did you, Emen. Please tell me you didn't.'

'No. I really didn't.' His voice was whining. 'I don't know anything.'

'But there was a van, wasn't there?'

'Look.' Emen stood and embraced Nina. He was roughly the same height as her – as in not tall enough. He held her tightly and she stroked the back of his head softly as he wailed into her shoulder.

'I didn't do it.'

'I know,' said Nina, feeling very detached from his firm embrace.

'I didn't do anything. Honestly. They're crazy.'

'I know.'

'I love you.'

'I know. Poor baby.' She held his shoulders and gently pulled him away from her. 'So where is the van now?'

Emen covered his face. He was a wreck. 'I didn't want to do it. I argued against it. I wanted to tell George but they told me not to.'

'George doesn't know?'

'No. No one other than Garfelli and Del Papa.'

Nina took a pace away from the sobbing heap that was Emen Trouville.

'And yet Frank's the one going to High Wycombe police station to get Jason.'

'Yes,' said Emen. He looked at Nina for a moment. 'Oh, God.'

35

'Case 312, your Honour, the Crown versus Jason John Nash.'

Monday morning, bright and early, up with the larks, Jason was washed, clean and ready for anything.

'And what is the charge?'

The magistrate was an elderly Pakistani with what Jason thought was a kindly, world-worn face.

'First-degree murder, your Honour,' said the clerk of the court, an equally old fellow. Not a lot of cut and thrust in High Wycombe, thought Jason.

'I see.' The magistrate looked down at his papers. 'How does the defendant plead?'

'Guilty,' said Jason without hesitation.

The magistrate looked at him over the top of his glasses. 'I presume there is going to be an application for bail?'

Jason looked at Lord Preston as he stood up. As usual the lord looked very well groomed – beautiful suit, immaculate cuffs. Jason knew how hard that was to maintain. He'd always had trouble with cuffs and had shied away from the whole white shirt thing as a result.

He discreetly checked his own cuffs. They were looking pretty smart, all things considered. At least he had managed to get into something other that the T-shirt and old jeans he had been given by the police.

The previous evening he had spoken to his sister on the phone.

Nina had left a message with the desk sergeant at the police station on Saturday night to the effect that he should call her. He was allowed to on Sunday afternoon. It was a very brief conversation.

'Jason, Emen has spilt his guts. It's very much in your interest to say nothing about what's inside you.'

'Oh, bit late. I blurted, but no one here believes me anyway.'

'Good. Well, you can lie and cover up, can't you.'

'I have a doctorate in the art, sis.'

'Okay. Garfelli may try something on the way back. Or Del Papa. You know how to mess things up, don't you, Jase?'

'You're talking to the king of the fuck-up.'

'You need to fuck up big time, brother.'

For thirty years she had been whining at him to behave, not to break things, not to be such a pillock. Now she was telling him to really screw up. He couldn't wait. He realised Del Papa would probably try and zap him with some data overload, so he would have to work fast.

'I'm on it,' he said with a smile. Then he hung up.

When he woke up on Monday morning, the cell was bright. He peered up at the glass bricks which looked out who knew where – somewhere that caught the sun. The cell door opened and along with his fried breakfast he was handed a suit and shirt.

The breakfast was followed by a visit from Detective Inspector Morris, the officer who had interviewed him the previous day.

'Mr Nash, something rather interesting has come up.'

'Oh, really?'

'There's a report in the paper today which says you have a silicon chip inserted into your brain which is controlling your every action.'

'Excellent,' Jason said as he stuffed his mouth with a standard British copper fry-up. 'It's total bollocks, if you'll excuse my French, Officer.'

'Well, in the statement you made to me you claimed you had a computer chip inserted in your neck.'

'Yeah, I know, but I'm in a desperate state. I've just killed my mother. I'm in some sort of denial. You'd have to ask a shrink for the correct analysis, but I'm barking, to put it bluntly.'

'Is it true, then, Mr Nash?'

'Does it sound very likely?' said Jason.

'Not really.'

'Exactly. It's just because Nash Systems is working on advanced cybernetics, everyone on the Web thinks I'm some kind of Terminator – you know, half man, half machine. So some tragic nerdy fellow in Wisconsin or Idaho has rung the papers and spun the story. It's like the animal rights nutters – can't believe a word they say. Tofu-heads, we call them. It's complete rubbish.'

'I thought so. Well, see you in court. I'll leave you to your breakfast.'

'Sure, sure,' said Jason.

When he was taken to the court building in the back of a police van, Jason was chatty with his fellow prisoners. There were three in all. One Chinese man sat with his eyes closed, while another swarthy-looking individual occasionally banged the back of his head against the side of the van and cursed. The man sitting opposite Jason was wearing a dishevelled suit and was looking very nervous.

'Cheer up, chief,' said Jason. 'What are they doing you for?'

'Drunk and disorderly,' said the man, clearly well educated, Jason noted.

'Trash a pub, did you?'

'No, my house. Well, the house where my ex-wife lives.'

'With her new boyfriend,' Said Jason knowingly.

'How did you know?'

'Oh, I was right! Wow. Cool.'

'What about you?' asked the man.

'Oh, I stabbed my mother fourteen times on Friday night.'

'Jesus,' said the man.

The rest of the journey was spent in silence. Even the swarthy-looking man kept quiet.

Lord Preston gave him a dark blue tie when they met in the cell. 'Put this on,' he said. 'You don't look too bad, all things considered.'

'Yeah, I feel quite optimistic,' said Jason.

Lord Preston looked at him gravely. 'Do you? I can't imagine why. Anyway, for goodness' sake don't *look* optimistic.'

'We would like to apply for bail, your Honour,' he confirmed a few minutes later in court. 'As you can see from the initial social enquiry report and the psychiatrist's notes, Mr Nash has led a very non-violent life until this point. He is a respected businessman and has a great many ties in this country.'

Lord Preston sat down as soon as he'd finished speaking.

'This is a very serious case, Lord Preston,' said the magistrate politely. 'First-degree murder is not a simple matter. There might be a great deal of public concern if a self-admitted murderer were allowed to walk the streets.'

Lord Preston bounced back up.

'My client is willing to live under any restrictions the court sees fit to impose.'

The magistrate raised his eyebrows. 'Is he now? Very well, bail is set at one million pounds and the defendant must reside at his home address and report to the police on a daily basis until the case comes to trial.'

Jason followed Lord Preston out of the small magistrates' court and into the corridor.

'There is a little bit of press interest,' said Lord Preston as they approached the exterior doors. Jason noticed they had been joined by Frank Garfelli and Michael Del Papa.

'Morning, guys,' he said cheerily. He had expected to see Garfelli; Del Papa was a bit of a surprise. 'What are you doing here, Michael? Undertaking a bit of security work now?'

'We're just making sure you get home safely,' said Garfelli. He got to the door first and held it open. Jason couldn't stifle a laugh as he saw what waited for him outside the entrance to the building. Nothing less than a horde of cameramen, flashing lights, TV crews, and people with microphones.

'Bloody Nora,' he said. 'What's all this about? I only killed my mum.'

'Are you a cyborg?' asked a young woman with glasses.

'My client is not making any statements,' Lord Preston shouted to the heaving mass of newshounds. He turned to Jason and whispered into his ear, 'Please don't say anything.'

Frank Garfelli forced his way through the crowd with what Jason thought was more aggression than necessary.

'Let's just get to the car,' he shouted back to Jason.

Lord Preston grabbed his arm and gestured for him to bend down. The lawyer was not a tall man, and Jason had to remain bent as he walked. 'I'm going in a separate vehicle. There's some sort of control device in the car you're in. I suggest you disable it at your earliest convenience. Take extreme care, and I'll see you back at the ranch.'

Jason looked at Lord Preston, who stared at him right in the eye. 'Thanks a lot, your Lordness,' he said with a big grin.

As Jason and Garfelli approached the pavement, a black Ford Galaxy fitted with tinted windows pulled up. The rear sliding door opened before it had fully come to a halt. A man in a grey suit wearing mirrored sunglasses held the door open and Jason was rapidly hustled inside.

'Are you the Terminator?' asked a young man who had pushed his way half into the vehicle. 'We've heard that you're the bionic man. Is this true?'

'I'm just the Nash, guys, you'd better believe it!' said Jason. The young man was roughly pushed out by the individual in the mirrored shades and the door slammed shut.

'Bloody Nora, what was all that?' said Jason as the car started to move off. He saw that Del Papa was sitting in front of a large flight case which had taken the place of one of the seats. Garfelli was in the front passenger seat. The driver, a large black man, didn't seem to take any notice of him and concentrated on getting the vehicle through the small crowd of reporters and camera operators.

'The media have gotten hold of some bullshit story and they're running with it,' said Garfelli. 'There's nothing we can do but ride the storm.'

'Hey, fellers, there's nothing I like more than riding storms.' Jason laughed as he slowly moved towards what was clearly designated 'his seat'. 'Been doing it all my life.'

'You seem kind of happy for a guy who killed his own mother,' said Garfelli accusingly.

'Yeah, I am, aren't I. But what do you know, eh? Frankie boy, things are never quite what they seem, are they, my old son. Whoops.'

Jason made himself fall forward as the vehicle turned a corner and put his hand out to protect himself. Unfortunately for Del Papa, what his hand grabbed was a series of firewire and RS232 cables plugged into the rear of the equipment in the flight case. As he fell, he ripped them as hard and fast as he could. They tore out with an ugly sound of breaking plastic.

'Shit. Sorry, Michael,' said Jason as he started to pull himself up. He held the wires in front of him, smiling broadly. 'Looks like I've screwed up again.'

'You shitball!' said Michael in utter disbelief. 'I don't fucking believe it!'

'Has it damaged the kit?'

'Damaged it! Damaged it!' screamed Del Papa. Jason noticed a line of spittle resting on his beard. 'It's totally screwed it.' He threw a small control box at the laptop screen in front of him. 'Shit!'

'What's this all for, anyway?' said Jason as he prodded the series of transmitter and condenser controls on the front of the machine.

'Leave it!' snapped Garfelli.

'Too late,' said Del Papa. 'We're seriously off line here.'

'Shit,' said Garfelli. Jason watched him start to turn. He didn't know what he was going to do but he wasn't about to wait for things to even start getting ugly. Although he was physically hopeless and 'chronically uncoordinated', according to his school games master, the pre-emptive fuck-up was Jason's spectacular skill, honed over many years.

'Whoops,' he said as he threw himself backward into the

arms of the man in the mirrored sunglasses. The man wailed as, quite by accident but perfectly in keeping with his physical insensitivity, Jason turned to try to push himself away, but in so doing landed his knee in the man's groin. He smiled at the now groaning individual. 'Hi, we haven't met. I'm Jason.'

The man grunted, both hands cradling his groin.

'Bit dark in here to be wearing those, isn't it?' said Jason, referring to the mirrored shades. The man looked at him. Jason could see his own slightly inane grin in each lens.

'Suit yourself. So, what's your job? You working at Nash Systems, are you?'

'He's with me,' said Frank Garfelli, who had moved around in his seat so that he was facing Jason. His arms were hidden, but Jason felt he was probably holding a weapon.

'Oh, you're with Garfelli, are you, and what does that mean?'

'He's been hired to ensure your safe return,' said Garfelli.

'Oh, like a bodyguard kind of thing,' said Jason. 'Cool.' He smiled at the man again. 'Are you tooled?'

'I'm sorry, sir?' grunted the man.

'Are you packing heat, carrying? Are you tooled up with an Uzi under your jacket?'

The man said nothing. Jason looked forward. They were approaching traffic lights. 'It's left here, isn't it?' he said. The driver hesitated a moment.

'Straight on!' shouted Garfelli. A car alongside them hooted as the driver changed lanes. He braked hard and in that moment Jason pushed the head of the man with mirrored shades as hard as he could, which was quite hard. As it made contact with the window, Jason quickly slipped his hand inside the man's jacket and immediately felt the butt of an automatic pistol.

'Shit, a real gun. Cool,' he said, extracting the weapon carefully.

'There's no need for that,' said Garfelli.

Jason looked at him and smiled. 'You are so right, Frank,

there really is no need for these things.' He waved the gun around casually. 'Which makes me wonder why Mirror Man here has got one stashed under his coat. Just tell the driver to go straight to Nash Systems. I'll sit back here with Pretty Boy and . . . oh, Frank, while I think about it, shut the fuck up.'

The rest of the journey was spent in silence. Jason stared out of the window at the anonymous countryside they passed through – Bedfordshire or Buckinghamshire or wherever. All he knew was the towns and villages looked like dreary quiet places that he was happy he had never lived in. Cookham was bad enough. But he didn't have to worry about it. He would never live in some windswept roadside house. He'd never have to – he'd be living in a prison. Didn't sound too good, but, boy, it was going to be fun getting there.

36

When she woke on Monday morning, the sun was shining and the air was truly warm for the first time that year. Nina opened her bedroom window and breathed in deeply. It was beautiful. The air seemed to sparkle in her throat, everything was so fresh.

She showered and dressed, taking care of her body for the first time in ages. She checked herself in the mirror in the bedroom. She was very thin, too thin. She turned and looked at her bum. Somehow, even though she could see she was too skinny, her bum still looked big. She smiled at herself and said, 'He's coming back!'

Once dressed, she went downstairs and fired up her MP3 player. She chose a Penguin Café Orchestra folder and danced around her house as she ate an apple. She then consumed an enormous breakfast of bacon, scrambled eggs, grilled tomatoes and wholemeal bread.

She drove to work listening for the first time to a Robbie Williams classic collection Jason had given her for Christmas five years previously. It sounded great.

All this because of one phone call, one short conversation. Just after Nina had flopped into her bed the night before, the phone rang. Initially she had left it – she didn't want to have to deal with another chapter in the unfolding horror. She had done enough telephone talk for one day; had been unable to get to sleep, there was so much going on. As the phone continued to ring, she cursed herself for not unplugging it.

Then a voice from her answer machine caught her attention. A voice from a long way away.

'Uh, hi, Nina.'

It was Pete Van Missen. Nina didn't think she had ever got out of a bed faster. She dived across the hall and flew down the stairs three at a time. Her feet slipped on the parquet floor as she dashed, stumbling, towards the phone.

'I guess you're not home, but I . . .'

'Pete! Pete, is that you?' she said, breathing heavily and speaking far too excitedly. She realised she had already given herself away totally.

'Hey, you're there.'

'Where are you?'

'I'm calling from my hospital bed.'

'Where, where?'

'Virginia,' he said, each word an effort. 'I've been trying to get you for a while but your lines have been busy.'

'Oh, Pete. You can use a phone! This is amazing.'

'No, sorry. Someone dialled for me. I'm wearing a headset.'

Nina sat down, disappointed but still thrilled to hear his voice.

'I've missed you,' she said suddenly, then bit her fist as she realised what she was admitting. She didn't know what sort of state he was in – this sort of approach might be completely inappropriate. She tried for an instant to imagine how she would feel if she were paralysed. It was impossible.

'I've been hearing that things haven't been going too well,' he said. She noticed he had to breathe in between every other word.

'No. It's been crazy.'

'Real sorry to hear about your mom.'

'Yes. Yes.' Nina knew she couldn't explain how complex it was over a transatlantic line. She didn't want to talk about it any more. 'How are you?'

'Well, I'm almost totally paralysed, so . . .'

'Can you get back here?' she said without thinking. 'I want to look after you.'

'Nina, I don't blame you. You have your own life to lead.'

'No, Pete, listen. I know I don't know who you really are or

313

where you're really from, but I want to help. We know the chips work, we know we can send signals from a mainframe to an insert. Boy, do we know we can.'

'Jason?'

'Yeah. It's very ugly. I don't even know whose side you're on, but I'm past caring, and anyway, it's all irrelevant now.'

'Why d'you say that?'

'Because the whole covert nature of the operation is about to be blown sky high.'

'Don't tell me any more,' he said sternly.

'Other people are listening?'

'You're learning,' he said lightly.

'Sod the lot of them. What is important is that it's only a matter of time before we can send signals from one chip implant to another.'

'I'm sorry, Nina. I don't know what you're talking abou . . .'

'If we insert a chip above the damage in your spinal cord and another below . . .'

'Oh my God.'

'We could do something good with all this stuff.'

The line went quiet for a while.

'Pete, are you still there?'

'Nina. Don't bullshit me. Please.'

'I'm not. It's experimental, I know, but we've got to try. I can't leave you like you are. I . . .'

'What?'

'I want you to walk again.'

Nina felt a lump in her throat. She didn't want to cry but something was welling up that she had no control over.

Pete said nothing. She bit her lip, then went on, 'I want to see you again. I have feelings for you.' Her whole body folded up in a knot of tension.

'Nina, I'm going crazy here. Hearing your voice. Your voice kills me. Nothing has changed in my head, it just doesn't have a body connected to it, and I want a body so . . .'

Nina's whole body was locked. She couldn't breathe.

314

'So I can hold you.'

Nina burst into tears. For the first time she could remember she cried. She threw her head around, trying to make the crying stop, but there was nothing she could do.

She could hear that Pete was crying too. She wasn't sure what he said, but it sounded like 'so badly'.

They didn't say much else – she couldn't really speak – but when she finally hung up the phone she felt as if she were flying. Her world had gone completely mad and she was happy.

He had promised to try to get transferred to England. He was coming back. Nina sat leaning against the wall for a long time, running through what could happen. Most of it was bad. She needed to act, and she needed to act immediately. She picked up the phone, then put it down again. She found her old leather coat in a cupboard near the top of the stairs. Checking her bag, she realised she had no loose change. She returned to the kitchen and found some in an old jam jar under the sink.

After a ten minute walk to a phone box outside a burger bar, and two phone calls to national newspapers, she returned home, feeling very nervous but slightly more in control.

When she pulled up in the Nash System carpark on Monday morning, it was immediately clear that events had already started to roll. A large crowd of reporters was standing around in front of the building. A police car was drawn up in her normal parking space, so she had to park in front of the freight delivery bay. As she got out of the car a young man ran up to her, carrying a microphone.

'Professor Nash?'

'No,' said Nina with a smile.

'D'you know Professor Nash?'

'Yes, she's wonderful,' said Nina, walking quickly through the crowd, everyone looking at her.

'That's her!' someone shouted.

'Professor Nash! Is it true?' said the young man with a microphone.

'I have no comment to make at this time,' she said. She was

smiling, which she suddenly realised could give a very mis-
leading impression. She wiped the smile off her face as fast as
she could. Cameras flashed in front of her. The journalists
massed together, completely blocking her way. She spotted the
policewoman who had told her of her mother's death trying to
make her way through the crowd.

'Make way, please. Stand back. Let the professor through,'
she said, being completely ignored by the jostling mass.

'Professor, did you put the chip in your brother?' asked a
woman with short blonde hair.

'Like I said, I have no comment to make at the present time.
Excuse me.'

The policewoman held Nina's arm and led her through the
crowd. Questions were being shouted at her, too many to
comprehend. As Nina reached the door, a man in a grey suit
opened it for her, nodding politely as she entered. Nina turned
to thank the policewoman, but she was already busy keeping
the journalists out.

'How the hell did they all find out, then!' screamed George as
Nina walked into the reception area. Amy was standing in
front of him, looking dreadful. 'I haven't spoken to anyone.
I've been staying with my mum!' she wailed.

'Good morning, George. Everything all right?' Nina's voice
oozed concern.

'Oh, Professor. I'm sorry,' said George, sounding genuine for
once.

'What have you done?'

'No, I'm sorry for this . . .' He pointed towards the journalists outside the front door.

'Oh, well, it's no less that I'd expect under the circumstances,' said Nina.

'You haven't seen the papers, I take it,' said George. Nina
glanced at the reception desk, where a pile of newspapers had
been scattered.

'TERMINATOR STRIKES!' said the *Sun* next a picture of
Jason taken from the company website.

'IT'S CHIPS FOR CYBORG KILLER,' said the *Mirror*, this time carrying a picture of Jason looking very drunk and dishevelled, probably from some dreadful dot-commoners party he'd attended.

As she lifted the paper she noticed the *Independent* underneath. 'CHIP INSERT BLAMED FOR MURDER,' read the headline. Next to it was *The Times*. 'MURDERER WAS CONTROLLED BY COMPUTER.'

'Oh, wow,' said Nina.

'Who blew the story?' said George. 'I'm going fucking crazy here. It has to be someone in the building. For once we know it wasn't Jason.'

'George, wouldn't our energies be better employed trying to work out how to use this story to our advantage?'

George Quinn stood glued to the spot. He said nothing, just stared at her.

'Why did you do it, Nina?' he said eventually.

'I'm only trying to protect my brother.'

'So, was it you?'

'I really couldn't say,' flirted Nina with a coy smile. George grabbed her shoulders and gripped her painfully.

'Professor, if you don't tell me what's going on I am going to seriously lose it!'

'Let go of me, George, right now.' She held his manic stare. He loosened his grip. 'There are at least fifty news reporters watching you assault me right now. I think this is referred to as fanning the flames. I suggest we go upstairs where we can exchange information on a one-for-one basis.'

George let go, managing to push her away a little as he did so. She stumbled backwards and half sat on the Spitfire wing that was the reception desk.

'Thank you,' she said as she straightened her clothes. She turned to Amy and smiled sympathetically. 'Amy, if you want to keep out of this, I quite understand. I'm going to tell George some things about what Jason did on Friday night, why he did them.'

'No, I need to know too,' said Amy weakly.

'Okay, let's go upstairs.'

The three of them climbed the stairs and walked along the concrete corridor to George's office. It was a mess, papers everywhere. He walked to the window and closed the blinds.

'What things?' asked George.

'First things first. Has Jason got bail?'

'Yes.'

'When will everyone get here?'

'They're on their way. About an hour.'

'Okay, we have to work fast. George, I will tell you what I know, but in exchange I want to know exactly who I have been working for at Nash Systems, and I want Pete Van Missen brought back here immediately.'

'You what? What's Van Missen got to do with it?'

'Never mind right now. Will you do it?'

'Well, I guess I can try.'

'No, George, you never try and do things, you do them. That's what I want.'

'Okay. Consider it done.'

'Good, okay.' She had to choke back a sob that was building in her throat. She breathed deeply. 'Listen carefully. Jason did not kill my mother single handed. Frank Garfelli and Michael Del Papa helped him – no, forced him.' Nina took the video-tape out of her bag. 'At precisely the time the murder took place a white VW van pulled up in the carpark of my parents' hotel. No one got out – they didn't need to.'

Nina slid the tape into the all-in-one VCR on the shelf behind George Quinn's desk. She picked up the remote and pressed 'play'. The now familiar black-and-white image of the van in the carpark played on the small screen.

'Inside this van I believe there was a directional transmitter which sent a data stream to the chip in Jason's neck. What was sent was a recording of flashback that Pete Van Missen occasionally has, a huge nervous reaction. Very traumatic for Pete when he has it, very traumatic for Jason when it fired into his central nervous system, but not as bad as it was for my mother.'

'Jesus.' George was transfixed by the TV screen.

'Now, I just want to make it clear that I know you tried transmitting to Jason when he had the fight with Garfelli, when you laced my coffee to keep me out of the building. I know you know about that, but I understand and want to believe that you didn't know about the van.'

'The van,' said George very quietly.

'They are completely out of control, George. I don't know who Garfelli is working for, or Del Papa come to that, but it's not for me.'

'You have proof of this?'

'All I have is this security tape from the hotel. It clearly shows the van arrive, wait, and leave immediately after the event.'

'Oh, Christ,' said Amy. 'Is there a chip in Jason's neck?'

'Yes,' said Nina, still watching George.

'Oh, my poor baby,' muttered Amy. 'That explains it.'

'What?' asked George.

'He went completely doolally before his mum came in. He was screaming and shouting and throwing things about. He kept telling me to get out of the way, but as soon as his mum came in he totally lost it. It was terrible – his body was twitching and moving in a really weird way.'

'So he didn't just attack his mother when she interrupted you and Jason,' said George. 'He was already affected before she came in.'

'Yes. She must have come in because of the noise,' said Amy.

'Amy, did you tell the police this when they questioned you?' asked George.

'Well, yes, but not in so many words. If I'd known about the chip, I would have said.'

'Okay. Jesus, this is going to take some handling,' said George, holding his head in his hands.

'It's terrible,' said Amy, clearly on the edge of tears. 'Poor Jason, he couldn't help it. He was screaming at his mum to get away, but she was trying to hold him.' She broke down and sobbed. Nina wanted to comfort her but felt herself shaking. She didn't want to hear this, didn't want to know how traumatic her mother's last few moments were. She knew she had thrown herself into solving what happened as a way of not dealing with these feelings. She couldn't let them overwhelm her now, she had to concentrate. She turned and looked at George, her eyes red rimmed.

'Fucking Garfelli,' he said. He stood still for a moment, looking at his telephone. 'Okay, I'm on this.' He went and sat behind his desk, picked up the receiver, then stopped and turned to Nina. 'Wait. Who's involved? Garfelli and Del Papa. What about Trouville?'

'He isolated Van Missen's flashback data, but I don't believe he was any more involved than that. He told me.'

'He told you?'

'In a roundabout way. He's very upset, not surprisingly. Pretty odd management system you operate here, George. Keep a lot of scientists in the dark long enough and they'll invent the torch.'

'Okay, give me five minutes.'

'What are you saying? Get out of your office while you make everything worse?' snapped Nina. 'I've always left things like this to you. No more, George.'

'Nina, I cannot allow you to stay.'

Nina laughed. 'What am I going to find out? That you work directly for the US government and this is a covert operation to develop technology for military use? D'you really think I'm stupid enough not to have worked that out already?'

'It's not that simple. And I don't work for the US government. I'm a freelance business manager. My CV is kosher, Nina. I am not a spook.'

'I didn't know you were doing that,' said Amy. 'I thought we were making things that helped people.'

'Yes, we all did, Amy,' said Nina with a kind smile. 'It's easier that way. All these stupid scientists with their ethical qualms can really hold up a project.'

320

George dialled a number. Nina watched him carefully.

'Hi, it's George.' He was silent for a moment, then went on, 'We have a problem.' Another silence. Nina stared at him – no emotion showed on his face. 'Okay. What do I do with Garfelli and Del Papa?'

Another silence.

'Yeah, both of them.'

George glanced up at Nina. Still nothing was revealed by his expression.

'Okay.'

'Van Missen,' Nina reminded him. George nodded.

'We also need Van Missen back here as soon as,' he said. 'Yeah, I know it's complicated, but if I'm going to keep this fucking shit heap from exploding I need him back and I need him back soon.'

George hung up.

'What was that?'

'That was the call I really did not want to make,' said George. 'These people do not fuck about.'

'Which people?'

'The people who supplied Garfelli, and Pete Van Missen,' said George. 'This is not going to be fun.'

37

'Can I borrow those shades? They are so cool,' said Jason as they turned into the Millford Business Park.

The man in the grey suit didn't move. Jason removed the glasses and put them on.

'Brilliant. Anyone got any hair gel?'

'What?' Garfelli snapped.

'Hair gel, you know, shit you put in your hair?' said Jason. He could feel the burn, the feeling he had known all his life, making everything that was bad so much worse so that the original bad was forgotten in the chaos. This was no longer clothes in the bath or the odd house fire; this was big time.

'I got some coconut oil,' said the driver after a moment. He wasn't American. Jason noticed a distinct London accent.

'Oh, yeah. Great stuff, chief. Where is it?'

'In the black bag, right behind you.'

Jason leaned towards the man sitting next to him and whispered into his ear. 'Remember I have nothing to lose. Your gun is pointing to your crotch and I'm crap at guns. Could go off really easily.'

He leaned over the seat and saw a black bag in the luggage area behind him. He pulled it over the seat, unzipped it and delved around. He found a pot with a label on the top which pronounced it to be 'Black and White hairdressing ointment'. He opened it. The smell of coconut greeted his nostrils. 'Oh, yes, this is the stuff.'

He took a big dollop and massaged it into his hair, pulling his hair upward and smoothing the sides back. The ointment stayed on his hands no matter how hard he rubbed it on his hair.

'Anyone got a tissue?'

'What the fuck are you doing back there?' said Garfelli. He turned to look at Jason. 'Oh, fuck,' he said when he saw the transformation.

Jason was wearing the mirrored shades, his hair was sticking up, he jutted out his chin and, adopting his worst Austrian accent, quoted the classic line.

'*Hasta la vista*, baby.'

'Give him a tissue,' said Garfelli. The driver passed a box of tissues to the man in the grey suit just as they pulled into the carpark at Nash Systems. Jason took a tissue as he looked through the smoked-glass windows. The carpark was swarming with people.

'Okay, here's how we do this,' said Garfelli quickly. 'We drive right up to the door, I'll secure one end of the vehicle, you take the other.'

The man in the grey suit nodded. The car drove slowly towards the entrance as the crowd of journalists swarmed around it.

'Hey, a welcoming committee.' Jason was delighted to see the sheer number of people. 'I need to meet my public.'

'For fuck sake stay where you are. We don't want any more trouble,' said Garfelli sternly.

'Oh, screw you!' said Jason. Without warning he pushed past the grey-suited man and opened the sliding door. He heard Garfelli shout something as he stepped out of the slow-moving vehicle. It pulled to a halt, but it was too late – the crowds had already engulfed Jason.

'Mr Nash, Mr Nash, over here.'

Jason stood as tall as he could, which as he was over six foot four was fairly tall. He turned his head very slowly, his mirrored shades giving him the courage to carry out his master plan.

'Is it true you are half man, half computer?' asked a young man.

'What is your name?' said Jason in his cod Austrian accent. 'I will find you.'

'Have you got a chip in your brain?' asked an old journalist with a bad comb-over hairstyle. Jason turned to him slowly, maintaining a very stern expression.

'You are bald, everyone knows. Accept it,' he said. 'Stand back or I will have to remove you.' The man looked genuinely scared and stood to one side. No one asked any more questions. They just moved alongside Jason as he strode towards the door.

'Get him inside!' shouted Garfelli, pushing people out of the way.

'Please take off the glasses. This really isn't helping,' said Michael Del Papa, now at Jason's side and trying to guide him forward.

A policewoman opened the door for them. Jason turned, saw that Garfelli and the grey-suited man were right behind him and pushed between them. The journalists and camera crews gathered around. Jason lifted both hands and there was instant silence.

'I'll be back,' he said, then turned and entered the building.

As soon as they were inside, Garfelli confronted him.

'What the fuck was that all about?'

Jason took off the mirrored glasses and smiled at the annoying redhead. 'It's called spin, Garfelli, you poor confused little minion. If I'd just walked in here and said "no comment", like all the other sad tossers who've fallen foul of the Old Bill, they would have been hanging around for weeks, digging and delving. They think I'm the Terminator, so what the hell? I may as well give 'em what they want.'

'I strongly advise you don't pull such a stunt again. It's not going to help you,' said Garfelli.

Jason sniffed. 'Nothing's going to help me, is it, Frankie boy? I'm fucked, so I may as well go down guns blazing. Eh? That sounds like what you'd do.'

Garfelli shook his head. 'Let's go upstairs.'

'What's happened to your hair?' asked Nina as Jason arrived

in the boardroom. She was standing at the far end next to George Quinn.

'Oh, wait, wait, you'll love this,' said Jason, taking the mirrored shades from his breast pocket. He slipped them on, stood up tall and rigid, then, adopting the same bad Austrian accent, said, 'Are you Sarah Connor?'

Nina screamed with laughter. 'Do it again, do it again!'

Jason responded. 'I am looking for Sarah Connor. Give me your clothes.'

'Jason, you are mad!' said Nina. She rushed across the room and embraced him. 'You okay?'

He took the mirrored shades off and looked down at his weird sister. 'Sure, sure. Where's Amy?'

'She's making coffee. She'll be back in a minute.'

'I need to see her.' He walked towards the door, turned and slipped the shades back on. 'I'll be back.'

He ran down the concrete corridor, hearing George Quinn shout after him. He ignored him, burst into the staff kitchen and picked Amy up almost before she could react.

'Oh, baby, baby,' she said into his ear as he held her off the floor.

'I'm so sorry,' said Jason. 'Really, I'm so sorry to have put you through all this. You don't deserve any of it. I'm so sorry.'

'No, no. It's okay. I love you so much nothing matters,' she said, clinging to him tightly. 'What happened at the court?'

Jason put her back on the floor, still holding her, but looking down at her face. 'I pleaded guilty. Should mean you don't have to be a witness. I don't want you to suffer any more.'

'Jason, you know whatever happens I'll wait for you.'

He put his hand to her mouth. 'Don't, baby, don't say anything. It's all going to be okay. The Nash is back on line.'

Jason helped Amy carry the coffee back to the boardroom. He walked behind her, watching her carefully. It all made perfect sense. He had found someone he could love just before he had totally and completely blown it. It was the pinnacle of his failure – he would never fail this badly again. Add to that the fact that she seemed to genuinely love him and he had achieved closure.

'Life is most definitely weird,' he said as he entered the boardroom.

'Okay, if we can all settle down, let's get started,' said George Quinn. Jason checked who was present – everyone from the top drawer of Nash Systems, as far as he could tell, except for Emen Trouville.

'What's on the old agenda, then, Georgie boy,' he quipped.

'Please, Jason, this isn't going to be easy for any of us,' said Nina. Jason raised his eyebrows and made an elaborate mime of zipping his mouth shut. George cleared his throat and put his hands flat on the table.

'People, we have a problem,' he said. He slowly turned and looked at Frank Garfelli. 'A major problem within the company. What I'm going to have to do now is something I really don't want to do, but I have no choice. Frank, I know what happened Friday night.'

Frank Garfelli looked up slowly. He said nothing.

'You are being recalled as of now,' said George.

Jason smiled. 'Oh dear, Frankie, you have been a bad boy, haven't you?'

George held his hand up. 'Please, Jason, this is very serious.'

'Sure, sure.'

Cindy Volksmann was looking around the room like a deer dazzled by headlights. 'What's going on? What are you doing, George?'

'Frank has abused his privileges as a Nash Systems operative, Cindy,' said George, glancing in her direction, but his attention was focused on Garfelli, who he turned back to immediately. 'He is totally out of line and I will not tolerate it.'

'You don't have the authority,' said Frank Garfelli slowly.

'Frank, would I be saying this if I wasn't sure I had the authority? Get the hell out of here now. Leave some real professionals to clear up the mess you made.'

Jason grimaced at Amy, who was nervously pouring coffee.

Old Georgie boy was definitely in a bit of a mood. He watched as George turned his gaze on Del Papa. 'Michael, we no longer need your services either.'

'What the . . .?' was all Del Papa said, although he was twitching violently in his seat.

'You know why, Michael,' said Nina. 'I won't make things worse by going over everything.'

'You can't, though, surely you can't,' said Del Papa. 'I mean, what about my contract?'

'Consider it shredded,' said George calmly. 'You operated beyond the parameters of the original agreement.'

'Hey, but this is outrageous. I assumed I was working well within the guidelines. I didn't do anything that wasn't in my remit. I worked with Garfelli under his instructions.'

'What the hell are you all talking about?' interrupted Cindy Volksmann. 'Jesus, this damn company is hard enough to run without this kind of screw-up. How come I didn't know about this?'

'None of us did,' said George. 'Frank isn't working for us. He's clearly working for another employer.'

'Yeah,' said Jason, although he didn't really have a clue who anyone worked for. It was as if no one really knew what was going on. He was used to not quite being sure what was going on at Nash Systems, but he'd always assumed everyone else did.

'This is bullshit,' said Garfelli. 'You've got no proof.'

'We have enough,' said George.

'Garfelli, you're a dead man as far as I'm concerned,' said Jason, staring at the neatly dressed spook.

'Don't threaten me, Nash.'

'Listen, chum,' said Jason, standing up, 'all I've got to do is get my big sis to play back a bit of Van Missen's fighting technique and I'll spread you all over this office like strawberry jam.'

'Please, Jason,' said George.

'Jason. Sit down,' said Nina. 'It's okay, it's all going to be okay.'

Jason straightened his suit without taking his eyes off Gar-felli, then slowly sat down. Everything started to make more sense as he stared at the two men opposite him. They were even more ruthless than he was.

'It's all clear to me now, Michael,' he said. 'Your little box of tricks in the people carrier. I mashed it, sis.' He turned to Nina. 'Mashed it up good and proper. I was a right pain, wasn't I, Michael? Just as bloody well, mate. You were going to data-zap me and rip the chip out of my neck in the back of the car. Well, pretty boy, the chip stays in. Anyone so much as tries to poke it and I'll do a full Van Missen. I reckon I've absorbed some skills. I don't even need a data stream.'

Michael Del Papa stood up and started jittering around beside his chair. 'This is utterly outrageous. I demand to see someone in authority.'

'I am that someone, Michael,' said George with a smile.

'How am I supposed to know that? How does anyone know who runs this goddamn place. For Christ sake, I was acting on behalf of the company. Don't tell me there was some fuck-awful committee up here deciding what was and was not ethical. Fuck your ethics, you hypocrites. Jee-zus! How can you sit there and pretend you're not involved!' Michael stared at Nina through his thick glasses. 'You, Professor Nash, you knew what we were doing, for fuck sake.'

'I knew what I was doing, I did not know what you were doing!' Nina shouted. 'How dare you try and implicate me in something I was deliberately kept out of, you fat fuck!'

'Yoh, get in there, sis,' shouted Jason. 'Give him one from me.'

Michael twitched some more, intertwining his stubby fingers in front of his comfortably sized stomach. 'I didn't know this was going to happen!' he whined eventually.

'What did you think was going to happen, Michael?' asked Nina sharply.

'I don't know. Your brother is a very disturbed individual. We had no idea this would happen. Sure, I'm really upset about it, but as far as I was concerned it was part of the programme.'

'That's bull, Michael, it's not worthy of you,' said Nina. 'You sent the most intense data we had on disk direct to his central nervous system when he was with his family to see if you could override all normal learned human constraints. To see if you and your fucked-up military cronies could control a soldier under any circumstances.'

George chipped in. 'I know this course of action was vetoed at the highest level, Michael. It was not part of any programme I was involved in putting together. Garfelli is clearly working for another agency. I have to protect this operation.'

'But why pick on me! Garfelli gave the fucking orders,' said Michael, now jumping up and down on the spot. 'This is not fair. I am a scientist, not some military crazy like him.' He glared at Garfelli, who also stood up.

'Will you shut the fuck up or d'you need some help?' he threatened.

'Oh, this is just getting silly,' said Nina. 'Will you all stop behaving like little boys and just go. None of the rest of us wants to be part of this. You are so thick, Garfelli. George is getting you out of a lot of trouble. If you don't go now you will be implicated in this case. Very heavily implicated, I'll make damn sure of it. I have enough evidence to get you convicted for aiding and abetting a murder at the very least. Don't you see what George is doing?'

'Overstepping his command.'

'What are you talking about? Command? He's not military,' said Nina.

'Who's being dumb now?' asked Garfelli flatly. Nina looked at George. Jason looked at George.

'Jesus, you are a spook!' said Nina.

'It's complicated,' said George.

'Oh, for fuck sake. What is going on here!' Jason shouted. He'd had enough – they were all barking. 'Can we start again, 'cos I don't have the first fucking idea what's going on.'

'Jason, I will explain everything if you will be patient.

Garfelli. I want you to leave now. There is a flight booked for you. I suggest you do the same, Michael. You have both been ordered to report to Virginia.'

'Why the hell have I got to report to anyone? I'm a scientist, for Christ sake. What is going on here?'

'Michael, you are in very serious trouble. I suggest you report to Virginia where your case will be dealt with.'

'Fuck you, fuck all of you,' said Michael. He got up and left the room. They could hear him muttering 'fucking Virginia!' as he stomped off down the corridor.

Frank Garfelli sighed very slowly and stood up. He put on his own mirrored shades, which Jason thought made him look faintly ridiculous, then, with no attempt at an Austrian accent, he said, 'I'll be back.'

He left the room, and George walked over and shut the door. 'Then there were five,' he said.

'Okay,' said Nina. 'Now we have started, let us finish. Who are you all, who do we work for, are the people we are working for going to continue to allow us to work as we want, and what are we going to do?'

George sat down and sighed heavily. 'I was given *carte blanche* by an American security agency to set up Nash Systems.'

'Why won't you tell us which one?' asked Nina.

'It's irrelevant,' George responded.

Nina looked up to the ceiling and wailed. Jason copied her.

Cindy raised her voice to be heard over the Nash siblings' noise. 'Truly, it makes no difference.'

'Of course it makes a difference, you stupid bitch,' shouted Nina.

Jason carried on wailing, then noticed Amy looking at him, obviously embarrassed. He stopped and cleared his throat. 'Sorry,' he said, then noticed Cindy Volksmann's hackles rising. She clearly wasn't a woman used to being called 'stupid' or 'bitch'. He thought he might have to intervene in a cat fight, but he was ready.

'Please,' said George. 'We are all on the same side here. The

330

object was to develop chip inserts for military as well as other uses.'

'What other uses?' asked Nina.

'Medical uses,' said George. 'Plus advances in the field generally – human–machine interface systems.'

'Oh, let's get real here,' said Cindy. 'There is a lot of interest in the possibility of using the data we have captured to create operating systems for mechanical fighting machines.'

'Jesus,' said Nina.

'Okay, sure, there're ethical implications,' said George.

'Oh, really,' said Nina, on irony overload.

'But the truth is,' George continued, 'the non-military applications are far more interesting, and the agency know that.'

'The agency, the fucking agency,' Nina muttered.

'They support what we are trying to do, and they are very unhappy with what happened to Jason. That was strictly not in the remit. Anyway, calm down about the whole military thing. The funding is channelled through a series of covert and overt operations. It is not a plain and simple military procedure. If that were the case, it would have been done in one of many facilities in the US.'

'I know that,' said Jason cheerily.

Nina looked up and stared at him. 'Do you?'

He stared back. He did now feel a little twinge of guilt. He had never really talked through the operation with George, but he could read between the lines. He had worked out that the kind of money they were receiving would not have come from the private sector – especially during the lull in the tech economy. Anyone from the sector knew that. Military money never dried up. He hadn't explained it to Nina because he knew it would scare her off. Now it didn't seem to matter. Nothing mattered.

'Well, I didn't exactly know it. I just worked it out for myself.'

'Before we all started here?'

'Yeah, I s'pose so.'

'Well, why didn't you work it out for me, you idiot? Why didn't you tell me?'

'Couldn't, could I?'

'Why not?'

'Because you're my ticket, thicko. If I'd told you what I knew, you would never have joined and I'd have been out and back on the dot-com dump. It's not that hard to work out.'

'Typical.' She turned to George. 'I am so dumb. There I was thinking we were doing medical research.'

'We are,' said George.

'Oh, of course,' snapped Nina. 'That's why we've been transmitting traumatic data messages to my brother, to see what he would do. Obviously there're reams of medical reasons for doing that.'

'Look . . .' George tried to interrupt, but Nina wasn't going to be quiet.

'Way to go, sis!' Jason cried, and punched the air. All those years hearing her strident tones, demanding attention and annoying him. Now it was turned on someone else, Jason found her determination positively reassuring.

Nina turned to Cindy Volksmann.

'How much do you know, then, Cindy?'

Cindy smiled. 'I guess I more or less know everything. Except for the shit Garfelli and Del Papa have been up to.'

'Jesus,' said Nina. 'Have I been stupid. Okay, who do you really work for?'

'I'm freelance, like George,' said Cindy easily.

'That doesn't mean a great deal any more,' said Nina. 'How did you get involved?'

'Okay, it's fairly straightforward. Nash Systems was set up through funding from the CIA,' said Cindy in a clear corporate-pitch manner. 'It's not even a secret. It's been in the public domain for some time that the agency is funding tech start-ups, before now in the fields of cryptography and code hacking. The chip insert technology that you have been working on has many applications, as you can imagine. Not all in the realm of the military. There are safety issues, like weapons that will only work in the hands of the legal holder. The police force, security companies and many others are very interested in that kind of thing. So yes, the CIA and various other government institutions have helped us.'

Jason scratched his hair. It was dripping with coconut oil. Amy was sitting very still, not saying anything. Jason noticed Nina looking at her.

'What about you, Amy?'

'What?' she said.

'How much do you know?'

'Nothing,' she said. Jason noticed a tear forming in her eye. She wiped her nose on her sleeve and looked at George, who nodded slightly. 'Well, I didn't know about all this. But George hired me and got me the job at Coventon's. I was supposed to find out stuff and tell him.'

'Jesus! Amy! You're a spook too!' Jason shouted.

'I'm not, I'm not, Jason, honestly. I'm a secretary. I did a three-month course in corporate surveillance, that's all.'

'Where?' asked Nina.

'At MIT in Boston. That's where I met George. Being a secretary can be very boring. I thought it would open up new avenues of work.'

'Oh, baby, corporate surveillance,' said Jason. 'That is so sexy.'

Amy sat in silence for a moment and looked at her hands which were clasped neatly in front of her.

'Well, George hired me earlier this year. I got the job at Coventon's to see what sort of state the company was in. I didn't do anything to damage Coventon's, if that's what you're thinking, I just had to report to George.'

'And was I one of your tasks?' asked Jason.

'No, of course not,' said Amy, tears now streaming down her face. 'Meeting you wasn't in the plan.'

'Oh,' said Jason. 'What a pity. I was hoping you were some

sort of kinky covert shagger who took down executives with your totally hot bod.'

'Oh, baby, that's sweet, but no.' Amy smiled at him through her tears.

'Babes, you being a spook, it's totally horn-ridden,' said Jason. He leaned over the table and kissed her on the lips.

'Jason, please, don't start,' said Nina. 'It was bad enough when you were in my kitchen.'

'May I possibly interrupt,' said Lord Preston. Jason turned to the learned barrister, who had sat quietly in the corner through the whole drama. 'I think we should try and concentrate on the matter in hand. We have to try and keep Jason from going to prison for twenty-five years – at least, I take it that is your collective desire.'

'Of course,' said George. 'But we can't use the chip as an alibi. We're really in a cleft-stick situation here.'

Jason snorted. 'You want to bet. I am not going down because some red-headed twat sent a signal to a chip that I didn't even know was in my neck which made me kill my mum. If I'm going down, you're all coming down with me. Big time.'

There was silence around the table. Jason could almost hear George and Cindy planning to wipe him out, but he didn't give a damn. The nothing-to-lose option had more advantages than he could contemplate.

Nina broke the silence. 'Look at it this way. If there's one thing we will achieve out of this going public, it's that we have incredible proof that the technology works. We can send signals to chip inserts which radically affect the nervous system. We can't go back and uninvent it – this technology works, and all we have to do is ensure it's put to beneficial rather than negative uses.'

'The public are going to freak,' said George. He jerked a thumb towards the window. 'Look at the press out there.'

'The public were always going to freak at some point,' said Nina. 'Let them freak. When they calm down, no one will ever ask "Nash what?"'

'Yeah, cool,' said Jason. He was sure the last phrase was due to his influence.

'The public weren't meant to find out about the military use of this technology,' said George. 'Only the medical side. My take on what Garfelli did is this. Someone in the system wanted to make sure we had to go public to screw the whole thing up. When people use the phrase "military industrial complex", it is just that. Complex. There are a lot of people pulling and pushing in a lot of different ways. There will be technology being developed right now that even I don't know about, technology that's making a call on funds, funds we are receiving. You guys have no idea how hard I've been fighting, trying to keep this set-up afloat. Guys like Garfelli are so dumb they'll always do what they're told, never think of the consequences. What better way to screw the whole thing up than totally blow it in the public arena? We are up against some powerful and hard-to-trace forces here, but maybe you're right. We go public and ride it out – either sink or swim.'

'Well, it will certainly make an interesting case,' said Lord Preston. 'I can't think of a lot of precedents as I sit here. I think Jason and I had better start putting a case together.'

'Great. I'll go out and make a statement to the press,' said George.

'I'll come and listen,' said Nina. 'Not that I don't trust you.'

'I'm going to be really mature and stay here,' added Jason.

Nina smiled at him as she stood. 'It's going to be okay, Jase. I can feel it.'

'Jesus, you feel things? Sure they haven't put a chip in your neck?'

Everyone left the room, leaving Amy and Jason alone.

'D'you know, Amy, I've had a bit of time to think while I was banged up, and d'you know what I've been thinking?'

'What have you been thinking, clever baby?' said Amy, standing up and walking around the table towards him.

'Well, not what you'd expect. I've been thinking that if nothing else a chip insert helps you stop smoking. I have had no craving to snout up once. Not even in the cell. I missed you terribly, but in a heart-based context, not a hard-core one.'

'Oh, that's so sweet.'

'And even though I find you highly stimulating in an adult action type of way, d'you know what I'd like to do now, more than anything?'

'No.' Amy was smiling and clearly up for adult behaviour.

'Just hold you,' said Jason. It was true – he felt a great need to be held by someone rather than adopt strenuous positions. Amy was immediately obliging. She fell into his arms and squeezed him tight.

'You know something, Jase,' she whispered in his ear. 'When I first saw you, I knew that this wasn't going to be just another job.'

'I know, sweets,' he said. 'A lesser man might have been disturbed by knowing that you shagged me for information and connections, but you're with the Nash now.'

'I know, baby. I know. The best.'

'That's right, the Nash is the best.'

'I'll wait for you, baby. I'll wait for ever.'

'I know. The Nash won't leave you. The Nash loves you so much.' And the weird thing was, what he said was true.

38

Nina arrived at Brize Norton airbase a full hour before the flight from America was due to land. The military police officer on the gate checked her papers – a letter George had given her, on US government paper, and a pass issued by the Ministry of Defence which had arrived that morning in her mail.

'Go straight ahead, Professor,' said the officer. 'Up to the main building there. On the left is the visitors' carpark.'

'Thank you,' said Nina. She drove as directed and pulled to a halt. As soon as she opened her door she heard a large jet roaring off down the runway.

'Good afternoon, Professor, the flight is on its way,' said a smart young RAF officer, who immediately approached her. 'The reception lounge is just over here.'

Nina smiled and followed the young man.

She entered a building and climbed a flight of stairs. As soon as she entered the spacious reception area she realised she was not alone. A variety of civilians and military personnel were sitting around the brightly lit lounge.

'There's a flight coming back from Kosovo in a moment,' said the officer who had guided her. 'Don't worry, they're not here to see you.'

Nina raised her eyebrows. Since the story had been confirmed by George after the last board meeting, she had become something of a celebrity. She had seen her own picture on the front pages of various newspapers, and only the previous evening a producer from the BBC news programme *Newsnight* had asked whether she would appear on the show. She declined, but couldn't deny that she had felt a moment of quiet glory. She wished she could have told her mother, but knew that even if she had been able to the old trout would somehow have managed to sour her moment in the light. She had thought about her mother a great deal since the murder, and had been pleased to discover that, although she cried and felt sad, she could still remember what she had really been like.

She followed the young officer to the far end of the reception lounge. He turned to her and smiled. 'There has been some interest from the press, but you don't need to worry about that,' he said. 'As soon as I hear an exact arrival time, I'll come and inform you.'

Nina looked out of the window as the young man left. She had a perfect view of the runway, bathed as it was in bright early-evening sunlight.

She had spoken on the phone to Pete Van Missen a further three times since the murder of her mother – long late-night calls that she never wanted to end. She had found out a lot about his life. He was single, he didn't have children, he was very close to his family, who lived in Colorado, and he had been in the US Navy since he was eighteen, but had quickly moved on through various arms of the military and intelligence community which he couldn't tell her about. But as he described it, it mostly involved sitting in dull places watching dull people do nothing. She had told him about her life, where she came from, what she wanted, which had been hard. He had pressed her, but she wasn't sure what she wanted. She eventually admitted that she wanted him, and he admitted that he wanted her. She could hear him breathe. He said nothing further and they sat on either end of a transatlantic phone line in silence – happy, expensive silence.

Life at Nash Systems had been, all things considered, very quiet. There was still a handful of journalists camped out in the carpark, but they were thinning out. Because of the court case, no one could say anything anyway. Jason was holed up in his flat in London working on his defence with the company lawyers, George and Cindy were up to their necks in crisis management, and Emen Trouville had been the most obedient scientist she could possibly have hoped for. Even by the standards of the 24/7 commitment most scientists like Emen worked by, he was breaking the boundaries of what was possible for the human body and brain to tolerate. She needed that kind of commitment. She wanted to complete her new project in record time – a chip that was capable of transmitting vast amounts of data coming from Pete Van Missen's brain and sending it to another chip capable of decoding it and routing it into his nervous system. She was approaching the holy grail of spinal injuries – the break bypass.

However, work in the laboratory had still gone very slowly. She didn't have Michael Del Papa to help her, and for all his annoying habits and stupidity he was impossible to replace. She had headhunted a group of five very bright but very inexperienced students, who attacked the problems they faced with fresh-faced zeal, but their inexperience slowed everything down. Nina's workload was enormous, but she had tackled the daily slog with joy. After all, for the first time at Nash Systems she knew what she was doing and she knew who it was for.

'It's coming in now,' said a voice behind her. She turned to see the young RAF officer standing beside her. 'These new planes are so fast.'

She followed his gaze out of the window. In the distance she could see a dark shape flying low over the Oxfordshire countryside. Four dark trails from its engines left wispy grey tails in the evening air.

'Goodness, what is that?' she asked.

'It's a C-23, a transport.'

'I've never seen anything like it,' said Nina, studying the strange wing design and sleek silver hull as the plane touched down. The rumble sounded through the building as the plane shot past, great clouds of white smoke whipping up from the wheels as they made contact with the tarmac.

'Very new – this is only the second time I've seen one. It's supersonic. Took less than three hours to get from Washington to here.'

'My goodness.' Nina watched as the enormous plane pulled to a halt at the far end of the runway, then turned and started to taxi towards the building she was in.

'Let's go and see her come in,' said the enthusiastic young man. Nina smiled as she followed him down a wide flight of stairs.

Two minutes later she was on the tarmac, wearing a pair of bright yellow ear protectors and a fluorescent vest. The plane was painfully loud, even with the ear protectors, and fearsomely huge as it approached.

A large vehicle fitted with a scissor lift pulled up beside it as it came to a halt. The lift rose as the door of the plane swung open. A few moments later a stretcher appeared, pushed by two uniformed men. The lift was lowered, and Nina walked alongside the vehicle as it moved very slowly towards a bay in the main building. She climbed a flight of stairs beside the docking area, her heart beating irrationally fast, then she saw him.

Looking pale and thin, covered in a thick blanket, was Pete Van Missen. He moved his eyes, looking for her, a rather odd expression on his face. She moved closer, into what she guessed was his field of vision.

She saw his lips move but could hear nothing. She said 'Hi,' but she couldn't hear her own voice. She felt tears stream down her cheeks.

Pete Van Missen winked one eye and smiled at her, and she knew everything was going to be okay.

39

'Are you seriously suggesting,' said Simon Fullbright, the prosecuting lawyer, who Jason had decided was much better at his job than the dozy Lord Preston, 'that you had no control over your body at the time of the incident?'

Jason smiled. 'I don't know why that should be so hard to believe.' He looked at the jury, who he had to admit to himself were displaying facial characteristics than gave out a strong impression of scepticism. 'The technology is there – we've proved that beyond doubt at Nash Systems. All that happened was that renegade elements managed to use it for some very dubious ends.'

'So you readily admit you murdered your own mother. However, you claim that persons unknown were situated outside the hotel sending signals to a computer microchip that was buried in your neck which, so you say, controlled your body.'

'Correct,' said Jason. 'I mean, it's so mad I wouldn't exactly make something like this up, would I?'

'That is for the jury to decide, Mr Nash.'

'Sure, sure. But my whole life has been destroyed by what happened. I was very close to my mother, and whatever happens to me I don't really care.' He felt a lump in his throat, which always happened whenever he actually admitted to himself that he had indeed killed his own mother, for whatever reason. 'I just want the world to know I didn't kill her with this.' He pointed to his head.

Simon Fullbright turned away from Jason and looked at the jury. 'You see, Mr Nash, even if it can be proved that the computer microchip in your neck could receive signals which affected your behaviour, it doesn't really explain what happened, does it? What I suggest happened, Mr Nash, is that your rather overbearing and difficult mother interrupted you and your fiancée during a passionate lovemaking session and you lost your temper. You have already told us that your mother didn't approve of Miss Muldoon, and when she was rude to you, you lost your temper, didn't you?'

'Very poor attempt at trying to paint a picture of guilt, if I may say so, Mr Fullbright,' said Jason as haughtily as he could. He wasn't going to let this little prick give him the runaround. 'As Miss Muldoon has already informed the court, I had already lost control of my body before my mother entered the room. In fact it was the commotion I was causing that led my mother to investigate. But then it was too late.'

'Tell me, Mr Nash, do you keep a twelve-inch butcher's knife in your bedroom?'

'No. I got that from the kitchen.'

'I see. So you lost control of your body and then ran down how many flights of stairs?'

'Well, my bedroom is on the fourth floor.'

'I see. Ran down four floors, went into the kitchen, picked up a twelve-inch knife and then returned to find your mother and stab her. Is that correct, Mr Nash?'

'Well, my mother was following me and I was telling her to get the hell away from me, but that's pretty much the top and bottom of it, yes.'

'Without control of your body?'

'It's hard to describe exactly what happens when your chip is receiving an intense data stream.'

'I'm sure it is,' said Simon Fullbright. He was smiling very openly at the jury. Jason refused to feel nervous. He knew he probably should, but he didn't want to and used every trick he'd ever learned to relax. Multiple pitch sessions and grillings by venture capitalists had hardened him to such experiences.

'I don't claim to fully understand it myself,' he added without prompting. 'All I was aware of was a burning sensation in my neck, which was the heat from the chip as it was firing massive amounts of data into my nervous system through wires inserted into my spinal cord.' Jason noticed a lady member of the jury grimace in horror as he said this. 'It's all really, really tiny. I mean the chip – even when it's housed in its bio-neutral satchel it's about the size of a match head.'

'A bio-neutral satchel,' said Simon Fullbright. 'Goodness me. What on earth does that mean?'

'It's a really special plastic scientists at Nash Systems have developed that doesn't react to the body's immune system, so bypasses the need for antibiotics when you plant a foreign body into someone.'

'Extraordinary.'

Fullbright turned back to his desk to pick up some papers. Jason sat placidly, occasionally looking at the jury, but taking care not to stare at any one of them for too long.

The build-up to the trial had been a busy period. The initial battle had been about whether or not he should claim to have been ignorant about the presence of the chip. It was all pretty clear that if he told the actual truth then he would land his precious bloody sister in serious shit. He argued that the fact that he didn't even know the chip was in his neck would clinch the trial for him. Lord Preston fought back – seeing as there was no precedent for such a case it was irrelevant and would only cause complications. He was eventually convinced by the argument that it would make him seem like a far better citizen if he was seen to be risking his own wellbeing for the sake of medical research. He could claim that he already knew that the chip was potentially dangerous because of what had happened to Pete Van Missen, but had brushed these concerns aside in a brave and manly way.

During this arduous period Jason had been living at his flat with Amy, which made the whole thing a great deal easier to deal with. They had got married discreetly at Kensington Register Office. No members of their families were present, other than Nina. Jason invited Tony and George Quinn, Tony as best man, which was hard work as he was wearing a purple fleece top with a feather boa. Amy invited a friendly fat girl called Naomi. It wasn't exactly romantic in the accepted sense, but to Jason and Amy it had been very special. Almost like a secret agent's wedding, as Jason had mentioned when they were hustled back into a car to return to the flat.

However, the highlight of the whole period was seeing Pete Van Missen walk into his flat the Saturday afternoon before the trial started. Walk was possibly a slight exaggeration – hobble would be more accurate – but he was standing, he had use of his body again. Jason also noticed that Nina looked very different. For a start she had put on a bit of weight – her face didn't look so drawn and pale. Jason had winked at Pete. Clearly the chip was working on one level. The old sis looked positively fertile.

Pete Van Missen was his salvation. When they called him as a witness he would save the day. The arrangements to allow Van Missen to stand as a witness had taken a great deal of time and money. He couldn't be identified owing to the nature of his work, which only made the whole case more intriguing for the press. But, as Jason often pointed out, the case was the best PR Nash Systems would ever get. It had put them on the map big time – no one who read the papers or watched the news could be in any doubt that chip insert technology was a reality, and it was about to change the world.

'So someone was sending you instructions as to what to do. Could you hear them? Was it like hearing a voice?' asked Simon Fullbright.

Jason laughed. 'No, for goodness' sake, it had nothing to do with my brain. I thought I'd made that clear. The signals are sent into the spinal cord, so obviously you get a mental reaction, but it's the muscles, the heart rate, the adrenal glands that are affected. The data they were sending . . .'

'And you don't know who "they" were, do you, Mr Nash?'

'No, but . . .'

'How convenient.'

Jason looked at Lord Preston. 'You could object every once in a while, couldn't you?'

Lord Preston looked pained as the judge said simply, 'Answer the questions, please, Mr Nash.

'Yes, your Lordship. I'll do my best. The data I received was from a flashback an ex-military person had experienced when we were originally recording with the first chip.'

'A flashback?'

'Yes. I was experiencing someone else's traumatic battlefield flashback.'

'Dear, dear me,' said the judge. Jason turned to look at him – a nice old boy, must have been seventy if he was a day. 'You've lost me now.'

'Well, you see, m'lud, Nash Systems made a record-only device which was placed into a man who will soon be a witness before the court. The data from his nervous system was kept on massive storage racks at Nash Systems' premises in Cambridge. Really cool disk array – you should see it. Anyway, while they were recording, old Van . . . the witness had a couple of flashbacks. You know, like hippies used to get from LSD?' Jason threw his head around and screamed like a madman. 'Aaargh, man, I'm having a flashback, that sort of thing.'

'Goodness,' said the judge.

'I would like to point out that I knew nothing of this at the time,' said Jason. 'I'm in marketing and general company management – all this tech stuff is at the very limit of my understanding too, your Honourship. So then parties unknown got hold of this data and zapped me with it when I went to see my parents. I assume that the purpose was military research, to see how far they could get an individual to go when receiving data. As you can imagine, there are a lot of social taboos about killing your own mother, especially if you are as close to her as I was, so, for their own twisted reasons, they must have wanted to see how far they could push an individual. It's all about control, that's their big thing – they're control freaks of the very extreme kind.'

'I'm still in the dark. Is all this entirely necessary?' said the judge. 'I thought this was a murder case, not an Open University science course.'

One or two of the jury members laughed quietly.

Jason answered more questions from Simon Fullbright, all of them clearly intended to make him look as if he had murdered his mother because he hated her, all of them to undermine his claim that the chip made him do it.

He answered all of them with complete honesty. Knowing he was telling the absolute truth gave him a great strength he wasn't used to.

The court was adjourned for lunch, and he was led back down to the cells. After he'd been alone for a couple of minutes, Lord Preston entered.

'Going well, isn't it?' said Jason as he stretched out on the bed.

'Not particularly. The jury don't like you, you're too cocky and sure of yourself, and the chip excuse sounds just like that, an excuse, even though we have proved that it was in place at the time. We've got an uphill battle.'

'No, it's fine,' said Jason. 'The Nash is working that jury for the long haul. I know I can ease them around. What's next?'

'I'm calling Van Missen as a witness this afternoon.'

'Sure, sure. Should be interesting.'

40

Nina held Pete Van Missen's hand as they drove into the rear entrance of the Old Bailey. The BMW they were travelling in had heavily smoked windows, but Nina could make out a couple of journalists trying to see inside.

Pete was wearing dark glasses and he'd grown a beard. He needed to maintain a certain amount of anonymity even though, as he had assured Nina on numerous occasions, he had resigned from all his former posts.

They were met in the lobby by one of the solicitors working for Lord Preston and shown into a small anteroom. Pete would be giving his evidence from behind a screen. He had been granted permission by the US government to appear as long as his identity remained hidden. A clerk entered the room and asked him to come into the court.

'Good luck,' said Nina, kissing him softly on the lips.

'Thanks,' he said. He looked at her with his deep blue eyes and she felt herself relax. She had never met anyone so sure of who they were, of why they were. So clear and open in every way – except of course about his work.

Nina sat looking out of the window, feeling wonderful. She was nervous, but she couldn't remember ever feeling more alive. The chip inserts had worked, although there was still an enormous amount to do to improve them. One particular area was still a big problem.

Pete's desire for her was unmistakable, but it wasn't manifesting itself in any physical way. Nina had spent a lot of time cuddling up to him in her now very untidy house, assuring him that it didn't matter to her. It was the only blot on an otherwise hopelessly happy vista. Nina was in love with a retired American covert operator. If she had ever been told that this was what would happen to her, she would have laughed, or turned away in horror. There was a side of her that wanted to know details of what he'd done before she'd met him, particularly in relation to the flashbacks she had now witnessed him have. He had awoken one night screaming, his body cold and covered in sweat. As she held him after he had woken up, he cried and thanked her repeatedly. He told her no one had ever held him as she was doing. He said nothing else about it, gave no details. Although she was desperate to know, she had to accept she never would.

The situation at Nash Systems had also changed dramatically in the three months that led up to the trial. The first change was when Nina moved her office and lab back into the premises formerly used by Coventon's. Building work started on a new chip fabrication plant next to the original building, capable of producing thousands of the newly designed chips. This was funded by Nash Systems' initial public offering, where the money raised made lastminute.com's offering look like chicken feed. Everyone and their rich uncle wanted a slice of the action.

Cindy Volksmann had recruited over three hundred employees, including, to Nina's relief, Hugo Harwood. Together they stripped the code and analysed it, finally finding a pattern and a system with which to extract the information they needed. Although the amounts of data were still enormous, they were far easier to manage, and using the code that the now very obedient and retiring Emen Trouville had devised, they started to be able to make sense of what they had discovered. Nina and her new team had come up with a method of constructing the chip with a blocking system burned into its circuits which controlled the input data the chip could receive. No longer could someone send something as intense and dangerous as Pete's flashbacks.

But this was only the half of it. The really big test came with Pete's two implants. The theory was simple – a transmitter and receiver chip, hard-wired across a three-millimetre gap. The wire was twice as thick as the chips it carried signals between, which was still pretty thin compared to the spinal cord it was effectively replacing. The transmitter chip had to know which information needed to be sent and which to ignore – that was where Hugo and his data analysis came in. They wanted Pete to be able to control his body, not lie on the floor twitching uncontrollably as all the wrong signals were sent to the wrong parts of his body.

The team worked day and night for two weeks, testing the chips, sending through every conceivable type of input and measuring the output. Eventually they reached a stage where there was nothing left but to test the device 'in the field'.

Roger Turnpike was called. He had two operations to do – one to remove the chip from Jason's neck under the supervision of a lawyer from the Crown Prosecution Service, and the other to place the two chips in the still-paralysed Pete Van Missen. Both operations were carried out successfully, although Pete's took over two hours. What was extraordinary was that even before Roger Turnpike had put the tiny stitches in his neck, Nina noticed his toes moving. Within four hours of the operation he was moving all his limbs, although with great difficulty, as he had suffered severe muscle wastage during his long period of dormancy. Within a week he was standing, and after another few days he had taken his first steps.

George and Jason were tearing their hair out with frustration as they couldn't use any of the copious video footage they had of the recovery for publicity purposes, but this pleased Nina no end. It would mean they would have to treat other patients and use them for publicity – she could keep Pete to herself.

'That was not a lot of fun,' said Pete when he emerged from the court two hours later.

'What did they ask?'

'They're not buying the fact that the chip could have controlled Jason. I could tell that much, even though I was looking at a green screen three inches in front of my face. The prosecuting attorney . . .'

'Lawyer.'

'Sorry, yeah. He's one hell of a bright guy.'

'Oh, God.'

'Even though I explained that I had been totally paralysed from the neck down, and now I was walking, and they had all my medical reports and a detailed description of how the new chips work . . . well, I could just feel it. The way our guy . . .'

'Lord Preston.'

'Yeah, he's like scrabbling around trying to grab any bit of evidence to hold up the case. I should go and get Garfelli and drag him here by the hair, the little shit.' Pete twitched in a slightly disturbing way as he spoke.

'Please, Pete,' pleaded Nina. She had a never-fading fear that with one false move Pete could collapse in a paralysed heap again.

'They just don't buy it that anyone was outside the hotel, even though they've seen the tape of the van arriving. I'm really worried for Jason.'

Nina sat down. She slowly looked up at Pete as he stood in front of her, leaning on his walking frame.

'I don't think it was the chip.'

She had waited a long time to say this.

'What?'

She looked at her hands. Her nails looked so good – she'd had them done for the first time in her life. She started to pick at the sides of her thumb, where a small piece of skin was sticking out. She must have bitten it without being aware of what she was doing.

'Jason is just too crazy.'

'You don't think it was Garfelli?'

'No. I'm sure they were there, and I'm sure they did send the data. It will have affected Jason, but it won't have made him kill Mum. He had to want to do that. It doesn't make sense. Everything we've learned about what the chips do militates against it. The brain scan I did of Jason when we were testing him with the new chip – you know, the coloured-circle test you did?'

Pete nodded slowly, another thing she had begged him not to do.

'There was nothing new going on. It doesn't affect the brain directly, or not in ways we can be sure of. It just pushed an already very unstable individual over the edge. He was already so close to the edge it didn't take much pushing.'

'You know what you're saying, don't you, Nina?'

'Yes. My brother is a murderer.'

Pete shuffled across to her as best he could and slowly sat down. He stared at the floor for a long time, then up at her. His clear blue eyes cut into her with such intensity she knew that without doubt she was hopelessly in love with this strange man.

'You can't think that,' he said finally.

'What d'you mean?' She was affronted. No one told her what to think.

'If you think that, even if you don't say it, if you think it in the court, you will communicate that and condemn your brother by default. Tell me this, Professor. If Del Papa and Garfelli hadn't sent the data to the chip, would Jason have killed your mum?'

'Well, no.'

'And if Jason didn't have the chip buried in his neck, would he have killed your mum?'

'I don't . . . no, I don't think he would.'

'Case closed,' said Pete flatly. He smiled at her. 'It's not your fault, Nina. You have been looking for ways to blame yourself.'

'Have I?'

'Sure. You did the wrong thing putting the chip in him without his knowledge, but whatever happened you did not mean to kill your mother, did you?'

'No, of course not,' said Nina. And yet her mother's passing had not, by any means, been the worst thing that had happened to her in her life. In fact quite the opposite. Since her mother had gone, more or less everything in her life had improved beyond measure. 'But it's complicated,' she added.

'Sure, you're a complicated woman. Really complicated, and I love you for it.'

Nina didn't feel reassured.

41

'Call Professor Nina Nash.'

Jason had been doodling on the legal pad that sat on the low table in front of him. He had been sitting in the court for what seemed like half his life, and was prepared to admit, publicly, that he was bored stupid. The way the two old duffers rabbited on about some fiddly little aspect of the law, the hours they had spent arguing over the fact that the trial was setting wholly new legal precedents that needed Acts of Parliament to clarify, was all so much shit.

'When is a murderer not a murderer?' as the smartarse Simon Fullbright kept saying to the jury.

Jason just wanted to get it over with, do his 'bird' and get out in a few years to start a family with Amy. He certainly wasn't short of money. That would still be waiting for him when he came out. He had even invested some of it quite wisely, in low-tech stocks and pharmaceuticals.

Nina took the witness stand and was sworn in. Once again, prompted by Lord Preston's questions, she went over the events as she knew them – her involvement with Nash Systems, an explanation of the chip and its capabilities, the flaws in the design that they had inserted into her brother.

Jason didn't pay much attention, although he was still bothering to look as if he was, more out of habit than anything else.

He noticed Lord Preston sit back down beside him. Simon Fullbright stood up and took the floor, like some old queeny actor, Jason decided. He'd really gone off the fellow.

'Professor, did your brother know the chip was in his neck?'

Jason watched his sister lie badly.

'Yes,' she said. It was bloody obvious to anyone over twelve than she meant 'no'.

'I see. Because it strikes me that what you were conducting at Nash Enterprises . . .'

'Systems,' Nina corrected.

'Yes. What you were conducting was highly dangerous, wasn't it? Charting unknown waters and allowing a patient – for that's what he was at the time, was he not – to wander around willy-nilly, knowing full well that he was capable of extreme acts of violence. In fact, further than that, he was extremely likely to kill someone. He was, after all, receiving signals which had been recorded from a man who worked, as the jury have already discovered, for a covert operation run by the US government which was so secret we were not allowed to know his name or see his face. A man who we can safely assume was also capable of extreme acts of violence, even if these were carried out in the name of his country.'

'It's not as simple as that,' said Nina.

'No, that's one thing we have learned in this case, Professor. It's not as simple as that. Or maybe it is. You were not close to your mother, were you, Professor Nash?'

'Yes, I was.'

'Well, from what I can gather from your father, you and she fought all the time. Your brother was your mother's favourite, wasn't he?'

'It . . . well, she was very fond of him, but she and I . . . well, yes, we argued, but no more than in any other family.'

'Your mother didn't respect your work, did she, and she didn't like the fact that you were having an affair with a man the same age as your father? She was very critical of you, wasn't she?'

'Yes, she was very critical, but . . .'

'Objection,' said Lord Preston after Jason had jabbed him in the ribs. Jason had decided that as the old duffer was half asleep he needed a bit of egging on every now and then. Lord Preston threw Jason a look that could not be listed under an 'affection' heading.

'Sustained,' said the old judge, who also seemed barely in the land of the living. 'Please stick to the case, Mr Fullbright.'

'Certainly, your Honour, that is precisely what I am doing. You see, Professor Nash, I put it to you that you hated your mother to such a degree that you deliberately used your brother as a weapon, if you like, tuning him in like a radio to "Murder FM"' Simon Fullbright smiled at the jury. 'You made sure he received a signal which would send him mad at just the time his mother discovered him *in flagrante* with his fiancée, is that not the truth?'

'No. I wasn't there. I was at home in Cambridge.'

'Oh, I have no doubt you were.'

Jason looked at his sister. She was really rattled – she was flushed in the face, and had lost all her bite. Maybe what the queeny old lawyer was saying was true – maybe she'd set the whole thing up. He fought to stop himself chewing his lip. He knew the jury would be clocking him – he had to hold it together.

'No, you are far too wily to be anywhere near the hotel at the time, but you knew it was going to happen, didn't you, Professor?'

'No, I did not,' she said, harder now, angry. Jason was baffled. He stared at her. Never before had he looked at her with such intensity. Had she done it? Was it her all along?

'I put it to you, Professor, that you hired persons unknown to go to the hotel. After all, you knew Jason Nash was going there, you knew the layout. You knew your mother was a fearsomely jealous woman who hated any other woman being near her precious son.'

That much was true, thought Jason. It was possible – she could have got Garfelli to do it. As he cast his mind back over events it all started to make sense. She spent hours with Del Papa and Trouville. They could have worked the whole thing out and set him up like the hi-tech patsy he was. Except that

Garfelli would have blown her cover, surely, when the whole thing came out at the board meeting. It was pretty obvious there was no love lost between them, but then maybe she had managed to dupe the red-haired tosser and make him think it was someone else. It didn't really make sense. For all her faults, and they were plentiful, she had never done anything so deceitful before, not that he was aware of. And Del Papa clearly didn't have a clue what was going on. He was such a loose-mouthed bastard he would have said something at the time. No, she couldn't have done it, but it was weird how much happier she had been since he had killed his own mum. He stopped thinking. He was suddenly aware that he might be giving himself away to the jury.

'But I was the one who got the security tape,' said Nina fiercely. 'I was the one who gave it to the police.'

'After two weeks,' said Simon Fullbright. 'Yes, after you had made sure your alibi would stand up.'

'Objection, m'lud,' said Lord Preston. 'The witness is not on trial here.'

'Sustained,' said the old judge, sounding as if he'd just woken up yet again. Lord Preston sat down.

'I quite agree, m'lud,' said Simon Fullbright. 'It is an absurd distortion of events. Of course the professor had nothing to do with it, other than the fact that she led the team which developed the computer chip. It's a tale using copious amounts of imagination only loosely woven from actual events, very much like the one my learned friend is trying to foist on the court.'

'Objection!'

'Overruled.'

'It is pure conjecture that a chip such as the one we have had so eloquently described to us would be capable of controlling someone to such an extent that he could carry out a murder. Not a sudden impulse, but a murder that required considerable running up and down stairs, finding knives in kitchens, chasing screaming victims. Not very likely, is it, Professor?'

'I . . . I don't . . . it's very . . .' Nina sputtered. Jason stared at her. She glanced at him. 'It's what appears to have happened,' she said finally.

'You have doubts, Professor?'

'I'm sorry. It's so complex . . .'

'Yes, we are fully aware of the complexity.'

'It's not . . . look, all I know is Jason would never kill anyone. Not like that, not deliberately. However the chip operated, it affected him enough to carry out a deed he would never have done in normal circumstances.'

'Normal circumstances?'

'Without a transponder chip attached to his central nervous system, a chip I . . . well, I feel very responsible for.'

'Oh, you do feel "very responsible" for it, do you?' repeated Simon Fullbright with just a slight impression of Nina's speech patterns. Bad move, thought Jason with a small inner smile. He had learned the hard way never to repeat what his sister had said in a patronising or teasing manner. He was right. She turned on the lawyer, her eyes alight with fury.

'Of course I feel responsible. The chip was my design, I helped insert it! Of course I feel responsible. Only an animal wouldn't. Jason is my brother. I lost my mother too.' Her eyes were red as she spoke, something Jason hadn't seen very often. 'For all the faults my mother and I found with each other, she was my mother and I loved her. I loved her very much, and her loss has been terrible. Not only that – my work is my life, and everything I had worked for was terribly affected because some . . .'

'Some what, Professor?'

'Some agent, some outside agent, bent on destroying what we were doing, intervened in the most hideous way. They used the technology for violent means. They were testing it to see if it could override normal human impulses of decency, loyalty, non-violence. All things my brother possesses in abundance, Mr Fullbright. In abundance. He is the most loving, open and emotionally expressive man I have ever known. A lot of men could learn a lot from my brother, Mr Fullbright.'

She almost spat out his name. Jason wanted to stand and cheer.

'No more questions, m'lud.'

42

Ingrid Neilson arrived at the lab early and was shown in by the new student, who had just joined the team that morning. Nina felt a wave of delight on seeing the girl. She had grown since they last met, had turned from a little girl into a young adult.

'Ingrid, it's so good to see you!' Nina felt herself almost running across the lab to greet her.

They shook hands and, as Nina held on, she inspected the limb she had developed and helped build. The prosthetic hand was very battered and clearly way too small for her. She had returned to have a new one fitted.

She looked into the girl's eyes. 'Goodness, I can tell you've been using it.'

'I wear it every single day except on Sunday,' said Ingrid.

'And why is that?'

'I just like to have a rest.'

Nina nodded and looked up at her father, Lars Neilson.

'Good to see you, Professor. I'm very sorry to hear about your mother.'

'Thank you.'

'This must be a very difficult time for you.'

'Believe me, it's wonderful to see Ingrid again. It makes everything that's happened worthwhile.'

Lars held his daughter by the shoulders. For a moment, Nina thought about her own father, alone in an empty hotel. She tried to remember him standing with her in the same way when she was a little girl. She couldn't recall anything like it.

Her father had returned to the hotel and tried, bravely, to pick up the pieces of his life. He didn't manage it, and after two weeks of hopeless confusion Nina had had to intervene. It wasn't fun. For a start she had Pete Van Missen to look after, and he needed constant attention. She had to hire a nurse to be with him while she spent three difficult days at the hotel trying to sort everything out. Then she had to convince her almost constantly silent father that the best option was to retire. They were lucky in that they found a small bungalow on the market on the outskirts of Cookham. The hotel was put up for sale. Somehow all the organisation had fallen to her. Normally this sort of extra work would have annoyed her, but now she managed it without getting angry. She felt she had grown up. She knew she could cope with chaos, and she needed to – the hotel was in a terminal state, with unpaid bills, piles of laundry in the corridors, staff in tears, bookings that needed cancelling into the following year.

Nina took Ingrid Neilson by the hand and led her to the bench at the far end of the laboratory.

'This is a very impressive set-up,' said Lars.

'It's a bit of a bigger operation than we used to have at Coventon's,' agreed Nina. She looked around the lab as she spoke. There were twenty-three scientists working in the lab – what had once been an echoing space usually containing three scientists had turned into a complex management exercise and a very busy workplace.

They stopped by a large white bench where Kashif Merchant, a young Indian computer expert who had worked there for a month, was operating a new arm for Ingrid.

'This is Kashif.'

'Hello, Ingrid. I've heard a lot about you.'

Ingrid smiled and looked at her new arm with wide eyes. 'It looks much better,' she said.

'It works much better too,' said Kashif proudly. 'What we've done is use the same data we originally recorded for your arm, Ingrid, but I think you'll find this one is a lot more obedient.'

Nina noticed she felt a lot more relaxed in the girl's presence. She wanted to talk to her, wanted to cuddle her, assure the brave little individual who had been through so much. She even considered telling her that she too had lost her mother, but discretion won.

Ingrid took off her old arm with help from her father. Nina felt a lump in her throat as she looked at the young girl standing before her, one sleeve of her pink sweatshirt hanging limp by her side.

'Okay,' she said with a sigh. 'Now, before we put this one on, I'd like to quickly check that everything is working. Can you wave at me?'

As soon as she spoke, the arm, being carefully held by Kashif Merchant, started to move. It made clear waving movements.

'Okay, now wiggle your fingers.'

The hand responded instantly, each finger moving independently.

'Point.'

Again the hand did as it was told. Ingrid was laughing hysterically – the pure delight on the child's face made Nina start to cry.

'Are you okay?' asked Lars Neilson. Nina nodded and pulled a tissue out of her lab coat pocket. Ingrid stared up at her.

'Don't be sad, Nina,' she said. 'It's the best arm in the whole wide world.'

Nina knelt down and held the girl, who responded with her left arm, squeezing her tightly.

'I'm sorry about your mum. Daddy told me.'

Nina smiled. Absurdly, she wasn't crying about her mother; indeed, she felt bad that her mother's death had been the least of her worries since the murder. She was crying because she wanted a little girl like Ingrid. So much had changed since the murder, since Pete's return, since the funeral. It was as if she had buried some part of herself with her mother, a part of herself that she now saw she really didn't need.

'Let's put it on, then,' she whispered into Ingrid's perfect little ear.

'Okay.'

Nina and Kashif gently attached the arm.

'It feels heavier,' said Ingrid as the arm started to move with her. She manoeuvred it in front of her, still fascinated by the fact that it moved as she wanted. 'But it's much better.'

'I have one thing I want you to try,' said Kashif. He picked up a small ball that contained a dolphin within its solid clear plastic body. 'Catch.'

He threw the ball up in front of Ingrid. Her arm snapped out with amazing speed and grabbed the ball as it passed her.

'Wow,' she said. 'Did I do that?'

'No one else did,' said Kashif.

Nina's pager buzzed. She picked up a wall-mounted phone as she watched Ingrid throw the ball up and catch it with her new arm.

'Professor Nash here.'

'We have a call for you, Professor. Connecting you now.'

'Hello, Professor.' It was Lord Preston. Nina felt her stomach turn over. The jury in Jason's case had been out for two days.

'Yes?'

'Not guilty on the murder charge.'

'Oh my God.' She looked around for something to sit on and flopped on to stool by a bench behind her.

'Guilty of manslaughter.'

Nina was silent. Manslaughter sounded worse than murder, and anyway her mother was a woman.

'Jason has been given a five-year prison sentence,' said Lord Preston without emotion. 'We're going to appeal, of course.'

'Oh my God! Five years!'

Nina noticed the Neilsons looking at her, along with about half the staff in the lab. She turned to the wall.

'How is Jason?' she asked as quietly as she could.

'He seems very happy. If he'd been found guilty of murder, Professor, he would be looking at twenty-five years plus. This way, even if our appeal fails, he'll only have to serve about two years if he behaves himself.'

Nina sat on the stool and leaned her forehead against the wall. There was an element of relief in the news. There was a side of her that wanted her stupid brother punished for what he'd done, even if he hadn't really meant it. He had screwed up so badly he needed to be sent to his room for a bit just to make it fair.

'Do you know where he's going to be taken? Which prison?' she asked.

'Not yet. As soon as I do, I'll let you know. I have to go now. I'll get a full court report to you today.'

'Thank you.'

The line went dead. 'Five years,' Nina repeated to herself. She stayed where she was for a while, not sure what to do. She was concerned that she might start crying again, which she really hated to do when she was in the lab.

She felt a hand on her shoulder.

'Nina, I just heard.' It was George Quinn. 'It's not as bad as it sounds.'

She turned to face him – George Quinn, the man who had effectively turned her life upside down, the man who she now worked with on a daily basis and was happy to do so.

'Five years, George.'

'Sure. It's bad, but not as bad as it might have been. It's also very good news for the company.'

'Everything is good news for this company,' Nina responded flatly.

'Thank God, that seems to be true at the moment. In some ways Jason's case was the best possible piece of PR we could have hoped for. The spin we'll be able to put on this outcome will be great.'

'George, don't be a prick,' said Nina.

'Sorry. Sure, I know it's rough on Jason, but from what I gather he's very happy about it.'

'Well, he's a prick too. It'll hit him when he's actually locked up.'

George nodded. 'We'll look after him,' he said with a gentle hand on her arm. He turned and looked at Ingrid Neilson, who was now playing catch with her father and Kashif Merchant.

'Who is this?' George asked.

'Ingrid Neilson.'

'What, the kid with the arm?'

Nina smiled. He couldn't tell that her arm was made of bio-neutral plastic and polycarbonate.

'You are kidding! That's not her real arm!' Or maybe he could, and he was just fooling her again. 'Jesus, Nina.'

She could never be sure with Quinn, she knew she never would, but she was now in a very powerful position in the company, so it mattered less.

'Bit better than a military control mechanism, isn't it, George? Makes you feel better in yourself. In the deeper recesses of your soul and all that. Or don't you have any of those?'

George looked at her and shook his head. 'If only you knew, Professor. This is the best thing I've ever seen in my life. I always wanted to do this sort of work, but I knew we'd never raise the initial funding. We had to prove that what we could do had potential and the military are the only option in those circumstances. It's been an ugly journey, I'll give you that, but we got somewhere good, didn't we?'

Nina smiled. She hoped so.

43

HM Prison Wandsworth was not a happy place in which to spend your time – Jason learned that very quickly. As an inmate convicted of manslaughter he was put into a cell on D Wing with two other men. One, he discovered, had killed a child in a hit-and-run accident. The other, a very overweight black man, didn't talk.

It was very boring being in his cell for fifteen hours a day, occasionally frightening when some scar-faced individual confronted him on the landing, but his spirits were still high. He knew never to show this – he just closed off as much of himself as he could, almost sitting down in the corner of his consciousness and waiting it out.

After his first week he was informed by a warder that he would be moved as soon as somewhere became available – he wouldn't be in Wandsworth for more than three months. He didn't know whether this was good news or bad. He decided it didn't matter one way or the other – even after a few weeks he knew that things could only get better. There was nothing worse that could happen. He'd reached the pit – the only way forward was up.

Amy visited him first. She was very upset, and he had to be patient as she slowly got a hold of herself. They sat opposite each other in the visitors' wing, a warder standing very close by the whole time. They drank sweet tea served to them by a man Jason knew to be serving life for killing a police officer.

'I've got some news,' said Amy.

'What is it, sweets?'

'I'm pregnant,' she said.

Jason stared at her, feeling an incredible sense of peace. 'That's good,' he said.

'You're not upset?'

He shook his head. 'Why should I be upset? It's fantastic. We're going to have a baby.'

'Oh, Jase. I've been so worried. I didn't know how to tell you.'

'How long have you known?'

'Two months. I just couldn't tell you while the trial was on.'

'You are such an amazing woman. Look at me, a convicted murderer, and you still stand by me. I love you so much, babes, you know that. If you'll wait for me, you know I'll look after you when I get out.'

They held hands over the table and stared into each other's eyes.

When Jason got back to his cell that night he hit a wall of depression. He wanted to be with Amy, to be with her when the baby was born, to see it when it arrived. He wanted to talk to it when it was still in her beautiful belly. He lay curled up in his bunk, trying not to listen to the two other men breathing. He wanted to be alone more than anything. Alone so he could at least cry. He tried to work out what it was that had brought the heavy blanket down. It was his mum. He wanted to show his mum the baby, and he never could because he had killed her. He turned over in his bunk, very slowly – he didn't want to talk to the others. He knew it was going to be difficult to get to sleep, and there was very little else to do but lie very still.

A week later his sister visited him. He didn't really want her to come, knowing that as he could only get one visit a week she was depriving him of Amy.

'Hey, sis. Look at you. Big, lumpy, radiant woman.'

They kissed on the cheek. She certainly appeared very different. Her hair was still cropped short, but she didn't look as if she were about to drop dead from malnutrition.

'Thank you,' she said. They sat opposite each other but

didn't hold hands. 'I've brought you some books. The guard at the entrance says he will get them to you.'

'Thanks. I'm actually pleased, can you believe it? The Nash starts reading at thirty. I hope they've got pictures in them.'

'No pictures, sorry.' She smiled at him. 'So, how is it?'

'It's prison, Nina. It's shit, but I'm fine. There's nothing to tell, to be honest. How's Dad?'

Nina sighed. 'Not good. He's living in Cookham, in the new bungalow. I've offered my place but he wants to stay there. The hotel's sold, new owners. Dad goes there quite a lot and sits in the bar, which is weird.'

'You're kidding. Poor bastard. He must hate me so much.'

'He does.'

Jason knew he shouldn't have looked for reassurance from the sis.

'How about Mr Van Missen? Looks like he's working wonders for you.'

Nina smiled. Her teeth glistened, her eyes looked happy – she had really changed.

'He is. He's such an amazing guy.'

'Who'd have thought it, eh?'

'I think that all the time. I keep looking for something that will show me that he's a pig. Something that will say, this man was a soldier who killed people for a living. But he's not.'

'Well, he obviously was.'

'Yes, but he's not what you'd think. He's incredibly well read, he's really kind and gentle. He listens, which isn't something a lot of men are able to do.'

'I listen.'

'Yes. Now you do because for once in your life you've got bugger-all to say.'

Jason nodded and laughed. He looked at his sister. She wanted to tell him something, he could sense that. He decided to try going through the list.

'Company okay?'

'Booming. We've got over four hundred employees now. I

went to see the new labs yesterday. You can't really call them labs – more like a science factory. Bit scary.'

'Great. Share price?'

'According to George, off the scale.'

'And how's old Georgie boy?'

'Same old. Untrustworthy, two-timing slimy bastard, but very good at his job.'

'So what is it, then?'

'What d'you mean?'

'Well, something is up. I can tell, sis. You can't pull the wool over the eyes of the Nash.'

'I wish you'd stop referring to yourself in the third person. Makes you sound totally mad.'

'I only do it to you, and Amy. She likes it.'

'She must be mad too, then.'

'She's pregnant. Did you know?' He could tell by his sister's reaction that she didn't.

'Oh, Jason, that's amazing.'

'Pretty incredible, isn't it? She told me last week. I get a letter from her every day. She is one very special lady, and now she's having my baby. She's having the baby of Nash.'

'Jason, I'm really pleased for you.'

'Pleased for me. That's nice. Sounds a bit like sister code for you bastard, you get everything.'

Nina looked at her hands on the table. She was wearing nail varnish – he couldn't believe his eyes. He was just about to goad her about it when she looked up at him, her eyes red.

'Pete and I . . . well, he can't.'

'Aha,' said Jason. So this was it. 'There is no adult action in the Van Missen–Nash household, then.'

Nina smiled. 'No, not much. I've tried everything. He's so patient and caring, and it's very obvious he wants to, but although it's a miracle that he can walk and do a hell of a lot of things, it's still very limiting.'

'It's bloody obvious what you should do.'

Nina didn't say anything.

'Play him a recording of the Nash.'

'What?'

'Nina, there is a data mass somewhere in that pile of code which is of me giving Amy the grade-A Nash special. Four courses of top-level adult action – the works.'

'What do you mean?'

'A shag recording. Can't you and the boffins extract a lump of top-class hump data?'

Nina scratched her head. She laughed, which was also a new thing, Jason noted. 'We could only record data from you when you were in the building . . .'

Jason smiled.

'What am I saying? You had sex with Amy in the building. Why am I surprised?'

'You can transmit to his chip, can't you?'

She sat motionless for a while, her eyes darting around the room as she worked it out.

'Nina?'

'I hadn't thought . . .'

'No, well, you need someone who thinks a bit laterally. So blinkered by all your cleverness you never look in the obvious place. I bet you've spent hours trying to get the signal through to the old Van Missen todger.'

'Please, Jason.'

'Well, if you want some cock, you're going to have to fire up a laptop stuffed with my fuck data. There's no nicer way of putting it.'

'Please, Jason.'

'I've just thought. If you can manipulate the data a bit, you can make him come whenever you want. Just pad out the run time with continuous thrusts until you're ready, then hit the button and whammo.'

Jason laughed. His sister was wearing the face he recognised – utter horror mixed with fascination. 'Actually there's got to be a marketing angle here. No more premmies.'

'Premmies?'

'Premature ejacs. You'd get a guaranteed perfect fuck every time. Ladies would pay serious money to get a sharpshooter hubby on that data stream.'

'Okay, that's enough.'

'You're going to try, though, aren't you?'

Nina said nothing. She looked up at him slowly, revealing a cheeky smile.

'Of course, there is one very tacky side issue.'

'What?'

'Well, effectively it's all a bit incestuous. Okay, it's only data, but in some ways you're shagging your brother.'

Jason watched as he pushed his sister's facial expression to a new, previously unseen level of pure horror.

'Oh, God,' was all she could say.

44

Nina Nash glanced around the doorway of the bathroom. Pete was in the shower, struggling away as usual. His arms were still very weak – just lifting the shower gel and squeezing it required a great deal of concentration, to say nothing of determination.

She walked past the doorway feeling slightly guilty, although she was doing nothing wrong – merely carrying her laptop and a small flight case. She put the laptop on the bedside table and the flight case on the floor, popped the catches and opened the lid. Inside, a small black transmitter sat encased in foam rubber. She pulled up the stubby antenna and switched it on. She then uncoiled a firewire lead, plugged the two machines together, and booted up the laptop.

Pete entered the bedroom with a towel wrapped around his waist. Walking awkwardly, he made his way to the bed and collapsed. Nina helped pull the duvet over him, then kissed him gently.

'You smell nice,' he said as he ran his hand slowly down her back.

'You look delicious,' she said. She saw him glance at the laptop.

'Still working?'

She smiled. 'You know me. I never give up. Just a second. I've got a bit of data I need to check.'

She pulled herself off him and touched the keypad. She heard him sigh and smiled to herself. The screen came to life and she opened the data program. She had set the whole system up at the lab earlier in the day. Whether or not it would work was anyone's guess, but it was worth a try.

She moved the cursor over the 'run' button and clicked. As

she moved back on the bed she glanced at the small row of LEDs on the transmitter box. They were busy. Very busy.

She snuggled up to Pete Van Missen, putting her head on his chest.

'Oh,' he said.

'What?'

'My neck feels hot. It's that weird feeling.'

'I'm sure it's okay.'

'Oh, my.'

Slowly, very slowly, Professor Nina Nash ran her hand down the stomach of the man she loved. What greeted her as she approached the end of the short journey was unmistakable.

'Oh, wow,' said Pete Van Missen. Nina looked into his blue eyes.

'Hello, baby,' she said as she kissed him softly.